THE SHE-WOLF OF BAKER STREET

BY

NARRELLE M. HARRIS

Clan Destine
PRESS

First published by Clan Destine Press in 2024

Clan Destine Press
PO Box 121, Bittern
Victoria, 3918 Australia

National Library of Australia Cataloguing-In-Publication data:

Harris, Narrelle M.

THE SHE-WOLF OF BAKER STREET

ISBN: 978-1-922904-39-3 (paperback)
         978-1-922904-40-9 (eBook)

Cover Design by © Jill Harris
Design & Typesetting by Clan Destine Press

Clan Destine
PRESS

www.clandestinepress.net

Dedicated with love to all the fierce women in my life,
and with fondness to my first TV Mrs Hudson, Rosalie Williams,
and to my most recent, Una Stubbs.

CHAPTER ONE

'WHAT THE HELL ARE YOU DOING? ARE YOU CUTTING THOSE plants?'

Audrey Hudson thrust her hands behind her back and looked innocent. Ish.

'I would never dream of doing such a thing,' she said as primly as she knew how. She fit the part. Smartly dressed older woman, salt and pepper hair; she looked like someone who baked and knitted and enjoyed a cheeky glass of white in the late afternoon and had a *darling* little herb garden. All of which was technically true.

The young man accusing her of floral vandalism was not appeased. 'What's that behind your back?'

Scissors, a snip of Aconitum lycotonum *and a set of claws when the mood strikes me.*

Audrey opted for stout denial.

'How dare you?' She was already peeling the glove off, inverting it over the stolen leaves to keep them off her skin. She pushed the scissors inside the glove as well, then balled the lot up and tucked it up her sleeve. Incriminating evidence hidden, she, annoyed – officious little sod; it's not like she went around lopping off roses in Kew Gardens – showed her accuser her empty palms, and an unintended flash of her wilder self.

The lad flinched from the sudden sense of *predator*.

'Sorry,' he said. 'Ah. Sorry. My mistake. I'll just. Just.'

And he *just*, as quickly as frightened feet would take him.

Audrey sighed, stifling regret. She wouldn't even be here, if she'd been able to find another source of monkshood in time. The full moon was looming, however, and residential London gardens were less accessible than the Chelsea Physic Garden. Stealing cuttings was bad enough; but worse to be sprung in someone's private garden, especially if their pets went berserk.

The lad didn't even know what she was. But then people didn't have to know, to cower at the sight of her.

She pushed away the self-pity, dusted her hands clean and transferred the inverted glove and its dangerous contents from sleeve to pocket. She'd have to start carefully cultivating the treacherous monkshood at Baker Street.

She still resisted calling it *home*. It was supposed to be a home, of course, but after three weeks it was just the place she lived. Alone. Again.

The nosy lad whose accusations, to be fair, were spot on, was returning with someone in authority. Audrey felt an oblique sense of shame, even though she'd done things much less civilised than pinch a few leaves.

The head gardener and the lad were angling across the lawn from the café. Audrey could hear the latter telling the former, in worried tones, that a dotty old duck had been mucking about near the poisonous monkshood. She supposed he meant well.

Audrey couldn't really leg it across the medicine garden to the main exit while they watched. Instead, she strode haughtily through the smaller entrance to Swan Walk. Once through the ivy-crowned gate, she turned left beside the high brick wall and loped off, with a slight limp, at a startlingly fast pace. She'd have run faster in her other form, but her other form did not have pockets.

Audrey was walking sedately, her limp barely noticeable, by the time she reached Baker Street. She unlocked the sturdy, steel-reinforced wooden door of the Georgian townhouse, but hesitated on the threshold.

Nearly a month and making that first step into the foyer was still an effort. The emptiness of this large house had weight, and the weight resisted her. The silence of it pressed on her ears; the scent of it was dust and neglect and loneliness.

However, it was still better in almost every way than the house in

Morningside on that last day. She'd alighted from the train from London to Edinburgh so hopeful, so happy. Yet from streets away, she'd sensed the horror waiting at home. Her taxi had pulled up short at the sight of the useless ambulances and out-of-their-depth police vehicles. She'd run to her pack, her children, heedless of danger, and no-one had been able to restrain her as she plunged inside her home – into hell.

The smell of blood and cordite and the tickling, bitter afterburns of silver and wolfsbane. The killer had known her family's secrets and their every vulnerability. Whoever it was had also butchered her children, post-mortem, to retrieve the silver bullets.

Audrey had lurched outside again, away from the unbearable sight, and been violently ill on a constable's shoes.

Now, carrying groceries she'd bought on the way home, Audrey made herself cross the threshold of 221 Baker Street, into the hall. She consciously ignored the apartment door on the left. That would have been Conal's flat, where he could guard the pack in her absence. She disregarded the staircase leading to the upper floors as well, where twins Travis and Tara had designed their perfect shared space. She was dreadfully aware of the basement apartment beneath her feet. That would have been Siobhan's room, accessible via the tiny back garden. Not now, it wasn't.

Audrey had already filled the flagstones in front of the door with trees in planter boxes – a bay tree, a kentia palm, some bamboo – all of which which would grow fast enough to conceal the entrance from a casual glance until the other foliage did the job. Even hidden, that empty room hurt.

Despite all her careful planning, she had left it too late to make their fresh start in London. All that remained was the bitter taste of shame and defeat, and a house that should have been full of anything but silence. Ignoring all the empty spaces took effort that was both a weight and a presence.

Audrey hurried to her own flat, the right-hand one on the ground floor, and slammed the door behind her.

In the kitchen, she washed her hands thoroughly then stored away the shopping; the freshest beef she held aside for tomorrow's full moon. Smaller cuts of beef and the lamb chops went into the freezer. A whole baking chicken and lean bacon for the week went into the fridge. Fruit and vegetables, because even weres needed a balanced diet, went into baskets or the crisper.

Then she pulled on a pair of latex gloves and retrieved the monkshood, which she knew better as wolfsbane, from her pocket and placed it in a small wicker pot. The leaves would dry in a few days, ready to use sparingly, highly diluted, in her personal tea blend. Like many dangerous plants, wolfsbane had medicinal qualities when used appropriately.

It was always possible to use it inappropriately, of course. Maybe if she ever found out who had slaughtered her pack in Edinburgh, she'd stop thinking about that.

Audrey scrubbed her hands again and shoved the wolfsbane-tainted clothes into the washing machine. She changed into a comfortable skirt with pockets for her keys and wallet – handbags would hinder any necessary getaway – and left the house. She was determined to enjoy the sunny afternoon in Regent's Park rather than curling up, metaphorical tail between her legs, stewing in her impotent grief.

Audrey Hudson been a werewolf all of her adult life and her senses were acute even when she wasn't in her other form. She'd go and smell the roses in Queen Mary's Gardens, and certainly not steal any cuttings from them, because that, as she well knew, was the act of a barbarian.

The lawn through Regent's Park was perfectly pleasant but too tame for Audrey's tastes. Most English parks, with their neat grass and pretty but regimented plots for flowers and shrubberies, had nothing on the rugged beauty of Scotland.

She'd give Regent's Park this, though: it smelled better than a lot of London. No doubt its proximity was why Audrey's very last Alpha, her Ruby, had bought the townhouse: in case the need arose for a London bolthole. Audrey had forgotten it was part of her inheritance until she'd begun to plan the retreat from Edinburgh. Baker Street was far from the escalating turf wars in the north – London was too tumultuous and over-filled with both humankind and Others for any one pack to claim it – and had the benefit of nearby gardens. Hampstead Heath was only thirty minutes on the train; an hour on foot if necessary.

The paperwork had finally been ironed out, the renovation completed, and she was returning home with the new keys when bloody events had overtaken them. Another week and they would have been safe. Another *day* even. Perhaps just another *hour*.

Audrey shook off that useless train of thought. As a *were*, she had many gifts, but turning back time was none of them.

As the afternoon cooled, Audrey's hip began to ache. She rubbed absently at the old scars. A sound caught her sensitive ears – a footfall on grass, rather than on the path behind her. Someone was breathing too fast; sweating too. The scent of both wolf and human. And *fear*.

Ahead of her was the odd little statue of the helmeted child astride a vulture. The vulture looked fed up rather than threatened. She knew how it felt. She held still and listened.

The footfalls crept behind her, moving away. A soft foot on earth now, followed by a sharp hiss – whoever it was had stepped in a garden bed and promptly been scratched by a rose bush.

'I won't hurt you, you know,' she said softly, knowing that it would carry sufficiently for whoever was trying to sneak away.

'I know who you are.' His voice was tremulous.

'I'm just minding my own business,' Audrey said. 'Smelling the roses. Looking at the weird statues. Have you seen the one of the boy and his frog?'

'I know what you did.'

'I didn't do anything. That's the whole problem.' Audrey turned slowly.

Hunched by the bed of pink roses was a young man, quivering like a whipped puppy, red hair bright against his blanched skin.

'I was warned about you,' he said. 'The Cursed Alpha.'

Audrey blinked. She'd gained that name forty years ago, along with her gammy hip. Her family never called her that, but others who hardly knew her used it like a weapon; or a shield.

This poor boy hadn't a clue. A new werewolf, maybe. Turned without consent, perhaps, as she had been. As most of them were. She'd have thought him abandoned to the dictates of his very first moon, except that he knew who she was. He'd been with a pack long enough to learn that.

Audrey hadn't realised anyone in London would know her, but clearly news travelled fast. Probably through smartphones, she thought sourly. Bloody things. In her day, wolves tracked each other the old fashioned way, by word of mouth, not with *apps*. The young ones were responsible for that. Not like vampires, some of them so old they still struggled with the concept of landlines and television. Ridiculous, prideful, pitiful creatures.

Had Siobhan talked about an app? MonsterWatch or NightstalkerGo! or AngryCryptids. She might have been joking. Siobhan had liked teasing Audrey about modern tech. Poor bairn.

'You should run home to your Alpha,' Audrey said steadily. 'Unless you've no Alpha to run to.' Her heart thudded fast. She'd brought home strays in the past, pardon the expression. Offered a home to the lost ones. She'd built a pack and made herself an Alpha. She'd lost all of them, true, but that house was so empty. She was so lonely.

'His Alpha's here,' growled a new voice. A woman, steel-grey hair, scowl of fire, arrived on the path. She held out an imperious hand and the cub darted to her side. 'He's not for you. He's not packless, and even if he was, he wouldn't need you and your bad luck.'

'I'm only here for the roses,' Audrey said.

The boy's Alpha – den mother, Audrey thought with sudden fondness, which was what Conal had always called her – drew the lad away.

'If I meet you here for the moon, I'll know what to do about it.'

'This prissy little park's no good for the moon run,' Audrey sneered, though it was more for show. She'd rather liked the idea of having her run so close to home. Hampstead it would have to be.

The Alpha jerked her cub by the elbow. Audrey watched them go.

The whole encounter had robbed the roses of their sweetness. Audrey moped among them for a while, but the rigidly ordered flower beds made her cross. She meandered west, skirting the open air theatre – Shakespeare in the Park had been Travis's joy; she couldn't go without him – and stopped when she reached the boating lake.

A regal white swan began paddling like a steamboat at full throttle to get past her. A duck flying in to land on the water banked suddenly and nearly crashed in the reeds. Audrey sighed. Animals mostly coped fairly well with her, but when the full moon was due, the scent of her rising wolf drove them into panic. Either that or they'd got wind of the whole "cursed Alpha" thing.

And suddenly, her whole body flooded with grief. It hollowed out her legs and her stomach. She couldn't even laugh at her own stupid damned jokes any more. She couldn't walk in the damned park without. Without. Without…

A grey heron high stepped into the shallows on the opposite bank, sensed her presence and took off with a panicked flap of wings and vanished into the trees. Despite herself, she laughed at how gawkily foolish it looked.

Someone stood beside her on the bank, laughing low along with her.

'They're all neck sometimes,' said the man. 'The swans are worse. Like snakes glued onto an exercise ball or something.'

The man's cologne made Audrey's eyes water and she stifled a cough. He grinned at her, bright and friendly.

'You're new around here, aren't you?' he said.

Audrey tried holding her breath. 'Yes. I moved nearby a few weeks ago.'

'I'm Bert,' he said, holding out a hand.

'Mrs Hudson,' she said, shaking it briefly. The gold ring she wore glinted in the light. *Let him think I have family waiting at home.* His hand was dry; the grip, surprisingly strong.

He nodded gallantly, like withholding your first name from a stranger was fair enough.

'Bert's an old fashioned name,' he said, 'but it's short for something much worse.'

'Really?' She let herself be amused, since he was so intent on being amusing.

'Adelbert,' he said. 'Told you it was awful.'

'German, isn't it?' He had the faintest of accents, softer, however, and more musical than German.

'Austrian,' said Bert. 'It means "shining nobility" I'm told.' His eyes twinkled.

Audrey retrieved a handkerchief from a pocket and coughed delicately into it, but his cologne still tickled her throat. Underneath the smell of something citrusy and spicy with a hint of cedar was the smell of the grass and the trees and the lake; the smell of humans. Nothing supernatural in the air since the *weres* in the rose garden.

Still. Something about him made the hair on the back of her neck prickle. Adelbert of the Shining Nobility reeked of cologne and danger.

Either that or she was paranoid, primed to howl at strong scents by the overwhelming memory of Edinburgh and the subtle whiff of wolfsbane underneath the blood. She repressed that urge thoroughly. It wouldn't do, to have a 65-year-old woman howling at the sun in the middle of Regent's Park.

The lake was quiet now. Audrey suspected even the fish and frogs were giving her a wide berth.

'So,' said Adelbert. 'If you like, I can give you some local tips. Cafes, libraries, bakeries, that sort of thing. There's a wonderful Indian place just off Park Road and my favourite bookshop is *Daunt's* on Marylebone High Street.'

'I do like a good bookshop,' she admitted.

Beyond Adelbert, among the trees, Audrey saw a wiry man with a stylish undercut do, the crown gelled backwards over his skull. He watched her with feline-sharp eyes, pounce-ready.

A slight movement further away led her keen eyesight to another man skulking in the shadows. This one was tall, athletic, slender, with untidy black hair and a hawkish nose. His sharp gaze shifted between Bert and the other.

Adelbert. Undercut. Hawknose. All three, hunters.

Audrey smiled faintly. All *four* of them. Who, she wondered, was hunting whom?

'It's been lovely meeting you, Bert,' she said, 'but I should get home.'

'Of course, of course, I didn't mean to hold you up. Perhaps we'll meet in the park another day.'

'Perhaps.' She blinked her stinging eyes, nodded goodbye and withdrew along the Inner Circle path.

Undercut was following her, by the sound of it. Adelbert held back. Hawknose was, surprisingly, too quiet to hear.

Audrey reached Ulster Terrace, aware of the traffic ahead and the three men ranged somewhere behind. Away from Bert's overwhelming scent, she could gather more subtle clues; all three were human. Whatever they were up to, they were no real threat to her.

A black cab stripped of its insignia was parked in the shade alongside the park. Not liking the look of it, she turned away. If she crossed towards Baker Street via Marylebone Road it would give her a clear run, if necessary.

No need to get claws out in broad daylight: yet her painted nails transformed anyway, polish flaking off as they changed. Audrey hadn't needed the moon to shape herself since well before menopause.

The strong cologne had dissipated, but exhaust fumes now interfered, and the noise of traffic and pedestrians on the path meant she couldn't distinguish hunting footfalls from any other.

She strode purposefully to the intersection. In the event she was being hunted, her best option would be to turn again, rather than lead them to the townhouse. If only she knew the neighbourhood better. Perhaps she could lose them in the cluster of buildings coming up on the left, circle back over walls and come up behind them to...

One set of footfalls hastened behind her, and she turned instantly – her brown eyes flashing a supernaturally wolfish tawny, human teeth bared on the verge of becoming sharper – and received a face full of aerosol, wielded by the wiry Undercut. Instinct made her gasp.

The sweet odour of disinfectant and the bitter bite of aconite swamped her senses. Wolfsbane. The same smell and taste that had lingered in Edinburgh (beneath the silver and all that blood).

Undercut strode past her as her knees buckled; as though it had nothing to do with him.

Then the pungent cologne hit her as well.

'Oh,' said the Austrian, filled with satisfaction. 'It works even better than he said it would.'

He stooped to help her up, pretending kindly assistance to his fragile relative, but his grip was too firm. Through her swimming vision, Audrey saw a plain white van drawing up to the kerb. So much for the unmarked black cab. So much for cleverness.

Part of her wanted to give up, to succumb to fate. She *was* the Cursed Alpha. She had let her pack be murdered.

But Undercut had used a debilitating spray that may also have been used on her family in Edinburgh. It was a clue. She wasn't giving up now.

She let her body become an unwieldy dead weight, playing for time. Adelbert's grip never faltered but other hands suddenly took her arm and helped lower her to the grass. She peered at him: the man with the hawklike nose. His grey eyes were full of concern.

Audrey tried to say "help". She sounded like she'd had a stroke.

'Should I call an ambulance?' Hawknose asked Adelbert.

'Nanny's all right,' said Adelbert soothingly. 'I'll call her physician when she's home.'

The van door slid open. The interior looked comfortable and friendly, and not at all like a trap.

Audrey grasped Hawknose's arm, pressed a finger against his wrist and tapped anxiously, hoping to be steady enough. Three fast taps. Three slow taps. Three fast again.

His grey eyes seemed to pierce her through, then his hand folded over hers and a long forefinger tapped a subtle reply. In her fuddled state, the meaning escaped her, beyond the fact he had understood her SOS.

His other hand fumbled as he knelt with her, holding something small between forefinger and thumb.

'You can leave her now,' said Adelbert, the friendliness gone. 'I can look after my own nanny.' His hand under Audrey's arm, he jerked her upright.

She bumped against Hawknose's elbow. The thing in his fingers fell to the road with a barely audible ping.

'She really needs an ambulance, I think,' said Hawknose, rising with her, trying to steady her. His concern held an undercurrent of frustration.

'Fuck off,' said Undercut, returning to assist. Adelbert hissed something at him in German, but Undercut's chagrin only lasted long enough for Hawknose to insist on reaching for Audrey again. Undercut punched him in the face, and Hawknose went down like a log.

Audrey pulled free of Adelbert, but dizziness felled her again. She lay on the ground panting but, near the van, she saw what Hawknose had dropped. It looked like a little battery.

A wee transmitter. A bug, like the spy shows on the telly.

Pretending to attempt to find her feet, she palmed it and then, still struggling, she slipped the little device between her lips. And swallowed it.

Meanwhile Undercut had taken another vicious swipe at Hawknose, which left him bleeding on the footpath. He then helped Adelbert strap Audrey into a seat inside and slammed the door shut.

Exhausted, trapped, she sagged. Her captors joined the driver in the front, and they drove off, leaving Marylebone and her failed rescuer far behind.

Chapter Two

About ninety minutes later, the van stopped and Undercut opened the door and pumped more wolfsbane-laced chloroform into Audrey's face. She held her breath for as long as possible, but even werewolves have a breathing reflex. She gasped for air as he released another dose, rendering her giddy and useless again.

Undercut and Adelbert unstrapped her from the car and bound her again straight after. She slumped, feigning greater debility to save her scattered energy.

They brought her into a dark house that smelled of age and wood polish, and then on down flights of stone stairs. Audrey resisted a little and was rewarded when Undercut scraped an elbow on the rough-hewn walls. She longed to bite him for daring this outrage, but she pushed the savage instinct away. She wouldn't get far, impaired as she was, and a short-lived satisfaction now might ruin better chances of escape later.

Besides, she was in no mood for misguided mercy that would merely create another bloody werewolf with poor impulse control. If she took tooth and claw to these bastards, she wouldn't leave them alive to transform at the next full moon.

Finally, she was bundled into a plain room with plaster walls and dumped on a thin mattress. Undercut loosened the straps around her torso and arms without taking them off. She heard the snick of the door closing behind them again, and the faintest hum of an electronic lock.

Audrey decided not to struggle out of the loose straps; she'd wait for her head to clear. For all the grief that had gnawed at her will to live these last weeks, she now very much wanted to find out who had supplied Shining Arsehole Adelbert with this gas designed specifically to incapacitate werewolves, and if they had been behind the slaughter of her family.

For if she could find who had done that to her poor cubs, she would even that score; oh yes she would. Without mercy, misguided or otherwise.

Audrey woke in the morning, curled up on the mattress. She'd finally shucked the straps from her body so that she could sleep in relative comfort. She'd also taken off her walking boots, so that she could shift, unhampered, if need be.

In this deep basement, she only knew it was morning because her blood knew when the sun was up. Her captors had left food, but her senses remained too fuddled to know if the water and meat were drugged. Salivation had to be hydration enough for the time being.

She examined the sparse room in more detail. A metal toilet and basin stood in one corner, without any privacy screen. The thin foam mattress was new and clean, but she had no bedding otherwise. The bare bulb which was her only light was unrelentingly bright, and beside it hung a small camera that panned whenever she moved. Three of the walls were smooth and beige.

The fourth wall contained the door with the slot for delivering meals. The slot, like the door, was electronically controlled. The door was solid; reinforced with steel, probably. To the left of it was an indentation that might have been a window, except that it was opaque. Her keen eyesight, pressed close, had identified filaments in the glass. She didn't know the name for it, but she'd seen glass like it in a disconcerting toilet at a very posh restaurant in Manchester, once. Clear until the lock was turned, when a circuit was completed and made the glass opaque. What kind of scatological sadist made a loo wall out of something that would become see-through in a power failure?

Adelbert probably. She already knew he was a pretentious little shit.

When she couldn't put it off any longer, Audrey lifted the negligible weight of the mattress and angled it across the toilet and basin so that she could have some privacy for her ablutions. She left the mattress up afterward and sneered at the pervert behind the roving camera.

She was considering whether to put her shoes back on for warmth when the opaque window became suddenly clear, and beyond it stood her captor, smiling smugly.

Rage responded before caution: Audrey snarled and leapt at him. The glass held but she left great scratches down the panels with her claws. Adelbert's smile became positively gleeful.

'You may try to escape, of course,' he said. 'It will be fascinating to capture your efforts on camera. But you won't.'

Audrey contained her fury with effort.

'You are my first live werewolf, but not my first cryptid,' he explained, delighted to have her undivided attention. 'I have an unparalleled spirit museum, so many fascinating things in jars. One or two surviving live specimens. I have a dragon in a neighbouring chamber, contstructed to be impervious to every flame, tooth and claw she has brought to bear upon it.'

Audrey stood in the centre of the room. Fingers grown hairy and taloned were curled ready to rend, mouth full of sharp teeth distended in a snarling snout. He appeared so elated with her monstrous aspect that she forced herself to calmness, to her human form, until at last she stood before him: a barefoot, 65-year-old woman with disarranged grey-streaked hair and brown eyes luminous with wrath.

Adelbert stood closer to the glass to inspect her. 'You are such a beautiful addition to my cryptid collection. I am presently negotiating for a preserved werewolf paw, but truly, it's nothing like having a live specimen. I must send him a thank you card for alerting me to your presence in London.'

'Who?'

'Oh, an acquaintance who knows of my proclivities. He has helped me to find items once belonging to Alistair Crowley, John Dee, even Madame Blavatsky. Many others of course.'

'Nasty little hobbyist,' she said. 'What do they call people like you? An *anorak*.'

He scowled, pride stung. 'I am a *collector*, of many things, some even quite respectable. Nobody could object to the rare porcelain I keep in another of my houses. I have priceless collections of stamps, also of cars, displayed where fellow aficionados may visit without an inkling of my more esoteric interests.'

'Braggart.'

'I do like the looks on their faces, when they see what I have. In fact, I have a particularly delicious brag book where I keep my collection of humans. Beautiful and pure. Well. While I have them, they are.' His oily little smirk repelled her. 'I do mar them a little afterwards. Nobody will ever have them again, the way I had them. Their purity will always remain only mine.'

This shining fart loved the sound of his own voice, Audrey noted. She remained silent and let him witter on.

'My cryptids I never share either. My brag books are for me alone. I have prepared one for you,' he said. He held up a gorgeously bound hardcover notebook, the paper of it heavy and expensive. He displayed the flowing calligraphy of the handwritten title to her.

Audrey Hudson, Werewolf
Held in the Private Collection of Adelbert Gruner

'See? A record for my very own werewolf.' His proprietorial gaze on her was foul.

'I am not yours.'

He opened the book and held it up for her to see that he had already pasted an image, taken from the surveillance camera, on to the title page. Even in that photograph, she was obviously not the dear old lady she seemed to be. Her grey skirt was wrinkled, her dark blouse with the little blue flowers at the collar dishevelled beyond belief. In the photograph, her walking boots were lined up beside the wall and her bare feet made her look vulnerable, when being unshod was the exact opposite. She was looking at the camera, and any assumed air of helplessness about her was countered by the wildness in her glare.

Adelbert turned the page and began to read.

'Audrey Hudson, born in 1958 to Stewart and June Green in Newton Abbot, Devon. Younger sister to Ingrid. Schooled locally. Won a few trophies for sport. An unremarkable scholastic career.'

'Where did you get this?'

'Birth certificates and school records are easy. I had to pay a little more for what follows. You were bitten by a werewolf in London in 1974, having snuck away to the Big Smoke with friends for a weekend. You were a wild thing, even then, weren't you?'

She'd been a pretty typical teenage girl, in fact. True, she'd lied to her folks about going to Torquay – London was so much more exciting for a post-A-level exam weekend, with its theatres and night clubs. She, Betty and Joyce had enjoyed a giggling afternoon tea at Fortnum and Mason; a thrilling musical at the Garrick. Then they'd gone dancing.

Joe Clarke followed them back to their cheap hotel; had leered and chased her when she ran; had grabbed her and bitten her arm with terrifyingly long teeth while she fought him off with a squirt of perfume to the eyes. He'd run like a coward when Betty and Joyce arrived with the police.

Joe Clarke had irrevocably changed her life but was nothing more exotic than a rapist with a particularly horrific transmittable disease.

A wild thing? Not by choice, but not tame either.

'Soon after, and in disgrace,' Adelbert continued his version, 'you leave school and little Newton Abbot to live with your pack in Bristol, with your Alpha, Gordon Edwards.'

That day before her first full moon, she'd wandered Dartmoor to settle her restless feet. The moor ponies she loved shied from her and galloped away in alarm. Her little dog Chester had tried to keep her out of the house when she returned to Newton Abbot.

Next morning she'd woken up on Dartmoor beside the carcass of a moor pony, its blood in her teeth and down her tattered dress. She'd had to bathe in a creek before staggering home, her feet bruised and bloody because she had no idea what had become of her shoes. Her parents were beside themselves with worry, after hearing of her assault in London. Ingrid lectured her about protecting her reputation, and Ingrid's by default. Chester was back to his normal friendly doggy self.

Gordon Edwards showed up a week later and explained the infection and the nature of her permanent new state. He had treated her like his property – 'I sired Joe, so that makes you mine too' – but she went with him, terrified by what she might do to the people she loved if she stayed.

'And then in 1980,' Adelbert was still talking, stripping her life bare and yet missing every important point, 'the Edwards pack engages in a turf war with Alpha William Ormstein.'

Not a war *she'd* wanted, but the two Alphas were determined to prove their ultimate authority and power. A pissing competition with deadly consequences.

'And then in a different war, just a month ago, the eight members of your new pack are defeated...'

Murdered.

'...and William, styling himself as the King of Bohemia, leaves you wounded but alive – to show his mercy.'

'To tell others what kind of mercy to expect when William Ormstein wants to make an example of you,' she corrected him.

'Quite.'

'I know all of this,' Audrey said stiffly. 'I lived it.'

'And you're wondering how I know?'

'I assume you're a nosy, prying little prig.'

'This is true,' Adelbert said mildly. 'I like to learn things, and I have contacts with many unusual people.'

'Including William Ormstein?'

'I have not yet had that pleasure,' Adelbert confessed sadly. 'I hope, one day.' He returned to his notes. 'Again, I hope to fill in the many blank pages of your story with your help. Here for instance, in the late 80s, you are associated with Ruby Stockton, a Lone Wolf, as they say, until she met you. Her fate is unrecorded, though rumour has it she died of poisoning. Were you too wild even for her? Then you too disappear until two decades later, you appear in Edinburgh using the name Hudson, with a little pack of your own.

'Why Edinburgh?' he asked suddenly. 'My recent research shows that Ruby Stockton left monies and London property to you. Why did you spend so long in hiding, only to emerge so far north?'

Audrey crossed her arms and refused to reply.

'My sources believe you were pregnant when Ormstein attacked, yet there's no record of a baby or any children since then. You have a limp, I know. Were the mutilations deliberate, to ensure that you couldn't have...' he huffed an amused laugh. '...*cubs*. Werewolf patois is charmingly trite. I suppose King Bill wanted no descendants of the pack to challenge him for the Bristol territory again. Or was it mere malice?'

Audrey quivered, pale with rage that this creature was pawing through her pain in a tone of mild curiosity.

'Did you kill my family?' she asked in a low growl.

'In Edinburgh? Oh no. Not my doing at all.'

'You know who did.'

'I spoke to people, well, I don't know if they are really *people*, who were part of that. They told me about you.'

'Give me their names.'

'Perhaps another time. Tonight, I shall film as you transform. It shall be history-making. We'll talk again soon.' Adelbert snapped the book shut.

'You can whistle for it,' snarled Audrey.

He laughed, like that was a joke, then toggled the glass to opaque again.

Later that night, more food was inserted through the slot. Her recovered senses detected nothing tainted, so she sipped the water and she ate the raw steak daintily. She was a werewolf, not an animal, and she needed the nourishment.

Audrey's blood sang at the rise of the moon. Normally, she would be somewhere safe by now. Hampstead Heath had been her plan. In Edinburgh, she and Conal always walked with the others across the causeway at low tide to Cramond Island in the firth of Forth. The incoming tide would cut them off from the mainland overnight, leaving them with 19 acres to run with the moon without people getting in the way. They would take off their clothes and leave them folded somewhere safe in the centre of the island, ready to dress again with the dawn and take the causeway back to Cramond village.

Well, she'd be damned if she'd strip for this ghoul and let him slaver over her old body as it changed. Scarred, drooping and wrinkled with years and experience in its human form, rangy and hairy and grizzled as a wolf, and all the twisted, unnatural shapes in between – every phase belonged only to her, and Adelbert Shining Creep couldn't have any of it without a fight.

Adelbert regarded her with avid curiosity, pencil at the ready over a rough notebook. He obviously meant to write up more polished notes in the official hardcover later, in a precise copperplate hand to match the title. He glanced at the camera which tracked her movements in the cell, ready to record every step of her transformation.

Audrey had smoothed her clothes and put on her walking boots again. She refused to hide behind the thin mattress she'd propped in front of the facilities.

So far, the little disk of Hawknose's bug hadn't gone through her system, but she didn't know if her system had proven too much for it. Did it still transmit? Had it ever transmitted? Had any signal been able to breach the stone walls of this underground room? She had to act as though no help was coming. It probably wasn't.

'You should disrobe to preserve your clothes,' Adelbert told her helpfully, an armchair expert in lycanthropic change. 'I shan't be fetching you anything new from Baker Street when I move in there. Don't make things harder for yourself.'

So. He planned to steal her home as well. Audrey added it to her short list of Reasons to Hate the Shining Fart.

The moon rose in the unseen sky. Adelbert rolled his pencil between his fingertips then tapped it on a blank page. The surveillance camera filmed his unmoving captive.

Audrey Hudson lifted her chin and glared at him.

Adelbert checked his watch. Frowned. Made a phone call to check the time and frowned again.

Audrey Hudson remained stubbornly human.

'What are you doing?' he demanded.

'Nothing.' Her thin smile was savage.

'Stop it.'

'No.'

'How can you even do this? We have a full moon. You are a werewolf. You have to change.'

'Make me.'

But he stayed beyond the window, confused and enraged and frightened. If he came inside and she changed, she could rip him into pieces. At best, she could bite him and transfer the curse to him. He wanted a captive werewolf, sure, but he didn't want to *be* one.

Audrey's cool smile did much to hide the effort it took, but a careful observer would have seen the perspiration, the lines of strain around her eyes and jaw, the clenching of her soft and hairless hands.

Audrey Hudson was fourteen when she had her first menses. Becoming a werewolf at seventeen had strengthened her natural monthly ties to the moon, but as the decades passed she fell into a rhythm, not fighting the change nor rushing headlong toward it like the male *weres* often did. She accepted the cycle into her blood and went with – she'd always found the term funny – the flow.

Now she was 65 and had been in menopause for over a decade.

In short, she was not the moon's bitch. Not anymore.

The moon waxed and waned, but Audrey Hudson was a constant, and stubborn, she could change – or not – at will, and she did not consent to give this awful man the gift of her pain.

When her bones ached and she felt the itching under her skin, Audrey closed her eyes and breathed deep, just as Ruby had taught her. She had no wolfsbane-laced tea to assist in the suppression of her cycle, but her captors had dosed her several times. In meditation, she reached for whatever residue remained in her body, and heard Ruby's voice.

You are the mistress of your soul. The wolf is in you but does not own you. You run with the moon when you can. You must run with the moon soon. But tomorrow's moon will be enough. The moon can wait, and so can you. Breathe, Audrey, breathe my darling. Breathe. Be calm. Be still. Let the moon wash through you for now. You are wild and you are free and you are yourself. Breathe.

Audrey was aware of Adelbert shouting at her, but she'd closed her eyes and breathed through the pain and the effort. She fought the pull of the moon not with the savage resistance of muscle and claw, but with the fluid strength of her mind and the memory of her beloved Ruby.

Breathe, my darling.

Who knew how long she could resist the curse of the wolf? But like a wolf, she existed only now: not yesterday, not tomorrow. She would inhale and be herself; exhale and be herself, and tomorrow would see what tomorrow became.

It was not effortless. Sweat pooled in the hollows of her body, at her throat, in her armpits, the small of her back. She trembled, she resisted, not as stone resists, but as the tree bending in the wind, as the water flowing over the rocks.

She hurt. But she did not change.

And then she felt it, the moment the moon slipped under the horizon and the sun bloomed over it. The sudden release of pressure. Her body ached, but the fight was done.

She fell, crumpled like an empty bag, onto the hard floor, and she wept for everyone she'd lost, and for herself, because she didn't have any fight left in her.

She couldn't see the rage twisting Adelbert's face, but she expected he'd come in to make his displeasure known. Her life had been full of men who'd made their displeasure known when she didn't hand them what they wanted on a grateful platter.

The door clicked as it opened. Adelbert's shoes made a sharp sound on the floor as he entered. Audrey tried to gather her limbs under her; readied herself to bite.

And then a house alarm sounded that Audrey thought would shatter her bones.

'You can wait,' snarled the Austrian. He slammed the door shut again on his way out. She couldn't hear his retreating footsteps over the strident alarm. She covered her ears.

And then...

And then the alarm fell silent. The silence was so profound that she couldn't even hear the sub-aural hum of the electrical system keeping the window opaque and the door locked.

She heard footsteps in the hall outside. Limbs still trembling, Audrey removed her hands from her ears and opened her eyes. With brutal effort, she rose snarling to her hands and knees. Her nails grew sharp. She would fight while she could.

The window was clear, though nobody was visible through the pane.

The door opened, and surprise blunted her nails and teeth.

The man with the hawk nose was bruised, and his mouth swollen where he'd been beaten by Undercut, but he beamed at her, pulling his split lip and making it bleed afresh.

'There you are! Brave lady. Let's get you out of here!'

Chapter Three

Audrey couldn't help thinking this knight in shining armour would be more impressive if he didn't have blood in his teeth, a black eye and a marked limp. The cheap polyester backpack slung over his battered leather jacket and the blood spotted over his blue trainers didn't instil confidence either. He seemed much younger, paler and more vulnerable than she remembered from the park.

Hawknose's grin widened at her appraisal. 'I let them think it was worse than it was,' he confided.

'You came for me.'

'I had another commission to fulfil, but yes, I thought I'd better get you first. Sherlock Holmes, at your service. Adelbert Gruner hasn't made you sign anything, has he?'

Her lip curled at the memory of the Shining Fart talking about moving into Baker Street. 'I'd have bit him if he'd tried.'

'That's the spirit. Among his many objectionable habits, Gruner's been abducting isolated home owners and coercing their signatures on property deeds. He's occupying several other suddenly empty buildings. Let's hope the real owners are imprisoned rather than dead.'

'Yes,' she replied drily. 'Let's.'

'Ah.' He didn't quite blush but he seemed to know he'd spoken thoughtlessly and changed the subject. 'Marvellous work, pocketing the tracker when I dropped it, like an idiot. Led me all the way down here to you. Where is it now? It's a useful bit of kit if I can get it back.'

'I swallowed it.'

He opened his mouth to speak; glanced at her belly; blinked.

'You can have it back in a day or two, I imagine.'

'No, no, no, that's fine. More where that came from, I'm sure. It's time we were moving, Mrs... ah. Everyone upstairs should be properly distracted by now, if Shinwell's done his job.'

'It's Audrey.'

Mr Holmes had poked his beaky nose out the door to examine the corridor. 'Hmm?'

'Audrey Hudson.'

'Lovely to meet you, Audrey Hudson. Time to go.' He beckoned with a forefinger and stepped into the corridor.

Audrey followed him but then glanced back, to three other cell doors, all closed. Hers had been closest to the stairs, and therefore logically the first Holmes checked, but there were other prisoners. *I have a dragon in a neighbouring chamber*, he'd said. Their matching windows clear rather than opaque; perhaps the doors were unlocked, too.

'Have you checked the other rooms?'

Holmes was peering up the stairwell. 'After I disabled the power supply.' He waved towards a fuse box mounted on the wall at the foot of the stairs. The case was open and the wiring eviscerated. 'Seemed the fastest approach to the locks. Nothing alive inside the others.'

Audrey backtracked down the corridor, opening doors. The first two really were empty. In the third, its walls scorched and torn with claw marks, a worn pile of scrap leather appeared to have been thrown into a corner.

A head lifted wearily from the pile at Audrey's intrusion. Red ember eyes stared forlornly from a fine head of black scales glinting gold in the light. Audrey had met only one dragon, a bluff, deep red Welsh fellow, the size and shape of a VW Beetle. This petite dragon, with her delicate fronded snout and claw-tipped wings, was not from Wales. As far as Audrey could tell, this dragon was not even an adult.

'Get out while you can,' said Audrey softly. 'And don't hurt the tall man on the stairs. He came for us.'

The little black dragon didn't waste a moment. In seconds she had unfolded her crumpled body. Wings outstretched, she launched herself over Audrey's head, and flew like a bullet out of the room, down the corridor, over Holmes' head and up the stairs.

Audrey limped achingly after her, to find Holmes gazing up the stairs.

'The giant bat looked dead when I found it, poor creature. Clearly I need to learn more about chiropteran life signs – but later! Places to be, things to steal. Come on.' He jerked his chin towards the eerie silence of the upper floors.

Audrey stumbled up the first step. Her bones felt brittle and every joint ached. She'd never defied the moon quite so thoroughly before; she wouldn't try again for a while.

The entryway and sitting room upstairs were deserted. Audrey raised her chin, sniffing discreetly, grimacing at the indiscernible odours. Was that smoke? Was that stink of ozone and burned plastic from the fuse box or something else? Somewhere was the smell of varnish and wet wool; something else was redolent of rotting plaster, and was that the musty funk of rats living in the walls? Gruner's wretched cologne was mingled in there too. Overlaying everything was the blood smearing Holmes' face and clothes, his sweat and grubbiness from a night spent, apparently, prowling the grounds outside. She could only be grateful that so few sounds were adding to the overwhelming jumble.

Oh, that didn't make sense. No sounds?

'Where are they?' she asked.

Holmes mistook her confusion for anxiety. 'Don't worry, I won't let him hurt you again, Mrs Hudson.'

She'd never said Mrs, but so many assumed the title because of her age, and her ring – a gold band, true, but with a ruby inset in the centre. Not truly a wedding band, though not, she supposed, truly not. She let it pass. 'It's not me I'm worried about.'

He grinned again. 'Oh, I'm fine. I have a black belt in bartitsu which I'll certainly use if Alec Reidl comes at me this time. I let him get a few good hits in at the park – I wasn't ready for them to realise who I was yesterday, but that's less important now. As for the emptiness of the house – I've organised a friend to create a distraction. Gruner and his cronies ought to be attending to the small explosion at the stables by now.'

'Stables?' Audrey hadn't realised it was so large a house.

'No horses were harmed in the making of this bomb,' Holmes said, 'though the same can't be said for his vintage cars. A shame, but you can't steal evidence from a foul little serial toerag without breaking a few tail lights, hmm? Ah, this looks like the library. Won't be a tick. Stand guard, would you?'

While he vanished inside the wood-panelled room, aiming to fulfil that other commission of his, Audrey stood guard. She was trembling all over but daren't sit down in case sudden action was required. Instead, she leaned against a polished display cabinet full of elegant bowls and figurines. Part of that porcelain collection he'd mentioned. Audrey was spitefully inclined to smash it all, but it wasn't the pottery's fault that Adelbert Gruner was a serial toerag.

Then she spotted something ancient and fascinating. A tiny bronze figure of the she-wolf suckling the infants Romulus and Remus. The metal was worn and pitted, but some detail had remained – the wolf's distended teats, the scores on the body to denote her hair, the attitude of her head, jaws open, snarling at the viewer as if to warn them from approaching her adopted cubs.

'Ah, you found my amulet. I'm sure you identify with her.'

Audrey's head shot up at the sound of Adelbert Gruner's voice, and she realised just how exhausted and muddled she was, as she'd not even heard his approach.

'They didn't stay with their wolfmother,' Gruner continued. 'Shepherds raised them in the end. Nobody ever says what became of the wolf.'

He was holding a gun. 'Silver bullets,' he said. 'I had hoped to keep you as a living specimen, but you'll taxidermy just as well.'

'Silver bullets,' she echoed. 'Someone used silver bullets on my family, just as they used the gas on them. And you know who it is.'

'Perhaps.'

Audrey's fingers curled into fists. Her body really wanted to change to grow claws and teeth and hair; she wanted to tear the smile right off his face. But even if she changed now, he'd likely shoot her dead before her claws could sink in. And she needed him alive to learn what he knew. Impasse.

'Shoot me, then,' she said. 'I'll die as I am and you can stuff and mount a 65-year-old human woman on the wall and explain *that* to your guests and neighbours.'

The library door opened again and Holmes appeared with a large, elegant journal tucked under one arm. He stilled.

'Come now, Gruner. You aren't going to fire that gun,' he said.

'I don't see why not. Self defence against intruders in the home.' Gruner shrugged elegantly. 'I don't know who you are, Mister Nosy, but I thought Reidl saw to you in the park.'

'As you see, he failed,' said Holmes, spreading his arms, which revealed the journal he'd retrieved.

'How did you–' Gruner began, furious, and then, 'Ah. That bitch, Winter. She did see where I put it, after all. I should have seen to her more rigorously.'

'You should have let her be,' replied Holmes darkly.

'Give me the book,' demanded Gruner, hand outstretched. 'Or I'll shoot.'

'Will you though? You're not a murderer. Yet.'

A peculiar silence followed, in which Gruner failed to hide a smirk, and Holmes' eyebrows rose.

'Oh. Your first wife. I wondered about that fall in the Alps.'

'A filthy slander,' said Gruner. 'Give me the book. It's no use to you.'

'My client begs to differ. If anything will get his sister to break the engagement, this will.'

Gruner scowled. 'She won't believe you. She loves me.'

'*Au contraire*. It's one thing for Kitty Winter to be rejected as a witness, seen only as a vindictive ex-lover, especially after the way you destroyed her reputation. It's quite another to see your cruelty and depravity detailed in your own handwriting. A person may consent to be the focus of their loved one's obsessions; few would be pleased to find they're just the latest in a long line of abuses.

'And this–' Holmes flipped open the book at the most recent page, containing a new photograph and a name, '–will be the clincher that she's just part of the ongoing collection. A new target already, Gruner? To work on before or after you marry your current victim?'

Gruner raised the gun. Audrey tensed. A silver bullet would kill a human man as easily as any other kind of ammunition. Even if it meant her own death, she wouldn't let Holmes die. She hardly knew him, but he'd come for her. He'd come to help others. The foolish young pup. The clever lad.

She steeled her aching body for the leap, and almost did herself an injury by aborting at the last minute when a small, curvy spitfire stomped into the room wielding an upraised – and rapidly descending – crowbar. It collected the unsuspecting Gruner on the left shoulder, causing him to pull the trigger with the impact.

The shot went wide of everyone and straight through a glass cabinet full of delicate china.

'You utter bastard!' the spitfire shrieked.

'Kitty, no!' shouted someone beyond the sitting room door.

Before Audrey could act, Holmes lunged at Gruner, using the corner of the journal to bruising effect in an upward swing that connected with the soft tissue of Gruner's throat. He followed the swing through and tossed the journal to Audrey, shouting 'Catch!' (she caught), and then deftly seized the Austrian's armed hand. A twist and Gruner, howling from the triple outrage to his person, was disarmed.

A heavy-set man blundered into the room, reaching for the spitfire – who had already kicked Gruner in the ribs and then found another target for her displeasure.

'No!' cried Gruner, a heart-cry, as though witnessing the slaughter of a beloved child, when Spitfire Kitty smashed the crowbar into a cabinet of china and grinned like a demon at the pretty tinkling sounds it made.

'Shinwell, get her out of here,' barked Holmes.

'It ain't like I'm not trying!' Shinwell replied. Spitfire Kitty had slithered out of his grasp and put the crowbar through what was surely an authentic Georgian Royal Crown Derby tea service.

Gruner scrabbled to the defence of his pottery collection. 'Stop! Stop it, Kitty! That's collection is priceless! Irreplaceable!'

Shinwell managed to wrest the crowbar from Kitty's grip. Kitty gave it up with a fight at first, then all at once. Diverted from immediate destruction, she grinned devilishly at Gruner, her hands on her hips. 'As irreplaceable as your car collection? All that vintage glass and metal is as wonderfully smashable as your fancy bloody dinnerware. Put that shit on social media, you arse.'

'I'll ruin you,' Gruner snarled at her.

'You did that already,' she said, and spat on him.

'Shinwell,' Holmes said grimly. 'Get Kitty out of here. The police will be on the fire brigade's tail any minute.'

'You burned my cars,' Gruner wailed.

'Yes I did,' said Kitty, not resisting Shinwell's attempts to steer her out of the building. 'Welcome to cancel culture. Prick.'

Audrey clutched the journal to her chest and tried to think. The expression on Holmes' face delivered the far from reassuring conclusion that none of this was in the plan. His eye was on Gruner's gun, which had slid across the room in the scuffle, and he bent to collect it.

Audrey's eye fixed on Gruner. Gruner's eye was wide and frenzied, first on the smashed china, then on the gun in Holmes' hand, and then on the crowbar, which he lunged for.

A supremely unladylike growl rose in Audrey's throat – she felt her larynx morphing, harnessing the unspent energy of the defied transformation – but the sound was drowned by someone else bursting into the room.

She could swear that Holmes rolled his eyes theatrically at the inconvenient chaos of it all.

'How's it taking so long to pop a granny in the skull, Gruner?' the newcomer roared. He screeched to a nearly comical halt to find the granny in question glaring at him like a feral beast. Audrey recognised Undercut at once, and the look she gave him was distinctly un-granny-like. He took an involuntary, stumbling step backwards.

'This is low, even for you, Reidl,' Holmes remarked. 'Demanding money with menaces not thrilling enough anymore?'

Reidl turned and ran. Gruner, who had regained his feet, hurtled outside after him. Audrey followed Holmes on their heels.

The van which had brought her to the mansion was parked on the drive. Reidl made straight for it, Holmes in pursuit. Gruner, crazed with fury about his precious collections, had angled in the opposite direction towards the stables and his vintage cars, above which a plume of black smoke roiled into the sky.

Within the building, a black shadow flickered in the shifting firelight. Periodically, a stream of flame belched from its head, combatting the efforts of the fire engine parked on one side of the building. The hoses poured a plume of water over the exterior of the wood and brick stables; two of the fire crew were fetching foam extinguishers to attempt dousing the fuel and cars within.

Through the open stable doors, Audrey could see that, unfortunately, most of the cars were nowhere near the flames, though she was gratified at how many windows, mirrors and lights Spitfire Kitty managed to break before expressing her wrath on the porcelain. The single crew of firefighters would have the fire under control before long.

'My Bugatti!'

Audrey sincerely hoped his Bugatti was a ball of melted rubber, shattered glass and twisted metal.

Gruner darted through the door, too panicked about his Precious to heed the shout of the firefighter trying to stop him. Next thing, the Shining Fart was dancing about an elegant and admittedly beautiful long-bodied car, the crow-bar scored paintwork bubbling on its sleek 1930s chassis. Gruner finally managed to open the hot door and fit himself behind the seat. She hoped he was wriggling because glass from the broken windscreen was embedded in his bum.

A fireman tried to rescue the vile idiot, and Gruner almost ran him down as he got the car going.

He was getting away.

Audrey was having precisely none of that.

She dropped the journal – it was obviously important, but Holmes could fetch it later – and despite her body's protestations, she managed to leap onto the running board of the car as it passed.

Gruner glared at her, enraged and fearful and full of panic, and slapped at her hands to make her let go. When that didn't work, he pressed hard on the accelerator.

Whatever speed it was meant to reach, the Bugatti hadn't taken to the sudden surge of activity after the intense heat. It gained speed, but only sluggishly. Audrey clutched Gruner's arm.

'Who sent you after me?' she demanded 'Who killed my family?'

Gruner wrenched the wheel left and right, slewing the vehicle down the drive in an attempt to shake her off, but she held tight.

'Let go!' he shrieked.

'Tell me!'

The Bugatti was hurtling down the drive when Audrey and Gruner both heard, dead ahead, a gut-churning, hissing, rattling roar, like someone was shaking a tin bucket full of water and red-hot rocks.

The incoming dragon made a relentless beeline for the driver of the car, wings spread, red eyes gleaming, teeth bared. From that wide maw, a ball of boiling red and orange started small; grew large.

Gruner slammed on the brakes. Audrey let go of the car and landed relatively softly in the English boxwood hedge lining the drive.

The infuriated dragon unleashed a fireball straight through the empty rectangle of the windscreen frame and onto Gruner's exposed face. Then, with a final guttural shriek, it vanished into the sky.

Audrey ran to the car. She used the hem of her skirt to open the door, pulled Adelbert Gruner out of the smoking ruin of his car.

She bent over the blistering ruin of his face. 'You know who murdered my family,' she said, voice breaking. 'Tell me. *Tell me.*'

His eyes were scorched sightless and his grimace might have been a grin. 'Wh-wh-what's i-in it. F'me?'

'Anything you want,' she promised recklessly. 'Ask and it's yours. You can film me. You can study me, if you want. But tell me.'

'Aaaah,' he sighed. Multiple pairs of feet crunched hurriedly down the drive towards them.

'Please,' she begged.

'Mmmm.'

'Tell me.'

'Mmmoran. Sssssto...k-k-k. Mmm....'

'What does that mean? What do you mean?'

The reply was a sibilant gurgle, and then arms closed around her shoulders and drew her away. Holmes, handling her gently. 'You can't do anything more for him.'

Or to him, Audrey thought bitterly.

Men in bulky firefighting gear knelt beside the burned man.

'Did you see that?' one murmured. 'Car just burst into flames.'

'Engine must've been cooking,' said another. 'He pushed it too hard.'

'Ambulance is on the way, sir,' said another gently, but Gruner was moaning piteously and well beyond hearing.

'The journal,' Audrey panted, resisting both despair and lethargy. At least one of them should get what they needed out of this awful mess.

'I have it,' Holmes reassured her.

She managed to arch an eyebrow, because his arms were around her and the journal was too big for pockets.

'Down the back of my jeans,' he said. 'The corners prod a bit.'

Audrey clutched at his hands, feeling for the moment very much the enfeebled old lady people kept mistaking her for.

'I want to go home.'

'Any minute now,' Holmes promised her. 'As soon as I've dealt with the police.'

Chapter Four

Sherlock Holmes turned, flipped up his jacket to reveal the journal tucked into the back of his jeans, and waggled his hips slightly. 'If you'd just... put that somewhere discreet until we go,' he said softly. 'My client needs it, and if the Old Bill get their hands on it, we won't ever see it again.'

Despite shaking fingers, Audrey retrieved it and then sat on it while Holmes shielded her. She concealed the horrid thing with the drape of her skirt. The corners prodded her, too.

Holmes spoke animatedly with the police. Fire trucks had doused the Bugatti in foam before continuing to extinguish the stables. An ambulance had taken Gruner away. Audrey refused to think of him as 'poor Gruner'.

Holmes was disavowing all knowledge of the conflagration. 'I came to negotiate with Gruner on behalf of a client,' he insisted to the lead detective.

'And you won't tell me who that is,' noted the officer drily, with weary irritation.

'You know that client confidentiality is my watchword, Detective Inspector Bradstreet. People come to me because I take that promise seriously. The client isn't here, in any case, and can't possibly be responsible for the fire.'

'Someone has to be.'

'Think of it as karma. It's merely excellent, or terrible, timing, depending on your viewpoint. I'm hardly the only one wanting to bring him to justice. Between womanising, underhanded antiques acquisitions, ruthless property dealings, and a willingness to take by force whatever he couldn't gain legally, Gruner had no shortage of enemies.'

'Nothing's ever been proved against him,' said Bradstreet.

'I infer from that phrasing that you've tried.'

'I couldn't comment on that, Mr Holmes.'

'Of course you couldn't. Still, I expect you're able to comment on Gruner's henchman – and how perfectly baroque of Gruner to have a *henchman* – Alec Reidl. He's tied up in the back of that white van.'

Bradstreet's eyebrows rose in comical surprise. 'You've assaulted a man?'

'I've restrained a thug with a history as an extortionist and standover man. Add "threatener of nice old ladies" to that charge sheet. He attacked me in Regent's Park, see?' Holmes tilted his chin to display his cuts and bruises to best advantage. 'Then they bundled Mrs Hudson into the van like a sack of grain and brought her here.'

'So you weren't just here to talk to Gruner.'

'I've just told you that that's exactly why I was here. Mrs Hudson is also a client.'

Audrey kept one highly sensitive ear on Holmes' conversation while she wondered if Reidl knew anything about her family. She wondered how to get five minutes alone with him to find out.

A shadow fell over her and Audrey looked up at a paramedic trying to get her attention. She allowed the woman to take her pulse; shine a light in her eyes.

'I'm all right. Thank you,' she managed. She was weary beyond imagining, and the journal poked uncomfortably into her thighs.

'You should come in for observation.'

'No, really. I just want to go home.'

The woman went away.

'Mrs Hudson, is it?'

She looked up again. A policeman looked down at her.

'Audrey Hudson. Yes.'

'I'm DI Bradstreet. Mr Holmes says he came to speak to Mr Gruner and found you being held prisoner here. Is that right?'

'Yes.' She considered the overheard conversation between Holmes and Bradstreet, played into it. 'Mr Gruner insisted he wanted to acquire my home on Baker Street. He wanted me to sign the papers.'

'Did you meet Gruner's associate, Mr Reidl?'

'Mr Reidl made threats. They frightened me.' She tried to remember how to look frightened, but she was shaking enough with fatigue that Bradstreet believed her anyway.

Bradstreet crouched; rested a gentle hand on her elbow. He was very gentlemanly. Very kind. Audrey felt a little bad for lying through her teeth.

'I'm sorry you've been put through all of this, Mrs Hudson. But I have more questions.'

To Bradstreet's dismay and her own bewilderment, Audrey began to cry.

'I tell you what,' he said, 'how about I visit you tomorrow and we'll talk then.'

'Thank you. Yes. I would like to go home now. Please.'

'I'll arrange for one of my team to take you back to Baker Street.'

'Mr Holmes said he would take me,' she said tremulously. 'He's been very sweet.'

Bradstreet snorted rudely then pretended he hadn't. 'All right then. Go with Mr Holmes, and we'll talk tomorrow.'

Holmes made a point of very sweetly and solicitously telling Audrey, 'No don't get up, you've had a terrible shock. Wait right there, I'll bring my car around.'

She almost arched an eyebrow and said "Hark at you, impressing the DI with your manners" but resisted. The whole point of sitting on a journal full of women made wretched by Adelbert Gruner was to keep it out of police hands.

Holmes drove up in an honest-to-God black London cab – a handsome vehicle with a golden light on top, a meter in the front cabin and the official green licence of a genuine London cabbie propped in the windscreen.

'I wondered who'd parked outside the gates,' said Bradstreet. 'Where's the driver?'

'I'm the driver,' Holmes replied. He'd taken off his coat and proceeded to drop it twice, his fumbling disguising how Audrey passed him the journal. They straightened and Holmes guided Audrey into the back seat. He dropped the journal discreetly from under the coat into her lap and arranged a blanket around her. She told herself she was playing along, ashamed of how fragile she felt.

'You have to be qualified to drive a black cab,' Bradstreet insisted.

'Oh, I've got The Knowledge,' Holmes said blithely, retrieving the green badge as proof. 'I've always aimed to have an exact knowledge of London, and the licence is handy. I have the green and all nine of the yellows.'

'Of course you bloody do. For those days when the consulting detective business doesn't pay?'

'I imagine so,' Holmes replied.

Audrey sat quietly while Holmes took the wheel and drove them away from Gruner's mansion.

'Are you really a cabbie?' she asked at length.

His grey eyes met her brown ones in the rear-view mirror. 'I'm a consulting detective, as you heard the man say. Unsolved crime is my *metier*. The cabbie thing is convenient for my work, sometimes. Nobody notices black cabs in the streets, really. They certainly never notice if it's the same one coming through every ten or fifteen minutes. People aren't very observant.'

As a woman who had been a werewolf for most of her life, she could attest to that.

'Will that young woman be all right? Kitty?' she asked.

'Shinwell whisked her away – thank you for not bringing her up, by the way. She's been through quite enough on Gruner's account, and was instrumental in helping me find the evidence I need to separate him from another of his victims. I don't know that I can repair the damage he did to her with that spiteful online campaign, but she at least is free of him now.'

'What are you going to do with this journal?' she asked. She'd begun to flip through it, but was so disgusted by the louche descriptions that she'd snapped it shut again. Gruner's precise hand on every page described these women in the most personal detail, footnoted with single sentences of how he'd marked them once he'd finished with them. A burn scar on flawless skin; explicit photographs released to the press. Kitty's entry was labelled "social media hack".

'I'll show it to the client's sister. Better me than him – she'll hate Gruner for his sins, but she'll hate whoever hands it to her just as much for destroying her faith in the man she thinks she loves.'

'You'd do that for your client?'

'Well, I am used to people not particularly enjoying my deductions, and he's paying me very well. He's covering the hire of this cab from its owner today, for example.'

Audrey wondered if she, too, was expected to pay for her rescue.

'Helping you was a bonus,' he said, reading her expression somehow, his eyes crinkling in a smile. 'Though I should put some thought into what I'm going to tell Bradstreet when he sees you tomorrow. He'll want to know if this has anything to do with Edinburgh.'

Audrey's breath froze in her lungs. She schooled her expression to neutrality again, though her hands trembled.

'What do you mean?'

'You're the Audrey Hudson whose family was killed in Edinburgh a month ago, are you not.'

'How do you know?'

'I told you. Unsolved crime is my *metier*, and that crime left so many bizarre clues it's frankly alarming that the police haven't found any leads.' He turned onto the motorway to London. 'I'm satisfied you're not a suspect, if you were wondering.'

Audrey quelled a growl. 'I was not.'

'I've read everything about the case. I even went up two weeks ago, but I don't understand the evidence yet. I know you were in London when the murders occurred. I know you had no motive. It's a puzzle.'

'That puzzle is *my family.*'

Holmes' eyes creased in dismay. 'Ah. I'm... Forgive me, Mrs Hudson. I get caught up in the intrigues of the case and I don't always think. I'm sorry for your loss.'

She nodded, not quite willing yet to forgive.

'What I meant to say is that I'm at your service, if you'd like me to look into it. I'm certain I could make headway if I had all of the facts. The case is so peculiar that surely, a truly complete account of the facts would lead somewhere concrete. Traces of silver were found in all the remains, and the toxicology results suggested aconite poisoning. And the, ah, post-mortem wounds. There seemed no fiscal or other rational motive for the murders, and your family had no known enemies, barring a brief fracas with some local toughs.'

Those *toughs* were the reason they'd been relocating to Baker Street. Another week and they would have been safe.

'Yet,' he continued, 'three people were shot and dismemb-aaaah. I'm sorry.'

'Dismembered. Yes. I know.' Her tone was clipped, crisp. Little bites of sound.

Holmes sighed and his shoulders sagged. 'I really am terribly sorry. I'm not trying to be unkind. I'm trying to understand. I know I can make sense of it, if you can tell me everything you know.'

'I've already told the Edinburgh police everything I know.'

'Everything that you *know* you know,' he replied. 'I suspect you carry the key somehow, even if you're not aware that you do.'

'How could you possibly learn a thing that I don't know that I know?'

'Usually it's in some small detail dismissed as unimportant. Most people are not very observant, as I said. I am, in most regards, the polar opposite of most people.'

Audrey smiled. Mr Holmes had described an escaping dragon as a bat; and she'd heard him tell DI Bradstreet about the large crow swooping at the Bugatti before it caught fire. So much, Audrey thought, for his vaunted observations. He was at one with most people, in that. The uncanny was infinitely deniable until it was unavoidable – like the first time the moon waxed full and your body twisted to obey the curse you didn't even know you carried.

She might have enlightened Holmes on the uncanny, but too often in her life, attempts to prove that the supernatural was real ended in terror, hysteria, absurd levels of denial, or wild attempts to kill her. She'd learned to avoid raising the subject.

She knew from experience that Sherlock Holmes' brand of secular logic would never accept the paranormal truth of what he'd seen today, which meant he couldn't possibly help her.

'I'll visit tomorrow,' Holmes promised her, tempering his eagerness with a kind tone. 'We'll discuss it further. I'll show you I'm right.'

Audrey was much too exhausted to argue further, especially when he *was* right.

'Fine. Not early. I plan to sleep in.'

He grinned. 'Splendid. Till tomorrow, then,'

Back in Baker Street, Audrey bolted the front door shut, then took several attempts to unlock her own flat, her hands were so shaky. Once inside, she dropped the keys. She was now shaking right down to her bones. Her skin itched; her nail beds ached; even her teeth hurt.

Unable to operate buttons or zippers, Audrey toed off her shoes before stepping, clothed, into the bathtub and turning on the shower. Her knees buckled and she sat in the tub, hot water streaming over her head and shoulders, over her clothed body and legs.

Over her snout, her ears, her claws and hairy feet.

She was not the moon's bitch, but defiance had a price.

Audrey curled under the warm water, halfway between human and wolf, and whined desolately to her bathroom walls.

More than a day passed before Sherlock Holmes came to Baker Street. Audrey answered the knock to find him on the threshold with a bulging suitcase on the path. A cab driver, manning the black cab Holmes had borrowed, was heaving a larger, heavier bag onto the path beside it.

'Sorry, mate. When I've lugged that French feller and all his baggage to Heathrow, I'll come back for you.'

'Perfect, Bill,' Holmes assured him. 'If I've finished with Mrs Hudson, I'll wait at the Pret on the corner.'

'Ey-up,' agreed Bill, and drove off.

Holmes responded to Audrey's inspection of his unexpected luggage with a proud tilt of his chin. His face still bore the healing cuts and bruises of his encounters with Reidl.

'A temporary embarrassment with regard to my lodgings,' he explained. 'Bill will be back for me in due course. Any objections to leaving my luggage in your hall in the meantime? Nobody could abscond with those bags in a hurry, they're mostly full of books, but it'd be tiresome to lose them.'

Audrey let him heave each of the bags inside. He limped in after them.

She had *so* many questions.

She started with the most obvious. 'How do you come to be at my door with what looks like all your worldly goods?'

'I had a bedsit in Montague Street. I thought I'd advised the landlord that I sometimes undertook chemical experiments in pursuit of my work. He disagreed.'

'I see.'

'He also took exception to my face.'

'It seems a perfectly inoffensive face to me.'

'Yes, well, you're not under the impression I'm conducting a meth lab in your spare room.'

She led him into her flat and waved him towards a kitchen chair while she put the kettle on.

'Was it a meth lab?'

He laughed. 'No. Not my poison, anyway. Not that I have a poison anymore. Ah.' He snapped his jaw shut and Audrey wondered what kind of life this odd man, full of contradictions, had lived.

'The limp is new,' she observed.

'Yes. My client's sister slams a mean door. I didn't get my foot clear in time.'

'At least she didn't give you a black eye.'

'Small mercies.'

She scooped tea into a pot and set out two cups on saucers, a sugar bowl, milk in the jug. A little plate of custard creams.

Holmes reached for a biscuit as she put the plate on the table and was half way through it before he realised his table manners were lacking. Audrey pushed the plate closer to him. 'Have another. They'll only go stale if you don't.'

He finished the first quickly but ate the second less like a starving animal. Audrey wished she'd thought to make cake, or sandwiches.

'It went well, then, apart from the door-slamming?'

'She's done with Gruner, if that's what you mean. I wanted to use the journal as evidence of his broader villainy, but she burned it. I should have expected that.'

'Are you sure?'

'Oh yes. She built a very effective bonfire, and after midnight I went through the ashes to be certain. I scaled the fence again just ahead of her dog!' Holmes laughed, delighted with his narrow escape, then sobered again. 'Just as well, really. No need to have that journal slip out of police hands into the media's. Kitty and the other women in that book don't need to be dragged through their trauma again. Kitty and I agree that its production wouldn't undo the harm he did her in that social media campaign.'

'Perhaps now she will be able to move on.'

'I think burning down his car collection's helping with that.'

Audrey poured tea and remembered that she had cheese and chutney in the fridge and savoury biscuits in the cupboard. She set those out too and watched him arrange a clock face of Ritz crackers on the plate, topping each with a lump of cheddar and a scoop of chutney. Then, following a pattern of opposites, he ate each one in a single bite. It afforded her a completely unreasonable level of satisfaction to feed him.

He gulped the first cup of tea, too, then drank more civilly, dunking a custard cream this time.

Honestly, she could watch him eat all day long. This was a bad sign. She did not need another stray cub to protect. Sherlock Holmes did not need protecting.

'Did Bradstreet make his threatened visit?' Holmes asked, arranging three more biscuits in a fan around his tea cup.

'He did. He recognised my name, but he was no trouble.'

'He's no doubt been in touch with Edinburgh and knows you're not considered a suspect there. Don't be surprised if he prowls around for a while, though. His instincts aren't terrible, though he relies too much on those and not enough on reasoning. He can be like a pig snuffling for truffles, however, and might pester you for a while.'

The interview with Bradstreet had involved leaving blank spots in her account of the day. Nobody had witnessed how she'd leapt onto the Bugatti's running board – Holmes had been busy dealing with Reidl, the firemen with the fire – but Bradstreet's arrival on the scene had coincided with what everyone had assumed was her rushing to Gruner's aid. It was awkward to be perceived as saint-like when her motivations had been far more desperate and personal.

Yet stolid, softly-spoken Bradstreet had emanated a confused distrust, as though embarrassed to be so suspicious, with so little foundation, of this nice, traumatised old lady. Some people were sensitive to her cursed nature: his instincts were sound.

'Back to business,' Holmes said brusquely. 'Your case. As I've been telling you, you do know something.'

'And as I keep telling you, I don't. And I've tried.'

'In your statement, you said that you'd returned home to find your house a crime scene. You'd been preparing your London residence for your family's relocation. Why was that?'

'The neighbourhood didn't feel safe anymore. Conal suggested, since my last tenants had vacated, Baker Street would be a good change for us.'

Her poor darling boy, her Conal. Fourteen when she'd found him. Saved him. Saved them all, so she'd thought at the time and for the years after. Until she hadn't.

'Why?'

'Pardon?'

He placed gentle fingertips on her wrist. She pressed the heel of her hand to her damp eyes.

'Why didn't you feel safe?'

'Those local toughs you mentioned were unpleasant, but the whole neighbourhood was feeling less safe, especially for Siobhan. She suffered from anxiety; and they upset her. Travis and Tara never cared where they were as long as they weren't separated again. Conal and I only ever wanted them to feel safe.'

It sounded very thin, spoken aloud, but it was the truth. The wolf in her had been uneasy at those rambunctious young men in the neighbourhood, catcalling Siobhan and Tara when they went to the store. Between them, Conal and Audrey had given the little buggers some second, third and fourth thoughts about their behaviour, but something else was at the back of it. The humans had perhaps been influenced by subtle but growing signs of the arrival of a new *were* pack. Audrey's hackles had risen at insipient danger before her mind had quantified the evidence.

She'd lost territory before. Turf wars had destroyed her first family, as warped as it had been; and killed the baby she carried – dear Hugh Hudon's baby – that she'd wanted despite the curse it carried in its blood.

Stupid Alphas and their stupid turf wars. She was having none of it. Turf was just a place to live. Family was what mattered. She and Conal had decided it together. Let the invaders have the turf. They'd save the family.

Only they hadn't.

'It was just a feeling,' she said at last, knowing it was weak. 'Instinct.'

'Instinct is often simply the act of assessing facts and likelihoods on a subliminal level. Unpleasant people in the neighbourhood, rising crime statistics, that sort of thing. Of course, there's the link with Gruner to consider as well.'

Audrey raised an eyebrow, not trusting to her voice.

Sherlock Holmes reached into his pocket and placed a bullet on the table.

'What is that?' she asked faintly.

'A very strange piece of ammunition I retrieved from Gruner's gun before I handed it over to Bradstreet. I left the other two for him, of course. It's only fair.'

Audrey's heart raced.

Holmes continued. 'Traces of silver were found in the autopsies in Edinburgh. I perceive that some assassin out there has a grotesque idea of a leitmotif.'

Audrey stared at the bullet like it was a manifest horror. He scooped it back quickly into his pocket.

'Silver bullets are associated with *The Lone Ranger*,' he said in a considering tone. 'Well, and the dispatching of werewolves, according to my sister's vast collection of folklore, but let's dismiss that ludicrous implication. The coroner didn't exactly check for wolf DNA.'

Who would even think to look for it? Audrey didn't even know what werewolf DNA looked like.

'The figure of the Lone Ranger is well out of the cultural zeitgeist, and frankly problematic,' continued Holmes. 'His signature bullet was a symbol of justice, which hardly fits the crime against your family. Ballistically, there's not much difference between this and ordinary bullets, except that silver bullets are marginally less accurate. It's all very peculiar.'

Audrey waited pensively for him to reach a conclusion. He certainly didn't require any input from her.

'Gruner's silver bullets and your loss may not be directly linked. Gruner wasn't in Edinburgh at the time of the murders. But silver bullets are odd and I don't believe in coincidences that strange. Perhaps Gruner's shady art and car dealer contacts in Scotland informed him of your situation – a vulnerable woman living alone in the city, in exactly the kind of building he liked to acquire.'

Holmes gave her an expectant look. Audrey set her cup into its saucer. 'I don't know what you expect me to say.'

'When you pulled Gruner from the car, you were shouting at him to "tell you". You believe he has a link to Edinburgh, don't you.'

'Yes,' she admitted.

'Did he tell you?'

'No.'

'That's a pity.'

'He might still tell me, if he recovers from his burns.'

'He might. But I wouldn't put much faith in a recovery.'

'No.' Satisfaction warred with regret. She would never know what Adelbert Gruner knew. Audrey, deep in that unhappy reflection and looking into her teacup, was surprised when Holmes' long fingers again reached out to touch her on the wrist, then withdrew.

'As I said, I do enjoy a puzzle.' He said it gently, like an offering.

She should've been furious. Conal's murder, Siobhan's and Travis' and Tara's – this wasn't a puzzle. They were her heart, torn out of her chest. They were her kin by choice, her – yes, all right – her cubs; her joys. And the were slaughtered like beasts.

But she looked into Holmes' eyes – steady, keen, full of curiosity, like Siobhan's had been. She saw he was trying to give her a gift. Or trying to relieve an ache, hers or possibly his, in the giving.

Sherlock Holmes was abrupt and too inquisitive. Too keen on solving this murder whether or not she asked him to. Obsessed about the puzzle without a thought for the people in it, for the pain of it.

But he had taken on the burden of telling his client's sister about her false love, so that her relationship with her brother wouldn't be damaged. He'd protected Kitty from the police and recognised that burning the book was another way to protect the women Gruner had harmed.

Sherlock Holmes was abrupt but kind. He was inquisitive but sought justice.

She felt exposed by the understanding in his grey eyes – that sharp mind saw her loneliness; but she saw his too.

'Where will you go?' she asked suddenly. 'With your bags?'

'Oh, I'll find somewhere. My sister has a sofa, even if she doesn't like people sleeping on it.'

'You could stay here.' It came out a blurt, almost pleading.

'I... could?'

'I have a whole, huge, empty house here,' she said firmly, trying to sound less needy. 'It's probably time I found a lodger or two.'

'It's kind of you,' Holmes said, 'but my means are limited.'

That's right. He'd been evicted from a bedsit in Montague Street.

'It would be a favour to me,' she insisted. 'Keep the predators at bay, if you will.' Oh, what a dreadful, wilful liar she was sometimes.

'If you take the upstairs apartment, there are two bedrooms. You can pay what you paid for Montague Street, and find someone to take the second bedroom for the same price. If you like.'

Holmes tilted his head on one side, considering. Audrey was worried that she sounded too keen for him to stay, too desperate to have him in her house, under her protection. Not that he knew he would be.

'My clients tend to come at all hours,' he said.

'As long as they wipe their shoes on the mat, that's fine.'

'I carry out chemical experiments, from time to time, in the course of my work.'

'Just don't burn down the house.'

'I almost never do.' He was grinning.

Audrey found herself smiling back; found herself liking this young man immensely. Ruby would have liked him too.

'I should fetch my lab equipment. My old landlord threw it into a skip, but I don't think he broke everything.'

'You haven't even seen the rooms.'

'If they look better than sleeping under London Bridge tonight, I'm perfectly happy.'

'They're furnished. You'll need to stock the cupboards.'

'And find a flatmate.'

She honestly didn't care whether or not he did, as long as he stayed, but articulating that would be weird. 'I'm sure you'll find someone you can tolerate,' she said lightly.

'And who can tolerate me?' He winced slightly, but brightened. 'Piece of cake, I'm sure.'

There was that note of loneliness again, alongside that sense of pride. He fancied himself a lone wolf no doubt, but Audrey knew how false that pretence was. Nobody ever really wanted to be the lone wolf. People said it to pretend they'd had a choice in the matter.

'I'll get my things,' declared Holmes, then clapped his hands together with energetic decision. 'And then I'll see what more I can discover about Edinburgh.'

Audrey wouldn't waste her breath on truths about werewolves, silver bullets and wolfsbane. He wouldn't believe her without proof; and his type probably wouldn't believe the proofs either. She'd seen people driven mad by their denial of all the proofs she had to offer.

But perhaps he could help. They could begin with trying to decipher what Gruner had meant by "Moran".

And why it sounded so familiar.

Chapter Five

Audrey had owned the dented shortbread tin, with its long-haired, heavily armed, brightly tartaned Scot staring boldly out from the lid, since long before she had taken her family to Edinburgh. Audrey had fled her Newton Abbot home at the age of 17 with a few changes of clothes and this tin of small treasures in her rucksack.

It had taken two days to realise the tin might contain some way to scratch that niggling itch of the name "Moran", and even then, she'd resisted the impulse to look inside. The contents might stimulate an elusive memory, but certainly it would stir a lot of other memories that she'd rather let lie, like sleeping dogs.

Audrey grimaced. There was no escaping the canine metaphors in her life. Might as well embrace them. Including the fact that she frequently caught herself referring to the new lodger as her cub, even though Sherlock Holmes was hardly hers.

Ah well, old dogs, new tricks, yadda yadda.

Audrey opened the tin.

With all my worldly goods, I thee endow, she'd said to Ruby once upon a time, revealing the precious scraps of her old life.

Her grandmother's gold bracelet, given to Audrey on her 16th birthday, which had been hocked and redeemed from time to desperate time. A pencil sketch of her own young face, inscribed *To my best girl, forever yours, Ollie*. A ticket to the Kinks 1972 Manchester show, stained with perspiration and a lipstick kiss, and oh hadn't she got in trouble for running off at 15 to dance and scream *I love you!* to Ray Davies and sing loud and gustily to *Lola*, which she loved even more after she understood the lyrics.

Most precious of all, the photographs. Her and Ollie. Her parents, grandparents and sister. She in her black and white mod minidress and knee high boots, hair teased out, eyes wide and mouth open, singing, and every cell of her joyful. Later, she'd added photos of Ruby; of Conal, Siobhan, Travis and Tara; but none of them had anything to do with that elusive memory.

The distant familiarity of "Moran" was smoke. She couldn't grasp it, except the scent of her past surrounded it. She just couldn't think how.

'*Mrs Hudson!*'

The good-natured bellow made Audrey twitch, as much with amusement as with sensitivity to the volume. She slid the closed tin back into its nook alongside the stove. She opened her door to the foyer to find Sherlock Holmes there, knuckles raised to rap on her door. His tall, wiry frame filled the space, his expression bright eyed and thoroughly braced.

'I may have found someone to share the rooms with me,' he announced. 'If you'll have him.'

In room-hungry London, it had taken Sherlock only three days to make this announcement.

'Well, tell me about him,' she urged, waving Sherlock into to the kitchen.

'A doctor, recovering his health after being invalided out of the army. He was supposed to have been sharing with an army buddy of his, but that's fallen in a heap at short notice. Our mutual friend Stamford whispered that the buddy has a drinking problem, among other issues she brought back from the war. Don't give me that look, I know better than to ask him about it.'

Audrey wasn't sure he did, but ignored that. 'What else?'

'He was shot while serving in Afghanistan. I surmised he was part of an extraction that went wrong; army doctors don't usually leave the base long enough to be shot at.'

She set about making tea. 'Does he have a name, then?'

'Doctor John H Watson,' said Sherlock, sweeping his long, floppy fringe back over the crown of his head. His grey eyes were alive with enthusiasm. 'A former colleague of Josie Stamford's at St Bart's Hospital. Do you know what this Watson did today when I deduced he'd been wounded in Afghanistan, before he'd even said a single word?'

'I'm all ears.' She fetched a container of the morning's fresh-baked biscuits.

'He looked surprised, and then he looked intrigued, and then he asked if I had any bad habits.'

'Did you tell him?'

'I did,' Sherlock said with an undeniable touch of astonished pride.

'And?'

'He matched them with a litany of his own vices, which he claims will change once he's recovered his health. I've no doubt we'll get on. He was in the army. They have to get on with everybody there. Well. Everybody who's on the same side,' he amended.

Sherlock's eagerness subsided at that thought and he nibbled pensively at a biscuit. Audrey quelled the urge to pat his hand. Sherlock tended to prickliness if he perceived his poorly concealed loneliness was eliciting sympathy.

'Do his vices include smoking?' she asked instead, pointedly.

'Not a smoker,' Sherlock conceded and he flashed a grin. 'So he'll keep me on the straight and narrow, if that's what concerns you.'

'Straight and narrow,' she scoffed, pouring the tea.

'Straight-and-narrow-ish,' he allowed. 'He's an occasional drinker, I think, but no tells indicating he's an alcoholic. He demonstrates a nice curiosity, too – asking all about the experiment I was conducting in Stamford's lab, and not apparently bothered that it was a human spleen in the dish.'

'Did he know it was a human spleen?'

'Yes. He asked if I was hunting for a cause of the enlargement, as it looked to him like cirrhosis and a rupture rather than parasites. He was delightful. Observant in his own field, even if not in a more holistic sense. I'm hopeful he'll be tolerable.' Or *tolerant*, his expression seemed to say. Then he added, 'He has a moustache.'

Apparently realising this detail was not important, unless you were the kind of man who liked other men with moustaches, Sherlock tipped extra milk into his tea to cool it, gulped it down and leapt to his feet.

'He's coming tomorrow morning to see the rooms, if that suits. I should go upstairs. A client's due by at seven, and he's not going to be happy with my findings.'

'Make sure *this* one pays you *before* you tell him the bad news, won't you?'

Sherlock waved his hand as though this was a paltry consideration.

Audrey shook her head. Perhaps an army doctor would have a better head for business than Sherlock, who, for all his intelligence, seemed without the slightest care for how money worked.

The scent of both foreign climates and the hospital still clung to Dr John Watson when he duly came to inspect the rooms. His wounded shoulder may have healed, but Audrey could detect even now the effects of the post-operative infection that had done worse to his health than the bullet had. He had the physique of a man who'd previously been robust. His fading tan and short brown hair, sun-bleached golden at the wavy tips, spoke of an outdoor life, but his clothes hung loose on him. An army doctor, without an army now; without a career.

Audrey felt an instant kinship with him. She knew what it was to be suddenly bereft of pack and purpose. But she liked him for other things. The way he slowly but steadily ascended the stairs, determined but not absolutely reckless to prove himself. When he caught her look of concern, he only smiled wryly.

'My physiotherapist says I need to be more active, but I can't bear the idea of the gym. All that running nowhere. Seventeen steps is a good start.'

'Plus fifteen more to the bedrooms,' Sherlock announced, having passed through the landing door into the sitting room. The doctor followed his potential flatmate inside and peered about.

'Sitting room, kitchenette, study at the back,' Audrey said, 'Though we could turn that into a bedroom and put the study upstairs, with Sherlock's room and the toilet.'

'No need,' said Dr Watson, stoic.

'There's room in the attic for storage,' she added.

'Not a lot of stuff to store,' he said. 'Books, mainly.'

'Ah, your medical library.' Sherlock was keenly interested. 'Basic anatomy, obviously. Toxicology? Traumatic injuries? They might be handy in my work.'

'Might they?' Instead of being alarmed, Dr Watson's wry smile became more openly amused. 'See a lot of bullet wounds in your line of work?'

'Bullet wounds, knife wounds, blunt force trauma, lacerations, burns. Poisons are common, too. It's not all murder and assaults of course.'

'Of course.'

The doctor regarded Sherlock with a combination of fascination, puzzlement and... enchantment.

Well, that's interesting, Audrey thought.

Sherlock cut a sharp glance at the doctor, whose gaze was suddenly fixed on the windows overlooking Baker Street.

'Nice to get some light in,' Dr Watson observed.

Sherlock, Audrey noted, was observing Dr Watson. His neck and shoulders and backside, particularly, but also his soldierly stance. And sometimes his moustache, which was neatly trimmed and suited the doctor's rather nice face.

Dr Watson turned suddenly. 'And the bedrooms?'

Sherlock just as suddenly found the wainscoting a source of deep significance.

The doctor trod up another flight of stairs, slow and steady.

He'll be running up those stairs when he's fit again, Audrey thought. *Nothing wrong with him some rest, a few good meals and something useful to do with himself can't fix.*

Dr Watson glanced briefly over Sherlock's bedroom. He took more time in the bathroom, noting the deep tub. Then he stepped into the second, smaller furnished room like he was ready to claim it as his own territory. The window looked over the back garden. A small skylight allowed a square of cheerful light into the room.

The memory of Tara claiming the space, smiling with her face tilted up into the light, caught Audrey in the throat. The soft shaft of light limning her dark hair with silver, illuminating the splash of freckles across her nose and her happy smile; brown eyes crinkling merrily; Tara laughing at her brother: *it's a little wolf den.*

Only if wolves love Nintendo and Monster Munch, Travis, her mirror but with shorter hair and sharper lines, had laughed back.

'...if I pass muster?'

Audrey blinked back into the present. Doctor Watson was trying to conceal his eagerness. The expression said loudly as words that he was used to disappointment.

'You'll do.'

The doctor's sudden, sunny smile transformed his weary features into something quite handsome. 'And of course, Mr Holmes, if you're still up for me as a flatmate?'

'Sherlock, please.' Sherlock waved his hand airily, despite the fact he'd scampered around in Dr Watson's shadow for the last half hour. 'And as the landlady says, you'll do.'

Audrey wanted to cuff him, but Dr Watson only seemed to find the attitude charming. 'Yeah. You might do as well.' He turned to Audrey, missing Sherlock's startled look.

'How soon might I move in?'

'As soon as you like,' she replied.

'Is tonight all right? Only, the friend I'm staying with is a bit keen to turf me out. She's, ah...' He faded out, flustered to have admitted his precarious situation.

'Not coping well with civilian life?' Sherlock offered in a surprisingly tactful rescue.

'Not that well, no.'

'Tonight, then, by all means,' Sherlock said grandly. 'Isn't that so, Mrs Hudson?'

'It is. Come downstairs to sign things, Dr Watson, and I'll get the other key.'

'I'll need the study as a laboratory,' blurted Sherlock suddenly, then stood haughty and defiant. 'Sometimes things explode.'

Honestly. It was like he was *trying* to make the doctor turn tail and run.

'Don't do it when I'm asleep, then,' replied the doctor with less hauteur but just as much defiance. 'I sometimes react violently to being suddenly woken by loud bangs.'

Good lord, were they having a competition over who could be the most appalling?

Sherlock, however, simply relaxed, as though Dr Watson had been confronted with a challenge and not been found wanting.

'I wouldn't dream of alarming you like that,' he said with absolute sincerity. 'My apologies.'

'We're good,' replied Dr Watson, at ease again.

Oh, these two are going to be a handful, thought Audrey. The thought made her happy like she hadn't been since Edinburgh.

The reasons why John Watson's army mate was not coping became more apparent when he returned in the afternoon with a box in his arms.

The mate was carrying John's duffel bag, but moving carefully on her prosthetic leg.

Audrey had intended to greet her, but the reek of stale smoke, unwashed skin and alcohol, all dowsed in an overpowering body spray and peppermint mouthwash, made her eyes water. She kept her distance, hovering by her own flat's door.

'Mrs Hudson, hello!' John greeted her cheerily. 'This is my friend, Nick Murray. We served together in Afghanistan. Nick, my new landlady, Mrs Hudson.'

Nick nodded curtly, a wary squint indicating she was aware of Audrey's scrutiny. 'Pleased to meet you. Hey, where do you want this, Johnny?'

'Leave it in the foyer here, I'll take it up later,' John replied. 'Thanks for the help.' He placed his box beside the bag on the carpet and went to hug her.

Nick skittered away. 'None of that, Johnny. Least I could do, since I bailed on you with my place.'

Feet clattered on the stairs above and then suddenly slowed, and Sherlock Holmes descended the staircase as though he'd never been in a hurry.

'Ah good, you're here,' he said smoothly, then lifted an eyebrow at the scant luggage at the foot of the stairs. 'Is that all you have? Oh, of course. Not much time to accumulate possessions when you're abroad, getting shot at, I suppose.'

'You're a charmer,' observed Nick drily.

Sherlock, who'd already realised how charmless he'd sounded, raked her from crown to boot-toe with a probing look. Nick smiled thinly and gave him the finger.

John's mouth twitched with tension, but he spoke lightly. 'Steady, Nick, that's my new flatmate you're flipping the bird. Sherlock, this is Nick Murray. Nick, Sherlock Holmes.'

Nick regarded Sherlock with the same frank assessment he'd just given her. 'Johnny told me you're uncanny at reading people,' was all she said.

'Uncanny implies the supernatural. It's pure science, I assure you.'

'Either way,' she said even more drily, 'you can keep your opinions to yourself.'

John's mouth twitched again, and Sherlock abandoned the skirmish for something kinder. 'John, I fixed the hinge on your bedroom wardrobe. It squeaked.'

That handsome smile lit up John's face again, bringing colour to his pallor and transforming the pain lines around his eyes into the laughter lines that had preceded them.

'Thanks.'

Sherlock shrugged, pretending disinterest, and John only smiled harder.

Nick's prickliness softened as she looked at her friend, and Audrey decided to like Nick after all. She might be all bristles and snap, but it mattered to her that John was happy.

'I'd best be off,' Nick said abruptly. 'You settle in, Johnny. We'll catch up at the pub.'

'Stay for a cup of tea, at least, Nick.'

'Nah. Time to dose up the lungs with a ciggie, anyway.'

'That stuff'll kill you, kiddo.'

'Let it take its best shot; nothing else has so far.'

They laughed together, as at an old and not quite funny joke.

'I'll see you out,' John said.

Nick said goodbye to Audrey, smirked at Sherlock, and stepped onto the street with John, who shut the door behind them.

Sherlock immediately picked up John's box of books and took it upstairs.

Audrey returned to her flat but, curious, stood by her front window to pry. Nick and John stood by the kerb. Her keen sight picked up their body language, and she heard every word as clear as a bell.

'He's a bit of a livewire, your new flatmate,' Nick said, amused this time. 'Tall. Pretty eyes. Just your type.'

'He's a bit of all right,' John agreed, 'but nothing's happening there. The only thing I've got to give right now is my half of the rent. Let's see what happens down the track when I stop flinching at loud noises and waking up with the sweats.'

'You'll be fine, Doc. And you've landed on your dainty feet, with this place. You'll have a proper bed here, anyway. Better than my lumpy sofa.'

'Didn't I tell you? I'd been planning on arm wrestling you after tea every night to see who got the bed, if I didn't get this place.'

Nick laughed raucously. 'I'd have wished you luck with that one, champ.'

'Well, now we'll never know who would have won.'

'You keep telling yourself that, Doc.'

'Every day and every night. Thanks again for helping with the bags.'

John tried to hug Nick again, and again she skittered away. A dark frown swallowed up her good humour.

'Don't, John.'

'What's wrong, Nick? You weren't like this when you got back.'

'That was months ago. I've been on some epic benders since then.'

'It takes time to adjust. Give me credit for knowing a bit about it, professionally if not personally.'

'I do, but I'm a mess and you know it.'

'You're having a rough trot, Nick. It's not like I'm going to hold that against you.'

'You bloody should. I'm sorry I ditched at such short notice but I finally realised I'm bad news, Johnny. You'll only get hurt if you stay with me.'

'You saved my life, Nick. They'd have got a better shot in and taken me out completely, or I'd have bled out in that bloody road, if you hadn't come for me. I owe you. Actually, sod that. Even if I didn't owe you my life, you're my friend. You know I love you, Nick.'

'Soppy bastard. I love you too. But you deserve better, John.'

'We all deserved better. You. Me. Percy. But none of this is about fair, and at least you and I made it through. We're here, at least.'

'In slightly less than one piece.' Her fingers twitched towards her prosthetic leg.

He held a hand out to her, an entreaty. She wouldn't hug him but took his hand and squeezed it.

'You'll be all right, Johnny. Better without me. With your pretty flatmate and your sweet little old landlady.'

'She is very sweet. I wouldn't say old.'

'She looks like she'll bake you scones every Saturday and tell you to put on your woollies so you don't catch cold, and tell long, involved stories about people you've never met. You and the pretty boy are probably the most interesting things to ever happen to her.'

Which only went to support Sherlock's theory, Audrey decided, that most people really didn't observe much.

CHAPTER SIX

The sharp rap at the door repeated three times before Audrey was able to divest herself safely of the hot baking tray. She abandoned attempts to make her hair more presentable when the fourth round of knocking began.

She opened the door to see John Watson, looking pinched about the face, trying to get DI Bradstreet to listen to him. Audrey knew the doctor had intended to register as a locum today, to supplement his meagre army pension. He seemed not to have had a successful day.

'I don't care what your business with Holmes is,' Bradstreet was saying brusquely, 'mine comes first.'

He, too, seemed to have had a very bad day.

'I'm very pleased for you,' said John stiffly, 'but I live here.'

'You live with Sherlock Holmes?'

'He lives with me,' the doctor conceded, unimpressed.

'You're that doctor he's mentioned. Army bloke. Moved in a month or so ago.'

John stopped glowering. 'He's talked about me?'

At that moment, Sherlock Holmes himself bounded down the stairs, his feet in slippers and a mouse-brown dressing gown thrown hastily over his trousers and untucked shirt.

John cast a distinctly admiring look over his flatmate's wildly untidy hair. Sherlock ran his fingers through it distractedly.

'Mrs Hudson, you've been baking parkin! John's favourite,' Sherlock declared. He gaze fell on his flatmate, examining John's exhaustion with concern.

John, as always in the past weeks, found Sherlock's scrutiny energising. He stood taller. 'Is this one of those mysterious clients of yours that come and go at all hours since I moved in?'

'An official one,' Sherlock said. 'DI Bradstreet, from Scotland Yard.'

'He's brought a juicy murder for you, has he?'

'I certainly hope so!'

John laughed instead of recoiling. Bradstreet gave the doctor a sidelong look.

Audrey stepped aside. 'Did you need me, Detective Bradstreet? Only, I have to get back to my ginger cake and I can't hold the door open all day.'

The baking was soothing her still jittery mind. It was a week past the full moon, and she'd taken a discreet run in Battersea Park's sub-tropical garden, which was close to home and nothing at all like Scotland. She longed for a wilder run, through the moors or a national park somewhere, but she was still too anxious to go so far from her potentially vulnerable new tenants and the cautious rebuilding of her life.

'I've no more news about Gruner or his doings, I'm afraid,' said Bradstreet, unable to move in or away, with Sherlock filling the door and John Watson boxing him in from the path, still waiting to go in. 'I'm here to consult Holmes on another matter.'

'Oh, excellent!' Sherlock cried. 'Come in and tell us all about it.'

The three men ended up gathered in the foyer.

'We've got a blood-soaked sitting room in Norbury, Holmes,' Bradstreet said to his little audience. 'The house is locked up tight, doors bolted from the inside, and we can't locate a body.'

Sherlock's interest was instantly engaged. 'A locked room mystery. My favourite.'

Bradstreet appeared tolerably irritated by this ghoulish observation, but Dr Watson was gazing at Sherlock Holmes like he was fireworks.

'Haven't you got a parkin to attend to?' Bradstreet asked Audrey gruffly.

'It'll keep,' she said, holding her ground. She wasn't about to be run out of her own foyer because a rozzer had the hump.

'Do you have any idea who the missing victim is?' Sherlock asked.

'The house belongs to one Sergeant Warburton, Her Majesty's Armed Forces, Retired,' reported Bradstreet. 'Divorced, no children. She lives alone with her assistance dog, Jack. Neighbours reported a loud bang and a scream at 10am this morning. Constables in the area were called to the scene and found the doors and windows all locked and barred. The only entry point is through a dog flap in the laundry, but that's clipped shut from the inside as well. No sign of anyone disturbing the back garden, and no-one's seen a blind woman, with or without her dog–'

Sherlock opened his mouth to speak just as Dr Watson said, 'You said assistance dog, not guide dog.'

Bradstreet was disinclined to elaborate, but Sherlock prompted him. 'A very good point. Which is it?'

Bradstreet checked his notes. 'The neighbour, Meredith Kershaw, said assistance dog. How is that different to a guide dog?'

'The term assistance animal is more usually applied to service animals for people with mental health issues, ' John explained. 'Anxiety disorders, post-traumatic stress disorders, that sort of thing. I know several veterans who have them.'

'I take it the dog is also missing,' said Sherlock.

'No sign of him, no. So. You want to take a look, or what?'

'Certainly. If Dr Watson is allowed to accompany me.' Sherlock was already tucking in his shirt, kicking off the slippers and shoving on the shoes he kept by the coat rack before pulling on the leather jacket that hung there.

Bradstreet scowled. John looked surprised.

'If you wouldn't mind, John,' Sherlock added belatedly, 'You've already proven useful.'

John's mouth pursed, making his moustache bristle slightly. 'If you think I might be of further help.'

'I think you'll be invaluable,' Sherlock assured him. 'Especially as Warburton's also ex-military. You won't be bothered by the sight of all the blood, will you?'

A soft scoffing sound was the response, by which time Bradstreet had resigned himself to having two inappropriate civilians on the case. 'Just watch where you step,' he muttered, 'and do what you're told.'

'Aye, sir,' said John impudently, which made Sherlock discreetly preen. John had perked right up at being included in this mystery.

Audrey watched them depart for the DI's car, pleased at first with how pleased those two men were with each other's company. Then she began to feel uneasy.

A blood-soaked sitting room, Bradstreet had said. It set all Audrey's instincts on edge, remembering the last such room she'd seen. A room like that was not merely a mystery. It was danger and death and grief for someone.

Ninety nine times in a hundred, a blood-soaked sitting room and a locked room mystery would be some outré human tragedy. The hundredth time...

The hundredth time could leave you packless.

And her lodgers, her boys, already dear to her, had gone willingly towards it, keen for an adventure.

Audrey knew her possessive anxiety for them wasn't appropriate. They were grown men, and not her responsibility. She worried anyway. Sherlock had been out till all hours last night, returning at three in the morning, wafting curious beyond-London scents with him.

She returned to her kitchen to take the ruby-set gold band off her left hand and leave it safely in her tin of treasures. That ring was why so many thought her a *Mrs*. Audrey supposed she was, really. She and Ruby had exchanged vows and rings, even though no legal recognition was possible back then.

She pocketed a folded shopping bag, her purse and her keys, and left the flat.

An Uber to Norbury would be a good start. She'd find them easily from there, with the noise and the scents. She wouldn't stay long. She just wanted to make sure her pack – her lodgers, rather – were safe.

Audrey stood outside the Norbury pub on London Road, listening.

There. Distant but distinct. The sound of police (speaking into their radios, the jingle of cuffs on a belt) and Sherlock's voice ('the house has been locked from the inside. The evidence of one person entering is there, there and there, footmarks on the path. Nobody has left. Ergo, they must still be inside. I know it's so because I know nobody has left this house.')

She followed the sounds. At the end of a crossroad, she saw the cars parked in front of a two storey house. Brown bricks on the upper floor. Whitewashed plaster over bricks below. Green tiles framing the front door of this house, and on the mirror-image house beside it.

Audrey inhaled, but she was too far away to discern specific scents over the odours of the city. She'd have to get closer.

Back in the pub's ladies' room, Audrey undressed and placed her clothes and shoes inside the shopping bag, along with her purse and keys. She stowed her things inside the unlocked cupboard under the sink. If someone nicked them, she could still run home, jump the back fence and let herself into Baker Street with the key she habitually left under a pot plant there.

Audrey was not a complete slave to the call of the moon; but she'd had an adult lifetime with enough moon in her cursed blood to have cultivated control in other ways, too.

Like now, only a week past the last full moon, when she could recall the moonlight to her veins and *shift*.

A few of the Norbury's patrons noted the oddly wild-looking dog trotting from the toilets to the back door. Audrey was alert for shouts of alarm, but there were none. Nobody expected to see a wolf in London, so nobody did.

Audrey loped from the rear of the pub to the main street and down to the locked brick house surrounded by police. The front door now hung open.

Outside, Sherlock enumerated observations and conclusions, but listened when John spoke softly but urgently.

The wolf skirted them to get closer to the house.

John was instantly alert to her presence. Sherlock's gaze followed his, and his eyes narrowed.

Audrey attempted to look doggier. More goofily friendly and less of a hunter. Audrey wondered if either of them had ever seen a wolf before.

'Some kind of Malamute/Alsatian cross, that,' said Sherlock. 'Jack's a springer spaniel, isn't he?' And he promptly dismissed Audrey's presence in favour of inspecting the garden by the front door.

John's eyes swept over her again, his penetrating gaze dwelling on the brown and black swirls of her pelt, her tawny eyes, her paws.

Perhaps he's seen wolves in Afghanistan, Audrey thought. Then she caught sight of her front paws: the claws were bright with the Punkin' Pink nail polish she'd applied that morning.

She lolled her tongue out, smiled and panted – more doggy than ever – and trotted away to sniff at the grass on the handkerchief lawn in a suitably urban-mutt fashion. She didn't look at her paws again. An urban mutt would not be checking out its tattered manicure.

Then she forgot all of that as the scents from inside the house hit her.

The sour bite of fear and adrenalin. The faint acidity of urine. The sweet metallic tang of so much blood. But cold; congealing, lying for hours, untouched. Dead blood.

She extended her *were* senses, alive to potential supernatural threats.

She detected at first only dead meat to accompany the dead blood. Then nearby, a living heart full of undiminished terror. Near, too, was Audrey's remote kin, a springer spaniel, standing guard over his human. The human's heart raced, as though she sprinted like a rabbit, away from danger across open fields.

Audrey pushed gently at the spaniel's mind.

Safe, the dog's mind spilled out at her in images and emotion. *I protect my sad-scared Alpha, my pack. Safe safe safe.*

Help is here, Audrey pushed in reply, a sensation rather than words. Dog minds were too simple for more complicated communication. In her head, she sensed a hopeful, wagging tail.

No monsters here, Audrey thought. *Well. Apart from the obvious.*

Satisfied with that, she loped back to the pub and the ladies' room. Ten minutes later she emerged, neatly buttoned, though with an urge to growl at the puzzled, staring barman.

Late in the evening, Audrey listened to her lodgers' return. John was laughing as he came indoors. Sherlock's deeper voice was laughing in counterpoint.

'And when you found the hidden door to the panic room, the expression on Bradstreet's face! Why does he consult you if he doesn't want to believe a word you say?'

'You only consult a specialist when you can't address a problem yourself. Some professionals find it galling.'

'They don't have to like it,' observed John, 'But in my profession, the patients are grateful at least. Poor Warburton.'

'Yes, but we found her, even if we weren't in time to save her abysmal boyfriend.'

'Mason was very much not prime boyfriend material,' agreed John drily. They'd closed the door and were hanging their coats downstairs. 'I should feel sorry for him that he shot himself. But I don't.'

'Aren't there rules about being an officer and a gentleman or something?' Sherlock teased.

'People unused to firearms shouldn't go messing about with them,' replied the doctor. 'And given he intended to murder Chrissy Warburton, I consider it karma that the gun malfunctioned.'

'You're positively philosophical, Dr Watson.'

'You learn to be,' John replied. 'What you did was incredible, though. You read the events of that room as though you'd been an eyewitness. It was the most extraordinary thing I've ever seen.'

Audrey could imagine how Sherlock would preen at that praise. He always was amenable to flattery, and John was proving amenable to delivering it. She stood closer to her door, all the better to hear them.

Sherlock, unfortunately, had adopted a tone both bright and serious. Underneath it she detected his rapid heartbeat and every sign of panic.

'You see, of course, why I have always eschewed romantic entanglements,' he said, like a pure born idiot. 'Warburton was blind to Alec Mason's treachery. Mason was able to manipulate her until the last, relying on Warburton's loneliness to forgive a lot of his behaviour until it was almost too late. For the trained reasoner, the florid intrusion of notions such as love or passion is anathema to a finely adjusted mental temperament. Time and again, I've witnessed how high emotion results in jealousy, clinginess, misunderstanding, misery, and motive for murder. It leaves reason maladjusted in the best people. To indulge would be grit in a sensitive instrument.'

Audrey jerked her door open, too late to prevent this foolish pronouncement. John was looking like he'd been slapped, and that thick-witted cub Sherlock was looking like he wished someone had slapped him.

'An interesting case, was it?' she asked, trying to keep it civil but she couldn't help the acerbity.

John cleared his throat and his stunned expression. 'Fascinating, but with a tragic ending.'

'I thought we'd established that Alec Mason had it coming,' said Sherlock crossly.

'I mean Chrissy Warburton,' said John. 'I've no doubt she'll be back in therapy for a while. This will have been a major setback.'

'Oh yes.' Sherlock frowned. 'Bradstreet should have come for me sooner. We could have found her hours ago. You were exemplary, though, in calming her and extracting both the Sergeant and her spaniel. First class work. I was very glad to have your company today. It made a significant difference, to me and to poor Warburton. Thank you.'

John was mollified by the compliment, proving he was as sensitive to praise as Sherlock. 'Any time, Sherlock. Always happy to provide a professional opinion if you need one.'

'Or an unprofessional one?' suggested Sherlock.

However he intended that little jest to go down, John only blinked at him. 'I'll be up in a minute,' he said, his tone very neutral. 'I need to speak to Mrs Hudson.'

With a defeated sigh, Sherlock went upstairs alone.

John didn't broach any topic of conversation until they were in Audrey's kitchen, and she'd placed a warmed slice of parkin on his plate, next to a cup of tea.

'He didn't really mean that, you know,' she said.

John blinked at her, confused, then his expression cleared. 'He's right. He shouldn't be getting involved. Especially not with me.' He tipped two spoons of sugar into his tea and stirred with grim concentration.

'Don't sell yourself short, John. He likes y–'

'What were you doing in Norbury today?'

'I wasn't in Norbury today.'

John pointed at her Punkin Pink nails with his wet teaspoon. 'You were in Norbury. As a wolf.'

She wanted to tell him it was nonsense, but he was clearly having none of that.

'The polish is a giveaway, but so was your fur. Those striations on your fur don't happen with natural wolves. Those are Blaschko's lines. Perfectly normal signs of cell development in human skin, but usually invisible. They show up in some skin diseases. And in werewolf fur. My mate Percy had them.'

'I see.'

John's expression softened. 'He was a good mate, Percy. Gentle. One of the best army nurses I've ever served with. Then one night while we were taking a few days leave in Kabul, he got bitten by a dog at the market. I cleaned his hand up, and Nick and I laughed about how quickly it healed. You've got such a pure heart, Nick said, even the dogs don't like to bite you hard. A few nights later, Nick was driving us back to the hospital base from a visit to a local clinic, and Percy went nuts. Screaming and writhing around like he was trying to climb out of his own skin.'

Audrey closed her eyes, remembering. Bones breaking and reforming. Muscle twisting and reshaping. The agony of it. The terror of the first time. The animal madness of it.

'Did you try to shoot him?'

'Of course we didn't bloody shoot him. He was our mate. Our Perce. Nick stopped the Land Rover and we helped him out onto the side of the road because he was banging himself up on the doors and roof of the car. And we watched him turn into a, a creature. A wolf on two legs. His eyes had changed colour but they were still Percy's eyes, and he was so fucking scared.'

'Did he attack you?'

'You're not listening. This was Percy Phelps. Sweetheart Phelps, everyone called him. Our company angel. Everyone loved Percy. And he took one look at us looking at him, finished turning into a wolf, and ran off into the night. Nick and I had no damned idea what was going on, but we knew what we'd seen. So we waited. He came back next morning, naked and shivering and in a state. But he was Percy again. We took him back to base and told everyone the car had broken down, and we looked after our mate. And we did that for the whole tour, and the next one.'

'Where is he now?'

'Dead. The Taliban got him in the ambush where Nick lost her leg.'

'I'm sorry.'

'Me too. He was a beautiful person. A bloody clever werewolf as well. He'd go out on the full moon and find out where the Taliban snipers were holing up, so we could avoid them. He saved a lot of lives. So, Mrs Hudson, I know what a werewolf is. And I know they're not necessarily monsters. And I'd really like to know why you were at Norbury today.'

'I wanted to make sure nothing there could harm you and Sherlock.' Audrey said stiffly, and waited for his protest.

John Watson only nodded curtly, then sipped his tea. 'Sherlock says your whole family was killed up in Edinburgh. All werewolves, were they?'

'Yes.'

'Hell.'

'Quite.'

'Does Sherlock know?'

'No.'

'No,' agreed John thoughtfully. 'He doesn't seem the type to believe easily. I wasn't, until I saw Percy with my own eyes. That's going to make it difficult for him to help you find the murderer, isn't it?'

'Yes. Not as difficult as if I tried to tell him. I could show him, but not everybody reacts with such equanimity as you did.' She'd had experiences in her desperate youth – and everyone had stories – which had ended very badly; including serious injury (hers) and institutionalisation (Ingrid's). She was exceedingly cautious with the paranormal truth these days.

John contemplated his tea. 'It was Percy. Me and Perce and Nick were the Musketeers.' He smiled crookedly. 'The shit we'd seen together.'

Audrey contemplated what three people might have seen in a guerrilla war that one of them turning werewolf before their eyes didn't reduce them to puddles of existential terror.

They could hear Sherlock upstairs, sawing away on his violin in graceless agitation. Thumping followed the cessation of violin torture, a bad tempered stomp around the flat. They heard when the upstairs door was flung open and Sherlock clattered down the seventeen steps to the foyer.

Audrey wondered if he would disappear until the small hours once more, but she could hear him breathing and a gentle, rhythmic thumping.

She left John to his tea and opened her door to witness Sherlock banging his forehead softly but repeatedly against the newel cap of the stair banister. Fortunately, it was round and not lumpy and he didn't seem to be doing himself an injury. He stopped when he saw her watching him.

'I'm fine. It's fine. It's all perfectly fine,' he said.

Not even a magnificent lie. Audrey almost felt sorry for him.

'John was superlative,' Sherlock said in a perfectly commonplace tone as he stood straight. 'Not in the least bit bothered by all the blood, despite his history. He understood the purpose of the assistance dog. Warburton has been diagnosed with post-traumatic stress disorder. The dog is trained to keep her calm, alerted by various stress signals. When the boyfriend Mason threatened Warburton with one of her own guns and forced her to open up the panic room, the dog got between the gun and his mistress.'

Sherlock fell silent. Audrey closed her door and joined him in the foyer.

'Do you know what a squib load is? Also known as a "pop and no kick"? John does,' Sherlock resumed, not waiting for an answer. 'It's what happens when a gun is dirty and doesn't fire correctly. If it malfunctions, a bullet can end up lodged in the chamber. Do you know what happens if you fire another bullet while one is stuck in the chamber?'

'Nothing good,' Audrey suggested.

'No. Nothing good at all.' Sherlock mimicked a muted explosion, puffing out his cheeks and demonstrating with a slow-motion flex of his hands, expanding ever out.

'That was all the blood,' he said, 'Mason thought he could just pick up a handgun that his ex-army girlfriend had kept in a trophy cupboard and just fire it at people without ensuring it was clean. He was very wrong. He bled to death mostly in the hallway, until Warburton, who had fallen into a deep and distressing fugue state, dragged his body into the panic room and locked the door, under the stress-induced impression Mason was a wounded comrade.'

'That's terrible,' said Audrey.

'No. What's terrible is that Mason convinced this woman that he loved her, solely because he thought Warburton had a secret stash of gold in the house – when what she had was a panic room stocked with bottled water, energy bars and a chemical toilet because electrical storms make her feel like she's under missile attack.'

'I meant for her.'

'Ah. Well, yes. For Sergeant Christine Warburton, it's been very terrible. But Jack did everything he was trained to do. That dog sat in Warburton's lap and looked her in the eye and kept her calm. Well. As calm as she could be with the dead boyfriend who'd tried to shoot her in the opposite corner.'

Sherlock tugged violently on his hair, punishing himself for his stampeding mouth.

'I located the panic room. I deduced that Warburton was the victim, not the perpetrator. But it was John who sat outside the room and talked with her and her dog until we could extract them safely and retrieve the body. He's expressed interest in joining me on other cases. His medical knowledge and calmness in a crisis will be of great service to the work.'

The last statement was delivered with dignified professionalism, and then Sherlock winced as though it hurt. 'I suppose you heard what I told John. In the hall. About the work. About. Entanglements.'

'Yes, Sherlock. I heard.'

'If you'd be so kind,' he said, 'The next time I go swanning about declaring how cleverly I've solved a case, just whisper Norbury in my ear. I expect it'll be enough to remind me that even the cleverest people need to check the mouth-brain connection sometimes.'

'If you say so.'

'It was like a verbal squib load.' He mimicked once more the explosion with sound and hands. '*Bhccchchchchchchhwhwhhh*.'

'He's in my kitchen, you know.'

'I know. I suppose he's been telling you that he doesn't think he can continue living with an idiot.'

'Not at all. He's been telling me about an old army friend of his. Percy Phelps.'

'Ah. Yes. An old army friend. Possibly a boyfriend at one time, though a long time before John was invalided out of the army, I think. Perhaps when they were at school together.'

'Why don't you come in for tea?'

'Would he like to have tea with an idiot, do you think?'

'I'm sure he'd tolerate it fairly well.'

'I have something to show you, as it happens,' he said, straightening his spine. 'He might have some insight into it.'

'I'll make a fresh pot,' said Audrey, and returned to John and her kitchen. 'He's coming in for tea.'

'Right.' John seemed to be girding himself for it.

Sherlock joined them a moment later, thoroughly composed and not as if he'd been banging his head on the banister five minute ago. Instead, he smiled with a hint of triumph and dropped a hardcover journal on the kitchen table.

Audrey at stared the familiar thing with horror. Across it were written the words:

Audrey Hudson, Werewolf.
Held in the Private Collection of Adelbert Gruner.

'I visited Gruner's house last night,' confessed Sherlock.

'They let you in?' asked John, surprised.

'I let myself in.' Sherlock smirked and John smirked back, obviously finding Sherlock's felonious streak as admirable and enchanting as everything else about him.

'Mrs Hudson and I believe the man who kidnapped her last month is connected with the person or people who killed her family.'

John nodded.

'I found this journal in a locked room, much like Warburton's panic room. It contained a bizarre collection of artefacts. A pile of ash under a glass dome labelled as *Thomas Belford, vampire*. A cleverly assembled animatronic forefinger wriggling around a little cabinet like an inchworm, with the plaque *French zombie, name and origin unknown*. A ten-inch square of seal fur labelled *Selkie*.'

That last one made Audrey's stomach churn. The selkie to whom it belonged, if she lived, would never return to the sea, with her coat so destroyed.

'That's a very strange collection,' John agreed without much inflection.

'And this is a very strange book. I'd like your professional opinion on the man who wrote it.' Sherlock flicked open the pages, revealing to John the awful, shallow truths it contained.

'It's all nonsense,' snapped Audrey, and it was. However true the basic premise, the bare facts didn't tell anything like the whole story, and Gruner's interpretation of it had been ugly and wrong.

'Of course it is,' said Sherlock kindly. 'But once we have eliminated the impossible – and you'll agree Gruner's assertions are certainly impossible – whatever remains, however improbable, must be the truth.'

'What improbable truth are you implying?' asked John.

'That Adelbert Gruner had an *idée fixe*. Perhaps a *folie à deux*, if someone was supplying him with these fake artefacts. It seems likely that whoever fabricated an anatomically accurate and mobile facsimile of a rotting human finger is just as capable of convincing Gruner that you, Mrs Hudson, are a werewolf.' Sherlock snorted at the absurdity of the very idea.

John Watson looked Audrey Hudson right in the eye and then said, deadpan as you please, 'That sounds like a lead to me.'

'And to me,' grinned Sherlock. 'And then there's this.'

He took from his pocket a folded sheet of paper, which he slapped onto the kitchen table. It was a letter demanding a ludicrously large sum of money for "a genuine werewolf artefact, recently obtained".

The letter was from a man named Dr Roylott. His address: Stoke Moran, Dartmoor.

CHAPTER SEVEN

John found a few days' locum work here and there; Sherlock had a sudden flurry of urgent cases, with pressing demands on his time from the Met. Suddenly, weeks had passed and Audrey had two days until the full moon. She told her tenants she was visiting an old friend.

She was, in fact, visiting an almost forgotten rumour. It had taken a few more days for memory to unspool, a few more to dig into an online search for details, then time to book and prepare for her first trip to Devon in decades.

No wonder Gruner's tortured 'Moran' had sounded familiar. Audrey hadn't the first idea who Grimsby Roylott was, but his address, *Stoke Moran*, had stirred up schoolyard memories of spooky stories and silly dares.

The kids of South Devon used to swap stories of Helen Moran, Witch of the Hall. Crazy Nell, it was said, lived half wild at the hall of Stoke Moran in the middle of the Dartmoor National Park. The Hall had fallen to ruin; bats flew out at night through broken roof tiles; foxes and feral cats lived in the blackberry and dewberry brambles that overtook the grounds. Those high, dark stone walls hid a tantalising world of wildness and dread.

Rumour was that Helen Stoner had black-widowed her husband, Alexander Moran, with hemlock from the moor. Rumour was that in a jealous snit she'd fatally pushed her twin sister, Julia, into traffic when they were both eight years old. Rumour was her only child was as feral as she; that she'd taught them how to catch rabbits in their bare hands and kill them with their teeth.

Rumour was, frankly, an ass; nothing but malicious gossip about a lonely woman who had lost her sister in an accident and, after her husband died, was too poor to maintain the old hall but had nowhere else to go. Audrey didn't know if Helen Moran even had a child, only that the tales grew in cruelty and grotesquery as the years went on.

Perhaps they were even more cruel than she remembered. The letter from Grimsby Roylott had referenced a recent and genuine werewolf artefact. The implications, given the rest of Gruner's collection, turned her stomach.

Before Audrey could let Sherlock Holmes further pursue what he thought of as a bizarre case of fake paranormal artefacts, she had to find out more.

Fortunately, *Cherry Brook B&B* wasn't more than a mile from the hall. It had charming stone walls and colonial grid-pattern windows with lacy cream curtains and probably served cream teas. Not that she'd get to sleep in the cosy little bed.

Before sunset, Audrey went to the nearest pub and ordered steak, extra-rare. Then she went to the conifer woods east of the eponymous Cherry Brook, took off her clothes and stowed them at the base of a fir tree in a small cloth bag, along with wet wipes and a hairbrush. She covered those with a mound of fallen, fragrant needles and cones and waited to give herself to the moon.

The pain of it was almost welcome, these days. Once her body had twisted itself, breaking and warping bones, muscles and soft tissues, she raised her muzzle to the rising moon and howled at the curse of it: and the freedom of it too.

Then she'd set off east, crossing the B3212 highway in an easy run. Moor creatures scattered at her coming, from the ponies and sheep to the rabbits and badgers, the ravens and the owls.

It had been ages since Audrey had last had a really good run, and among werewolves it was accepted that Dartmoor, like most national parks, was neutral ground on cursed nights.

Audrey had a shaky history with Dartmoor. She'd avoided it for years, being too close to her childhood home in Newton Abbot. Only once had she succumbed to nostalgia. Five years ago, she'd brought Conal and the twins here for a moon run. The morning after, they'd found a young girl sobbing by the body of a moor pony, blood in her teeth. A child abandoned in her monstrosity.

Of course Audrey scooped her up, brought her home. Coaxed and comforted, with kindness and experience. Made Siobhan feel loved again. One day, Audrey hoped that Siobhan might even feel safe again; safe enough to let go of the boiling rage she harboured at her fate. That boiling rage was Audrey's now, whenever she remembered holding that trembling eight-year-old child, hungry for love, for shelter, for a place where she didn't have to be afraid of herself anymore.

All of that seemed rather moot at 10 o'clock at night as Audrey loped across the moor towards Merrivale – with the peculiar yet unmistakable feeling she was being hunted.

It was unnerving. Natural animals normally gave *were*-creatures a very wide berth. What kind of animal, Audrey thought, stalks a *werewolf*?

A desperate one, she decided. One that had *issues*.

This one had the peculiar odour of the tiger enclosure at the zoo.

Dartmoor was full of legends. The Hairy Hands that forced drivers off the B-road she'd just crossed. Old Crockern on his skeleton horse. The ghost at Jay's Grave. Big cats living secretly inside the woods. The first three were much more likely, in Audrey's experience, but the creature keeping pace with her under the moonlight was definitely a large wildcat of some kind.

It was a clever predator, too, because she lost the scent of it in a wash of the wind sweeping across the moor towards West Dart River, ahead of her.

She supposed she'd better deal with the stalking wildcat before scoping out Stoke Moran. A werewolf could certainly best a tiger in a fight – well, probably – but what damage might the tiger do the inhabitants of Devon?

Audrey ran through Dartmoor, slow enough for a hunter to track, and let her instincts and intellect collaborate on a strategy. Both took her to the edge of a copse of malformed oaks limned in moonlight, growing among mossy boulders. Wistman's Wood.

She paused at the fringe of the trees, ears twitching. The sound of padded footfalls on grass was barely audible. Any sane predator would have abandoned the chase as hard work by now, conserving energy for an easier target. Not this beast.

Wistman's Wood was another witchy place from her childhood. The boldest of her schoolmates had stolen into this grove in the darkness to tie strips of cloth and trinkets to the boughs of an inner tree. Some swore they'd been granted faerie blessings in return.

The wood was dense and dark, the tangled branches and rock-strewn ground a barrier to ponies and cattle alike. But not to werewolves or, it turned out, cats of any size.

Audrey leapt between the gnarly, lichen-wrapped trees to land on mossy boulders. She altered her shape subtly, hands and feet becoming more prehensile to hold herself steady on the uneven surface. Crouched, she sniffed the cloistered air.

The smell of the cat was powerful here, where it had obviously been sheltering during the day. Somewhere nearby was the bloody stench of a dead moor pony.

The cat followed her into the trees. Audrey watched its shadowy approach.

That's it. Follow the leader, puss. That was more a feeling than a thought, with the wolf high in her blood: a predator funnelling its prey into a trap.

Astonishingly, it really was a tiger, though a fairly moth-eaten specimen. It was half-starved, spine, ribs and hips jutting from its matted pelt. Its eyes gleamed faintly by moonlight, before it slunk deeper into the woods.

Audrey sensed that this ruin of a tiger was half mad. That impression coalesced when she found the mauled pony. The tiger had opened the poor thing's belly and throat before dragging it among the trees and boulders: but despite starving, the tiger hadn't eaten more than a mouthful of its kill.

Now that they were deep in the wood, the tiger's passage was unmistakeable to Audrey's uncanny senses. The animal smelled sourly of neglect and abuse, infected wounds and faeces. The human part of Audrey felt sorry for it. The wolf had other ideas.

The tiger was cunning. The werewolf was smarter and had strange powers to call on. Audrey prowled over, between, around boulders, all black-ink-dark underneath the twisted oaks. Moonlight fell only in faint chinks and needlepoints. The tiger squeezed into clefts and crannies, left and right of her, mostly behind her now, imagining perhaps it drove its quarry rather than being led.

Having chosen her ground, Audrey stilled; held that ground. She knew when the tiger coiled for the leap. When it sprang.

Audrey changed shape, shedding the humanoid and dropping to all wolfish fours. Claws swiped harmlessly through the air where Audrey's throat had been, well above her now lowered head.

Unfazed, the tiger landed, tight-turned, crouched. But it had made a mistake. It was penned in by the rocks and clustered trees. The wolf loomed in the only clear way out.

The tiger, undernourished and agitated, didn't know it was already beaten. It lunged, slashing. That was nothing to the werewolf, which reared beyond reach. Even in the grip of the hunt, Audrey wondered if she might defeat it without killing it – but then the animal leapt, terrible teeth bared, claws outstretched, intending to kill. Almost simultaneously, the werewolf surged to meet it.

Audrey twisted mid-leap, intercepting the cat's trajectory. As she leapt, she changed shape again: her wolf body rising upright, spine straight; paws turning into hands with no right to exist on the ends of those lupine legs; those rough-pelted shoulders more flexible than a wolf's withers, giving her reach.

Her snout stayed long and full of teeth as the upright werewolf seized the tiger in its strong hands and arms. All those teeth sank into the throat of the cat, silencing its piercing yowl.

Blood blood blood blood blood.

This part of the hunt didn't need grammar.

The tiger struggled, but its diminished strength was no match for a mature werewolf. And then it was dead, a limp weight in the werewolf's arms. With a low, satisfied growl, Audrey Hudson shook her prey by the throat, tasting the last pulse of blood, then let go, tipping the body back onto the rocks. The scrawny body tumbled to the ground, belly stained with its own blood, no light in its golden eyes.

Slaughter my ponies, will you? Audrey knew she was transferring her rage about other deaths to this creature who could pose no further threat.

She was about to lift her head, to howl – triumph or despair or some other primal thing – when her voice was stayed by a distant scream.

Prehensile hands and feet became paws again. She dropped to all fours and picked her way to the edge of the wood. The moor was silent hereabouts, everything living in hiding or running away from Wistman's Wood.

Sound was tricky on the moor, but Audrey knew the cry had come from the west. That way lay Tavistock. Before Tavistock, the old Dartmoor Prison at Rundlestone and then Merrivale – and Stoke Moran.

Audrey bounded across the rough, boggy moor to the rock-strewn bank and into the West Dart River.

The faint plash of something disturbing the flow of water came to her ears. Audrey hunkered into a deeper pool in the shallows, perfectly still, to listen. Upriver was an inky, almost invisible, human-shaped blot, smelling of mud, grass and even dung, with only the tiniest whiff of human underneath. This hunter had disguised their scent well from natural beasts, and almost well enough to hide from her, too.

The human shadow crawled almost soundlessly from the river onto the east bank and stilled. She waited. It waited. Finally, the figure grunted and rose to a crouch, revealing a rifle in its right hand. The hunter sniffed the air and touched a finger to the soil. 'Heh.' A masculine huff of wry laughter followed.

'Here, kitty, kitty,' the man breathed, sly and vicious.

Too late, Elmer Fudd.

But Audrey waited until he'd made his padfooted way towards the wood before she emerged from the Dart. Her brief sojourn had rinsed her hide of blood and sweat.

The scream she'd heard didn't repeat but Audrey continued westward towards Stoke Moran Hall.

She smelled the hall before she found it. Ripe with the pungent odour of an unkempt zoo. A hedge of brambles, stone and wire ringed the overgrown acreage. Audrey explored the perimeter until she found where the tiger had escaped and through which the human hunter had followed. She wriggled through the gap.

She emerged into undulating, rocky ground and a grove of ash trees, all ink and silver in the night. She could smell the tiger and the strong, unpleasant musk of other creatures. Those unfamiliar scents made her hackles rise.

She padded through the grove, alert, and emerged to find a baboon scratching itself among the shrubs. It opened its mouth wide at her, all teeth. She responded in kind. It shrieked and scarpered.

Too bloody right.

Ahead was a stone house and stables, linked by a gravel drive, both within a secondary barrier of storm fencing. Stoke Moran Hall was in indifferent repair, topped with gables and with half its windows boarded up. The portico and lintel were recently repaired, the new stone cleaner and brighter than the rest. Several chimneys were obscured by wooden scaffolding, indicating more work in progress.

The fencing was three metres high; to keep the tiger and the baboon out, no doubt. Werewolves, not so much. Even one with a gammy hip.

With a short run-up, Audrey leapt straight over the barrier and almost instantly recoiled at a strong reptilian stink. She skittered away, growling, and then stood stiff-legged, angry with herself for being spooked. She was a werewolf. *She* was the spooky one.

At her feet was a trail, barely visible in the dirt, but alight to her nose. She sniffed the trail, snuffling the width of the track. A very big snake, the undulating trail easily half a metre wide. She listened, but the only evidence of the creature was this trail. If it was still loose, it was in some other part of the grounds.

The faint 2am hum of the few cars on Pork Hill Road reached her. Or perhaps it came from nearer Princetown, or even the motorway further west. Sound being tricksy again.

Audrey circumnavigated the old house, ears pricked for the hiss and glide of a giant snake. A circular folly of a ruined Roman temple lay just inside the barrier. A smaller fence around it kept a handful of fat goats penned under its shadow. They cowered by the artfully scattered stones, too frightened of her to even bleat.

Further along the path she found a mass of bone, horn and hide, which stank of goat and snake. Well, she knew what the snake ate, at least.

Mingled with the powerful mammalian and reptilian odours criss-crossing the grounds, three human scents were detectable. One suggested the hunter she'd encountered on the moor. Another had a peculiarly infused odour, as though it handled the monstrous snake so often they'd absorbed its essence. The third seemed kin to them both.

Muffled voices came from inside the building. An aggressive Englishman with a gruff voice. Another man whose complaining tone annoyed her before she'd even met him.

The national origins of the third voice, not British, was hard to place; frightened weeping didn't have much of an accent. Desperate begging was scarcely more informative. 'Please. Please, no. Please.'

'Well, you're hardly any use to us now,' said Whiner.

'I beg of you!'

The sound of a fist on flesh and a painful cry, and then Gruff said, 'Don't kill him yet, you idiot. He may have learned *something* we can pass on.'

Audrey rose on her hind legs, eye level with a gargoyle of a doorknocker in the centre of the heavy wooden door. She morphed a hand to test the door handle, which moved easily under her grip. With a wary push, the door soundlessly opened: undoubtedly left unlocked for the hunter's return. They obviously didn't expect a breach in their defences. Helpful of them to have refurbished the entrance and oiled the hinges as well.

Audrey shouldered the door open enough to slip inside and dropped again to four feet. Her claws snick-snicked on a marble floor. The entrance was filled with the dead: a black bear mounted in a corner, a lion skin pinned like a substantial butterfly on one wall. Hunting trophies of deer, big cats, zebras, giraffes, bears, even eagles, empty-eyed, empty of meaning or value, peered down at her. Both the human and predator in her were disgusted at the waste of all that life.

'What did she tell you?' demanded Gruff, followed by the sound of another blow, another cry, from beyond a door to her left.

'His Nibs'll be pissed off if he doesn't talk, Da,' warned Whiner anxiously.

'Oh, he'll talk. *What did she say?*'

An agonised yelp followed hard on the question, and the panicked reply: 'She said nothing!'

Audrey now thought his accent might be Greek. She'd had a brief fling with a Greek sailor, once.

'Yabbered a lot for someone saying nothing.'

'She begged for her life,' said the Greek thickly, through probably a cut and swollen mouth. 'I am not sure of the rest.'

'You speak ancient Greek.'

'I *read* ancient Greek,' the poor man cried out. 'Hearing it spoken is different. I could not–'

A blow. A cry.

'Please, please, no.'

Audrey threw back her head and howled. The terrible sound throbbed and echoed around the hard surfaces of the entrance, up the stairways, off the ghastly trophies. A howl not forlorn, but full of rage and teeth; full of the sound of *coming for you*.

The cry had the desired effect. The beating ceased.

'What was that?' the Englishmen were saying.

'What in the name of God was that?' echoed the Greek in further terror.

But then Gruff said, 'Sounds like a wolf to me.'

'We don't have a wolf, Da,' replied Whiner. 'We don't even have the bloody tiger any more. I told you we should have fed it more.'

'When will you learn that a hungry animal is a motivated watchdog,' Gruff replied patiently. He and Whiner seemed remarkably unconcerned by the howl.

'Well it bloody got out looking for something to eat, didn't it? And now Seb's gotta deal with it before it eats a bloody tourist.'

Gruff made a dismissive noise. 'Seb'll see to it.'

'If the bloody tiger doesn't eat him first.'

'Like to see Tigger try.' Gruff laughed, gravelly and uncharming. 'Never mind that, Gus. Let's sort this out and dump the bodies.'

The Greek broke in, 'Please, I beg you. No. Please, no.'

Gus-the-whiner replied: 'His phone call probably didn't get through, Da. The reception out here is rubbish. We've got time. We should wait for Seb. I should go help him.'

'He'll probably mistake you for a rabbit and shoot you in the dark.' Another grating laugh. 'No. If anyone's going to have a hunting accident one day, he'll be on the receiving end.'

'Seb wouldn't shoot me.'

'You always were an idiot. But you're my idiot, so do as you're told and you'll be looked after. Now, let's put this thing to sleep, hmm?'

'Please!' The Greek's fear ratcheted up another notch. 'I will say nothing. Nothing. Please!'

'Of course you'll say nothing. You need a tongue for that.'

Audrey sprang at the closed door, crashing into it hard enough to make a splintered dent in the wood as it rattled on its hinges. She fell back and howled again, her aim to unnerve before throwing herself at the door again. This wasn't her first run under the moon. She knew how to frighten people when she had to. Surely they'd be properly frightened now.

'Wolf at the door, Da.' Gus seemed sourly pleased to be making the joke.

'Bloody werewolves. Running on my moors every month. Pests. Grab this useless bastard, Gus, and we'll throw him to the dog. Might make a good excuse for failure, for His Nibs.'

And against all expectation, the door opened. Gus and his Da held the terrified, bleeding Greek in front of them, his hands bound before him with a zip tie. The Englishmen were each armed with a pistol.

Audrey stood in the hallway, striated grey pelt bristling, teeth bared. She had to grudgingly admire people who would face her under the circumstances.

The bound prisoner's knees buckled and his captors let him fold.

'Aren't you a beauty?' said Gruff, the older of the two, with wild white hair and wild, cruel eyes. This, no doubt, was Grimsby Roylott. He stared at her in amazement. In avarice. His smell hit her then, that stink of the zoo: tiger, baboon and snake smeared all over him. Her skin crawled with it.

Roylott pushed at the kneeling Greek's back with his boot. 'Got a hankering for some human flesh?' he offered mockingly. 'Be my guest.'

'Give him to me,' she rumbled.

Roylott hauled the Greek close to his chest and pressed his pistol to the man's temple. 'Try to get him and see what happens. Gus, get my wolfing gun.'

Gus, a younger, less wild copy of his father, nodded nervously. He began to edge back into the recently vacated room, behind his father, and Audrey didn't dare lunge at any of them, too aware of the gun, and of the possibility that if, in the melee, she scratched or bit the Greek, he'd have a whole new set of problems.

And then Gus' mobile phone rang. Gus froze behind his father; answered it.

'Seb! Are you–? What?' He pressed the phone to his chest. 'Da, Seb says something got the tiger already.'

Roylott, eyes fixed on Audrey, scoffed, 'Well, der.'

'And the Department of Fisheries is parked at the Two Bridges pub. He thinks they're talking to the landlord.'

Audrey, still calculating what to do, was startled by the sudden intrusion of the Department. Who'd brought them into this?

Roylott Senior pushed the gun barrel hard into the Greek's cheek. 'You little shit. How did you know to call the Department?'

The Greek sucked air in through his teeth, too busy dribbling blood and staring fearfully at Audrey to reply.

'Tell Seb we'll have to run for it. Rendezvous at the Club.' Then

Roylott addressed the Greek again. 'You arse. Making me leave my house. At least I can leave them your body with hers. Matching bloody pair.'

Audrey's jaw quivered with a bowel-watering snarl, drawing Roylott's sudden attention. 'Not paying enough attention to you, sweetheart? You'll have to wait your turn. One execution at a time, love. Gus, my wolf gun?'

He turned slightly away and Audrey seized her moment. She leapt, knocking the Greek to the ground as Roylott fired – the bullet stung as it grazed her flank, but it was only lead and the furrow healed as she landed. She straddled the Greek protectively and snarled again, her snout drawn back, all long fangs and bristling fur. The saliva that glistened in sticky strings between her teeth was a curse waiting to strike.

Grimsby Roylott was clearly aware of this, and that his gun was useless against her. She would certainly bite one or both of them before Gus could fetch the gun with the silver bullets. Roylott grabbed his son by the collar and dragged him towards the front door.

'Get the car, Gus.'

'I can't leave you here with–'

'No-one's leaving anyone. I'm right behind you.'

Audrey was quivering with the rumble of her enraged growls, and with the effort of holding herself back. Oh, how she wanted to leap, to bite, to tear, and to pass on this curse.

But the poor man curled, whimpering, between her paws reminded her that she was here to protect, not attack. The impulse to shield was always much stronger in her than the one for blood.

Audrey bristled and growled until Gus and his Da had backed out of the room, out of the house, and down the gravel path. She heard a car start up, doors slam, and she loosed a wild howl.

The car took off in a welter of squealing tyres and spitting gravel.

The instinct to chase – *hunt, catch, devour* – was intense, but Audrey took command of it. With Roylott's terrible smell gone, she shook her bristling pelt back down against her skin.

The Greek curled beneath the shelter of her body, arms over his head, still saying, 'Please, no.'

Audrey leapt aside and sat on her haunches a short distance away, and waited.

Shaking, he sat up. The side of his face was bloody from a wound over his eyebrow and his mouth was swollen and cut in several places. His hands trembled. He stared at her.

'G-g-good d-d-og. W-wolf. G-good w-wolf.' He held out his bound hands, not for her to sniff but to keep her, however ineffectually, at bay. He tried to rise but his knees wouldn't lock.

She stayed right where she was.

He tried to rise again. Stood swaying for a moment and then limped back into the room in which he'd been held. Curious, she followed. He noticed, stopped, limped onward. She kept a measured distance between them.

A woman lay on the carpet of what appeared to be a library and office, her light brown skin waxy in death. Her pale yellow hair had streaks of green dyed into it. She was dressed in a simple brown cotton summer dress that revealed the cuts and bruises of blows to her face and body. The fingers of her left hand were broken, except where they were missing. Her cooling body reeked of fear and despair.

And of trees.

Audrey cocked her head. Bent it close to the corpse and – ignoring the Greek's cry of disgust – sniffed at one broken hand.

What she had initially perceived as protruding bone was – wood. The colour of birch. This poor woman had been a dryad.

The Greek's expression was puzzled and anxious. Audrey dropped to her belly to make herself look as harmless as a werewolf could. It was like a volcano pretending to be a sandcastle.

He swallowed then nodded, as though resigned to his fate, before turning his back on her to poke through ashes in the grate. He retrieved a half-burnt mobile phone. Its screen was cracked and the plastic had melted. He sat on the floor, cradling the device, but he couldn't make it activate. After a while, he prodded gingerly at his battered face and hissed with pain.

'Aren't you going to eat me?' he asked her, speech slurred from his injuries. His gaze shifted between the dryad and the werewolf.

Audrey couldn't bring herself to loll her tongue or wag her tail like some dopey little terrier, so she dropped her chin to her folded front paws and watched him with her tawny eyes, willing him to say something – anything – that would explain what had happened. She might have asked him outright, but a wolf opening up conversation with 'so, what's all this then?' tended to result in screaming rather than enlightenment.

Audrey tried a delicate whine with an upward inflection. The wretched man, too exhausted to overthink such a subliminal prompt, wilted.

'She looked so young,' he said, 'but she only spoke the Greek of the ancients.'

Audrey forgave the poor sod for not noticing the corpse had birchwood for bones and hair like spun leaves and how she had bruised and broken but not bled. He'd had a rough night.

'They made me ask her again and again about a well,' he continued. 'Where is the well, they wanted to know. Make her tell us where to find the well. And all she would say is that she would die before she betrayed her sacred trust.'

A tear spilled out of one blackened eye; he winced at the sting of it.

'I understood more than I told them,' he continued. 'I tried to ask my own questions between theirs. She said her name was Sophia. She said it was her honour to tend the sacred grove. She said.' He swallowed and more tears spilled. 'She said she didn't blame me. That none of this was my fault. The poor girl said the Garland King would forgive me.'

He dropped his head into his hands. 'I didn't try to save her. I didn't know how.' And he wept.

The crunch of tyres on gravel made both man and wolf raise their heads, alert. The rumble of an extremely well-tuned and otherwise very quiet vehicle, and another with a louder engine, followed by the faint snick of a van door sliding open.

The Greek staggered to his feet and out into the morbid marble foyer. Audrey followed a distance behind. Through the open front door, she could make out a dark vehicle, barely visible behind the blazing headlights. Those lights threw a wash of illumination on a white van with *Fisheries, Wildlife & Parks* written on the side in dark green.

'In here!' cried out the Greek.

The unexpectedly rapid arrival of the Department startled Audrey out of her curiosity. She hunkered low and slunk across the entrance to the shadows opposite. She'd have to find another way out. She had no intention of being netted by the Department of Fisheries, Wildlife & Parks like a common or garden variety feral dog.

Three people emerged from the Fisheries van.

'Mr Melas?' called out the woman in the lead. She was carrying a shockstick in one hand and a lasso in the other.

'Yes.'

'You all right?'

'No. And. And there's...' he swallowed. 'There's a dead woman. Much older than she looks, I think. And a wolf.'

'Damn. Well, good thing we brought the van.' Shockstick Lady and her companions stepped onto the porch. 'You're a mess, aren't you?'

'How did you find me? The call didn't get through.' Mr Melas was crying again as Shockstick Lady carefully examined his face and placed a gentle hand on his arm.

'It did, for a few seconds. After that it was investigation, triangulation and brain-iation. You know what the boss is like.'

'Not really,' Melas laughed feebly. 'I only started last Monday.'

'Hell of an induction.'

'It's all really true, then?'

"Fraid so. The boss is in the car. She'll debrief you.' Shockstick Lady tilted her head back towards the dark car.

'I thought, I mean I heard she never attended scenes.'

'Almost never. She wanted to check this one out herself, first hand. There's rumours about this place.'

'Yes,' he agreed. 'True, I think. There was talk of a tiger.'

Time to not be around. As Shockstick Lady and her colleagues stepped into the entrance with Mr Melas, Audrey made herself thin as shadows and padded softly away, unseen, following scents of spices and baked-in grease to a kitchen at the rear of the building.

The Hall's zoo smell was strong here. Audrey made her paw into a hand, unlatched the back door and slipped outside. She circled round to the front path again and, pressed close to the stone walls, she studied the placement of the Department's officers and watched for an opportunity to escape.

One of Shockstick Lady's team was helping Melas to the dark car. The automated rear passenger window hummed down.

In the illuminated interior, Audrey could make out a pale, sombre woman wearing her dark hair in a bun. She wore smoke-tinted glasses in the middle of the night. Audrey could hear her racing heartbeat and the effort she was making to breathe evenly. Underneath the anxiety, the woman's scent reminded her of someone, though Audrey had never met her before. The association tickled at the back of her brain. *Why does she seem familiar?*

'Mr Melas. I'm sorry it took so long to find you.'

'You came, ma'am. Thank you.' A little sob. Audrey was cross that they wouldn't let him sit.

'You mentioned a wolf.'

'Yes, ma'am. It... I think it saved my life. They would have shot me. The wolf wouldn't let them.'

'Any sign of other creatures? A tiger, perhaps. Or a snake?'

'The youngest man said a tiger had escaped onto the moor. Another man took a gun and went out.' Melas swallowed. 'The oldest told me to ask the girl questions and translate the answers. The youngest. He. He beat us. He killed the girl. She was...' Tears spilled from his dark eyes. 'She was so brave.'

The anxious woman reached a gloved hand through the window and hesitantly patted Melas' own.

'I'm so sorry, Theo. Sit by me, I'll take you to our doctor. No more questions for now. Perry, help him in.'

Perry led Melas to the other passenger door and helped Melas inside. He closed the door quietly.

'And Perry, have your team send their report to me after you've cleaned up.'

'Aye, Ms Holmes.'

Oh. Oh. A *sibling* scent.

The unseen driver drove away while Perry returned to Stoke Moran to assist his colleagues.

Audrey made her own way down the drive to the gates of Stoke Moran – left yawning open by Roylott's rapid departure. Well short of the road, she angled onto the moors, heading east.

The mists swirled around her out on the rolling slopes. Somewhere out there, other werewolves were running, or perhaps keeping to the hollows and shadows, aware of this night's strange events. Audrey was too weary to race, so she loped unsteadily back to Cherry Brook. So many shifts of form had left her prickling and throbbing with pain. Her gait was uneven now, with the spasming ache of the old hip wound. She would have howled if she'd had the energy.

She returned to where her clothes were bundled under the pine needles. Best to be ready when the sun rose: a woman of mature years wandering naked on the moor would excite comment. By the time she limped into the conifer woods, pre-dawn light was glimmering on the horizon. She slumped under the trees, almost tasting the rising sun.

When the first light touched her, Audrey surrendered to the familiar agony of her twisting skeleton, muscles, skin. The moon was leaving her bones as painfully as it had entered them. It was a curse, after all.

As a teenager, the change had put a wall between her human and wolf selves and she would wake naked in the undergrowth in some remote woodland, with no clear memory of the night. Her wolf and human selves were more aligned these days. That, too, was a blessing and a curse.

When the moon was done with her, Audrey curled naked in the grass, drawing sharp little breaths as her body settled and the pain dissipated. Then she stood, brushed her skin free of twigs, grass and wandering bugs, dressed in the frock and slippers she'd hidden, brushed her hair, and made her way back to her room in the *Cherry Brook B&B*.

A large breakfast, a long soak in the bath, and a good long think were required. What was the meaning of the dead dryad? What was the well that she'd died for, rather than reveal the location? And who was "His Nibs", who would be so unhappy about the result?

And did Sherlock Holmes know that his sister served in the infamous Department of Fisheries?

Chapter Eight

'Good morning, Mrs Hudson! Did you have a good sle– Oh.'

From the B&B landlady's aborted chirpiness, Audrey gathered that she looked like something the wolf dragged in, despite her attempted soak in the bath. Now she smelled too strongly of hibiscus and was filled with bath foam regret. Her face probably also betrayed her crabby certainty that a continental breakfast was not going to cut it after the night she'd had.

'I have a bad hip,' Audrey explained, attempting to sound apologetic, 'and I forgot to bring my pills.'

The sterling woman accepted the explanation. 'It wasn't the noise kept you awake?'

'Noise?'

'Wild animals making a ruckus on the moors. They do, on the full moon – gets in their blood or something. Some people find it unsettling.'

'I thought it was the pipes.'

The landlady blinked, not knowing how to take that. Audrey smiled thinly. The landlady went abruptly away to make bacon and eggs.

Audrey sighed. The morning after the moon, she was always a bit snappy. Especially after a rough night. She should probably bring some flowers back for her hostess later on. Or a bottle of wine. Or a dead rabbit.

She really needed to get her teeth into a sausage.

Despite her ravening hunger, Audrey managed to eat her dainty portion of two eggs, three rashers and white toast very nearly like a civilised person, before going out to find more muscular fuel to replenish her strength.

Half an hour later, she'd downed sausages, eggs, mushrooms, roasted tomato, bacon, black pudding and beans at a nearby hotel café, only realising as she finished packing away the extra-large helping that she had an awestruck audience of two waiters, four ramblers and an Australian backpacker, who rather rudely took a photo. The upstart colonial vanished rapidly after that. Audrey assumed the woman had a developed a sense for predators in her nation full of things that wanted to kill you.

Audrey had moved on to a new café location to drink tea and slake the remains of her hunger without an audience when company finally arrived.

'Mrs Hudson!'

Audrey looked over the lowered rim of her teacup at Sherlock Holmes. Goodness, he liked to bellow a greeting. He strode down the narrow road towards her table, his expression exasperated.

John Watson kept pace a fraction behind him. He had a slight limp today, though after two months in Sherlock's dynamic company, his face had lost the pinched look of long illness. In fact, despite favouring his left leg, he gave the impression of a horse left too long in the stable, itching for a gallop. Even his moustache was bristling with impatience.

Sherlock flung himself into a seat opposite her. 'I thought I might find you here.'

'Why did you think that?' she challenged him. 'This isn't where I'm staying.'

John declined a seat, instead warily surveying the landscape, before resting an expectant, affectionate look on Sherlock. Sherlock preened under that admiring scrutiny.

'You claimed you would be visiting a friend in East Barnet for a few nights, but you wore your walking boots,' Sherlock explained. 'That might indicate you planned on walks with your so-called friend, but you've never mentioned them previously and gave no details of your planned visit. I've never had a landlord or lady so un-prone to gossip, but this was terribly tight-lipped, even for you.

'A tip for next time: if you're lying about paying a social call, a smidge more detail without over-gilding that lily would serve you well. I can give you some tips on body language as well. An unblinking stare does not convey sincerity so much as an attempt to dominate and convince, when you're talking about a flit to suburbia for a phantom sleepover. Touching your mouth and throat at the same time are definite signifiers. Added to this the discovery of Roylott's letter, your own researches as well as mine, that you grew up near the moors, in Newton Abbot, and that I know perfectly well there are things you're not telling me, it wasn't hard to realise where you were really headed.'

She opened her mouth to speak, but Sherlock continued with hardly a pause for breath.

'Or if you mean, how did I know I'd find you at *Badger's Holt Café* – that was serendipity, deduction and research. Yesterday morning, I heard our neighbour, Mrs Turner, telling you on the steps outside 221 that the scones at a teahouse she knew in Dartmoor were better than yours. I don't know why you told her your true destination–'

'She ran into me at the train station when I was booking the ticket.'

'–but I know that you are inordinately proud of your scones, and no really proud baker would ever leave such a claim unchallenged. And who boasts they have the best scones in Dartmoor, using a secret recipe? *Badgers Holt*, according to the internet. You may already have visited to test their claim, but you would have arrived in Dartmoor too late yesterday for a Devonshire tea, and a Devonshire tea is not a suitable breakfast. This is your first opportunity to taste the competition.'

He gestured at the plate bearing the second half of the café's Secret Recipe Scone, strawberry jam and clotted cream.

Audrey arched an eyebrow. 'How do you do that without stopping for breath?'

'Practise,' suggested John, his gaze still checking the periphery out of habit. His cheeky grin saved him from Sherlock's exasperated glare. 'And your verdict?' John continued, indicating the scone in question.

'It's hardly for me to say, is it?' She pushed the plate over to them. Sherlock took a bite of scone and handed the rest of it to John. John, the second unbiased judge, ate a portion and closed his eyes in bliss.

'Well?' Audrey challenged, hiding a smile.

'Not bad. Not as good as yours,' declared Sherlock.

John was contemplating his scone more seriously, sucking slightly on his tongue. 'Not quite as good. You use champagne and cream in yours, don't you? And your jam's better.'

'Flatterers.'

'I never flatter,' Sherlock said sternly. 'Flattery is an affront to logic.'

John's sideways glance at Sherlock was full of amusement.

'And now, to business,' announced Sherlock. 'Have you been to Stoke Moran yet? I gather you came ahead of us to refresh your memory of the area. You clearly hadn't immediately realised Gruner's last words referred to Stoke Moran or you would have acted sooner. Even if,' he added sourly, 'you wouldn't tell me sooner. You're still keeping secrets.'

'I don't mean to,' Audrey said, keeping a whole lot more of them after last night. She was mindful to blink, to not touch her mouth or throat, to keep her breathing even, as per Sherlock's excellent advice.

'I'm... I'm struggling since Edinburgh. Poor sleep, poor appetite, poor memory. I wanted to see if I could knock something loose. I left Devon when I was a teenager and this is my first time back.'

Sherlock's expression softened and he patted her wrist. 'Trauma can have unpredictable effects on all of those things.' His eyes flicked momentarily towards John. 'But be assured, I'm going to solve your case, Mrs Hudson, even if you're being your own worst enemy in the process.'

Audrey wondered if this was Sherlock being kind or stubborn or both. John had stopped bathing him in admiring looks, but his eye on her now was hard, his moustache bristling with the disapproving moue underneath it. Audrey supposed it couldn't be comfortable for him, holding as he did the missing clue about werewolves.

'You don't need to solve it,' she said, though she'd love it if he could.

Not for the first time, she wondered what he would do if she told him the truth. If she showed him the truth. He couldn't deny the evidence of his own eyes, if she changed her shape while he watched. She had refused to put on a show for Gruner, but she might for Sherlock, if she thought it would do any good.

But it might only do harm. It had done harm in the past. Audrey had tried just once to explain things to her family. As an adult she tracked down her sister in Manchester. Ingrid was furious with what she said were Audrey's delusional lies, then deeply concerned. So Audrey decided to show her the truth. The reunion ended with Ingrid screaming in terror and then trying to run Audrey over with her brand new Ford Cortina while shrieking 'Stay away from my children!' Audrey's bumper-bar injuries had healed quickly; Ingrid's nervous breakdown had taken longer to manifest and longer to heal.

Siobhan was only eight when her terrified family abandoned her on the moor. Conal's friends had attacked him, "defending" themselves with cricket bats until he fled. Travis and Tara had fared better, by some measures. Their family refused to believe a word of it, and when presented with irrefutable evidence decided it was some wild hoax. The twins were sent to separate institutions. When Audrey found Tara, after her third escape, she'd kept Tara safe and helped her find Travis.

All her life, Audrey and the *weres* she knew had been vehemently disbelieved or, when proofs were offered, violently rejected. John Watson's reaction to his friend Percy was a rare exception to the general rule that humans did not cope well with *were*kind. Perhaps Sherlock, so committed to his idea of logic, would be like John. But maybe he'd be like Ingrid. Audrey didn't want to take the risk; she didn't want to hurt him or drive him to unreasoning terror or even to abject denial. If only he would somehow deduce it for himself, and be able to accept it. If only John would tell him. But John wouldn't. He knew it wasn't his secret to tell.

'Are you telling me to drop it?'

Her lack of reply was reply enough.

'Normally,' Sherlock said, 'I would. I dislike cases with mysteries at both ends as well as in the middle. But,' and here Sherlock leaned close, eyes twinkling, 'I like a challenge. And I like you. And this is the most interesting challenge I've had in a long time. So if there's something you're willing to share about your time here yesterday, we can go on from there.'

'I walked around Stoke Moran hall yesterday,' Audrey offered, relieved to have a version of the truth to contribute. 'It's walled and the gates are locked, so I couldn't get in. The garden was terribly overgrown, though I could see some repairs were being made to the chimneys. I thought I heard animals inside.'

'Ah, yes. I hear Roylott keeps a menagerie to dissuade trespassers.'

'Where do you hear that?'

Sherlock settled back in his chair, hands folded over his stomach. 'John and I arrived yesterday evening – we headed here from Baker Street once it was clear you'd come ahead of us. We had a profitable pub crawl, encouraging chit-chat.'

'Making up stories in one pub just to get people to correct him, and passing the new tidbits on in the next pub like he had a scoop,' laughed John.

'A technique I picked up at my grandmother's knee,' said Sherlock, unabashed.

'He really is the most dreadful gossip,' John confided in a tattletale whisper, having recovered his good humour. He remained standing, though he'd stopped scouring the perimeter as though it were ticking. 'People will tell him anything.'

'And they did,' Sherlock said. 'Stoke Moran was once the home of the profligate Lord Alexander Moran, who died young in the late 1960s and left a widow, Helen Moran, and an infant son, with a large property in disrepair and larger debt. Lady Moran paid off the creditors but was lumbered with a mouldering home she couldn't afford to repair or to leave. Little Sebastian grew up with his mother sinking deeper and deeper into depression and was, by all accounts, a surly child who liked to kill small creatures on the moor – first with a slingshot, later with an air rifle. When he took pot-shots at the livestock, the police gave him his first warning.

'While attending mandatory group counselling with her son, Lady Helen Moran met one Grimsby Roylott, a doctor of archaeology recently returned from some years in India and, either through the power of his personality or, less likely, some stunning tendresse, he won her over and they married in 1976. With me so far?'

'When I was young, the rumour was that she'd done away with her first husband, and that her child was a savage,' said Audrey.

'The rumour mill was half right. Sebastian was a hellion, encouraged by his stepfather. Peas in a pod, and the boy was devoted to Roylott. They garnered a shared reputation for misanthropy. After Sebastian attacked a boy from his school, Roylott sent him to a military academy in Kent, which seems to have agreed with him. From there, the heir to Stoke Moran joined the army and honed his skills as a special ops sniper until his discharge. He became a big game hunter and guide in South Africa, Namibia, Zimbabwe and the like. It's odds-on the hunting was a cover for mercenary activities.'

'People really will tell you anything,' Audrey said, startled that Sherlock had learned so much.

'Well, credit where it's due, the military history aspect is courtesy of John's connections. He made a few calls to former colleagues in army bureaucracy for ex-Colonel Moran's inglorious past while I was winkling out the local history. Really, he's becoming invaluable to the work.'

John quietly glowed.

'While Moran was off covering himself in ignominy,' Sherlock continued, 'back in the decaying pile of Stoke Moran, Lady Helen unexpectedly had another son – Augustus Roylott – whom Grimsby doted on: "like a prize hound" one wit put it. Within a year, and while Sebastian was in the army, Lady Helen died of a snake bite. Which is curious as the adders on Dartmoor are rarely fatal.'

'So Helen Moran may not have black-widowed her first husband, but it's possible her second Bluebearded her,' Audrey noted.

'Colourful, and accurate,' Sherlock conceded. 'As for recent activities, Sebastian Moran has lately returned to the fold. Some gossips say he's still under his stepfather's sway. Others think he's becoming resentful of the preference Roylott's now showing for his biological son. Generally, the busybodies concur Sebastian accepts Grimsby Roylott's entrenchment in the family seat, though they disagree how long that will last. In the past he's fully supported Roylott Senior's efforts over the decades to fund the restoration of the hall while obsessively maintaining his privacy with a vanguard of unsanctioned wild creatures. Accounts further suggest he is up to unspecified no good behind the brambles and the beasts.'

'I can believe it.' Well, she knew it for a fact.

'The stories are astonishing.' Sherlock adopted a tattling tone: 'Watch out for the wild animals! That Grimsby Roylott's a bad lot. Sebastian Moran and Augustus Roylott are hardly better! We had such high hopes when the old family finally returned to their traditional seat, only for the Morans of Stoke Moran to turn out to be unsociable thugs. I blame their stepfather. Roylott's not right in the head. Is he allowed to keep a zoo on the moor? I hear he keeps a tiger; I hear he has an ape; it's said his anaconda ate a moor pony! Histrionics. Local pubs, mark my words, are the best places to gather hearsay, if you can't get to a wedding.'

'I'll make a note of that.'

'So, I propose we go to the hall and try to obtain entry, with permission or by scaling a fence or two.'

'You mean to trespass where a man has gone to great lengths to repel intruders,' Audrey said drily.

'Well, I didn't say it would be simple.'

'Quite.'

'Before we go,' said John firmly, 'I'd love a cup of tea. Maybe some toast?'

Sherlock rose, declaring with good humour, 'Ah, John, I went and boorishly dragged you out of our lodgings before breakfast. Tea and breakfast it is. Excellent fortification for an Englishman before storming another Englishman's castle. No, you stay there. Sit and tell our landlady what we've been up to this morning; she might reciprocate.'

He dashed into the café. Audrey could see him inspecting the board for specials, and noted that John's gaze was, as ever, on his flatmate.

'What were you up to this morning, then?' she asked.

John's expression was solemn. He finally sat down.

'We were following up rumours of wild animals escaping from the hall. A sheep had been mauled by something with very large teeth and claws. People spoke last night of wolves howling and lions snarling, monkeys, even. A regular safari out there on the moor in the night. Sherlock had to stop telling people we don't have wolves and lions on the moors because the arguments were slowing us down. This morning we followed the trail of a slaughtered animal – Sherlock thinks a pony from the clumps of hair, hide and blood – being dragged into Wistman's Wood. Nothing to do with you, was it? It was a full moon, after all.'

'I had a lovely moon run, thank you,' Audrey said acidly. 'Wonderful weather for it.'

'I didn't mean–'

'I don't hunt ponies, Doctor. I despatched the emaciated tiger that did, however.'

John whistled, long and low. 'Jesus. So the rumours of Roylott's menagerie are true, then?'

'Oh yes. I got onto the grounds last night. When you scale that fence, be on your guard. He has a baboon, a herd of goats, a very large python, and lord knows what else.'

'Goats?'

'The bite of an annoyed goat is no laughing matter,' she deadpanned.

John laughed. 'All right. I'll do my best to appease the angry goats.'

'Good man.'

'Anything else we should know?'

The Roylotts murdered a dryad and tortured a Greek interpreter and Sherlock's sister arrived to mop up the aftermath, she thought. But that was too much to unpack yet. Not until she knew what Ms Holmes' role was in the Department of Fisheries, and whether she was murdering werewolves.

'Nothing comes to mind.'

John relaxed a fraction, but his gaze wandered away again, beyond the café tables to the rolling hills and clumps of trees beyond. He stretched his leg out underneath the table and flexed his toes.

Audrey was reluctant to ask after his health. John Watson was a grown man and a doctor and not under her protection, technically.

'Do you need something for the pain?' she asked anyway.

'I took something. It only plays up occasionally. I've got a metal pin in my left leg.'

'I thought Sherlock said you'd been shot.'

If John thought it was tactless, he didn't object. 'The medical convoy was ambushed. I got shot when I stupidly left our ambulance to triage the wounded from the escort truck. Then the other truck was blown up with a mortar and I got peppered with shrapnel. The only reason I'm not dead is that Nick – she was our driver – dragged my sorry arse to safety and stopped the bleeding. She kept me alive until an extraction squad got us to the base for surgery. My femur needed a pin, and my right wrist. A fragment went into my lip–' he gestured over his moustache. 'Then an infection set into my shoulder and knocked me for six. I was in rehab for months. Long enough for Nick to be wounded too, then invalided out with her prosthetic before I got mustered out. I still get the shakes when I'm fatigued, so I was medically discharged as unfit for duty.'

'And then Sherlock runs you ragged hither and yon all over the moor.'

John grinned. 'Actually, I'm loving it. It's fantastic to be useful again, after being so bloody useless for so long. I won't be able to go with him when I have locum work, which is a shame. It's fun. I mean, he's good company.'

'The flat share is working out, then?'

'It's great,' he beamed. 'It was fine, staying with Nick for a few days. If it had worked out, we could have helped each other for a bit. But,' he shrugged. 'It's probably best I left. She didn't want me see how much she was drinking. She, ah, she knows my late brother, Hal, was an alcoholic. She knows it bothers me that she drinks so much. I think she worried that I was starting to drink too much, myself.'

A self-deprecating laugh followed that. 'Sherlock wanted me to drill you about your morning, and you're just getting way too much information about me. You're a sympathetic listener.'

Audrey wondered if it was more that he knew her secret and honour demanded that he share a few in return.

'You've been through a lot,' she said.

'Yeah. In a way, getting wounded was the least of it. Not being able to get about like I used to has been worse. I'm a doer. I used to be, anyway. I did rugby, boxing and rowing at school and university. I used to ski, hike, rock climbing for a while. Then between a bullet in the shoulder and shrapnel everywhere else, that all stopped. All through my recovery, and after my discharge, I've been... not myself. It was like I stopped being real; like I'd died out there and they only brought back my ghost.' John shook off the introspection.

'Except with him. I've only known Sherlock a couple months, but I know who I am when I'm with him. He doesn't know what I was. He sees who I am now. He sees what I can do, not what I can't, and he shows that to me.'

'I'm glad.'

'Me too.'

John fell silent as Sherlock returned with a number on a stand and slotted in beside John at the table. 'Any discoveries?'

'Mrs Hudson now has a full account of our morning, and she was giving me hers.'

'Nothing to report, really,' Audrey said. 'A lie-in, a stroll, a scone.'

'You're telling such bald-faced lies for such a very nice lady,' Sherlock said with good humour. 'All the tells of a poor night's sleep and of a rapid and haphazard toilet indicate otherwise. The scone is incontestable, though.'

At her raised eyebrow, he said, 'You have bags under your eyes, despite your concealer; you have unusually flyaway hair and chipped nail polish; and your brow creased when we spoke of Roylott. You're also biting your lip and looking for exits, the way John does. Ah.'

John shrugged. 'It'll come in handy when I see the goats making their sneak attack.'

'What?'

John grinned. 'Mrs Hudson was warning me about the cranky goats on the moor.'

'Goats. Right. So what was she really saying about her morning?'

John cocked an eyebrow at them both. 'You've read Gruner's book on her. It was a full moon last night. Mrs Hudson turned into a werewolf and hunted Dartmoor's grumpy goats.'

Sherlock's disgruntled reply was: 'And I'm a vampire who sleeps in a coffin of earth, and you're a zombie–'

'Ghost, Sherlock. Or I was. You cured me.'

For all it sounded like an argument, Audrey could see they were thoroughly enjoying the ridiculous discussion. Then a waitress brought a full English breakfast for John and buttered toast and jam for Sherlock.

'That's hardly a fortifying breakfast,' John noted, digging into his bacon like it was his life's work.

'Digestion takes too much energy away from my thinking.'

'Hunger buggers up my concentration until all I can think about is breakfast.'

'Yes, yes, I dragged you out shamefully early. Eat your eggs, then we'll visit the hall.'

John cheerfully ate his eggs.

CHAPTER NINE

'WHERE HAVE YOU PARKED?' ASKED AUDREY WHEN BREAKFAST WAS done and she felt, literally, more human.

'Just down the lane,' said John.

'Would you mind giving me a lift to the B&B? I'd walk, only my hip is acting up. I'm afraid I've overdone it.'

'We're due at Stoke Moran shortly,' Sherlock said pointedly.

'He says *due* like he made an appointment,' said John, 'when he just means to show up and shove his oar in, which is his *modus operandi*. He reminds me of a sergeant major I had, who liked to spring inspections and make everybody jump.'

'I'll come for the ride then.' She rose and limped a few steps, exaggerating, but not much, for effect.

'Mrs Hudson. We're working,' said Sherlock impatiently.

'On my case. Don't be a fusspot. I'll read a book in the car while you work. You won't even know I'm there.'

Nothing as crude as scaling fences was required when they drove up to Stoke Moran. The unlocked front gates were manned by a worker in overalls. Sherlock leaned out of the window and said, 'Holmes. Home Office,' and she waved them through.

I'm not the only one who tells bald-faced lies, Audrey thought.

Sherlock read her expression like a particularly wide-open book. 'It isn't a lie. I said my name and the name of a government department. I left it to her to draw inferences.'

Before she could refer to hairs and how to split them, Audrey was disconcerted to see a Fisheries van parked in front of the hall steps. A man stood at the door; not one of last night's crew.

Sherlock led John to the steps while Audrey watched from the back seat.

'Holmes. Home Office,' he repeated and the fellow raised an eyebrow.

'I thought you was a *Missus* Holmes.'

Sherlock spread his arms to indicate his very much Mister-ness and the Fisheries worker shrugged.

'Sit-Rep?' Sherlock prompted.

'The team got here soon as we could after we got the call about the animals, about eight this morning. The goats were trucked out about an hour ago. There was a mastiff in bad, bad shape. We found a civet as well, and an alligator – a bleedin' *alligator.*' The man grimaced. 'Mr Roylott's bonkers. Where the 'ell he got a Caiman and 'ow he smuggled it onto the grounds is anyone's guess. Only a juvenile female Speckled, according to the zoo vet, thank Christ. Less than a metre and easy enough trapped with a chicken sandwich for bait. There went someone's lunch, eh? Vet's taken it and the civet off. We found traces of a big cat, tiger maybe, and tracks of what the vet swears is a humongous rock python. Haven't found it yet. And could be more animals.'

'How hard is it to find a humongous python?'

'Surprisin'ly 'ard,' was the wry reply. 'Maybe the missin' tiger et it.'

Sherlock strolled back to warn Audrey to stay inside the car. 'Somebody alerted the Department of Fisheries, Wildlife & Parks about Roylott's bizarre collection of wild animals. Some are still at large. Best keep out of trouble. Don't want an irritable badger to take a piece out of your ankle.'

As if it would get half a chance. But Audrey nodded. 'What are you going to do?'

'John and I will look for any more paperwork of the type Roylott sent to Gruner, offering hoax curios to gullible collectors. We'll be back in half an hour or so.'

Audrey waited obediently in the car until Sherlock and John were inside the hall and she was certain that none of the more "specialist" Fisheries employees were around. She suspected they'd vanished after covering up last night's events – otherwise the hall would have been cordoned off with a police investigation into kidnapping and murder.

A moment later, Audrey was pacing along the front path. She circled the building again.

Stoke Moran Hall looked less disreputable and more tragic by daylight. The stonework of the once noble edifice was cracked and stained with age and neglect. Here and there were further signs, however, that it was being restored. Some damaged walls had been repaired with new stone; dead ivy hacked away from the side of the house. Lines of fresh soil showed where new water and sewerage pipes had been laid. The work was the merest drop in a renovation ocean, but it presented Roylott's dogged intent.

The strong scent of reptile permeated the place. In daylight she could easily see the tracks of a gigantic snake all around the building. The trail was so interwoven with old and new scents, it was impossible to determine where the creature had gone to ground.

Her limp was hardly noticeable by the time she reached the front door again, but on sighting a woman there, she hissed in theatrical pain and limped up to her.

'So sorry to bother you, dear. Would it be a terrible inconvenience for me to come in?'

'I don't think I'm allowed. The owner is away. How did you get here, anyway?'

'I came with the gentlemen who arrived earlier.'

'Ah yes, Mr Holmes and his colleague from the Home Office.'

'That's him. He's giving me lift to my B&B when he's finished here. But, I, well, I do rather need to use the loo,' she said in an anxious *sotto voce*.

The woman winced in sympathy. 'Come on in. I'd better escort you, though. Sorry.'

Audrey suffered to be escorted, preparing an innocent face for Sherlock and John should she encounter them en route. She needn't have bothered. Sherlock was busy scouring the side room that last night had contained a dryad corpse and an assault victim. He was tossing impatient commentary over his shoulder at the previous door guard who was now overseeing Sherlock's invasion of the house.

'If your people hadn't tramped back and forth over the scene like a herd of cows I'd be able to determine how many animals are secreted in this building and where!'

'How did you even know about the badger?' grumbled the man.

'Are you joking? Wildlife management is your job, and you missed the prints on the marble, and the long hairs caught in the suit of armour at the bottom of the stairs? Oh, what's this?'

Sherlock dropped flat on his belly and took a pocket magnifying glass to something enthralling on the carpet. John watched him with a puzzled frown.

'The loo's that way,' said Audrey's escort.

Audrey followed her to the downstairs toilet. She could hear the man from the Fisheries asking what the hell Sherlock was doing, digging around under the furniture and in the fireplace, the silence where Sherlock refused to answer, and the murmur of John being placatory.

After entering the loo, Audrey listened to her escort's footsteps recede as she went to view Sherlock's performance as a spectator sport.

Audrey slipped back into the corridor. Unsure where to start, she did what wolves do best. She followed her nose, tracking the persistent stench of snake up to the first floor. The powerful, eye-watering musk, redolent of decomposing goat, led to a master bedroom. Audrey searched for coils of serpent around the bed, without success.

She ran her hand across the top of a six-drawer pinewood tallboy before trying each locked drawer. The cupboard seemed an unlikely receptacle for wads of cash or valuables. Audrey exerted her *were* strength and tugged energetically at the lowest drawer. The lock broke and it opened.

At once she was overwhelmed with a new scent. A familiar scent. A *beloved* scent.

She recoiled from it, her skin crawling with dread and despair. A howl curled in her chest and clawed up her throat. She kept her jaws clamped on it as she opened the drawer fully to reveal the horror inside.

Waxed cloth wrapped around a long, slender object. The howl slid over her tongue and prowled around the back of her teeth. Her arm had sprouted claws and fur, which stood on end as she folded back the wrapping.

Nestled in the cloth was a severed wolf's paw.

Even without that dear scent, she'd have known it by the black pelt with the smattering of white hairs, and the scar across the pads of two of the toes. She'd have known blind and deaf, whose paw this was. Whose hand.

A genuine werewolf artefact, recently obtained.

99

This was *Conal's* hand. Her adopted son and loyal second, Conal Dunn, dead, defiled, his hand a trophy for this snake-stinking bastard Grimsby Roylott.

The uncontrolled howl broke out of her. A tumble of wild grief and rage filled the room, filled the house, rattled the windows. The sound spilled out across the tors where ponies and cattle, small mammals and the birds, ravens and sparrows and hawks all, started and fled in terror.

When the keening faded, Audrey was kneeling by the drawer, tears spilling from her eyes, her face almost as wolfish as her hands.

'Mrs Hudson?' John called up the stairs. 'Did you hear that? Are you all right?'

Audrey folded the cloth over the gruesome trophy. She held it against her heart for a moment, and then gently put it inside her shirt and folded her hands over her stomach to keep the parcel in place. She wiped her eyes and smoothed down her hair and breathed in and out, in and out, until the wolfishness went away.

Fully restored to her human-seeming self, if not to equanimity, and with her hand firmly pressed to the precious, awful thing under her clothes, Audrey walked regally downstairs, through the foyer and onto the front landing.

Her erstwhile guide rushed to meet her before she could reach the car. 'Where've you been?'

'No soap downstairs,' she said; another glib lie. 'I went to find another loo so I could wash up. But did you hear that terrible noise?'

John and Sherlock had joined them outside, along with the man from the Fisheries. John's eyes on hers were full of alarm and concern.

'Didn't know that bugger Roylott had another dog here,' was the Fisheries man's observation. 'We already had to put that poor bloody mastiff down.'

'It came from inside the house, didn't it?' asked the woman.

'Oh, I hope not!' Audrey couldn't fake blanching but she looked around fearfully for effect. 'I'm sure it came from the moor. Wild dogs chasing after those poor ponies. It's dreadful.'

'That was like no dog I ever heard,' Sherlock asserted.

'It was a wolf,' replied John automatically, with unassailable certainty, then belatedly clamped his mouth shut as though that would make it unsaid.

'You've heard wolves, have you?' Sherlock raised an eyebrow at him.

'In Afghanistan,' said John, unwilling to be thought a fantasist. 'Grey wolves. We used to hear them at night. Our translator showed me how to read wolf and dog tracks after we got trapped with an extraction team in a village in the Maiwand district. The first time we got trapped in Maiwand, anyway.'

'Wasn't that where you –'

'Got shot? Yeah. It gets a very poor Trip Advisor rating from me.'

'You can read tracks, you say?' Sherlock stepped off the landing and indicated prints in the soil around the house. 'What are these, then? The footprints of a gigantic hound? Or a wolf?'

John inspected the prints and said, 'Wolf.' He spared a fleeting glance for Audrey but, after having outright told Sherlock that their landlady was a werewolf, he had obviously decided on a policy of honesty.

'How do you know?' Sherlock prompted.

'Dogs generally track all over the place, following numerous scents,' John explained. 'Wolves tend to track in straight lines, going directly to their target. Longer stride, narrower chests. See how close the tracks are, left to right, and how the hind prints land almost right over the front paw prints? The toes are pretty much the same size, and there's no toenail drag, like you get with dogs. Even big dogs.'

'How certain are you it's a wolf?'

'I'm not actually an expert, Sherlock.' But at Sherlock's intense scrutiny he conceded, 'Pretty certain.'

Sherlock, impressed, regarded John like he'd solved a locked room mystery all on his own.

Audrey was suddenly exhausted. She hugged herself. 'I'll go back to the car.'

In the next moment, Sherlock had an arm supportively across her back. 'Roylott may have plotted against your family. Of course you're distressed to be here. I should have insisted you stay behind.' The brusqueness of his manner was offset by the gentleness with which he guided her towards the car. 'Wait here while we look for the wolf.' He shook his head in wonder. 'A wolf. Good God. Better wind up the windows.'

She let him help her into the back seat. Once the door was closed she leaned her forehead against the glass and watched Sherlock, John and the Fisheries workers follow the tracks that she knew would lead nowhere but in circles and then back to the moor.

But those lads weren't safe, she realised. The tiger was dead, but the snake hadn't been found. What else was lurking out in the brambles and tangled shrubs of Stoke Moran? She took the precious burden from under her shirt, wrapped it in her cardigan and reluctantly left it on the car seat. Then she followed them, her skin prickling.

Sherlock, John and the others were approaching the circular folly which rose above the empty goat pen.

'No wolf tracks here, but look,' Sherlock said, indicating another set of marks.

'Is that the badger, then?' asked the Fisheries woman.

'Not a badger,' said Sherlock. He walked up to the folly. The fake Roman tower had been built with an artfully broken pillar, an incomplete wall and half a tiled roof. A tree grew flush along one wall. Sherlock stepped inside the circular space, hands pressed flat to the 18th century stones.

John Watson became hyper-alert. 'Sherlock?'

Sherlock poked his head back out into daylight. 'The prints end in here. There's a trapdoor. And it contains,' it creaked as he opened it, 'nothing. That's disappointing.'

The hairs along Audrey's arms and scalp rose up. 'Sherlock!' she called out. 'Be careful.'

'Who has the time?' he called back cheerfully, returning to the shadows to inspect the cavity below the trapdoor. 'God, it reeks in here.'

Audrey couldn't help the way her stance changed, ready to spring at any danger with a moment's notice. Sherlock had cornered himself in that stupid tower, with barely room to move should something attack, and John was too close by, ready to join him in the danger.

She nearly howled again as a spindly body made of matted hair, wickedly long teeth and fury leapt, shrieking, from the half-roof of the folly into the empty goat pen, trapping Sherlock inside the tower. The missing baboon, mad with hunger and fear, had found them first.

It lunged towards Sherlock, a feint, then prepared to attack in earnest.

At the first sight of it, John had shucked off his jacket. Now, before Audrey could act, he flung the garment over the head of the terrified and terrifying baboon. Swiftly and decisively, he bundled the shrouded ape towards the folly, shouting, 'Keep back, Sherlock!'

Sherlock stood clear enough to allow John room to shove the confused, shrieking ape into the tower and through the trapdoor. Sherlock slammed the trapdoor lid down. John promptly stood on the lid while Sherlock fastened it shut and the ape shrieked and thumped ineffectually from below.

'Better call a zookeeper,' said John, breathing heavily.

The Fisheries man was already on the mobile.

'Let them know there may be a tiger, too,' Sherlock said. 'We're after a wolf and a python as well.'

'I'm going to need more coats,' muttered John, but he caught Sherlock's eye and they began to laugh.

Audrey returned silently to the car and sat, heart crushed under the weight of cradling Conal's swaddled, severed hand in her lap.

Sherlock was full of talk as he drove the three of them back to *Cherry Brook B&B.*

'Some very strange things have been going on at Stoke Moran,' he said, handing John a selection of items in plastic bags from his pocket.

'To begin with, someone was recently assaulted in the office off the main foyer. Blood spots in the carpet and the skirting boards, though most of it had been cleaned off. Not enough blood to indicate a major blood-loss injury, but someone's gone to the trouble to eradicate evidence. It was a very efficient operation. MI5-level efficient, which is deeply peculiar.'

'What's this?' John had extracted a short stump of wood from one plastic bag and held it up to the light.

'I found that under the easy chair.'

'Weird. It looks like a fossilised finger. Made of wood.'

Audrey pressed her hands over the bundle in her lap. That would be one of the dryad's severed fingers.

More tears spilled. It was easier to cry for that poor creature than for her own deep losses.

'I expect it's one of the faux cryptid artefacts Roylott was selling to the deluded. The filing cabinet in that office has been swept almost as clean as the skirting boards, as it happens. The only thing I found was those paper fragments in the fireplace. Rather warm for a fire at this time of year, so I suppose we know what happened to at least some of the missing documents.'

John examined the fragments through the plastic. 'I can't quite read this. Orm-something? And a few letters and numbers. Oh, like an address. Was this from an envelope?'

'Well spotted, John. Do you recall the name Ormstein from Gruner's ridiculous book about Mrs Hudson? I suspect those figures are part of the postcode for a district of Edinburgh. EH38 belongs to Midlothian, if I'm not mistaken.' His tone suggested that he was never mistaken.

Audrey's stomach churned. William Ormstein. She still carried the physical scars from his attack, over forty years ago. The mental and emotional ones too, if she was honest. It was his fault she carried that awful name, The Cursed Alpha.

If he'd murdered her family, she'd see him dead. Perhaps she would cut off his arm and send it to his loved ones as a souvenir.

Oh, my darlin' girl, she heard Ruby's voice in her memory. *Don't play his game.*

Audrey drew a deep breath and wrapped herself in Ruby's memory; in the life they'd shared in the cottage near Bellingham, on the edge of Northumberland National Park. Her beautiful, wise, wonderful sweetheart had brought Audrey so much joy, after too much loneliness. Ruby had scoffed at the notion of Audrey's *curse*. When it became clear William Ormstein was encouraging the spread of that awful epithet – as though Audrey were to blame for the death of her Bristol pack – Ruby had hugged her close.

'Don't play that bastard's game, Audrey, my lovely. Let 'im and everyone else think what they like. Show them who you are with how you live.'

Audrey had huffed a laugh against Ruby's soft neck. 'Happily in love with a beautiful woman?'

'That's it, my sweetheart. For better or worse.'

'Definitely for better.'

Audrey had leaned up to kiss Ruby – tall, graceful, full-figured, full-hearted Ruby – and run her fingers through Ruby's short curls, just beginning to grey. Audrey had been 26 at the time; Ruby 40. Audrey remembered hoping she'd age as gracefully as her darling.

Next full moon, the curse twisted them to wolf-shape – but larger, more terrible, more savage-seeming than a wolf. Wild and powerful as they were however, they did not hunt. Sated with meat before the run, instead they shook off the pain of transformation and delighted in their power; and in each other. They raced joyfully side by side across hay meadows and in the shadowed valleys, the moon-bright hills, along and across Hadrian's Wall to the south. They stopped by the lake and pounced not-quite-playfully on each other, nipping at tail and ear, nosing and licking at throat and belly, pressing close, seeking and giving pleasure and all their heart to each other.

What a wonderful, wonderful life it had been.

Ruby had taught Audrey the champagne-and-cream trick for scones and the words to *Someone to Watch Over Me*, changing all the pronouns, and to laugh at being 'a little lamb lost in the wood', and how to leave the past behind.

Audrey closed her eyes and brought Ruby close again. The scent of her perfume and the warmth of her dark brown skin and darker eyes, her capable, expressive hands and the sway of her body when they danced together. Ruby was gone, but also with her always; in her memory and heart, and in everything Ruby had taught her about being a *were*, being a woman, being alive to the moment.

When they reached the B&B, Audrey said a wan goodnight and vanished to her room. She placed the wrapped bundle on the bed. On the table. Unwrapped it briefly then, almost sick with horror, bundled it up again and put it back on the table.

She couldn't take it home. It should be buried with her boy in Edinburgh. And since that was not possible, it should at least be buried.

She waited until 3am and crept out of her room, out of the lodgings, onto the gravel drive.

Where, to her intense surprise, she found John Watson staring at the stars.

'What are you doing here?'

'Can't sleep.'

'I mean here, at *Cherry Brook*. Didn't Sherlock say you had lodgings?'

'Sherlock has a tendency to state things a little ahead of the facts,' he said, amused instead of annoyed like he should have been.

'Last night I slept in the back of the hire car and he bivouacked by the side of the road. When we got here he decided a mattress was nicer.' He laughed softly. 'They said they didn't have any twin rooms left, when he asked, so he said he'd take whatever. Turns out it's a double room. With. You know. A double bed.'

Audrey thought that John Watson was wasting a perfectly good opportunity, but it would be taking a liberty to say so. 'Snores, does he?' She knew perfectly well he didn't. 'Drools in his sleep?'

'He looks like a fucking angel.' The observation was heartfelt, and John cleared his throat, embarrassed to be so obvious. He changed the subject.

'Are you all right? I mean. Obviously not. Roylott's carnival of animals was hell on wheels for a start. Do you know what went on there last night?'

'Some of it.'

'Want to share?'

Audrey considered the role Sherlock's sister must have played in the clean-up. 'Not yet. I have a few things to work out first. Roylott and his sons left in a hurry, though.'

'We gathered that much. Did you find anything when you were poking about?'

The look on her face was clear, even by moonlight.

'That bad, huh? Is that it?' He nodded at the bundle in her hands.

'Yes.'

'What is it?'

She hesitated before saying, 'It's the authentic werewolf paw he'd promised to Adelbert Gruner.'

'Shit. Did you, ah, know the werewolf it belonged to?'

'Yes.' She swallowed. 'It's Conal's.'

John inhaled sharply. 'Conal. One of your family.'

'Yes.'

'Oh, Mrs Hudson. I'm so sorry.'

He regarded the bundle with pity and apprehension. Grief too. It struck Audrey that, with his military history, he had similar, heart-curdling memories of his own; of people he cared for reduced to fragments. His friend Percy. Nick, with her prosthetic leg.

She found his pity suddenly less offensive.

'Will you take him home?' John asked.

She flinched. 'No.'

'No. No, of course not. I'm sorry.'

Audrey calmed herself. 'I'll bury this on the moor.'

'Would you care for company?'

Audrey found that she very much would. 'Yes, Please.'

They walked down the gravel path. As they passed a garden bed, with tools left carelessly outside, John casually took up the spade.

A good, practical thinker, John Watson. Conal would have liked him.

Wistman's Wood was not terribly far away, as the crow flies, though crossing the foggy moor made the going more difficult. Audrey knew the way, though, by instinct and scent. John was quiet, respectful of her distress. He never flinched at the sounds that drifted through the fog, no matter how uncannily they struck the ear. Perhaps he was truly as fearless as he seemed.

Perhaps he was simply confident that, to bastardise an old psalm, 'though I walk through the valley of the shadow of death, I will fear no evil – for the bad-ass-est wolf in the valley art with me'.

The clinging mist had penetrated the twisted oaks of the wood. Audrey and John picked their way carefully among the boulders. John used the shovel as a de facto walking stick at times. She led him well around the place where the tiger had died, going deeper and deeper into the tangled darkness. Finally, satisfied she'd found a place undisturbed by humans, *weres* or scavengers, Audrey stopped.

She gently placed her wrapped bundle on a boulder. John rested beside it while Audrey exerted a burst of strength to dislodge a large stone from among the visible roots of a stunted oak. She sat with the bundle then while John dug into the bared earth with the shovel.

Audrey placed the bundle in the hole. John pushed the dirt over it again. Audrey placed the stone back on top, mossy-side-up to conceal the tiny grave.

John stood beside the spot, hands folded, head bowed. Audrey didn't know if he was praying for Conal or simply observing a minute's silence. It nearly made her cry, either way.

She patted the stone. 'Goodbye, my lovely boy.'

The tears fell then, and she wiped them angrily away. Questions burned in her mind and heart.

How had Roylott ended up in possession of Conal's hand? Had William Ormstein sent it? That was gruesome, even for that bastard. Did Ormstein murder her family? To do that, to leave her alive and grieving yet again, struck her as vilely in character.

John, bless him, made no promises that they'd find the people who'd done this. But his solid presence and the knowledge of Sherlock's bright, inquisitive determination made her feel that it was possible. With Sherlock and John to help her, she might yet answer the most important question, which had haunted her ever since that awful day in Edinburgh, mere hours before she was due to take them to safer shelter.

Why?

Audrey and John limped home in the dark, reaching the B&B as the sun began to rise.

Sherlock was waiting in the drive to greet them.

'Insomnia?' he suggested mildly. 'Was the shovel helpful in driving it off?'

'In case we met the wolf,' John explained serenely, placing the tool back in the garden.

'Nothing to do with whatever Mrs Hudson took from Roylott's house yesterday, then?'

John dusted his hands and put them in his pockets. 'She found that werewolf artefact Roylott wrote about,' he said, easily enough. 'Neither of us could sleep. We decided to bury it.'

Audrey realised that John, like Sherlock, was adept at telling unconnected truths and letting the listener invent plausible connections.

'It would have been useful to see it,' grumbled Sherlock.

'I'm going to pack,' Audrey said, unwilling to discuss it further, and limped inside. The last thing she heard was Sherlock speaking to John.

'I apologise for the sleeping arrangements. I didn't intend to make you uncomfortable.'

'It's fine. It's not the first time I've had to bunk up with a colleague.'

'Next time, I'll go for the 3am ramble in the fog; you deal with the too fluffy pillow.'

Next time, we'll toss for it,' John replied. 'Fluffy pillows are the worst.'

Chapter Ten

AUDREY PRETENDED TO DOZE AS SHERLOCK DROVE THE THREE OF them back to London. She suspected he knew better, but he let her be. She was grateful for the respite.

Sherlock didn't say much either, leaving John with no conversation, but the good doctor had the soothing habit of not feeling compelled to fill silence with chatter. Occasionally, when some unidentified item loomed by the side of the road, he grew still and wary, then relaxed as they passed it, unmolested. Whatever occupied his mind remained unspoken.

From underneath her artfully drooping eyelids, Audrey saw how often Sherlock glanced surreptitiously towards John; how often John likewise glanced at Sherlock's hands or at his profile. It was a bloody miracle, frankly, that they never managed to catch each other looking.

Her own thoughts whirled around the metaphorical roadside bombs that had torn apart her life and which had begun to feel less random and more like a vendetta.

Ormstein, the self-styled King of Bohemia, had murdered sweet Hugh Hudson and their unborn baby along with the pack into which she'd been thrown (never chosen). Here he was again, his links to Gruner muddy but, through Roylott, perhaps connected with Edinburgh.

At least he couldn't have been responsible for Ruby's death. Ormstein's methods were vicious but direct. Ruby's slow then sudden decline from Creutzfeld-Jakob disease was not his style at all.

Ruby's end came at her own hand, the only answer available to her fear that she might lose herself so completely she could cause unintended harm one full moon. Ruby had, with characteristic courage and compassion, opened her arms to death instead.

Ruby had changed Audrey's life and made it wonderful. Audrey wasn't sure how she'd found her matching courage, except that Ruby needed her, and she would always do anything, everything for Ruby. Even that. To hold Ruby as she breathed her last, and tell her how much she was loved, treasured, adored.

Audrey stayed in the north long enough for the funeral. Then she left and never went back.

She and Ruby had never understood how only one of them had ingested the infected meal that made Ruby ill. Their supernatural senses had warned them away from tainted meat for all the years of the mad cow disease crisis before.

No. Ormstein could have had nothing to do with that. Could he?

Audrey swore and gave up all pretence at sleep.

'Is that a commentary on my driving?' asked Sherlock, weaving through London traffic.

'You could watch out for that bicycle,' remarked John calmly.

'Oh, he's got plenty of space.'

'Inches of it. At least two.'

'I missed him, which is the important thing.' Sherlock steered them into Baker Street.

John shook his head but Audrey could hear the soft laugh. 'You are, as my gran used to say, a caution.'

'I have many attributes, John, but caution is none of them. I am, however, an excellent driver, and almost never run over anything I don't mean to,' he said as he drew up outside the house.

Where did caution get anyone anyway? Audrey thought. She'd been cautious for so long, and still here she was. With nothing.

'Mrs Hudson.' Sherlock was at her open door, offering his hand like an Old World gentleman. She graciously let him assist her from the car, then open the front door.

She watched him and John fondly as they climbed the stairs to their flat.

Maybe not *nothing*.

Poring over mementoes was a useless way to spend the day. Emptying the almost full bottle of scotch was just as bad. Instead, Audrey put on some old clothes, a smock apron, a headscarf and a pair of thick rubber gloves and she cleaned. Carpets, kitchen, loo, bedroom, rugs. She'd sunk as far as polishing the brass fixings on the townhouse door when a greeting broke into her retreat from unacceptable things.

'Afternoon, Mrs H.'

Nick Murray was walking up the path, fretful and determined. Even through the polish, bleach, and Nick's own haze of cigarette smoke, Audrey could smell her fear.

And something else. Today, Nick was not wreathed in the fumes of stale alcohol, sour breath and general neglect. Its absence meant that Audrey could definitely scent that Nick Murray was –

Oh.

Oh dear.

'Good afternoon, Ms Murray.' Audrey kept it casual.

'Just Nick, eh, Mrs H?'

'Of course. Nick.'

'I'm looking for Johnny. Is he in?'

'He was called out for a job interview about an hour ago.'

'Oh.' Nick jammed her hands in her pockets. Misery leaked from every defeated line of her.

'Can I help?'

'I don't think so.'

'I'll try that again. Nick, I can help you.'

Nick laughed bitterly. 'Hardly think so.' She turned away.

Audrey held out her hand – the way Ruby had done one night in Northumberland, so long ago, offering help when Audrey had been too proud and too afraid to ask for it. 'I've been a werewolf for decades, dear. I can tell you everything you need to know.'

Nick froze; slowly turned her head, her expression wary.

'You'd disguised it stupendously well when we first met – booze, smoke, body spray, mouthwash,' said Audrey, not too gently. She didn't think Nick would respond to pity at all. Honesty couched in humour was more this woman's style. 'I couldn't smell the wolf in you at all under all that. I almost couldn't breathe.'

That approach worked a charm. Nick huffed self-deprecatingly. 'That wasn't a clever disguise. It was me hitting the skids after those bastards blew off my leg and killed Percy. I tried to clean my act up when they invalided John out, so he could stay with me without being revolted. And then. Fuck. And then the full moon happened and a whole lot of really confusing shit suddenly made a whole lot of sense.'

'Come inside,' said Audrey. 'I'll make tea. You can tell me about it.'

Nick followed her inside almost without hesitation. Audrey could almost taste the relief that rolled off her.

Nick studied her own hands rather than look at Audrey making tea, setting out biscuits, pouring milk into a little jug.

'You're very civilised,' Nick commented, still not looking up.

'What did you expect?'

'I dunno.' Nick looked furtively around the kitchen. 'A kennel?'

Boiling water in the teapot, pot on the table with a delicate clunk. Audrey sat opposite her guest. 'Are you trying to impress me with bravado?'

'Nah. I'm just an arsehole sticking to what I know best.'

'I won't take it personally, then.'

'Don't. It could be a long bloody afternoon otherwise.' Her gaze skittered everywhere but Audrey's face, finally resting on Audrey's brightly painted nails. 'Is there a reason I keep wanting to lie on the floor and show you my throat, or is my subconscious really just fucking grateful to have someone to talk to.'

'A bit of both, I imagine. I didn't curse you, but I'm older and very settled in my *were*dom. The wolf in you recognises that. I take it you haven't been a *were* for long.'

'About seven months.'

'And the *were* that made you – are they dead or alive?'

'Oh, Percy's dead. Super fucking dead. They made sure of that.'

'We'll talk about him later. Tell me why you've come to see John two days after the full moon.'

'I thought. He might know... what to do about me. How to keep me from hurting anyone.'

'Have you hurt anyone?'

'Not so far. Or, if I did, I don't remember. I think this full moon was only the third time I wasn't drugged or drunk to the gills for it. I've only really known I've been changing for that long.'

Audrey poured the tea. 'Let's hear the whole story.'

Nick spooned five helpings of sugar into her tea, made it milky, then drank it down in three quick gulps. Audrey began to feel that Nick was an uncivilising influence on her inner wolf, rather than the opposite.

'It starts with Percy Phelps, I guess. We were all in the Medical Brigade, part of the 335 Medical Evacuation Regiment. Doc Watson, Nurse Phelps, Driver Murray. The queers have a way of finding each other, and we were besties. Johnny and Perce had known each other at school. They might have had a thing back in the day, but out there we were just all good mates.'

Nick made a second cup of abominable tea and resumed. 'Then Percy was bitten by a dog that wasn't a dog in Kabul and next thing you know the full moon hits while we're on our way back to the base and he's got fluffy ears and a tail. Hell of a thing. Should have scared us shitless, I suppose, but honest to fuckin' god, your mate turning into a wolf is weird shit, but at least you can see what's going on, not like wondering if the next rock or the next market stall or the next 12-year-old you see is going to blow us all to kingdom come.' Nick huffed a humourless laugh. 'Uncertainty's the killer. This was fucked but it was *happening*. And he was still our Percy, his expression anyway, even if he had claws and teeth all the better to eat you with.'

'Weren't you afraid?'

'Terrified, but you know, that's kinda the status quo out there when you're not bored out of your gourd. You stand up, though. You put the fear away for your mates, and our mate was even more scared than us. He kept saying 'help me'. With that doggy mouth and too much tongue. So fuckin' weird. *Help me*. Jesus.' Her forehead creased in a deep frown at the memory. 'Christ, I could use a fag. Can I smoke in here?'

'No.' Nick's white skin was clammy and her hands shook. Audrey was on the verge of allowing it, just this once, but Nick began disassembling a biscuit into crumbs instead.

'What happened after he changed?' Audrey prompted.

'He took off on all fours into the hills. We could hear him howling all the way. Johnny and I figured, we've seen the movies. We thought, even if only some of it is true, maybe he'll be himself in the morning. We decided to wait. We could hardly go back to base without him. How would we explain that? Three going AWOL for the night we could almost make fly. Truck breakdown, time to fix it, safer to take cover till dawn, all that.

'He come back at first light, stark naked and expecting us to plug him in the back of the head. John and I just hugged him until he stopped crying.

We found a pair of greasy overalls in the truck and got back to base. Got a bollocking for being away overnight, but John's such a smooth little bastard he talked the Sarge out of confining us to barracks or anything. After that, Johnny and I looked after Percy every full moon. Taking our Wolf for a run.' She ended with a lopsided smile.

'You speak like it was funny.'

'That's army life for you. You make jokes about the unspeakable just to get through the day. And that shapeshifting business was brutal. Horrible to watch the gentlest guy you've ever met, screaming while his body turns inside out. Even the extra hair growing out of his skin hurt him. Every goddamn month. I don't know if anyone ever deserves shit like that, but if there's a list, Percy's name should have been at the bottom of the last page at the end of fucking time. So Johnny and I went with him every month. If we couldn't protect him, then at least friends don't let friends turn into werewolves all on their own.'

'But he bit you.'

'No he didn't.'

'You said–'

'He didn't bite me, exactly. Look, we did this for months, driving out to the perimeter. He'd wolf up in agony, come back to us in the morning a wreck, and we'd hug him till he could face coming in.

'Got away with it, too. The team thought it was hilarious, the way Perce, Johnny and me went out together every month. They thought we were having three-ways out there. Suppose that made more sense of the state of us than "the bender and the dyke have got a gay pet werewolf". Nick's face twisted in bleak humour. 'I think our comrades fundamentally misunderstand the whole gay and lesbian solidarity thing.'

Audrey heard the front door open with a key and John's distinctive, slightly uneven footfall as he entered, then paused instead of climbing the stairs.

'John's home,' Audrey said, rising to answer the door before he'd begun to knock.

John Watson was holding several letters. 'This one was on the carpet. Hand-delivered, I think.'

John handed her a midnight blue envelope, addressed simply to *Audrey* in silver pen. She couldn't imagine who it was from. She had no correspondents, only various utilities and their stubbornly regular bills.

Audrey turned the envelope over, feeling the quality of the thick paper on her fingertips, but it bore no return address. She considered letting Sherlock do his thing with it, but as quickly decided against it. The paper carried a scent that was alien to her, yet it made her chest ache with near-familiarity.

Audrey could hear Nick in the kitchen – taking out a packet of cigarettes. Flicking a lighter flame on and off.

Audrey put the letter aside. 'Come in, John. Your friend Ms Murray is here.'

'Hey Johnny!' Nick's usual gruff greeting hailed them as he and Audrey entered the kitchen. 'I've been telling Mrs H about Perce. His werewolf thing. I suppose you kno– ooh. Ah.'

Nick's gaze flicked anxiously to Audrey, obviously tense with resisting the urge to blurt truths that might be important to her best friend's wellbeing without outing anyone.

'Yes, Nick, I know my landlady's a werewolf. How did *you* know?'

'Easy peasy, ' she began glibly, then seized up. 'Thing is, mate. Thing is.' Nick took a steadying breath. 'So am I.'

John quickly smothered his surprise. 'Ah, shit, Nick. Shit. I'm sorry.'

'The funny part is it took me months to notice. How fucked is that?'

'God, Nick–'

'Typical Nick Murray SNAFU, eh?'

John went straight to where she sat, wrapped his arms around her shoulders and drew her against his body. He rested his cheek on her hair and rubbed her back. Nick clung to him, pushed her face against his stomach, then abruptly let go.

'Don't Johnny. I don't want to blub about it.'

John accepted the withdrawal with silent concern, then took a seat.

'How'd it happen, Nick?'

'I was just telling Mrs H about wolf patrol.'

'Did Percy bite you?'

'He didn't mean to,' Nick snapped, defensive.

'Of course he didn't,' John said gently in his best bedside manner.

'I was just about to say how Percy decided to make the best of a bad situation. He'd go off scoping the territory, Mrs H. Roaming all over the joint to look for ammo dumps and sniper nests, or if he'd seen Taliban work parties setting up IEDs and shit. He'd drop hints to the recce crews about where to look. We're a superstitious lot in the army. He'd just have to say he had a spooky feeling and someone would check it out. By the third time his hunch paid off, nobody questioned it any more. They just said, Sweetheart Intuition's kicking in again. That's probably what made them come after us.'

John's brow creased. 'You didn't say you'd been targeted.'

'No,' Nick agreed. 'I never put that in the report, once I was able to make one, because I'd have to explain why, and that was never going to happen. After that I was on morphine or getting well and truly trolleyed and it slipped my mind.'

Audrey, who'd been thinking that scotch was a more appropriate beverage for these revelations, pushed the bottle back into the cupboard. This was way more information than she'd expected, but Nick had talked about an impulse to bare her throat to the Alpha in the room, and that, more or less, was exactly what she was doing.

'Go on,' she encouraged, firm but kind. She had a pretty good bedside manner herself, when it came to gathering nervy strays.

'Percy didn't foresee the ambush that John and I got caught up in. He felt rotten about that. Used up another of your nine lives there, hey John?'

'One in the field, one on the operating table,' John said lightly. 'I still have at least five left.'

'That left just me to have Percy's hairy back on the next full moon, a few weeks after you were evacced out. So there we were at the edge of the base, where we weren't supposed to be, but it had always been fine before. But this night...' Nick shuddered. 'One of them was dressed in a wolf skin with those patterns on it; what d'you call 'em John?'

'Blaschko's lines.'

'Yeah. So that's how I knew this Taliban bastard was wearing a werewolf skin. That they'd come for Percy.'

Audrey shuddered. *Weres* reverted to human form when they died. Pelts and paws could only be taken from a living *were*, still in their wolf form.

'The moon was almost up. Percy'd stripped and folded his uniform – he was always so neat about his kit, wasn't he, after he started howling out? Like he was trying to make up for being a scruffy mongrel once a month.'

'I remember.' An underlying tone indicated that John would quite like to howl about now, too.

'There he was, Sweetheart Percy, in the buff when they lobbed grenades at us out of nowhere. The first one landed by my foot and that was me, done. Lower leg blown clean off, me bleeding all to buggery.'

John winced. Nick paused to work on her pretence that this was old news and not fresh hell.

'Another grenade landed nearish and Perce threw himself on top of me. Next second, all at once, he's all wolf. He set a record, with that change.'

'It's not common, but imminent danger can accelerate it,' Audrey explained, 'especially if... if members of the pack are threatened.'

'How about that? We were pack, Johnny.' A weak smile before continuing. 'So I am in literal pieces and this prick in the wolf skin is coming with a half dozen armed arseholes either side of him. Perce dragged me behind the truck with my jacket in his teeth and then he did this super weird thing – his front paws turned into hands and fixed a tourniquet so I didn't bleed to death half as quickly as I ought to.'

'Half-shifting is much rarer in a new werewolf,' Audrey said in wonder. 'Most are decades old before that's possible. His adrenalin levels and his drive to protect you must have been phenomenal.'

Tears glittered in Nick's eyes. 'They were still lobbing grenades over the truck but they didn't have our range yet. Wouldn't be long, though. I thought were going to die. Then Perce got his paws back and went out to stop them. And he almost did. Johnny, that beautiful bastard of ours nearly stopped them.'

She had reached for John and they sat, hands clasped tight, while Nick told the rest of her story. 'They shot him, a dozen times at least, but it didn't even slow Perce down. Our sweet boy just tore them open. I couldn't see much, and I shut my eyes after a bit. I couldn't... our Perce, Johnny. Doing that. To save me. Making himself a nightmare to buy me time.'

No stopping the tears now. 'Even with them shooting him point blank, he took the kill squad down, but that prick in the wolf skin waited till Percy was almost on him, and he pulled out a handgun and shot our boy right in the head. And fast as he'd wolfed up, he fell down. Naked as a baby. Just Percy again, with a big hole in his beautiful head.'

She leaned against John, who embraced her in silent solidarity.

Finally, Nick pulled away, putting her brave face back on. 'Right. So that fucker comes up to me with his pistol and he says, "the plan failed. He was supposed to destroy your base from within".

'And I say, fuck you. And I've no idea why, but he just walked away laughing and left me to die, knowing they'd done this to Perce on purpose, that day in the market. He was supposed to have gone feral at the base next full moon and bitten anyone in sight. Not our Perce though. Always more sweetheart than wolf, eh.'

Weres don't have to be beasts, Audrey wanted to say. *Ruby taught me that*. Instead she asked, 'What happened next? '

'Someone from the base heard the ruckus and came looking for us. They got me back to base, and Percy's body. I heard later they'd found a silver bullet in his skull. That kills werewolves, right?'

'Yes,' agreed Audrey tightly.

'So they had to have come especially to kill him.'

'I'm afraid so. I'm very sorry.'

John held Nick's hand. 'How did Percy infect you?'

'I didn't realise till later, but when he dragged me behind the truck, his teeth must have scraped me. It was a scratch more than a bite, and it healed quickly, but it was enough. Bodily fluid transmission, eh, Mrs H?'

'Yes. *Were* saliva has to meet an open cut to get into the bloodstream. A bite usually, but a nip like that, however unintentional, would do it too.'

'Told you he didn't mean to,' Nick said firmly.

John held Nick's hand against his own chest, giving himself comfort as much as his friend.

'And you didn't notice you'd been cursed?' Audrey asked.

'I spent the first month doped to the gills on morphine, antibiotics, all kinds of shit, while the docs did what they could with my stump. I suppose I was too medicated for the transformation to take hold, or even that dozy lot would have noticed a fuckin' great dog in my bed. Can that happen?'

'Apparently.'

'Huh. Teaching an old dog a new trick, here, Johnny! Ah. Sorry.' This at Audrey's baleful look.

'When the stump was mostly healed and I wasn't so medicated, I woke up one month in the loo; another time in the hospital garden, aching all over. The nurses couldn't work out how I was crawling out there, except it was on my charts that I had bad nightmares. I had no idea it had been the full moon, even. I barely knew what day it was back then. They sedated me a lot at night so I didn't wake up my fellow crips with the screaming.' Nick delivered that information with a wry shrug.

'I got my first prosthetic after that, which was bad news because once I worked out how to walk on the thing, I could get to the pub. Next full moon I was drunk. Well, I was drunk most nights. Drunk and doped up a lot of them, actually. Absolutely basted. My doctors give me lots of lectures about it.'

Nick scrubbed her hands over her face. 'And then Johnny finally got his medical discharge – after me because he got an infection that just about killed him.'

'Life Four,' John said gamely.

'You are a stubborn little fucker, all right,' Nick agreed. 'I tried to clean up my act so I could give you a place to stay, Johnny. I really did. I figured we could at least be a couple of wrecks together, and talk about the good ol' days when you, me and Perce were the Musketeers. That was the only plan I had.

'Except before you could move in, two months ago, I was sober and unsedated for the first time since I got blown up, and I fucking *changed*. Right in the middle of a scrub. I was left slipping around my goddamned bathtub. I'd been trying to get veterans' funding to change it to a shower because getting in and out was a bitch when I took off my tin leg. And there I was, a three-legged mutt in a slippery tub of lukewarm water, howling like the deranged. And in the morning I worked out that Percy must have nipped me. So I got good and stinking drunk and told you that you couldn't possibly stay with me.'

'You could've explained. I would have helped.'

'Oh, god, no.' Nick's voice shook with pity and despair. 'Tell you our lovely Percy had accidentally given me the wolf equivalent of VD? You were having too many bad days yourself. I didn't want to lay that on you.'

John took the hand he held and kissed her knuckles. 'And you call me stubborn.'

'One fuckwit to another, Johnny.'

Audrey leaned closer to them. 'Why did you come to see John today, then?' she asked. 'What's different about today?'

Nick sighed. 'These last two full moons I've spent in a lock-up I'd hired to keep me off the streets. I got drunk again the first time. Tried to be sober for the one two days ago, to see if I could control anything. I remember most of it. I didn't try to get out, but I know I was angry. The walls were all scraped with claw marks. The garage door's dented where I threw myself at it, three legs and all. Percy never hurt anyone until the end, but Percy was a saint and I'm an arsehole, and what if I get out? I need Johnny to find a better place to lock me in. Or to have the vet put me down.'

Now, at the end of her story, Nick raised her chin and glared at Audrey.

'So, Mrs Landlady Werewolf, what do you reckon? A nice padlocked kennel for me, or do we get John to tell our mates that I've gone to live on a lovely farm where I'll have rabbits to chase and a doggy bed of my very own?'

'I think,' said Audrey sternly, 'we can start with you not feeling so sorry for yourself. Your friend cursed you when he saved you, but you're no more a savage than he was, or I am. Sober up, take responsibility for your actions, and I'll teach you what I know so you do not in fact have to be sent to that great kennel in the sky.'

Nick blinked. Stared. Blinked some more. Looked at John, who shrugged. She started to laugh, then harder, then she folded up wheezing with it, shrieking with laughter, tears rolling down her cheeks. She tried to steady herself but took one look at Audrey and went off again.

Audrey lifted an eyebrow. Nick calmed herself briefly.

'Christ, Ms H. And to think I thought you were nice old lady when I first met you.'

'I am a nice lady. Not old, thank you.'

'No. Not old. Not that nice, actually. But I like you.'

'One day, that sentiment might even be mutual.'

Nick began to laugh again. 'Christ, Johnny. I think I'm in love.'

Audrey's double raised eyebrows only set Nick off into guffaws again. She placed a hand on Nick's head, and stroked her short, dark-blonde hair. And again.

'It's going to be all right, Nick. I'll look after you. I'll teach you what I can and I'll make sure you're safe, to others, to yourself.'

Nick's laughter had turned to sobs. John held her close and rocked her in his arms while Audrey stroked her hair. 'It's all right.'

A packless Alpha will sometimes make pack out of the unlikeliest people, Audrey thought. Lost children. Consulting detectives. Former army doctors. And disabled army drivers too, by the look of it.

Chapter Eleven

Cars, cabs, lorries and buses traversed Baker Street constantly, it being a connecting thoroughfare to Marylebone Road. Few but the buses stopped, and none in front of her house. The sound of a car halting outside therefore captured Audrey's immediate attention, prickling the hair of her neck.

'Put the kettle on, John,' she said. She ignored his enquiring eyebrow and rose to peer through the sitting room curtains.

An elegant black sedan was parked by the kerb. The uniformed driver had opened the passenger door. Alighting was Ms Holmes, wearing tinted glasses, gloves, a hat with a brim pulled down over her eyes, and a grey scarf. She was taller than her brother, and heavier set.

But where Sherlock moved with sinuous grace and energy, Ms Holmes' gait was less assured. If he was the King of Cats (and knew it), she was a ponderous feline counterpart, slow-moving and suspicious of open spaces. What Audrey could see of Ms Holmes' pale skin was unhealthily blanched and her hands were clasped tight together, betraying anxiety.

Audrey had no idea what brought her here, but Ms Holmes held a significant position at the Department of Fisheries, and therefore her presence was alarming.

Audrey returned to the kitchen, took her house keys off the kitchen bench and pressed them into John's hand.

'Take Nick through my back door into the yard and use this key to get into the basement room. Move the bamboo to get to the door, but put it back as exactly as you can. Nick, stay there with John and don't make a sound.'

She half expected a protest, but they were alert, attentive, and aware this was an order, not a request.

'It may be a problem,' she said curtly. 'It may be nothing. Stay hidden until this car leaves.'

Nick had taken up a kitchen knife and held it at the ready in a firm, dry grip. John, unarmed, led her towards Audrey's private exit to the yard. Audrey watched from the door as they slipped silently behind the bamboo.

The knock on the door came, then Sherlock's footsteps clattering pell-mell down the stairs. 'Myca? What are you doing here?'

'And hello to you too, little brother. It's a fine day, I know, but I'd rather not spend it on the doorstep, if it's all the same to you.'

Audrey heard Ms Myca Holmes step into the hall, followed by Sherlock saying, 'You can't blame me for being surprised. You're not exactly keen on visiting.'

'You're not exactly keen on having me round for tea,' Myca responded evenly. 'You insist on a builder's brew and terrible biscuits and going on and on about how I'd be a wonderful detective if only I would get off my lazy backside to do the grunt work.'

'Well, you would,' replied Sherlock, as the siblings ascended the stairs. 'I can't see why you waste your talents and time as a public servant. You're much smarter than I am, if only you'd make the effort.'

'I'm much smarter than you without any effort, thank you very much.'

'And yet, so lazy. Or usually.'

'Quite. I need to speak with you about your visit to Dartmoor.'

Once the door closed upstairs the siblings' conversation became much harder to overhear. Satisfied that Nick was away from prying eyes, Audrey stood in the entry hall, listening hard, hoping to learn what had brought the Fisheries to her door.

The siblings spoke so quietly she only caught snatches of their conversation. Was Myca Holmes aware a werewolf lived downstairs and might eavesdrop?

Between the driver outside and Ms Holmes on the floor above, caution kept Audrey from creeping upstairs or part-shifting to elongate her ears. Discovery would mean disaster. Even if Ms Holmes suspected Sherlock's landlady was *were*, she couldn't know his flatmate was a friend to werewolves, or that a new-minted werewolf hid in the basement. Events at Dartmoor had made her too freshly aware of her losses to risk anyone else.

Audrey withdrew to her own flat. She paced, then forced herself to stillness. Her eye landed on the midnight blue envelope she had placed with her ordinary mail. She examined the latter first. Everything but the bills went straight in the bin.

The hand-delivered letter stood out in every way, not just its disquieting scent. The timing of its arrival was troubling, too. Audrey strained for any sound of danger, even allowing her ears to lengthen, cupped wolf-like and angled upwards, but she could make out only murmurs.

She opened the envelope and eased out the letter. Cream coloured paper, as expensive as the envelope. She opened the single page and her eye landed on the signature.

Irene Adler (nee Stockton)

Audrey drew a sharp breath. Irene Stockton. No wonder the envelope's scent was faintly familiar. That familial scent had carried through.

Ruby's daughter Irene, child of two werewolves, was ten when her father took her to Germany in the mid-70s. Back then, Audrey was a new werewolf, only a teenager, reluctantly living with Gordon's pack in Bristol. Ruby had rarely spoken of them, though she kept photographs. Irene would have been 18 by the time Audrey met Ruby in Northumberland. Irene had always been a mystery, but not a secret. Why would she be writing to Audrey now?

The letter was very short.

A great danger hangs over your life and mine. It has already cost us much. Meet me at Tower Hamlets Cemetery. 9am.

The sparse message explained nothing and filled her with dread.

The sound of a heavy footfall on the stairs startled Audrey back to awareness. She shoved the letter onto a shelf underneath the other mail. Put a book on top of that. Part of her wanted to bury it under the hydrangeas in the back garden.

Oh, get a grip.

Her hackles were rising and a growl rumbled at the back of her throat. Irene's warning. The Fisheries at her home. The Roylotts. So much danger, from so many angles, and she had no idea how to protect herself, or Nick, or John and Sherlock. But she'd tear throats with claw and tooth and fight to the death to defend them.

Three raps on her door made her jump. Instinct told her to run, but she stayed calm. Her freedom, Nick's – perhaps their lives – might depend on it.

Surely any Great Danger wouldn't knock first, like a man come to read the gas meter. Perhaps it was merely a Middling Danger.

Audrey adjusted her hair, checked her nails were not claws, and opened the door.

There stood Ms Myca Holmes.

'Mrs Hudson. We need to speak.' So much for pleasantries.

Audrey assessed this woman from up close for the first time.

Myca Holmes was regally tall and generously built, like a grand operatic soprano. She was shrouded in her hat, scarf and gloves despite the heat of the day. Her eyes were hidden behind the smoked lenses of her glasses, but her hands clenched and unclenched at her sides. She radiated confusing signals.

'I know you're a lycanthrope, Mrs Hudson,' Myca said with soft-spoken authority. 'You've been on our radar for many years. I offer you no harm.'

Audrey's heart pounded but she spoke calmly. 'That is not your reputation.'

Myca swallowed, the anxious movement visible through a gap in her scarf, at the soft point under her chin. She suddenly seemed less a danger; more an anxious recluse being forced to have new experiences.

'A reputation is a useful thing sometimes,' Myca said, her voice steadier than her body language. 'You have one of your own: The Cursed Alpha.'

Audrey damn near snarled.

'Quite,' said Myca, unflinching. 'Labels so often exaggerate or misrepresent us. The Department knows who you are, but we also know not all cryptids are a danger to humans. Historically, we have nothing against you personally. More recently, you saved the life of my Greek interpreter. Theo Melas was very clear on that, and he and I are grateful for your intervention. I would rather that's the last we see of you in relation to the Roylott family. We have our own investigation underway.'

'Roylott was involved in the murder of my family.'

Myca tilted her head sympathetically. 'We're looking into that, too.'

'Without telling me?'

'The Department's cryptid work can be complicated, operating in secret as it does. I'm very sorry for your shocking loss, Mrs Hudson. But it's part of a deeper issue and it would be best if you didn't involve yourself in it. I've suggested as much to my brother.'

'My family were slaughtered like beasts. I'm going to learn why and by whom, and your damned pack of civil service hunters and killers can go hang.'

Myca's fingers went to the arm of her glasses. She didn't take them off, though.

'We are hunters and killers in the same way that you are the Cursed Alpha.'

'My reputation is built on truth. My first pack was killed in a turf war. My partner Ruby–'

'Yes. We know about Ruby–'

'*Don't you say her name.*' A growl slipped out behind the demand. 'Then my new family was executed with silver bullets. I *am* cursed. And your Department is full of the monsters that monsters are afraid of.'

'Who else should be responsible for the cryptids and uncanny forces of the United Kingdom but the Department of Fisheries, Wildlife & Parks?'

'We are not fauna, to be corralled and culled by you. Some of us were fully human, once.'

Myca glanced up the staircase. 'I'd rather discuss matters inside. My brother is an inveterate eavesdropper, but he also stubbornly mistakes the absence of evidence for the otherworldly as evidence of absence. Or do you want him to know what you are?'

'He's been told,' Audrey admitted grimly.

'And does not credit what he hears. He never has. But for now, I'm at peace with his ignorance. It has so far kept him safe. The knowledge of it can be a terrible burden.'

Audrey felt a wholly unexpected pang of sympathy. She stood aside. 'Do you need to be invited in?'

'I'm not a vampire.'

'Prove it.'

Myca stepped across the threshold with a disgruntled huff. 'Satisfied?'

'What are you, then?' Audrey closed the door.

'Merely a minor government official with a very specific purview.'

'To imprison people like me.'

'To protect humans and cryptids alike.'

'We don't see you lot disappearing humans to keep *us* safe.'

'Humans are handled differently.'

'You say that like you're not one of them.'

'My position requires a dual perspective. These days, human people are less a direct threat to the fae than the other way around.'

'These days?'

'Once upon a time, as they say, the strictly human and this island's more esoteric inhabitants clashed frequently. But then the industrial revolution began and iron, always problematic to the fae, criss-crossed Great Britain from John O'Groats to Land's End. Most of it, over land and underground, was consecrated – if I may use the word in this context – with the sacrificial blood of the men who dug the tunnels, laid the tracks, built the engines.'

No need to wonder where Sherlock got his propensity for long and flouncy speeches, then. It was clearly a family trait.

'The English – I won't necessarily include the Irish, Welsh and Scots in this summary – assumed most of the fae meant them harm, and so harmed first. But this network of consecrated iron–'

'Rail tracks are made of steel, aren't they?'

'Which is primarily made of iron, yes. This network of consecrated mostly-iron spread for 150 years. The fae retreated from the cities to their natural habitats, then even further from the mortal realm. They diminished. They hibernated.'

Audrey had crossed her arms. 'You Holmeses do like the sound of your own voice. John thinks Sherlock rehearses his speeches. He has a point. You've definitely rehearsed this.'

'It's in the induction for new employees. If I may continue?'

'Amble to the point in your own time. It's not like I've got things to do.' Snark, delivered piping hot, with a side order of acid and ice.

'The point is,' snapped Myca, 'that ancient forces slept, beings of power found more subtle ways to guard the land from below the rocks and lakes, and so few other cryptids were active that both they and humans were generally safe from each other. Then that bloody Beeching tore out half the rail network with his damned cuts and disrupted the balance.'

An aggravated Myca Holmes wasn't the best outcome, but Audrey was too angry to care. 'The fae, diminished and in hiding. Is that the balance you mean?'

The little of Myca's skin on show was no longer pale but flushed red with ire.

'They didn't threaten the human population and, of equal importance, the human population ceased to hunt and destroy the fae. It was a Pyrrhic victory, but once Beeching's cuts took hold, the fae awoke.'

'The railway tracks are still there.'

'Some are still there, but the blood sacrifice made on them was rendered impotent by his act. You know perfectly well that for the supernatural, words and acts have deeper meaning. Beeching deciding the railways weren't needed effectively rendered the protection of consecrated iron worthless. The fae began to stir, but emerged into a world largely unfit for them. Whole forests have vanished, the sacred waterways are polluted or were diverted for farming and industry. The Clean Air Act is the only environmental improvement we can count on for the airborne spirits, but little else is conducive. The roads are full of cars and the skies are full of aircraft – steel again, if you're wondering – but the iron isn't fixed. It roams and disrupts randomly, leaving moveable holes in the network. This is no less of a hazard.'

Myca stopped abruptly. A peculiar dappled light briefly flickered behind her glasses then vanished. Myca swallowed again and Audrey could almost believe she'd imagined it.

'You made me lose my temper,' Myca said mildly.

'Yes. Well. You've been testing mine. And I'm still not sure of your point.'

That unexpected sound was Myca Holmes, laughing. 'I see why Sherlock likes you so much. All right. To be less cryptic: it is my job to know and understand the folklore of this Sceptred Isle in order to protect fae and human alike and keep them, as far as possible, from wilfully harming one another. Forces are at work to disrupt the balance which it is my duty to maintain.'

'What forces?'

'That is the matter under investigation. From what Theo told me, the Roylotts tortured and murdered a dryad, who bravely would not betray the location of the sacred well she and her sisters safeguard. Theo's report leads me to believe the Roylotts are doing another's bidding. I further believe this motivating force is behind a number of other sinister events. The Department of Fisheries, Wildlife & Parks, reinforced by the authority of the Home Office, will seek this menacing force and deal with it. You, Mrs Hudson, should therefore keep your remarkable nose out of it, lest it be snapped off by something more dangerous than you are.'

'What? You?'

Myca was amused. 'Not me. But something wicked is at the murky heart of this business. I haven't yet grasped the extent of it, but the danger is great, Mrs Hudson. You must drop it. You must withdraw.'

'I see. Well. Thank you for your advice.'

'You're going to ignore it, aren't you?'

'Why would I? Not now that I know what a good and kind organisation you represent. Keeping the balance. Protecting all us poor, diminished, reduced creatures of folklore. I wonder you have such an evil reputation, with benevolence shining out of your every action.' She'd almost said *arse*.

Myca rubbed her forehead. 'I cannot guarantee your safety.'

'The arrogance of you,' snarled Audrey. 'As if you ever have. As if you ever could. You can leave now.'

With stolid dignity, Myca Holmes departed to the foyer. Audrey followed and pointedly opened the door onto the street.

'I can see myself out,' said Myca with a faint smile.

'I like to be certain that unwelcome guests have gone. Goodbye, Ms Holmes. If you visit your brother again, a note ahead of time will enable me to lock the door.'

Then the "minor government official" who ran the Department of Fisheries, Wildlife & Parks was gone.

Audrey locked the door, pressed her back to it, then stood shaking as though she'd unexpectedly won a game of cards with the devil and wondered what hell she'd pay for the privilege.

Chapter Twelve

Audrey easily overheard John and Nick's argument as she approached the basement room via the back garden.

'I'm not in love with Sherlock Holmes!'

'You fancy him rotten. Worse than that, Mr Three Continents Watson, you are besotted down to your ten tiny toenails. Look at how you keep that ridiculous face fungus of yours waxed and polished within an inch of its life, 'coz you know he likes it.' She wiggled her finger at his carefully maintained upper lip.

'That's *Doctor* Three Continents Watson to you, Murray,' John said, self-consciously. 'And for God's sake, don't tell him that's what you reprobates in Afghanistan called me.'

'I knew it! In. Fucking. Love.'

'Nick, I've only known him for two whole months!'

'So? You don't just like him. You *like* like him. I can tell. It's the way you look at him like he's the first cold beer after a week on patrol. Clean pants on a Sunday. A letter from home that isn't asking for money. You're an open bloody book, frankly.'

They didn't notice Audrey as she stealthily shifted a potted bamboo plant to get to the door. Rattled by Myca Holmes' visit, Audrey couldn't help treading carefully. Listening to their illuminating exchange was a by-product of being alert for signs of danger.

'Right, Nick. And if the most observant person I know can't read this open book, then he's not bloody interested.'

'You didn't see the way he looked at you the day you moved in. He definitely thinks you are one tasty snack. You should tell him you fancy him.'

'I'm not telling him I *like like* him. I'm not fourteen, and he'd think it was sentimental twaddle.'

'He'd *say* it was sentimental twaddle. That's not the same thing. I can see the thirst even if you can't.'

'I don't *li*-...you know, I'm not saying that phrase again. I just like him, okay? I'm grateful to him.'

'You should be. He's absolutely changed your life, John. You're talking about the future again. You're smiling again, especially when you talk about him, like you don't even know you're doing it. You even text like you're a happy man. About him, mostly, I should point out. It's all Sherlock says, and Sherlock does, and Sherlock is. It's fucking adorable.'

'I don't. All right. Maybe I do. He's fascinating. But I don't think you can base a romantic relationship on gratitude.'

'True. But those aren't the looks you're giving him, unless you are immensely grateful for his pert young bum.'

'Well, it's a lovely thing and *someone* should be grateful it exists.'

They both jumped when Audrey tapped lightly on the door. John let her inside.

'The coast is clear,' Audrey reported. 'You can come back up.'

'Care to share a sit-rep?' Nick asked. 'Who was that? Why did we have to hide? And... I suppose you know your left hand's hairy as a coconut's arse.'

Audrey was startled to see this was true. Now acutely aware of her heightened anxiety, she took a calming breath. Her claws, with the polish cracked over the shape of them, became nails again, the paw-like hand became human again. She was so inured to the discomfort of the shift she hadn't noticed when it happened.

'I need tea,' she declared, voice rough with heartfelt desire for normality and comfort. Time for tea meant no other crisis was lurching out of the darkness. Tea meant time to think and consolidate. And she had a very specific blend in mind.

Ensconced once more in her cosy kitchen, Audrey put off discussing Myca's brief, strange visit. She reboiled the kettle and put out a cup and teabag and then a teapot with matching cups.

'That's for you,' she said, pushing the single cup with its PG Tips bag towards her lodger. 'Nick, we're having the pot. You need to learn how to make a cup of tea.'

'You're kidding.'

'No. Pay careful attention.' She retrieved her small wicker pot from the shelf, opened it and wafted it under Nick's nose. Nick recoiled like someone had tried to slice her face off.

'That is wolfsbane,' said Audrey, replacing the lid. 'Also called monkshood or aconite.'

John was instantly alert. 'That's extremely poisonous.'

'Yes it is,' Audrey replied, 'and as deadly as it is to ordinary humans, it's potentially twice as lethal to werewolves. However, as you will appreciate, Doctor Watson, many harmful things – in small, altered and controlled doses – may also be beneficial. Swallowing wolfsbane can kill, especially the roots and seeds. Are you listening, Nick?'

Nick attempted to sniff at the pot again but withdrew. 'Is this the suicide option we're talking about?'

'No it bloody isn't,' snapped Audrey. 'Pay attention. I've had a *morning*. I've had a bloody *week*, and I've been a werewolf so long that if I've had a particularly distressing time, I–'

'Sprout random wolf parts?' offered Nick. 'Something to look forward to, I guess.'

'If you live long enough, which may depend on how well you listen.'

Nick looked marginally contrite, and Audrey continued. 'Judicious use of a small piece from a single leaf of wolfsbane, diluted in a large pot of herbal tea, can help to suppress the effects of the curse. It can't stop you changing with the moon, but usually it can help to delay the worst of it until you're in a secure place. After the first decade, your wolf is prone to emerging when you experience extreme spikes of adrenalin or emotion.'

Audrey spooned a fragrant blend of lemongrass, rosehip and aniseed infusion into the teapot.

'Like what happened to Percy, then,' said Nick, 'when he got his hands back to fix up my tourniquet.' She was solemn, white-faced but calm, as she said it.

'Yes,' replied Audrey, abandoning the lecture for a kindlier tone. 'Even in a young werewolf, intensely heightened emotion may incite a shift, though it's unpredictable. Protection of family is a strong instinct for humans, wolves and *weres* alike. There's no doubt how much he loved you,

Nick, because despite how recently he'd been cursed, he was able to do that for you.'

Nick took refuge from her emotions by expressing disgust at the very notion of herbal tea. 'Muck for hippies, that stuff. Grass soup. And it smells nasty.'

With a pair of delicate sugar tongs, Audrey placed a portion of dried wolfsbane leaf in the infusion basket. 'You're welcome to try it with black tea, but it's unspeakably foul,' she said placidly.

'Whereas in herbal tea you expect it to taste merely foul?' Nick grimaced. 'Can I put it in my bottle of scotch?'

'And ruin a perfectly good scotch? Are you a complete barbarian?'

Nick grinned. 'Very nearly.'

Audrey poured boiling water into the pot and John's mug as well.

John inhaled the steam from the teapot. 'It smells fine to me.'

'Humans can't smell the wolfsbane,' Audrey pointed out. 'But don't ever make the mistake of drinking it. Even in this small dose it could make you very sick.'

'Stay off the aconite. Got it.'

Nick treated her first sip of the infusion like a six-year-old being forced to eat her sprouts. The gurning was epic and the ridiculous woman dipped her reluctant tongue into the tea first, scalding the tip of it.

'I strongly suspect you're not an actual idiot, Nick. Correct me if I'm wrong.' Audrey's exasperation already held fondness. Nick's antics reminded her of Travis, the first time he'd tried the infusion. Tara had smacked his arm and called him a drama queen. Their impersonations of the late Queen and the Prince Consort keeping a stiff upper lip while at tea with werewolves had reduced them all to giggles, even sombre little Siobhan.

Nick only waggled her eyebrows at her. 'You need to ask Johnny about my heroic levels of stupid.'

John rolled his eyes. 'God, where would I begin? It might be with pranking the Americans by stitching a Union Jack over the stars on their flag. You nearly started a minor war with that one. Or that time when your two girlfriends showed up at the same time to greet our furlough flight home and there was a brawl in the *Pret a Manger* at Heathrow.'

'To good times,' toasted Nick, and drank her tea.

Audrey served biscuits to help mask the taste of the tea and Nick, like the entertaining heathen she was, stirred her tea with one and slurped the soggy mess quickly down before she dropped it.

'Too lazy to chew, I see,' said Audrey drily.

'Time's a-wasting,' Nick declared, then did it again.

John gazed at her with a peculiar combination of amused horror, fondness and concern. Audrey guessed Nick's manners got proportionally worse with anxiety.

Audrey drained her own cup and examined her now wholly human hands. Dreadful table manners were probably a better anxiety response than randomly were-shifting body parts.

A business-like triple-rap on the door of her flat was more alarming than it needed to be. But nobody had rung or knocked from the street, which meant it must be Sherlock. He was clearly in a mood.

The man at the door was not at all her socially awkward, garrulous tenant who normally bellowed 'Mrs Hudson!' like he had exciting news to share, and laughed easily, and was secretly kind underneath his shroud of intellect and bravado. He was instead very much Mr Sherlock Holmes, Consulting Detective, and On The Case. His grey eyes were full equally of curiosity and suspicion.

'Good afternoon, Mrs Hudson,' he said.

'Hello, Sherlock. Come in. John and Nick are having a cup of tea.'

The guests in question had emerged from the kitchen on hearing his voice.

'Yo, sup?' Nick greeted. Sherlock tilted his chin up. 'Ha. Your boy's in a snit,' she confided to John, very much out loud.

'He's not my b–' John began to protest, then fell silent at the scouring gaze his flatmate raked over him, head to foot.

'May I come in?' This morning's Sherlock would simply have bowled cheerfully, chatteringly inside. This terribly polite Sherlock was disconcerting.

'What's wrong?' Audrey asked.

'I thought with your bad hip, Dr Watson's shoulder and Ms Murray's prosthetic, a seated discussion would be more comfortable, but we can discuss it here if you like.'

'Sherlock?'

'I'm curious, you see, about how the three of you know Myca. And why you, Mrs Hudson, took pains to hide my flatmate and his friend in your basement. I've been sorting my facts, testing theories, re-examining behaviours and inferences, and the only conclusion I can reach is that everyone, from my sister onward, has been lying to me.'

'That's not–' John tried.

'Please don't insult my intelligence, Doctor. I saw everything from our window, from my sister's arrival to her departure, and the three of you skulking in the back garden. Mrs Hudson was acting like she expected to be attacked at any moment.'

John's mouth opened. Closed again. Then: 'That was your *sister*?'

'That is not the point I'm making.'

'You might have mentioned you had a sister.'

'Really? *This* is the issue for you?'

'You could have mentioned her when, for example, you were rather rudely deducing the existence of my late brother from a pocket watch.'

'For which I apologised when I understood your distress. But that has nothing to do with Myca. Wait. You didn't know she was my sister. Then why the hell were you hiding from her?'

Audrey, caught on the back foot, didn't know how to approach the issue. Blithe honesty or stout denial? 'Your sister represents an authority that I don't trust,' she said, to see what he'd say.

'My sister is a public servant. She holds a specialist analyst position at the Home Office. Conclusions of the sub-departments are brought to her, and she foresees the unforeseen consequences, across a very broad range of activities. How exactly is she a threat to you?'

'I think *she* should explain that–'

'How would you even have met her? Myca's much smarter than I am, but she's been acutely agoraphobic since her early teens. Her haunts are normally confined to her home, her office, and the Cynics Club off St James' Square. Her visit today for a private conversation with me that could have been a phone call is as astonishing as if the Eurostar had pulled up in our parlour. I could never have predicted such a visit, so her arrival must also have been a complete surprise to you all. You'd have been long out of the way, otherwise.'

'Don't even know the woman,' muttered Nick. 'John was just showing me around–'

'No more lies, Ms Murray.'

'Not a word of a lie,' she said, palms spread. 'I don't know her. You don't know her either, do you Johnny?'

'Nope,' John agreed, popping the "p".

Sherlock gave him a hard look. 'So why hide? '

John flicked a glance at Mrs Hudson; another to Nick, and then his gaze settled back on Sherlock. 'I can't really say.'

Sherlock's gaze on him intensified. 'Not can't, *won't*,' he deduced. His cool grey gaze turned to Nick. 'It's about you.'

'Oh, yeah, ' Nick agreed with bluster. 'Everything definitely revolves around me. I'm the bloody chosen one.'

'That's not an answer.'

'No it's not. And it's not your business.'

'It's my case,' he snapped, and then his voice took on a more troubled tone. 'This is my *home*. My landlady and my frie... flatmate. It's my *sister* you're hiding from! How can all of these secrets not be my business?'

'Coz they're *our* secrets. Though apparently your sister knows the story, so I'd start with her.' Nick's defiance faltered at the look on John's face. Exactly the look of a man caught in a fight between two people he cared about.

Sherlock's eyelid twitched. 'I can at least start with the reason for her visit to me. It seems our expedition to Dartmoor interfered with a departmental investigation into an illegal trade in poached wildlife and even animal parts fraudulently presented as specimens of dismembered cryptids. Werewolves. Dryads. Dragons. Utter nonsense.'

He paced the carpet, disturbed as he recalled recent events. 'She asked me to steer clear, and I refused, which hardly surprised her. She didn't need to come in person to know that's how it would go. It wasn't a reasonable request. So why go against an adult lifetime of avoiding travel by coming here? The moment she left me, she knocked on your door, Mrs Hudson. She remained here for some time in discussion. So the reality is she came in person not for me, but for you, and for a pressing reason. Were you expecting her?'

'Not expecting, no,' Audrey said.

He quit pacing. 'A visit you feared, then. Because when Myca's car arrived, long before she knocked on your door, you sent these two into hiding, and while they were furtive and purposeful, they were not obviously alarmed. Although both had clearly been in some emotional distress.'

His gaze softened with puzzlement and a confused compassion. 'You were both wiping tears away. You hugged briefly, clearly for comfort. You spoke and pressed your foreheads together, before moving and replacing the plants, swiftly but exactly. Nothing about your actions indicated fear, and you've admitted not knowing my sister. So, you hid away on Mrs Hudson's instructions rather than your own concerns.'

Audrey wondered how close he would come to the truth, as he unravelled *what* had taken place in the search for *why*.

'I'll tell you what I do know,' Sherlock said to Audrey, moving on with his thoughts, picking through events. 'I know your family was murdered with silver bullets and some form of aconite poisoning. I know the forensic report shows that before Conal Dunn died, his forearm was severed and removed from the crime scene. I know that you and Doctor Watson removed and buried something from the home of Grimsby Roylott, which itself was the scene of a violent altercation, and that Roylott had offered Adelbert Gruner the preserved leg of a supposed werewolf.'

Go on, Audrey thought. *Take it to the illogical conclusion.* She might have risked his having a panic attack to show him what a werewolf looked like – but she couldn't. Her ability to shift had just been shut down by a cup of wolfsbane tea; and, as a still-new *were*, Nick could only change under the full moon or extreme duress. Or her own dose of special tea. Right now, only the possibility of an open mind, a willingness to accept the unacceptable, could alter his perception.

But Sherlock didn't, or couldn't, weave those unacceptable threads together and so:

'I know that everything we've seen is interconnected – Edinburgh, the Roylotts, Gruner, these fake artefacts – but there is something else; some*one* else beyond the obvious. Every scheme in which the Roylotts and Moran are involved has one aim in mind: the restoration of Stoke Moran. They lack the overarching world view required to organise a scheme of the scale and breadth which seems to be taking place. Gruner's kidnapping and extortion ring, arcane murder weapons to uphold a bizarre pretence of cryptozoology which may support a grotesque illegal trade in exotic animal parts. And my sister's investigation is somehow intertwined with these repulsive people.

'And, with you,' he glared directly at Audrey. 'Though why Myca's arrival prompted you to hide John and Nick downstairs, in a place you hold as... almost sacred. It's all highly suggestive and yet stubbornly unclear.'

He finally stopped for breath, the colour high in his cheeks, his grey eyes glittering with frustration. Audrey saw the hurt in them, in the pull at the corner of his mouth.

'What I don't know,' he said to their collective silence, 'is what connects you all. I've already told you my connection: this is my case, my home, Myca is my sister. I'd like some answers. No more lies. Please.'

John's voice, as he replied, was flat and controlled. 'I've never lied to you.'

'No.' Sherlock sounded sad. 'You've concealed things, I think. You've told tall tales in doing so, rather than more subtle lies.'

'I've left things unsaid,' John agreed. 'Not everything is mine to tell. But every single thing I've told you is true.'

'Mrs Hudson is a werewolf. And you're a ghost.'

'That was a metaphor,' John said stiffly.

'I suppose Myca's a vampire.'

'Not that, no,' Audrey said thoughtfully, remembering the flash of light behind Myca Holmes' dark lenses. 'I don't know what she is. Though she is certainly something.'

Audrey was startled to see how her comment seemed to hit Sherlock like a blow. He almost flinched, then went on the attack.

'Oh, very funny. Is Nick Murray a werewolf as well, or is that another metaphor?'

'It's a condition transmitted through bodily fluids, often through violent assault,' said John, as though providing a diagnosis. 'I suppose it could be a metaphor for something. But that's not what I mean.'

'Ghosts are a metaphor but werewolves are real.'

'I didn't say ghosts weren't real. I said I'm not really a ghost.'

'You're mad.'

'Is that what you think? Is that what you've observed?' John's tone was clipped.

'Not in the slightest, but no other conclusion fits the facts,' Sherlock bit back.

'One other conclusion does.'

'I'm not in the habit of enabling fantasists.'

'You have no idea what's out there, beyond cosy little London. The things I've seen in war zones–'

'Hallucinations brought on by fear, exhaustion and trauma. Heightened stress plays tricks on the mind.'

John's calm finally broke. 'Well thank you very much for the medical warsplaining, Sherlock, drawn no doubt on your years of deep personal experience,' he snapped in the parade-ground bark of an officer to an upstart underling. Sherlock was so startled he drew away. 'Or, you smug prick, you could give me credence as both a medical professional and a soldier for examining and understanding what's real and what isn't in my own lived experience.'

Sherlock struggled to regain ground. 'What you experienced as you've stated it is impossible.'

'And maybe, despite how you go on about absorbing facts without bias and not theorising ahead of the data, you're so hidebound by bias that you can't accept that there's more to the world than only what you want to see. Maybe you should re-examine your idea of what's impossible.'

'We can prove it.'

Audrey, John and Sherlock all fell silent at Nick's sudden interruption.

'Well, not me, probably, until the next full moon, but Mrs H can. Do that thing. Like downstairs. With your hands.'

'Do you remember what I said about the properties of the tea we just drank?'

'No, I– Ah, the wolfsbane. Shit.'

'Quite. The wolf has been very thoroughly suppressed for the time being. No shapeshifting, even in part, for a few hours at least.'

For just a moment, all the haughty anger drained from Sherlock's features and that awkward, lonely boy stood on her carpet, suddenly bereft of the few friends he thought he had.

'I don't know why you are doing this,' he said, helpless and hurt and furious. 'Tell me why you're doing this. Make me understand. Mrs Hudson? John?'

'We're not doing anything, Sherlock,' John said, sounding just as helpless and lost. 'It's the truth. I don't know why your sister was here, or what she has to do with anything, or who's behind all of this–'

'Whoever it is, murdered my family,' said Audrey. 'But I understand if you can't help me anymore.'

Sherlock stared from one to the other, and again, and then he shook his head.

'This whole thing is untenable. I think.' He winced as he looked at John. 'I suppose I had better pack. If I may leave my things here for a few days while I find new lodgings? Thank you.'

'Sherlock!' John lurched after his receding flatmate, but stopped.

'Well, fuck,' said Nick with feeling.

Chapter Thirteen

Next morning, Audrey attempted to disguise her sleepless night with careful attention to her hair and make-up, but even a very good foundation couldn't render her bright eyed and, as it were, bushy tailed.

Anxiety, confusion, worry for Nick Murray, and complex heartache for Sherlock and John, whose instant and adorable bond had splintered last night, had kept her from sleep.

Insomnia was compounded by the unsubtle sounds of John drowning his sorrows, with Nick for company, upstairs. Sherlock had vanished with nothing but whatever he'd had in his pockets.

She had to accept that she looked like the *Wreck of the Hesperus* as she quietly headed out to meet Irene Adler, nee Stockton, at Tower Hamlets.

'Heya, Mrs H.'

Audrey turned to glare at Nick Murray, who was hunched on the bottom of the stairs. Damn her exhaustion and preoccupation; she should have heard Nick's breathing if nothing else. Audrey couldn't afford to let her vigilance slip.

Nick flashed a weary grin at her. 'Ha. Gotcha. Boo.' She sobered again almost at once. 'Sorry. Waitin' for Johnny to drag his arse downstairs. I bet him if he couldn't hit a target from ten feet with a knife throw, he'd have to come play five-a-side rugby this morning. My bet is the bastard's fallen asleep with his head over the toilet bowl. And sorry about your wall. He got a bit stabby to make a point. I forget what point it was.'

So much to unpack in that sentence. Too much for now.

'Has Sherlock come home?' Another thing Audrey should have heard, and hadn't.

'Christ, no. Johnny's in a state about it. He spent half of last night wondering if vampires were also a thing and if Sherlock was all right out on his little lonely-ownsome when he was so unprepared for the risks.'

Nick's tone had devolved into scornful baby talk but then she covered her face in her hands. 'Sorry. Don't mean to bitch it up. I'm worried for John. I know he's only known that lanky sod, what, eight or nine weeks? But my boy has fallen hard for Mr Pretty. I mean, it's probably not *love*-love yet. They've hardly had time for that. But,' she shrugged, 'my grandparents met at a dance one night, got married within the month, and it's not like there was a war on then. It was just "this one for me" right off, and they went all in. I think John's like my grandad. Sailing along for years, never anyone right, and then, BAM! It's "this one for me" and that's that.'

Audrey didn't comment. She and Ruby hadn't been quite as quick off the mark as that, but quick enough. Sometimes, you just knew. Even if it took a while for it to come together. But she'd known, that first week, that Ruby was the person for her. "This one for me" indeed.

Nick, caught up in the telling, though, went on.

'All the things that happened to us in Afghanistan; John was a hundred kinds of messed up by the time he was discharged, like he was an old man already, resigned to being alone. And then he met Sherlock Bloody Holmes and he came back to life. It's been beautiful. He's been texting me for weeks about his amazing flatmate. How he's felt really, properly seen. Accepted. How he thinks he might still have some use and purpose in this world. And Johnny needs that. He's a good man; a good mate. He deserves to be happy, and it's been like he finally got to be that. But now he's...he's back in the dark. He doesn't know what to do. He doesn't know how to make it right. He doesn't know how to make Sherlock believe in all this madness.'

Nick sighed and rubbed at her eyes. 'I wouldn't either, if Percy hadn't sprouted a hairy forehead, killer gnashers and a wet nose right in front of me. If he'd just told me, I'd have thought he was taking the piss.'

This dilemma was new to Nick, but Audrey had dealt with these coming out problems for years. The only thing for someone like Sherlock was to show him, not tell, and hope it didn't break his reason. And that couldn't happen until he came home.

'I'm sorry, Nick. We can only give it time. Right now, I have to go.' Nick looked ready to protest. 'Private business. Will you be here?'

'Sure. Someone's gotta turn John right-side-in again after he's finished puking his guts out.' Nick sighed in defeat. 'Rugby's definitely off. Shame, that. I figured if Sherlock got an eyeful of John in his rugby kit, he'd break records to kiss and make up. The wanker.'

'I'll be back in a few hours.'

'I'll try not to let loverboy's hangover kill him before then.'

Audrey regretted taking the Underground to her destination. The usual jostling crowds combined with the accumulated station smells of grease, dust, cleaning fluids, metal and urine were overwhelming her senses. The noise was almost as bad – coughing, chatter, the beeps and hisses of the train doors at each stop, 'Mind the Gap!' and an indefinable background electronic whine. She was relieved to alight at Mile End with a handful of other, unfamiliar passengers, and set off at a rapid pace.

As she passed through the gates of Tower Hamlets Cemetery Park, the high brick fence reminded her of slipping out of the Chelsea Physic Garden, just over two months ago. Only two? It could have been two months or ten, time had become so elastic.

She only knew Ruby's daughter Irene from a photograph Ruby had kept. In it, Irene's youthful, dark skin was only slightly lighter than her mother's. Her eyes were an unusual colour, passing for the rare golden-brown of a human, but they were the tell-tale amber of a natural-born werewolf: a child born of two werewolves. Irene's father, Dieter Adler, had taken the girl away when she was only ten. Ruby had a photograph of Dieter too, a handsome white man with dark hair and laughing brown eyes. Ruby spoke of Dieter occasionally, but even more rarely of her lost daughter. Those reminiscences were always full of longing but no recrimination.

It was from Ruby that Audrey had learned of the shadowy, relentless threat of the Department of Fisheries, which had forced Dieter and Irene's withdrawal to Europe. Myca Holmes could claim her department was for the protection of all until doomsday: Audrey did not trust them.

Alert for any threats – *great danger hangs over your life and mine* – Audrey passed the entrance into the graveyard. Down the path, she loitered by the war memorial and watched for anyone following after.

141

Two women ahead of her, one tall and willowy, the other rounder and prettier, were dressed for gardening. They were laughing with a stooped, white-haired priest. A too-thin man in layers of grimy clothes had followed them into the cemetery park. The slender woman gave him a pear from her voluminous bag. The priest said something, his body language inviting trust, but the man shuffled away, gnawing at his pear. Everyone was downwind from her, the breeze carrying their scents away, but they seemed innocent enough.

Audrey veered right along a path shaded with tall ash and oak trees, interspersed with juniper and holly. Irene hadn't specified where to meet, but Audrey knew it would be at the grave of Ruby's mother, Mary.

The grass and ground plants had partially swallowed the gravestones along this stretch. Hedgehogs, birds, fieldmice, even foxes, fled ahead of her, rustling through the undergrowth: giving the apex predator space and then some. They didn't know she meant them no harm.

Then Audrey saw Irene waiting down the path. Even in profile, this woman in her fifties was unmistakeably Ruby Stockton's kin. She was tall, wide-hipped and curvaceous, like her mother, her head held proudly high, the shape of her chin and her nose and her forehead heart-hurtingly familiar. Where Ruby had worn her hair in a short crop, however, Irene's was plaited in cornrows that hung down her back.

She turned at the sound of Audrey's footfall. Her eyes were golden brown. Beautiful. She waited until Audrey came alongside her before speaking.

'You came.'

'Of course.'

'Were you followed?'

'No.'

They turned together to face the gravestone half buried in the grass, under the shade of the horse chestnut trees. The inscription was worn but legible.

> *In loving memory of Mary Stockton*
> *6 October 1922 – 4 May 1958*
> *Beloved mother of Ruby*
> *Sleeping safe now in the arms of the Lord*

'I suppose the stonemason couldn't fit "murdered by a werewolf" in there. My poor Oma. I wish I'd known her. You have to admire a woman who fought a werewolf with her bare hands. Not that she saved my mother from the curse, but oh she tried. Do you think that's why Ruby let me go? Trying, like Oma, to protect her daughter? I've often wondered.'

Audrey frowned at Irene's cool tone, if not her slight German accent. 'Papa said so. He told me often that it wasn't safe for me in England.'

'Your letter said we were both in danger.'

'Yes. I am getting to that. Walk with me.'

Audrey was glad Irene didn't speak in anything like Ruby's warm, affectionately teasing East End accent. At least, it hurt in a different way than if Irene had sounded, as well as looked, like her mother. She fell into step beside Irene and they wound through the rambling tracks of the woodland park. At one point, Irene stepped off the path and picked her away among listing headstones scattered beneath the trees. A cluster of bluebells bloomed on one grave and over the torso of a broken statue, seeming artful rather than neglected.

Other park visitors exclaimed over memorials and inscriptions and nature's reclamation of the space. The snip of garden shears indicated gardeners performing their Friends of the Park duties on old headstones.

'I used to blame you for Ruby's death,' Irene confessed quietly under dappled green shadows. 'How could she catch that terrible disease, but not you? In my grief, I was certain you had somehow given it to her. And she left everything to you. Her money, her houses, everything she owned. It was like she had forgotten me.'

'She kept your picture,' Audrey said, defensive. 'She told me she didn't know where you were and refused to even look when I suggested we try. She worried that the Department of Fisheries would discover you.'

'Ah yes. The Department. Papa and I also wondered if they had killed her. If you had let them do it, to save your own life.'

Outrage grew into actual rage, and Audrey's teeth grew sharp in her mouth. 'Never. I would never have hurt her. And I tried to find you myself, afterwards. I never wanted her houses or her money. I'd have given it all to you. I'd have traded every penny, every–'

'I'm sorry,' Irene interrupted, curtly yet somehow kindly. 'I know now you could have had nothing to do with it. You didn't kill my mother. Nor, I think, did the Department.'

Audrey, in pain from the salt in that still-open wound, unwilling to be mollified so quickly, glared. 'Really?'

'Really. England's Department of Fisheries could have no reason to pursue us, after all this time, into a country far outside their jurisdiction and decades after Ruby died. Papa confessed after he got sick that he took me away because several attempts had been made to abduct me as a child. I recall one of them now, many noisy men too close to me in the playground. I had misunderstood the incident at the time. I know Ruby stayed behind to distract the Department while Papa made an adventure of sneaking me across the Channel. I thought she would join us, but she never did. She stayed away, I think, believing it kept me safe. I had finally decided to visit her, to meet you, after my marriage, but suddenly, she was dead. After I stopped blaming you, I suspected the Department had done it, but Papa thought otherwise. Why would they wait so long to poison her after Papa and I had gone? Why wait decades more to kill Papa? It makes no sense.'

'Your father is dead?'

The next words fell from Irene's mouth like stones. 'Papa died a month ago. Of Creutzfeldt-Jakob disease. It was...' Irene bowed her head. 'It was a terrible death.'

Audrey felt she should shake her head to rattle her ears loose. Surely she hadn't heard that correctly. The coincidence was too much. Dieter Adler had died not long after her own family. And he died of the thing that had taken Ruby.

'We couldn't understand how he contracted the disease, twenty years after the outbreaks in England,' Irene continued. 'How did Gottfried and I avoid the infection, living as we did in the same house? On Cursed nights, Papa and I ate uncooked meat I bought myself from the butcher. And yet, he became ill and I did not.'

Irene's coolness had vanished, the shock of recent grief in her eyes. 'We had to lock him in the basement, those last few months, at the full moon. I no longer have to imagine how it was for you, to see my mother reduced.'

She killed herself before it got to that. She spared me without my consent. I would have cared for her to the bitterest of ends.

Irene stretched, attempting to shed the weight of loss. 'On the day Papa died, someone broke into the house. They destroyed the metal door to the basement – it was a foot thick, impervious to a great deal. They used explosives. But the house was empty. I could not stay where he had died. Gottfried and I spent the night drinking toasts to him at *Die Rote Bar*. Gottfried Norton is my husband,' she elaborated. 'He moved in with Papa and me when we married. He understood our need for a safe place.'

Gottfried Norton knew that his wife and father-in-law were werewolves, then, Audrey concluded.

'The break-in was the culmination of many strange incidents,' Irene went on. 'Papa was convinced someone was watching the house. I thought it was an effect of the disease, but then I too became convinced. Someone who understood werewolf senses was being very careful. Gottfried detected the same signs, but could not find who was stalking us. After Papa died, Gottfried took me away on a tour through the provinces. I am a singer, you know.'

Audrey hadn't known. It was a strangely public life for someone with a dark monthly secret, but then, some celebrities had kept worse secrets for longer.

'When we returned to Frankfurt, two men attempted to take me by force from the train station.' She gave Audrey a sidelong look. 'Two days after the full moon.'

Audrey was paying full attention now.

'They spoke English. The old one with the German accent and the knife said, "Got you at last; the chief has been looking for you for forty years". The one with the London accent and the gun told him to shut up. Herr German said, "Will you come quietly, or will we do for you as the chief did for your father and mother?"'

Cold spread from the pit of Audrey's stomach, down every nerve, to the tips of her fingers and toes.

'Mr London said to him, "The Professor wants her intact, you twat". Herr German wanted to argue, but Mr London was a true professional. He did not talk. He acted. He shot Gottfried and the German grabbed for me.'

Before Audrey could express stunned condolences, Irene went on.

'This was a mistake. Gottfried has been a vampire for years, now. Silver bullets are useless against him unless they pierce his heart. I freed myself from the German and we fought. The London assassin, realising his error, called for a retreat. They fled, but the German left his telephone behind.'

From the pocket of her slacks, Irene produced a mobile phone. Its clock was still set to Central European time and the symbols in the top right corner showed that it was set to aeroplane mode.

Audrey's snarl rose unbidden.

The lock screen image was blurred and off-centre, but it clearly showed

Tara, her hair and freckled face splashed in blood, standing protectively in front of Siobhan, who lay in a huddle on the carpet of their Edinburgh home. Trying, and failing, to protect her sister. The image was overlaid with a scarlet cross.

The reaction startled Irene and she turned the screen away. 'You know them?'

'My, my–' *My children, my little loves, my pack.* 'Mine.' No other words could make it past the howl in her throat.

'I am so sorry. I didn't mean to distress you. I didn't know who they were. Only that he had hunted them. There's more. Should I–'

Audrey did not want to see more, but she nodded. The hideous lock screen vanished to reveal a red-spattered wallpaper image thankfully obscured by app icons. Irene opened the photo app and began to scroll through images. The most innocuous were selfies showing a grizzled man in his 70s or 80s, with wild eyes and a wilder grin.

Another sharp jolt of recognition shot through Audrey. 'That's William Ormstein!'

'Ah. This was his phone. He's the one who calls himself the King of Bohemia, isn't he? Papa warned me about him. Do you know who the Londoner was? He was tall, dark-haired. A hard man. A soldier, I think, but wholly human.'

'I've no idea who it could be.' Or perhaps she had some idea. A soldier and a hunter. Wholly human. The Moran boy? 'Ormstein got away?'

'Yes. They separated instantly. We thought it best to see what we could discover through the phone instead of chasing them.'

'How did you break into it?'

'Ah.' Irene's smile was cool and not entirely pleasant. 'The German foolishly tried to wrestle Gottfried for it. Vampires are very strong. The German didn't only leave the phone behind. He left this.' She waggled her thumb meaningfully. 'We used it while it was still warm to open the phone, then added our own thumbprints to the memory. We've disconnected the phone from the network so it can't be deleted remotely. But this is the important part. This is how I know we are both in danger.'

Irene opened an album labelled "Targets". A sub-folder marked "D.O.A." contained not only the picture of Tara and Siobhan with the scarlet cross through them, and one of Travis and Conal, but dozens of others.

Among the strangers were faces Audrey had known, however briefly.

A werewolf who quietly ran a bookstore in remote Scotland and never hurt a soul; a vampire who'd definitely been a bastard and was now a pile of dust; a bedraggled Jenny Greenteeth water witch from Norwich, long green hair just so much limp weed covering her fishbelly-white face. All very much dead, with that red cross over their faces.

'And this.' Irene had backtracked to the main album. It was full of images with red or green circles over the face.

There was Irene – green circle. And Audrey – red circle.

And Sherlock Holmes – green circle. John – red.

It seemed Irene's fate to turn Audrey's heart and belly to water.

'Who are they?' Irene demanded

'Sherlock and John. They're my tenants.' Audrey didn't know if she should reveal that Sherlock's sister headed the Department of Fisheries. Was Myca the reason his photo bore a green circle for capture, rather than a red one for death?

'Where are they?'

'John's at home. Sherlock is out.'

'We had better hurry, then. I don't know if Ormstein or the London hunter are still in Frankfurt. I think they have that list to complete. Don't you?'

From the path beyond the trees they heard a scuff of shoe on pebbles, a small gasp. Audrey's head shot up, her nose in the air, her ears almost growing wolfish. Irene crouched slightly, ready to change, but all they saw through the trees was the elderly priest, clearing weeds from a grave on the opposite side of the track, murmuring a prayer.

Audrey caught a whiff of a familiar scent. This muttering old man smelled confusingly of dust, glue, talcum powder, mildew and – two different people. One of whom—

Damn. The odour of the clothing mingled with the white human hair that was probably a wig, and under it was the familiar but obscured scent of a *Holmes.* Was this Myca, Sherlock, or another sibling? A brother to them perhaps or, given the priest's apparent age, an uncle? Father, perhaps? His presence here could hardly be a coincidence.

He was gone again before she could confront him, and Irene took Audrey's arm before she could follow.

'I don't know why they are targets, but your tenants are in danger,' she said. 'We should go. At once.'

Audrey tried phoning the flat first. John didn't answer the upstairs phone or his mobile, and her own downstairs number rang out. Sherlock's mobile phone went straight to voicemail.

She tried all these numbers as she and Irene ran for the station at Mile End, deciding the direct tube line would be faster than any other transport. They emerged at Baker Street Station, shoving impatiently past the streaming throngs of passengers. Once above ground, they ran. From the end of the street they saw a man at the door of 221 Baker Street. Audrey recognised him immediately.

Grimsby Roylott.

A surge of adrenalin arrowed through her blood, calling on the wolf inside as her front door opened and someone let the devil in.

Audrey ran faster, ignoring the twinge from her hip, and Irene kept pace beside her. In the next moment, Nick's voice, raised in a furious, uncouth expletive, swelled out from the still-open front door. A deeper voice joined hers: 'Get the fu–' and dissolved into a deep, hoarse horror. 'Jesus Christ!'

'*John!*'

Nick's cry from within the house was echoed by one directly behind Audrey and Irene. Audrey glanced briefly back to see the elderly priest from Mile End sprinting across Marylebone Road towards the house.

Audrey and Irene reached the door first. Roylott's clothes were strewn across the entry. Just beyond, a monstrous black-banded grey snake rose almost to the ceiling, poised to strike the man and woman sprawled on the floor at the base of the stairs.

The snake lunged for John; Nick aimed an enraged kick at its face. The glistening fangs sank into the limb and stuck there, fast.

'*Mother*,' screeched Nick, grabbing an umbrella from the overturned hat-stand, '*Fucker.*' She whacked the snake over the head. '*Fuck.*' She jabbed at its head with the ferrule. '*Off.*'

The snake, trying to retreat, dragged his victim along the floor, teeth wedged in her prosthetic leg. Nick stabbed it in the eye with the umbrella.

John, on his feet again, hefted up the hatstand and swung it at the giant snake's head. He didn't waste breath on swearing, just got a better grip and smashed the hatstand repeatedly into the snake's body. A sudden whipping movement from that sinuous torso threw him sideways into a wall.

Irene hands had grown long and clawed. She bounded towards Nick, who was being shaken side to side as the snake tried to free itself. She wrapped her arms around Nick to anchor her and kicked with startling strength at the snake's blunt snout. Audrey's body had begun to change too but as she leapt to John's side, fear that she might accidently wound him in a fight made her shift abruptly back to her human form. Cornered between the wall and the bannister, Audrey whirled to face the serpent just as it shook free of Nick's leg.

The snake's hiss at Audrey sounded disturbingly like laughter.

John used the wall for leverage and lurched to his feet, his hands in fists. Nick, resisting Irene's attempts to retreat, took another whack at the snake with the umbrella. 'You stay the fuck away from my mate!' When the snake's head swivelled towards her, John and Audrey tried to dart out of their dangerous corner, but it had been a feint. With stupendous speed, it reared its body high and–

Sherlock Holmes – who had shed his aged priestly trappings – finally burst through the open door and barely baulked at the strange spectacle before him. He threw himself bodily at the serpent as it lunged for John. It thrashed again, trying to dislodge the man wrapped around its torso.

'John! *Run!*'

John did not run. As Sherlock was shaken off and fell with a bone-shuddering thud, John seized the splintered hatstand and smashed it against the snake's head, drawing blood. The five of them stood against it then: Irene and Nick, who could hardly balance on her damaged limb; Audrey and John, who was bleeding from a cut lip and a gash across his forehead; and Sherlock.

Finally conceding defeat, the monstrous snake twisted, fast as lightning, and slithered with uncanny speed back into Baker Street. Irene bounded out instantly in its wake.

'That was a snake,' Sherlock stared at the space recently vacated by the creature, so stunned he was stating the bloody obvious. 'A giant snake.'

'Look after them,' snapped Audrey, shoving him forcefully towards a swaying Nick. She dropped her keys, purse and phone to the carpet, and raced outside in pursuit of Irene and their mutual enemy.

Chapter Fourteen

Audrey could tell where Irene and Roylott had gone by the shrieks of alarm. Londoners are immune to so many peculiar sights, but even they found a middle aged woman pursuing a giant snake past the local *Pizza Express* startling.

Audrey kicked off her shoes before the intersection and looked for a place to transform without gawpers putting in their hysterical tuppence worth.

Traffic had squealed to an astonished, shouting halt on Marylebone Road. Audrey caught a glimpse of the snake twisting, rising and transforming into a naked man. Irene still appeared mostly human, but she was a born werewolf, with all the wolf's aptitude and instincts. With devastating, terrifying grace she leapt at Roylott, who was slow to dodge and Irene raked four lines across his back with nails that were now claws.

In a moment, man became snake again, writhing across the intersection, avoiding a red bus and a yellow lorry; but an Uber Eats cyclist was too busy shrieking to steer and crashed into, then over the centre of his long body.

The snake's forward undulation turned into a sudden sidewinding movement down the drive-through entrance to Baker Street Tube Station and vanished.

Irene, unfamiliar with the Underground, paused within the arched entrance to scour for their quarry, which allowed Audrey to finally catch up. A departing train cleared the platform and she glimpsed an aged back, pale bottom and hairy legs as Grimsby Roylott's human form darted across tracks to the next platform.

Irene vaulted the barrier. Audrey dismissed a faint feeling of fare-evading misconduct as she followed suit.

People were crying out again, signalling Roylott's transformation back into the serpent and his attempt to escape up the stairs. Too many people coming down entangled with those trying to run back up them, blocking that escape route. The snake became a man again.

'Ew, mate, nobody wants to see your shrivelled willy!'

'Oi, get out of it, ya mucky ol' geezer.'

Oh yes, Londoners may panic at the sight of a giant snake but they knew exactly what to do with a naked man trying to press rudely past people on a crowded staircase. Someone coming down it hit him accidentally-on-purpose in the groin with a skateboard and called him a 'dirty bollocking creeper'.

More screams rose as he reverted to snake form, hissed at his tormentors then folded back on himself to return to the platform.

Irene was there to meet him, having leapt straight across the gap from one platform to the next. Roylott coiled and shot off again, down onto the tracks and into the tunnel. Irene pursued, amber eyes glowing with the thrill of the hunt. On the platforms, officials were shouting, commuters echoing the horror of anything running into a possibly oncoming train.

Audrey followed them into the tunnel, remembering to keep clear of the electrified middle track. Finally hidden from the eyes of strangers, Audrey let the change surge through her. Adrenalin made it easier, but she still stumbled as her body twisted. Her stockings ripped and, to free up her movement, she tore away the frock she'd so carefully chosen for her meeting with Ruby's daughter, commending it and her comfortable underthings to heaven.

She loped on. Beyond a dark bend illuminated only by service lights, the snake was manoeuvring on the floor and walls of the tunnel. Four bloody lines showed where Irene's claws had raked him in the chase. His body seethed in perpetual motion in an attempt to keep off the live rails.

Irene, too, had shed her outer clothes. Her black-pelted wolf form, marked with brown-black Blaschko's striations, was large and handsome. She and Audrey poised on either side of the snake, snarling, shoulders down, ears flat, teeth bared and eyes blazing with rage.

'I've no quarrel with yyyou,' the snake said to Irene. 'Let me passss.'

'*Zur Holle mit dir*,' snapped Irene. 'I remember you. *Die grosse Schlange*. The snake that attacked me when I was small.'

The snake shifted in what would have been a shrug in his human form. 'His Nibss hasss an interessst in you. Sstill hasss. He can wait. He'sss a patient man.'

Roylott feinted towards Irene then whipped his tail to strike at Audrey, but Audrey darted under his head and scraped claws across his scales. He twisted again then hissed out in fury and pain as his body glanced against the electrified rail.

Audrey fell back into another attack-ready crouch. 'You killed my family,' she said through her wrath-wrinkled snout.

'Not me,' breathed the snake, tongue flickering. 'Sssilver bulletsss – not my sstyle.'

'Who?'

Roylott hissed another spine-crawling laugh. 'Ormsssstein's a busssy boy, I hear.'

Irene bristled. 'The King of Bohemia killed my father. Who gave him his orders?'

'His Nibsss of coursse.'

'And *who* is that?' demanded Irene but the snake only swayed and drew itself as high as it could within the confines of the tunnel.

'And did His Bloody Nibs set you onto my boys?' Audrey demanded.

'I wassss there for *you*, Granny Wolf. The othersss are my bonusss. Holmesss iss meddling in my affairsss. Damned busssybody. Missster M wantsss to sssend a messssage to that ssister of hisss, too, that damned public ssservicce Jack-In-Officce. I'll sseee to them all and reclaim my housse. After I've sseeeen to you.'

The great snake struck, but Audrey hadn't survived by being stupid or slow. She leapt to the left, aiming to pivot off the curve of the tunnel wall, onto the back of Roylott's head and to bite him through the spine.

Irene, of a more straightforward disposition, sprang straight for Roylott's throat as he struck at Audrey. Roylott missed them both and twisted rapidly. Audrey overshot the snake, though her snapping teeth tore scales from the top of Roylott's head. Irene was unable to sink her teeth into any vulnerable spot. She landed hard and turned, ready to spring again.

Roylott whipped around to face her, thinking the larger, younger wolf a more dangerous adversary. His body rolled over and around itself even as he positioned for another strike. Another sharp zap from the third rail made him thrash. A coil of his body caught Audrey as she leapt at him and threw her into the tunnel wall. Then he twisted over and around Irene as she went for him and tried to wrap her in the loops. Irene dug claws and teeth into his skin while Audrey, heaving for breath, clawed for his eyes, red slits in the darkness.

The rushing of the wind along the tunnel gave the first warning, pushed ahead of the sound. Perhaps Irene, technically a foreigner, didn't know what it meant. Perhaps Roylott, who preferred life in a mansion on Dartmoor, wouldn't know either. But Audrey, new Londoner though she was, knew exactly what it meant.

'Irene! Move away!'

Audrey abandoned her attack to reach the side of the tunnel, her sharp eyes looking desperately for one of the small alcoves cut into the walls. She shifted abruptly back to her human body, naked now in the dark and in danger.

'Now, Irene!'

Irene was beside her in an instant and followed Audrey's lead in reverting to her human form. Audrey seized her hand and dragged her to the nearest nook in the brickwork. She pushed Irene in first and pressed in close afterwards, hoping she'd tucked her bum in enough.

Electrified tracks weren't the problem down here – the live third rail hardly inconvenienced Roylott in his snake form at all – but the momentum and weight of an oncoming train was less forgiving, even for *weres*, and for whatever Grimsby Roylott called himself.

Audrey turned her face to see how close the snake Roylott was to killing them.

He'd heard Audrey's shouted warning of course, but didn't seem to realise that Audrey wasn't warning Irene about *his* next imminent strike. As much as his reptile face could display emotion, Roylott appeared smug and triumphant. He curled his thick, sinuous torso around and up to tower over them, his wicked mouth open wide, the venom beaded on the tips of his fangs.

Audrey wanted to look away and couldn't. Death was coming. She could feel the wind of it on her naked skin. She could hear the burgeoning whoosh and clatter of it hurtling down the tunnel towards the platforms.

Roylott's flat head turned sharply into the rushing wind, suddenly realising the danger. He shifted instantly to occupy less space, to become a much smaller, moving target: but he wasn't fast enough. The train was faster, no matter how the driver tried to brake.

The edge of the Bakerloo line's Mark 2 1972 stock engine face clipped Roylott on the heel and threw him into the air with violent forward momentum. He landed on the track seconds before the train ploughed over him and onward to the station.

He might have fared better as a giant snake. But then again, probably not.

The train shot past, brakes screaming. Audrey squeezed Irene's hand. 'We have to go.'

Audrey supposed that London Transport would halt all incoming trains to Baker Street until further notice, but she and Irene remained wary of oncoming trains as they trotted in wolf form down the tunnel towards Marylebone Station and escape.

Audrey was shaking with fatigue by the time the two of them loped back to Baker Street. A preliminary scratch at the front door demonstrated both that the door was locked and that the occupants, if around, hadn't heard. After a brief exchange, Audrey folded down on the stoop, panting and holding onto her shape with extreme effort, now that the adrenalin was draining away. Only her determination not to be discovered by her neighbours, a naked and trembling old lady, kept her out-of-cycle wolfishness intact. She muttered 'back door' and Irene disappeared around the corner.

Moments later, the front door was opened from the inside by human-Irene, wrapped in a too-small robe. Audrey suddenly felt aged and fragile, shaking with reaction, as Irene lifted her easily into her arms and brought her into her flat.

'It's dangerous to keep your key under a pot plant,' said Irene mildly.

Audrey was quivering too hard for a reply. Irene wrapped her in a blanket and sat rubbing her hands up and down Audrey's arms and back. Audrey felt that if for one second she lingered on how much that reminded of Ruby, she would fall to pieces and never be whole again. She shrugged away from the brisk kindness instead. 'Tea?'

Irene put on the kettle and, at Audrey's insistence, went to shower and find some clothes. When she was done and they'd had tea and cheese sandwiches, Audrey had recovered sufficient strength to shower and change too.

Then her home phone rang.

'Mrs H!' Nick said with loud relief. 'Are you okay? Did you get him?'

'The London Underground got him. He didn't give much away before it did, I'm afraid.'

'Well Sherlock Holmes reckons we've got a half dozen new leads here. You better come upstairs with that friend of yours, if she's with you.'

'Irene's here. We're coming.'

John let them into 221B at Audrey's knock. He held a cold compress to his bruised face as he limped out of their way. Sherlock was sitting at the microscope at their kitchen table, feigning disinterest, but Audrey caught him glancing towards his flatmate as John sank gingerly onto the sofa.

Nick half ran across the room to clasp Audrey in a sudden and then suddenly awkward hug. Audrey froze with surprise and then was sorry she had when Nick backed away.

'Sorry. Sorry, sorry. Fuck it's good to see you, though. I was worried I'd end up seeing you on *News of the World* being cut out of the belly of a dead anaconda in Regent's Park. Bet that'd ruin your shoes. Speaking of which, John found your shoes down the street when he finally got out to look for you, but there were sirens and vans all over Marylebone Street and he thought it best to come back.'

John waved feebly from his seat and shifted the ice pack slightly to cover his split lip.

'I just finished sorting out my leg – that snaky bastard bit right through the foot and split the plastic. John helped me gaffer tape it up for now – and I'd have gone looking for you only Mr Pretty said he'd seen a dog coming over the back fence.' Nick raised a sardonic eyebrow.

Mr Pretty himself sighed with irritation.

'He's been making himself useful, though, with all his clues,' Nick continued. 'The clothes Roylott left here, and the phones, and the stuff he wiped off the floor onto his slides. Even though he's insisting that thing was nothing more than a very big snake. Nothing weird about a giant snake, right?'

'What else would it be?' said Sherlock sharply, though everyone could hear the touch of desperation behind it. 'At least we know what happened to Roylott's missing pet from Stoke Moran.'

'And all of Roylott's clothes in the foyer are...?'

'I have not yet–'

'You're really bowling me over with your deductive skills.'

'Leave it, Nick,' said John tiredly.

'I refuse to believe–' Sherlock stumbled then tried again. 'I wasn't here, and your account of the event is insupportable.'

'*You're* bloody insupportable. Why John thinks you're such hot stuff is beyond me.'

'Leave him alone, Nick!'

John and Sherlock exchanged a glance that was fairly equal parts hope, despair and embarrassment.

'I have too little data,' Sherlock muttered, looking away. 'It's madness to theorise ahead of all the facts.'

'Excuses, excuses. A man arrived, he disappeared, a giant snake tried to kill us all. Good work tackling the fucker before it bit John, but pull your head out, sunshine. If it quacks like a duck...'

'Please,' groaned John, shifting the ice pack to another area blooming into purple and black. 'My face hurts. My shoulder hurts. My entire me hurts. I can't do this with the two of you as well.'

Sherlock's contrite expression rapidly vanished when he realised Audrey and her guest were watching him.

'You were at the cemetery,' Irene accused. 'Pretending to be a priest.' She lifted an eyebrow at Audrey. 'I thought you said you weren't followed.'

'Nothing is what you may expect to see, when I follow you,' Sherlock announced.

Irene snorted a laugh at that.

'He got in *ahead* of me,' said Audrey, stung. She hadn't recognised his Holmesian scent until she and Irene were leaving Tower Hamlets. John and Nick were extremely lucky he'd returned so close on their heels.

'And why would you follow her in the first place?' Irene asked.

'I got tired of having mysteries at both ends of my investigation.'

Audrey decided the best way to ignore the tension in the room was to create a fresh source of it.

'Irene, this is Nick Murray, Dr John Watson and Sherlock Holmes. Everyone, this is Irene Adler, the daughter of my late partner–'

'Ruby Stockton, yes. The name was in Adelbert Gruner's book; and you visited her mother's grave today.' Sherlock waggled a mobile phone with a cracked screen and minus its protective case at Irene. 'You threw this on the floor before you ran after the– the snake.'

'I dropped it,' Irene corrected him.

'You threw it, just as Mrs Hudson threw her own phone, keys and purse away when she took off after you. Anyone would think you didn't want identifying property on you while you chased a giant python through London.'

Audrey, retrieving her property again, didn't have the energy to explain that she'd left them behind because wolves don't come with pockets; not even werewolves.

'I don't have a phone of my own,' Irene said after a moment. 'That one belongs to our enemy.'

'One William Ormstein,' said Sherlock at once. He flipped the phone around to show the scratches on the back of it. 'Another name from Gruner's fantastical book. It looks like he scratched his name into it with a compass.'

'He would,' said Audrey darkly.

'I haven't turned it on. I don't want it being wiped remotely before we get a chance to examine the contents. In the meantime, there's this.' Sherlock placed the battered smartphone on the table and waved towards the microscope. 'I took a sample of the venom that soaked the carpet after the snake failed to bite anyone.'

'Oi!' protested Nick, as John said grimly, 'Not for the want of trying.'

Sherlock cast another flickering glance of concern towards John, and then Nick. 'Due to Ms Murray's fortuitous intervention, of course.'

'Cheers,' said Nick sourly. 'I feel lucky.'

'You and John were exceedingly lucky,' Sherlock said with feeling. 'The snake that attacked you had many features in common with the deadliest snake in India, the common krait, from the banded colours and shape of its head to the alarming properties of this venom – which features in a number of mysterious deaths over the last ten years.'

That announcement suddenly commanded everyone's attention. Audrey sagged into a chair, motioning for Irene to listen as well. It may not have anything to do with her own case, but it was something new.

Sherlock was almost startled to find he no longer had to wrestle for attention.

'Mysterious, how?' John sat forward in his seat, cuts and bruises forgotten in his eager interest. Sherlock turned instantly towards him, as though John were the only audience that mattered.

'Twelve deaths in thirteen years, John, all apparently unconnected other than for the apparent manner of death. Snakebite, except that only two of the victims could be proven to have had any proximity to snakes, of normal or any other size, and neither of those was the Indian krait or even an English adder. Another was found to have pricked a finger on the thorns of an American shrub called the Devil's Walking Stick, a fourth on a simple Chinese winged thorn rose. One is thought to have been pricked by a needle secreted in an anonymous package sent on the day of her death. The coroner's reports on the remaining seven state that it's not known how the venom was introduced to the victim. I came across the deaths in a journal two years ago, when there were only nine victims. The most recent three deaths, including the one who received the parcel, have occurred only in the last two years. The case for serial murder is quite clear.'

'But why?' John asked, hanging on every word.

'If I could work out the connection, John, I'd understand the motive.'

'What if this snake was the source of the poison, then?' John prompted. 'Roylott could well have been supplying the venom.'

'Exactly. The question is, was he the assassin, and if so, how did he benefit? Or was he simply the provider of the weapon in question to those who wished to dispose of a family member?'

Audrey, Nick and Irene were riveted to their exchange.

'Is there any pattern of inheritance?' John asked.

'In two cases, the beneficiary of the property died within a year of other, unrelated causes. Car accident. Tropical infection. In one case only, the wife who inherited died of the same venom two years later. In all other cases, the beneficiaries sold the land within 36 months, though to different buyers. Those who received cash and other assets have generally survived untouched, barring the usual and expected attrition rate.'

Nick cleared her throat, reminding them that other people existed. 'What are you saying then, hotshot?'

Sherlock blinked and sat stiffly upright, reminding Audrey that he'd also been slammed into hard surfaces during the struggle with the snake.

'I'm saying, Grimsby Roylott and his snake are supplyi–'

Audrey's mobile phone rang on the table where Sherlock had put it. Audrey snatched it up before Sherlock could do it.

The surprise caller was Myca Holmes. It was not a friendly kind of call. 'What the hell were you two playing at? In the middle of Baker Street tube station?'

'It was hardly my choice,' Audrey replied coolly. 'Roylott had his own agenda.'

'Roylott's currently being placed into several body bags, my team are wiping closed circuit footage as a matter of urgency and that poor bloody driver is soon to be seeking trauma counselling and anti-psychosis meds. God knows what we'll do about the smartphone recordings, though thankfully there are few enough of those.'

Audrey's tone shifted to ice cold. 'None of which is down to me. Roylott was at Baker Street, intent on murder – of *all* the residents, I might point out, partly to send a message to *you*. Surely you heard that on the footage.'

That news silenced Myca Holmes more effectively than any shouting.

'There is no sound on the tunnel recording,' said Myca, suddenly strained and breathless. 'Roylott didn't... Is Sherlock–'

'A little bruised, but fine.'

Audrey made the mistake of glancing at Sherlock as she said this, giving away the identity of the caller. Sherlock leapt to a very accurate conclusion before darting up and slipping the phone out of Audrey's hand.

'Myca!' He dropped into his chair with a pained grunt. 'You're calling my landlady, which is only slightly odd, given you visited her yesterday, which is much more odd.' He listened to her response, then said, 'Apart from tying Grimsby bloody Roylott to twelve unsolved murders and evading death by giant snake? Not a lot. Oh, very funny, why? If you insist.

'The first was a man by the name of Benjamin Castle from Hayfield in Derbyshire. His property, Oakenwell, was bought from the family six months later by a development consortium, though as far as I'm aware no actual development has occurred. Then it was Afan Bowen, who had a tiny sheep farm in Wales called *Bendithio Dwr*.' Sherlock's Welsh pronunciation was flawless.

'But– All right. Trevelyan Sands in Cornwall, Llanfair Farm in Anglesey...' He rattled off the other eight locations easily and then, his scowl dissolving into puzzlement, he handed the phone back to Audrey.

'Roylott's been acquiring sacred wells, standing stones, groves, and *you killed him before we could find out why*,' Myca blurted angrily once Audrey was on the line. 'You and Ruby Stockton's daughter.'

'We didn't kill him.'

'And yet, he's dead.'

'Sherlock said Roylott wasn't in the vicinity when any of those twelve deaths occurred.'

'I never said Roylott wasn't there; I said there wasn't usually a snake around,' corrected Sherlock automatically.

Audrey ignored him. 'In the tunnel, Roylott referred to "His Nibs". He talked about him at Stoke Moran too, when he had your man, Melas,' she told Myca.

'William Ormstein and Seb Moran attacked Irene and her husband in Frankfurt too, and said, what was it Irene? *The Professor wants her alive.* Today, Roylott said my family was killed on His Nibs' orders, then he said someone named Mister Em wanted to send a message to you by capturing your brother, so this Em knows who both of you are.'

'M. The letter *M*,' said Irene abruptly. 'There is an M on the contacts list of Ormstein's phone.'

Sherlock nimbly picked up the cracked phone and threw it to Irene, who snatched it out of the air.

'Hold on,' Audrey reported to Myca. 'We have Ormstein's phone.'

Irene pressed her thumb to the indent and the screen opened. Sherlock rose to look over her shoulder, stumbling slightly. John was on his feet in a moment, his hands on Sherlock's stomach and shoulder to steady him. 'Not so quickly, Sherlock. You took a wallop yourself; you may experience some vertigo.'

'I'm *fine*.' Sherlock winced in instant regret as John pulled away.

Irene scrolled through the contacts list. A few of the names were known to them: Adelbert Gruner, Seb Moran, Grimsby Roylott, Gus Roylott. None of those entries held an address or even a phone number, though each had an 8-digit number in the Notes field.

Under all the entries for M, only one was of interest. Prof M was accompanied by the usual 8-digit number and under Company, the entry read: *Napoleon 62765366.*

'That hardly helps,' Irene said in disgust.

'Let me see.'

Sherlock took the phone back and flicked through the phone apps to find, alone on the last page, a little blue square with a white V, suggesting a Napoleonic uniform. The app was named *Napoleon* but across the blue and white square were the words *pour les bêtes.*

Curious, he fetched his own phone and searched for the app then downloaded it. He opened it and was presented with *Enter the Code.* He tapped in the digits 62765366.

'These digits correspond with the word "Napoleon" on the keypad,' said Sherlock as he typed. The moment the app opened, a message flashed on the screen: *Invitation Only. Enter Your Personal Code.*

Sherlock drew up the 8-digit code that appeared beside Grimsby Roylott's name. The little wheel-of-waiting whirled and then a new dialogue box appeared.

This Entry is Unauthorised. Deleting App.

The Napoleon app vanished from the screen.

'Well, that's curious.'

Audrey explained the progression of events to Myca, waiting impatiently on the other end of her line.

'Keep hold of that phone. I'm sending someone for it.' Myca hung up.

Irene was not impressed with the idea of surrendering her only clue to the Department of Fisheries. Audrey agreed with her, but John made the argument for the resources at the Department's disposal.

'Maybe Sherlock could–' he added, but looking around, he found Sherlock was no longer with them.

Nick jerked her head towards Sherlock's bedroom door, beyond the kitchen. 'He went off for a sulk.'

John sighed and limped to Sherlock's door. 'Sherlock. Sherlock, we need to talk about this. Sherlock?' He knocked but after no reply on the third attempt he cracked the door open.

Then he pushed it wide.

The bedroom was empty and the window facing the back yard was wide open.

Sherlock had done another bunk.

Chapter Fifteen

Irene Adler expressed herself in earthy German terms when she realised that Sherlock had departed with William Ormstein's incriminating phone.

John Watson, displaying an equally keen grasp of Anglo-Saxon terminology, gave as his qualified medical opinion that Sherlock Holmes was a goddamned idiot to go clambering down two storeys of ivy-clad pipes and brickwork with multiple injuries and if he fell and broke his fool neck, he deserved it. Then he fretted.

Nick peered over the windowsill into the back yard. 'Well, he's not lying in a bleeding heap in the lavender bushes, so he's probably fine.'

'Of course he is. The man's stupidly dextrous and stupidly athletic as well as stupidly bloody clever. The twat.'

'He is a twat,' Nick agreed, sliding an arm around John's shoulders. 'An utter pillock. A total arse.'

'He's not that bad.'

'Your libido is a terrible judge of character.'

'I'm a great judge of character, thanks.'

Nick grinned at him and squeezed his shoulders. 'You are. Terrific. I'm your best mate so I should know.'

John sagged into her hug. 'You're a bloody menace.'

'Yep. And you. Laying into that bloody great snake with a hatstand.

My little scrapper. Grrr.' She knuckled him on the chest and mock-punched him with a nudge to the jaw, then followed up with a smacking kiss to the forehead.

The sudden ring of a bell announced a visitor. Audrey left Nick and John to their post-adrenalin-high mucking about and went downstairs, Irene at her heels, to give Myca Holmes the bad news.

The hall carpet was still damp where the snake's venom had soaked into the fibres and spots of blood marked where John had been thrown against the wall and Sherlock to the ground during the struggle.

Irene's lips were set in a grim line. 'Mama never liked this carpet.'

'No,' Audrey said. 'She thought it was too busy.'

'You should replace it.'

'Yes. I suppose I should.'

Irene opened the front door as though it was hers. Audrey flinched in sudden realisation: Irene had grown up here, before her father had taken her away to Germany. Her mother had died without leaving her daughter anything but memories. This house, the cottage up in Northumberland, a tidy sum in savings and bonds, had all been left to Audrey when, by all natural rights, they belonged to Irene.

'Gottfried!'

Standing at the door was not Myca or any representative from the Department of Fisheries, but a tall Black man with short silver hair and beard, dressed in a mulberry coloured suit, crisp white shirt and a matching patterned tie. Dark sunglasses hid his eyes but the scent of his condition was unmistakable.

'Irene, darling, are you all right?' Gottfried Norton held a hand out to his wife, but not even a fingertip threatened to pass the threshold.

'I am, but this is far from over.' Irene took his hand and stepped onto the street. She turned towards Audrey.

'I called him while you were showering. I don't intend to meet your friend from the Fisheries.'

'She's not my friend.'

'And since Sherlock Holmes has stolen that phone, I see no reason to wait for her. Whether or not that department hunted me as a child, I have no reason to believe they represent good will.'

'I expect that's wise.'

'We have more to discuss. Contact me or Gottfried at the *Langham Hotel* when you have dismissed the Department.'

'Irene–'

'Later.'

Irene turned her back on Audrey. Gottfried gave her a tight smile, revealing the tips of his sharp teeth against his lower lip, then smoothly, faster than the eye could see, was at the parked Bentley, opening the passenger door for his wife. Irene slid gracefully into the vehicle. She did not look at Audrey as Gottfried drove them away.

Audrey closed the door and leaned her forehead against the wood rather than look at the mess in her foyer. Then she went home.

She recognised Sherlock's scent at once. Annoyed, she strode into her kitchen, where he sat in a chair with a thousand-yard stare.

'What are you doing here, Sherlock?'

Sherlock drooped in his seat and studied his hands. 'God knows.'

'John is worried that you might have fallen. He's afraid you'll hurt yourself.'

'Is he very angry?'

'Not as angry as he should be.'

'Is he all right?'

'Of course not, but he will be. Nick's still with him.'

'Oh wonderful. The friend who let him down.'

'And you didn't?'

'John and I aren't friends like that. Not comrades. We hardly know each other.'

Audrey sat opposite him, scraping the legs against the floor for maximum screech. He flinched, but it wasn't as satisfying as she'd hoped. This blunderingly kind boy was in knots, storm-tossed by events and the conflicts of his intellect, his reason, his heart and his hope.

'Don't be silly,' she said gently. 'I've seen how you are together, as though you were friends who'd just been waiting to meet. And I see how you look at him. I know how you talk about him. Even now, despite thinking he's lying to you. You're very fond of him.'

'Yes. Hardly reciprocal though, is it?'

Give me patience. 'John cares for you too. Surely, with your observational skills, you've seen that. You saw it not half an hour ago.'

'Then why doesn't he do anything?'

'Why don't you?'

'Panic, mostly.' Sherlock folded his arms on the table and hid his face on them.

Audrey wondered how best to break into the shrinking world Sherlock was making for himself. She recalled conversations she had overheard, and said, 'I think he believes he's too war torn, to be good for you. He doesn't believe he has much to offer.'

'Then he's an idiot.'

'Yes, it's something you have in common.'

He pulled a wry face then looked at her, his expression dismissing that topic for some new hell.

'The dog which Nick rightly says I saw in your back garden. It wasn't a dog. It was a wolf.' It was almost a question.

Audrey decided on the John Watson strategy of Truthtelling. She'd answer everything honestly, whether or not Sherlock was able to believe it yet. 'Yes, it was.'

'I've been reading up on wolves, since Dartmoor. I've spent too much time watching them on YouTube, wondering what happened to the wolf at Stoke Moran.' He cleared his throat. 'Just before you returned from chasing that snake, I looked out the front window and saw two wolves coming up the street. The grey wolf was limping. They stopped in front of this house. The grey stayed by the front door; the black one continued on and around the corner. I was curious; suspicious, I suppose, and went to my room to see if it had circled to the alley that runs behind us. I watched it jump the rear fence and go to your back door. I lost sight of it then. The little overhang and all your damned bamboo got in the way.'

'I see.'

'I returned to the front window, to see if the grey wolf was still there. It was, and then a Black woman opened the door from within the house and carried the grey wolf inside. And, after a while – long enough to bathe and change, say – you and Irene Adler came upstairs.'

Audrey waited.

'After I closed my door on that ridiculous conversation just now, I climbed from my window into the yard and followed the wolf tracks to your rear door. Where they stopped. You shouldn't leave your key under the flowerpot, by the way. Anyone could find it.'

'I'm not generally very concerned about burglars.'

'No. I imagine not. Because you keep – wolves. Except, your house does not contain wolves, despite the fact that two wolves entered your flat, Mrs Hudson. Wolf tracks are distinctive; John taught me that. Their tracks lead to your back door, but not away. The traces I found in your apartment vanished mid-stride, it seemed. No other evidence. Two wolves, Mrs Hudson. That vanished without leaving.'

'Yes.'

'What are you really, Mrs Hudson?'

'I'm exactly what I say I am.'

Sherlock had begun to examine his fingernails, reluctant now to meet her gaze. 'My sister used to love the outdoors, you know. Climbing, walking, studying nature.'

Audrey tensed. She didn't know where this was leading, but she knew where it began. Myca Holmes, who pretended to be an eccentric human, but was also really something *other*.

'We were holidaying around Caenarfon when Myca–' Sherlock stopped short, took a breath, and began again. 'She was fourteen and very independent. She decided to spend a day walking in the national park. Being half her age and a pest, I followed her, from a distance of course, so she wouldn't tell me to bugger off. So I saw when she slipped from a path and fell into a lake. It was called *Llyn y Dywarchen* on the map, Turf Lake. I ran to her as quickly as I could and waded in, but she'd sunk below the water. No bubbles could even tell me where she'd gone. I ran for help. I was so certain she'd drowned, but when we finally got back to the lake, she was lying, soaking wet, on the shore, unconscious but alive. She woke up in the car on the way to the hospital, and every test indicated she was unharmed. She was never the same, though. She always hid from the open sky, after that.'

Finally he raised his haunted gaze to meet Audrey's.

'She started collecting books on folklore, finding obscure references, seeking tall tales from anyone who'd share them. She's incredibly smart, my sister. Her capacity for soaking up knowledge is almost miraculous. If she'd let this– this obsession interfere with her studies, our parents would have intervened, but it has run alongside her academic and government work for decades, without damaging her record.'

'Experiences that bring you close to death can change you,' Audrey offered.

'We went home soon after her accident,' Sherlock said, without addressing the suggestion. 'Myca was unusually quiet, but otherwise well. Then one night I dreamed that Myca was submerged in the bathtub, fully clothed, her face under the water while her legs hung over the sides. She was always too tall for that tub.' A quirk of a sad, fond smile was there and gone.

'I watched her, transfixed. In my dream. I watched for fifteen minutes – I timed it on my watch – and she never moved. I thought she'd drowned again and I was too late, again, to save her. I was afraid, in the dream, to find out if Myca was really dead. I didn't want her to be. I wanted her to wake up and be like she used to be. To play with me and teach me. When I couldn't bear it any more, I gathered my courage and touched her arm. It was warm. Under the water, her eyes opened and she looked at me, right into my brain, it felt like, and I was too afraid to scream or run. Then she sat bolt upright in the tub. Water sloshed everywhere, over the sides, over the floor, over my slippers and the legs of my pyjamas. Her eyes were so strange, the colour of the lake shifting with the sunlight and clouds on it. And she said. In my dream. She said, "Sherlock, I'm all right, and I won't hurt you, but you mustn't look". She said it without moving her lips. I ran and hid in my bed, with the covers over me, hoping she wouldn't ever look at me like that again.'

Audrey reached for his hand, but he pulled away.

'It was a dream, of course, but next morning Mama found me limp with fever. I spent days in hospital, hardly conscious, rambling, having hallucinations. The doctor diagnosed pneumonia, exacerbated by shock, probably a delayed reaction to what had happened at *Llyn y Dywarchen*. The fever broke eventually. It took time to rebuild my strength, of course, and I was terribly bored even after they let me go home.

'That's when I began learning how to observe what I saw, to seek signals below the surface of what people said and did, because everyone was tiptoeing around us and wouldn't talk about how our parents had nearly lost both their children in a month. I would study people, study ideas, apply them where I could. It was, in truth, the event that I can identify as the first step towards becoming what I am: a consulting detective. It all came from those weeks recovering.'

'Something good came of it, then.'

'You might say that. Curiously, I soon learned that the only thing nobody was ever able to understand or account for, the night I got sick, was how I came to go to bed and to fall asleep, wearing soaking wet slippers and pyjamas.'

The unspoken meaning of it hung between them. The dream that had not been a dream. But Sherlock wouldn't articulate it. He'd pushed the notion out there to look at but then refused to look at it. If she hadn't been so drained by the out-of-moonlight changes and the battle with Roylott, she might have been able to shift, to show him incontrovertible evidence – but Audrey also felt instinctively that if she tried to make him face it, he would retreat, perhaps into unbalanced denial. She approached the issue obliquely instead.

'You can let this break you, Sherlock, or you can let it change you. Knowledge is what you do. This is just new knowledge.'

Sherlock pushed away from the table and rose. 'You're all mad.' But he was clearly not convinced by his own deductions. 'And I'm almost as mad as the rest of you.'

Audrey followed him as he strode, limping, to the door. He headed for the street, only to jerk the door open to his agitated sister, standing there in her sunglasses, hat pulled low over her eyes, hand raised to the knocker. He stood back to allow her the immediate shelter of getting under a roof and away from the sky she so disliked.

'Sherlock.'

'Myca. You've come for Irene Adler's phone, I suppose.' He'd pulled it from his pocket and held it between them. Her hand closed on it but he kept brief hold of it. She lifted her chin, a gesture he read as one of inquiry.

'Are you still my sister?'

'Always, Sherlock. Always.'

He released the phone, shaking his head sharply, possibly at her answer, possibly at himself for even asking such a peculiar question. Then he sagged, too exhausted to grapple with these frightening, mysterious contradictions any further.

'I'm going home,' he said, and turned to trudge upstairs.

Audrey tilted an eyebrow at Myca. 'I thought you were sending someone.'

'My staff are occupied at present,' Myca said, 'and this is too important for delay.'

'It's full of photographs of Ormstein's...'

'Assassinations,' said Myca.

'Is that what they are?'

'It's one interpretation. He could simply enjoy killing for its own sake – his history suggests it – but recent events indicate a guiding hand at work.'

'Professor M,' said Audrey at once. 'That's how he's listed in the phone. What recent events?'

Myca pursed her lips.

'Stop it. Right now,' said Audrey sternly. 'Enough of your damned secrets. Too much is happening. Roylott came here to kill me, to send you a message by killing poor Sherlock. John and Nick were caught up in it too. Ormstein tried to kill Irene two days ago, in the company of Roylott's son–'

'Stepson. It was Sebastian Moran, not Angus. We don't know where Gus is, at present.'

'Right. And here we have evidence that the bully who called himself the King of Bohemia killed my family, has been killing others, and takes trophy photos.' The bile was bitter in the back of her throat.

'He won't be doing any more of that.'

The next angry comment died in Audrey's throat. 'What?'

'In addition to Sherlock's new leads regarding those twelve unsolved murders, my staff are presently occupied with Ormstein's death and the disappearance of Irene Adler and her husband Gottfried Norton after they left Baker Street half an hour ago.'

Audrey didn't want to sound stupid by saying *what*? again but she felt incredibly dense with confusion.

'William Ormstein's body was found in the Rhine this morning. The bullet to his heart had been removed, probably with a hunting knife, but the preliminary forensic report shows silver in the wound. I believe that in misplacing his telephone, Ormstein effectively exhausted his usefulness. The architect of these incidents must have instructed Sebastian Moran to eliminate the risk of further mistakes.'

'And Irene?'

'We tracked Mr Norton's arrival here – he's been on our radar for some years, though as a German citizen, if the undead might still be considered citizens, he's not strictly our concern. We know he and Ms Adler left a short while ago in a black car, which disappeared somewhere between Baker Street and their accommodation at the *Langham Hotel*.'

'*It's a ten minute drive.*'

'I am well aware. The walk would have been more convenient, given various road works. Our assumption is they drove to spare Mr Norton too much time in the sun. It wouldn't kill him, as you're doubtless aware, but sunlight reduces his strength and they were clearly determined that this not happen.'

'And yet, they've vanished.'

'And yet,' Myca conceded. 'I expect that at least one set of road works was bogus and redirected their vehicle. How a natural werewolf and a vampire were then overcome is the key mystery my team is trying to solve.'

Audrey threw her hands up. 'I can't believe I wasted so many years being so afraid of a department so riddled with farcical incompetence.'

'A little harsh,' said Myca.

'Prove me wrong.'

A heavy tread on the stairs and Nick's, 'Prove you wrong about what?' interrupted them. Nick halted at the last step. 'Ah, shit. I was supposed to be keeping away from her, wasn't I?' Nick lifted her chin and took on a fighting stance, despite the bruises and obvious bodily aches.

Myca looked Nick over from behind her dark glasses. 'A new werewolf,' she observed. 'You're not on my books.'

'And it better stay that way,' said Audrey sharply.

'I haven't been called on to fight an Amazon queen before.' Nick twitched her shoulders, loosening them, and held her fists in readiness. She was clearly appraising Myca's magnificent height and build. 'I'm game, though. I beat up a giant snake with an umbrella this morning. You look much more fun to wrestle with, at any rate.'

'Thank you,' said Myca drily.

Nick grinned suddenly. 'Nah, seriously, tall, dark and strapping is kind of what I like in a gal.'

Myca, nonplussed, looked to Audrey for assistance.

'Stop flirting with the enemy.'

'Is she, though? The enemy?' Nick asked, dropping out of her boxer pose.

Myca sighed. 'I am not.'

'Great. Let's head out for a drink, then, 'coz fuck knows I need one.'

'Are they fighting again?' Audrey asked, head tilted to listen but she couldn't hear raised voices from Sherlock and John's flat.

'Worse than that. I think they're making up. The second Sherl came in the door, he was all low-key hangdog, and Johnny was all solicitous bedside manner, wanting to look at his poor little ankle, and then they started muttering at each other. It was all very earnest and they were somehow apologising without either of them saying the S word and then Johnny said something to make Mr Pretty laugh, and then he said something to make John laugh and, swear to God, I think they forgot I was there. I snuck out while the going was good, which is slightly more dignified than waiting till they're actually snogging.'

Now that Audrey was listening carefully, it was possible snogging may already have commenced, and she was torn between feeling pleased for them and condemning their terrible timing.

'Pub,' insisted Nick.

'We could just sit in the park,' suggested Audrey.

'Don't go policing my drinking,' Nick snapped suddenly, then she was contrite. 'I'm also still a bit buggy around loud noises. Sometimes. I'm probably in enough disgrace as it is, without diving for cover if a car backfires. Jesus Christ on a Ferris wheel, Mrs H, why do I tell you these things?'

'She's an Alpha,' Myca explained, 'and she has a rather formidable personality.'

'She has at that. I'm just a mouthy arsehole.'

Audrey wondered why Nick kept saying such things about herself, though the mouthy part wasn't inaccurate. And perhaps she was also buggy about loud noises. Myca, she remembered, was a little buggy herself in open spaces.

'All right. The pub it is. We have things to discuss, Holmes.'

'We could just...' Myca gestured towards Audrey's apartment.

'Please don't let us be sitting there with all this supernatural hearing when your brother and my best mate are getting slippery,' Nick pleaded. 'I've had a hell of a day.'

Nick's vivid description sealed the deal. They left to find a pub.

Chapter Sixteen

NICK DOWNED HER FIRST BEER RIGHT AT THE COUNTER LIKE SHE WAS necking it for Olympic Gold, then belched with a hand over her mouth. ''Scuse. Fuck me, I needed that.' She signalled for another and carried it to the table.

Myca's expression was hidden under her hat and dark glasses, but Audrey had raised an eyebrow.

'Oh, don't,' Nick said, annoyed. 'I know I spent the last two months drunk as a fart, but I've been completely dry the whole damned week and that's just not normal. It's not like I plan to pickle myself.'

Audrey said nothing. Nick sighed. 'Fine, so I tried to pickle myself.' She sipped her beer, placed it carefully on a coaster and gazed at the slowly rising golden bubbles. 'Can't do that anymore, can I? Not if I'm going to go howling every month. God knows who I'll hurt without meaning to.'

Audrey tutted slightly and Nick huffed back. 'She knows, though, doesn't she? Holmes' mystery sister. Head honcho of the Anti Gremlin brigade. You know all about me, don't you, lady?'

Myca tilted her head in what might have been good humour. 'I had no idea you existed until you came down the stairs, though it's true I identified your lycanthropy at once.'

'Don't suppose you can identify why I couldn't wolf-up when that snake-rat-bastard tried to kill me and Johnny? Mrs H said new werewolves could, *in extremis*.'

'I said it was unpredictable,' said Audrey.

'We were pretty *in-fuckin'-extremis*, I thought. Percy could do it, and he was never half as much of a brawler as I can be.' Nick slugged down another mouthful, clearly distressed and angered by her inability to shift when she'd needed to protect her friend.

'Our research shows that sudden, un-mooned human-to-*were* transformations in new *weres* is much less common than the reverse,' said Myca matter-of-factly. 'Factors such as how many changes a *were* has previously undergone are significant. If you've previously been inebriated, your body will not make those out-of-cycle transitions easily, if at all.'

She noticed how aghast her audience was. 'What?'

'Your... research,' said Audrey stiffly.

'Research,' agreed Myca firmly. 'Observations undertaken with volunteers. Interviews and questionnaires. A literature review of historical information from our archives. I am not,' she said, coldly, 'in the habit of conducting live vivisections or involuntary investigative trials on sentient beings.'

Nick blinked at her. 'So I didn't wolf up because I'm not practised enough at wolfing up to have done it in broad daylight without a full moon in sight.'

'Precisely.'

'Well, that's a relief, I suppose. And bloody inconvenient.'

'I imagine being a werewolf is at least 90 per cent bloody inconvenience,' said Myca.

'Dunno. Haven't been sober enough in the last few months to find out.'

'But you expect to be so from now on?'

'Looks like.' Nick took another pull of beer and made a show of putting the glass back down.

'You aren't afraid I'm going to drag you away and lock you up for experiments?'

'Nah,' said Nick with a sudden grin. 'You're all right. Probably. Like Johnny, I am an excellent judge of character. If you haven't hauled Mrs H off anywhere, you're not going to haul me off unless I become a public nuisance, are you?'

'No.'

'Cheers. You're a very lovely Amazon Queen.' Nick raised her glass, winked and took a sip.

Audrey decided to rescue Myca, despite how much she was enjoying the woman's perplexed expression.

'What are you doing about Irene?'

Myca seemed grateful to not have to parse the continued, and still startling, flirting. She glanced at her phone and then back to Audrey.

'My team has found the car stowed inside a disused garage in the dogleg section of Seymour Mews. A false traffic diversion *had* been set up and subsequently cleared, which is how they became trapped. That section is a dead end behind Duke Street. There's evidence of a struggle but not as much property damage as I would have expected in a fight against a vampire and a werewolf. I suspect wolfsbane gas was used on Irene, perhaps a garlic equivalent for Norton. There's no evidence Norton was staked at the scene – no ash or other remains – so we must act at present as though both have been taken.'

'Who by?' Nick asked, grimly fascinated.

'My assessment is that Sebastian Moran has continued with his mission to abduct Ms Adler, having despatched of Ormstein for his incompetence. Speaking of whom.' Myca pulled out Ormstein's phone and examined the device but it stubbornly refused to budge from the ugly image on the lock screen. 'How did you access Ormstein's assassination photographs?'

Audrey winced at a term that was both clinical and brutal. 'Irene's clever. She used Ormstein's detached thumb to activate the screen, then programmed the phone with her own fingerprint. Now that she's been kidnapped I'm not sure how you'll manage.'

'I'm sure my brother found a way past that. He's passably good at cyphers.' Myca attempted several 6-digit codes which failed to produce a result. She sighed and slid the phone back into a pocket. 'I'll speak to Sherlock.'

She rose to leave, but Audrey seized her by the coat cuff and pulled her back down.

'No. We talk first. I want to know everything you know.'

Myca's crooked smile was smug as much as weary. 'Sherlock likes to joke that my speciality is omniscience, so I don't think that's entirely achievable. But regarding the matters in hand: it's clear that some driving force is behind Moran's actions – likely this Professor M that Irene Adler identified in Ormstein's contacts. Ormstein is dead; Roylott Senior is dead;

my people are scouring London for Sebastian Moran. Burdened with a captive werewolf and possibly a vampire, he ought to be easy to identify, but as nobody has called me yet, he's clearly smarter than that. The only other obvious lead is the other Roylott. The son, Angus.'

Nick sucked foam from her upper lip. 'I wonder where he's buggered off to.'

'He's not at Stoke Moran,' Myca said. 'We've had it under surveillance since we recovered Mr Melas. Ormstein and Moran went to Germany, but Angus and his father remained behind.'

'So where did Gus go while his old man came slithering around Johnny's place?' Nick said. 'Coz if that was my crew, I'd keep him around for back-up. One thing you can count on during a mission is that something's going to go tits-up, and that was one hell of a FUBAR situation for Snake-Eyes this morning, eh?'

Audrey reacted with alarm; so did Myca, who speed-dialled someone to demand a report on Angus Roylott's whereabouts. Her body language said everything that couldn't be seen in her eyes as she bolted for the door.

Nick abandoned her beer to race after Myca, then stopped to help Audrey along. Too long sitting had stiffened her hip, but as soon as they were on the street she shook off Nick's hand and dashed towards home.

Myca was on the phone as she strode along. 'Get to 221B Baker Street! Now! I have no idea, but if he was waiting as a back-up operative for his father's mission, he might well have moved on the occupants already.'

So much for omniscient, Audrey thought, bitterly.

They were a ludicrous sight, the three women hurrying and hobbling their way through Marylebone towards the Georgian mansion on Baker Street. Myca's surprising slow grace had vanished as she lumbered along in unaccustomed speed; Audrey's non-lunar transformation and battle exertions today had resulted in a bone-deep ache that could only be countered so far by panicked adrenalin; Nick, even knocked about after the fight and with a damaged foot, reached the front door first.

She bashed on the locked door. 'Johnny! John!!! Spit out your boyfriend and open this fucking door!'

Audrey elbowed Nick aside to unlock the door and throw it open, in time to hear Sherlock's voice in a heartfelt cry.

'*JOHN!*'

It was not a cry of passion – it was a roar of desperation, of fear and rage.

And despite what the day had already cost her, Audrey sprinted up those stairs two at a time, summoning all her diminishing strength. Nick and Myca were at her heels as she burst through the half-open door of 221B, already beginning to change.

Audrey was a strange, half-shaped horror of human-and-wolf wrapped in strained and tearing clothing. She could smell blood (John's and the intruder's) and fear (Sherlock's) and rage (everybody's) before she launched herself, still mid-transformation, at the likewise half-formed creature grappling with John and Sherlock in the sitting room.

Gus Roylott's body was still human, but the face on his bald and scaly head was noseless, its round black eyes lidless under scaled ridges. The lipless mouth was stretched wide, baring glistening needle-like fangs. He had one fist in John's hair; a gun was in his other hand.

John, in nothing but his boxer shorts, was pushing the heel of his hand into the soft vulnerability of Gus' pale throat, trying to keep him from getting closer. John's bruises from the struggle with Roylott Senior had already darkened, though a flush of stubble-burn along his collarbone indicated intimacies had been interrupted by the intrusion.

A long, thin gash on his chest was bleeding; a bloodied knife lay on the floor between them.

Sherlock, trousered but shirtless, revealing bruises and stubble rash similar to John's, was too enraged to be cowed by Gus' gun. He had brought the poker to bear with a snarl worthy of any wolf, and was feinting and lunging at their assailant, keeping him too distracted to bite John.

Audrey's bowel-curdling growl at this filthy reptile – who dared to enter her home and to attack her new family – dangerously distracted Sherlock and John; but fortunately, it diverted the snake-man's attention too.

'Yyyyyooou,' Gus said with a mouth not best made for human speech. He held fast to John with one faintly scaled hand, and aimed his gun at her heart.

Audrey was peripherally aware of a sudden radiant light glowing from the landing, flooding the apartment; and of Myca's voice chanting in a low register that also somehow burbled and rushed, a demi-song in the language of brooks and running streams, storms and showers, waterfalls and mists.

And from nowhere came a surge of energy, an almost painful sparkle along every nerve, in every blood vessel in Audrey's body.

Snake-headed Gus pulled the trigger but missed as Audrey shifted entirely into wolf, no longer occupying the space at which he'd aimed.

She leapt.

At the same time, another wolfish figure leapt through the door, limned in bright light, and joined her in knocking Gus Roylott back. John wrenched free of his assailant's iron grip, leaving Gus with strands of brown hair in his fingers.

The other wolf – Nick Murray, three-legged and wild with rage – dropped with a slam onto the floor and lost her balance. She scrabbled to her paws again and stood between Gus and John, her hackles raised and teeth bared. She snarled at all comers, even Sherlock as he tried to go to John.

Sherlock took a swipe at the wolf with his poker but John yelled at him. 'No! Stop! That's Nick! Sherlock, that's Nick Murray! Nick, you recognise Sherlock, don't you? C'mon Nick. Show me you're in there.'

Gus Roylott had recovered both his footing and a second gun from somewhere on his person, so now he was doubly armed. He pointed one gun at Audrey, the other at Sherlock. Venom gathered on the tips of the fangs protruding from his scaly, lipless mouth.

John darted to intercept; Nick pivoted on her hind leg and knocked him to the ground as Gus fired again, and missed again.

Heedless of the danger, Audrey rushed Gus. Her teeth closed on the wrist of the hand holding the gun. She bit hard, crunching through skin and flesh and tendon and bone, and Gus screamed, a combined shrill shriek and hiss, and dropped the weapon.

Audrey shook him in her mouth, snarling, and when the crushed and broken hand went limp, she released it and dragged him away from her boys by his shoulder. Muscle tore under the power of her jaws, bone cracked, and blood filled her mouth. She shook him. One of her wolf paws became a hairy, clawed hand as she groped for his second gun.

Gus, yelling in agony and fury, pulled the trigger of the gun now trapped between them. He might as easily have shot himself as her. But for once, he hit his target.

A lead bullet would have meant nothing but a moment's pain; even point blank, it would have passed through her body; bled for a few seconds; and a minute later, her skin wouldn't even be scarred.

But this bullet was silver and it *burned* a searing channel through her thigh. The skin of it was fire in her flesh, igniting the cells and veins around it. It burned, and the strange energy that had compelled her transformation fled her body.

Almost mindless with agony, Audrey yelped. Gus tried to stagger away from her but her predator instinct knew he would escape, would hurt her again, would hurt her cubs. She would die before she lost anyone else. She would kill before then, too, to protect them.

Audrey snapped at his throat, teeth sinking through scales and flesh. Venom dripped onto her fur as he struggled. Before he could break free, she braced herself, jerked her long chin, and tore his throat out.

His blood sprayed over her snout and into her eyes as he fell away. He made an awful gurgling noise as he died.

Audrey collapsed the other way, her body transforming again as her howl of pain morphed to the gasping cry of an old woman in terrible distress.

'Nick, get *off*, I'm fine!'

Audrey felt hands on her shoulders and she snapped feebly before she realised it was John. He had taken up the hem of her torn dress and ripped it to gain access to the wound in her thigh.

Audrey was suddenly aware of Sherlock frozen in place, eyes round, staring at her with horror. It broke her heart and she would have cried if her body had room for grief as well as agony.

She was aware of Nick, too, also suddenly in her human form again; bemused and horrified, half naked and terribly vulnerable in her torn clothes and the stump of her amputated leg pushing on the carpet as she tried to rise.

Audrey was shuddering against the silver in her wound, but even in that state she was alarmed by the glowing creature who had entered the room.

Myca Holmes looked like the goddess of the drowned. The hat, scarf, coat, glasses were gone, revealing bedewed pale skin that glistened and shone. Her long, dark hair flowed about her face like reeds in a riverbed. Her eyes. *Oh, her eyes*, were rain upon a mere, were the dapples of light and shade on a cheerful brook, and at the same time they were the still, dark, deeps of a fathomless underground lake. And she glowed with light, with phosphorescence.

'We are...' she began, her voice like clear water, but her mouth did not move.

A sudden crack of glass interrupted her. Her body jerked briefly forward and she looked down with surprise at her unblemished chest.

Myca turned unhurriedly, graceful as a slow and rolling wave. Across the room, the bow window had a neat hole in it, where the sniper's bullet had punctured it, before puncturing her back. Audrey could see the blood blooming between Myca's shoulder blades.

Myca, untroubled, lifted her phone, dialled, and said in her human voice, softened with a musical lilt, 'Sniper in the empty house across the street. Moran, I expect. Go.'

She dropped the phone and turned back to those watching her. She lifted her hand to her mouth and, ever so delicately, spat a small pebble and a quantity of bloodstained water into it.

Not a pebble. A compacted bullet.

'Myca?' Sherlock cried out in a small, frightened voice; the voice of a little boy fearing his sister had drowned in the lake.

Myca smiled at him. 'I'm all right, Sherlock. Silver doesn't hurt me.' This time, her lips moved.

'What are you?'

'I'm your sister. And I'm someone else too. I'm all right. We must look after Mrs Hudson now.' And she didn't look like a drowned spirit any more, only like Myca Holmes, bedraggled and exhausted with wet hair straggling over her shoulders.

She cast a worried look at Audrey, and Audrey knew how awful *she* must look because Myca instantly tried to hide her reaction.

'Silver hurts your landlady, however. You'll need to get it out, Dr Watson. Quickly.'

John shook off his wonderment. 'I need a knife,' he said in the sharp tone of command. 'Something long and sharp. Or get my bag if you can find it. Sherlock?'

Sherlock unfroze, though he stumbled as he went to the kitchen drawer. He came up with a boning knife.

John held out his hand for it and Sherlock placed the tool in his palm.

'Be careful,' Audrey warned John weakly, the drive to protect them overcoming her pain. 'Don't get... my blood in your cuts.'

John nodded acknowledgement but his focus was on triage. Sherlock, who seemed acutely aware of everything now, whipped his shirt off and wrapped it across John's bloodied chest, tied it at the back.

'Sherlock, I'll need water to irrigate the wound in a while.' Sherlock retreated to the kitchen to fetch it. 'Hold on, Mrs Hudson,' said John in a gentle, firm voice. 'This will hurt.'

'Already hurts. Get it out. Get the silver out. Please.'

John carefully probed around the injury. Blood, abnormally congealing, oozed from it. 'Usually, I'd do this a lot differently,' he said as he worked. 'Ordinary bullets in ordinary people should stay right where they are until I can get you into surgery. Does more damage digging them out than leaving them *in situ*, half the time.'

As he spoke, he used the knife to cut the entry wound wider. More congealed blood, blackening now, spilled. Audrey cried out in pain.

'*John!*' Nick wailed. She tried to rise again but she fell with a cry. 'John, let me help!'

'Stay put, Nick,' he told her firmly, then he resumed his quiet commentary. 'Mrs Hudson, I'm going to take this out with my hands. It's the fastest way to get the silver out, and it's clearly toxic to you.'

John's thumb and finger were in the bloody furrow. Audrey felt them moving, felt when he'd snagged the lump of silver and began to draw it out.

'I learned from Percy that a werewolf's natural healing capacity is pretty amazing. I'll get antibiotics in there as soon as I can, but this comes out first. Sorry it's so clumsy.'

Audrey wanted to tell him it was fine, she understood, but she could only whimper and grit her teeth against the need to cry out.

Then the pain was suddenly reduced as John removed his fingers, and the bullet, from her thigh.

Myca walked past them to kneel beside the keening Nick. 'There, there,' said Myca awkwardly, patting Nick's shoulder. 'Dr Watson is looking after her. She'll be all right.'

With the bullet removed, Audrey's whimper became a strained sigh. It hurt less now, but not by much.

Sherlock had returned with the kettle. 'It was boiled earlier, but it's cool enough now.'

John held the deep gash open with his fingers and poured the water into it, sluicing out the traces of silver along with clumps of congealed blood. When he ran out of water – and Audrey's blood was flowing healthily red again – he sent Sherlock for more, from the tap this time.

Finally, John dared to place his fingers on her cheek. 'There, now. Has that helped?'

'Yes.' She blinked at him, tears in her eyes. 'Is that Roylott bastard dead? Really dead?'

He stroked her hair. 'I haven't checked.' With a corner of her torn blouse, he tried to clean her bloodied face.

'He's dead," says Sherlock in almost his normal voice. 'John. More water.'

Another sluicing of the wound followed. Audrey sighed as her heart rate slowed and the burning quietened to an ache.

'It's healing already,' John told her. 'What else do you need?'

'She needs iron,' said Myca. Somehow she had ended up on the floor, holding Nick in her steady, no-nonsense arms. Nick's face was pressed into Myca's shoulder. 'Beef, lamb, any raw red meat.'

'There's raw mince in the fridge, Sherlock,' John said. He was gently stroking Audrey's dishevelled hair. 'Can you get it?'

Sherlock brought the mince along with the blanket that normally lived, folded, on their sofa, which had ended up on the floor long before Gus Roylott had broken in. Sherlock covered Audrey with it. That's when Audrey realised that Myca Holmes was the only one of them still fully dressed.

It'd been a hell of a day, but at least John and Sherlock had had better reason to be semi-naked at the start of all this.

John pinched some mince in his fingers, rolled it into a ball and held it to her mouth. She took it carefully, afraid of biting him accidentally; chewed and swallowed. Almost at once, she felt better.

'Be careful of the blood,' she said again to John.

'I know,' he said, calm and confident, even though she could scent the adrenalin still coursing through him. He fed her another bite-sized ball of mince. Blood from the shallow cut in his chest had begun to seep through the shirt wrapped across him, in a thin, sporadic line.

"We should see to that," Sherlock said.

'It's not deep. I won't need stitches.' John inhaled then exhaled a slow breath. 'Stings a bit. Are you all right, Sherlock?'

'Fine.'

'You don't sound fine.'

'I'm... reassessing.'

'Okay. Well.' He didn't push. 'I should get my first aid kit.'

'And put on some trousers,' said Audrey, then opened her mouth for the next ball of mince, like a baby bird.

John fed her then pushed the remaining mince into Sherlock's hands. 'Look after her,' he said. 'I'll be right back.'

Sherlock settled by Audrey on the floor and lifted her head into his lap.

Despite herself, tears glistened. 'Don't be afraid of me, Sherlock. I'd never hurt you.'

'Well, of course not.' He rolled a small ball of raw mince and helped her to eat it while John retrieved and donned his trousers.

Sherlock picked up a shirt from the floor – John's, all its buttons torn. Sherlock soaked a corner of it with water from the remains of the jug of tap water and began to wipe her face and throat clean. He washed the patch of hair matted with venom and let all of it – water, blood, poison – seep into the rug. It was ruined anyway, drenched with the blood of the dead man-snake behind them.

John stopped to kiss the top of Nick's head. 'We're all okay, Nick. Let me get my kit and check you over.'

'Y-y-y-you see to that c-cut,' Nick admonished him, teeth chattering. 'If you let one of us wolves b-bleed on you and you c-catch this thing I'll b-bite your bloody ears off.'

'Gotta catch me first,' he said with a wry grin. He nodded at Myca, even managing to look into her water spirit eyes with only a slight wince. 'You all right?'

'I am always all right.'

He nodded. 'Right. Back soon.'

He went to the landing to bring in Nick's prosthetic leg and her suspension sleeve, which had fallen free of her stump as she'd transformed, and left them beside her before going to the bathroom to find the first aid kit.

While he was gone, Sherlock, still feeding raw meat to his landlady and cleaning her face, looked towards his sister.

'Myca. What did you do on the landing to turn these two into werewolves even though it's not the full moon?'

'You're not going to ask why a bullet didn't kill me?'

'Drowning didn't kill you; I assume that's more of the same. You glowing like a beacon and letting supernatural beings change shape on an average Tuesday is new level of weird. I'll need the full *Penguin Study Notes* later, of course, but let's get me up to speed on this, at least. Who or what else is living in there with you, sister mine?'

CHAPTER SEVENTEEN

Myca's expression as she gazed at her little brother was far from unfathomable. Normally so controlled, hidden behind her glasses and austere mien, now she seemed full of vulnerable hope.

'She is a mermaid of the mere. A lady of the lake. Morgen is another name, though it's not precisely fair to say she and her sisters lure people to their deaths.'

'How did she lure you into the lake that day? Precisely?' asked Sherlock, brisk and business-like. Having chosen to accept what he'd seen, he seemed intent on gathering data.

'She didn't lure me. I fell. She means no harm.'

'But she drowned you and moved in to your body. Didn't she?'

'I invited her in. She saved me from drowning.'

Audrey closed her eyes wearily, and listened. Sherlock was too preoccupied to continue feeding her, but that was fine. She was sufficiently recovered, and this was important; and not only to Sherlock.

'I slipped on the path and fell into the lake,' Myca said. 'The water was freezing. My clothes and shoes filled up with it. I became so heavy, I sank. When I finally tried to fight it, I was too deep. I was swallowing water. My legs were tangled in the weeds at the bottom of lake, keeping me down. And then she was there, shimmering with green light. I was too surprised to be afraid. Her hands touched my face, even colder than the water, and she smiled. Such sharp teeth. And her eyes were like a storm. She spoke and I could hear her in my mind. So clever, she said. So young. We need someone like you. Will you help me? And I told her...without speaking aloud, I said, I'm dying. And she said...I can save you, if you let me in. She was so beautiful, Sherlock. Terrifying and beautiful. And I could hear you calling for me. I wanted to go home. I said. Don't hurt my brother. She smiled, like the thought hadn't occurred to her until I put it there. She said she didn't want you; a boy, even a clever boy, was not for her.'

'So you invited her in. She would have let you die, otherwise.' His tone was brittle.

'No. No, I don't think so. She had no reason to save me, I suppose, but she was curious about me. At least as curious as I was about her. I held out my hand and I thought, come in. Come in and I'll help you. And the next moment, she was in my mouth and blood and eyes, and I was on the shore, and you'd brought help.'

'She doesn't sound as beneficent as you think,' Sherlock said, troubled. 'And you – *she* – had the power to force Mrs Hudson and Nick to transform, days after the full moon. I can only assume that's not a normal occurrence.'

'Not for me it bloody isn't,' muttered Nick.

'I called upon the Lady's resources to save you from the serpent, Sherlock. It was necessary and I had no time to seek permission.'

'I suppose not. Still. I know I'm terribly ignorant in these matters, but I'm not aware of any folklore giving the Lady of the Lake powers over werewolves. *Le Morte d'Arthur* is strangely silent on the subject when discussing the troubles of Sirs Marrok and Gorlagon.'

'The Lady has certain affinities. Water and the moon have long been drawn to each other. It's one of the reasons why I am not comfortable outside anymore.'

Sherlock shook his head in protest. 'I am not convinced that the being that inhabits you is benign.'

Myca's gaze fell to Audrey. 'It's a balance,' she said in appeal. 'I strive to keep a balance. You understand. I explained.'

Audrey wasn't at all sure she believed that. She wondered if Myca or the water spirit spoke. 'So you say.'

'I could harm you, but I don't. The Fisheries could take you in for your own safety, but–'

'Don't you fucking dare.' Nick, draped in her torn shirt that only part covered her thighs, paused in the midst of pulling her leg on over her

THE SHE-WOLF OF BAKER STREET

sleeve-encased stump and glared at Myca. 'You keep your flippers off Mrs H. I don't care how beautiful a mermaid or water nymph or what-the-fuck you are. You're not touching Mrs H.'

'No, that's what I'm saying,' said Myca, flustered to suddenly be out of favour with the one who'd been flirting so hard. 'The world of humans and the world of the fae are out of true. She and I seek to restore balance. Sometimes that work is difficult and maligned, but it's done for the sake of all. Mrs Hudson is in deep need of protection–'

'We'll protect her. Me and Johnny. Sherlock too, if he hasn't gone off his nut by now.'

Sherlock grimaced, as though he wasn't sure of that himself.

'He appears perfectly rational,' Myca said, apparently to reassure herself as much as Sherlock, 'and you are leading us from the subject. Someone is trying to undo all we've worked towards. William Ormstein has been murdering his fellow *weres*; he has been part of a campaign of death and disharmony. Sherlock has uncovered a secret, concerted effort to control sacred water sources. We–'

Her phone rang, a prosaic jingle interrupting her explanation. Myca's impatience showed as she spoke to the caller before she took a breath. 'Well, do you know where he went?' The answer made her no happier. 'Did you discover any sign of Irene Adler or Gottfried Norton? Very well. We have a dead naga here on the second floor; Roylott's son. He doesn't appear to have been capable of a full transformation, like his father, but we cannot allow an ordinary police investigation to take place. Send two teams.'

John's return – carrying a spare pair of his own khaki joggers and a T-shirt retrieved from the drier for Nick – coincided with the end of the call. He gave the clothes to Nick and began to ask after her injuries. She shook out the joggers but waved him onward. 'I'm good, John. You better check your boy hasn't tipped over the edge.'

Once Myca's focus was back on her work, Sherlock's business-like expression had faltered. A muscle twitched at the corner of one eye as he gazed into space, his mind clearly in tumult. He'd pressed his lips tight shut to control the trembling, but it emerged anyway in the tight set of his shoulders.

'Sherlock,' John said carefully, coming close but not crowding. 'Let me help.'

Sherlock's gaze went straight to John's face, the sharp scrutiny tinged with anxiety. 'It's all true,' Sherlock said in a low rasp. 'Everything you said.'

'I know it's a lot.'

Sherlock huffed a hard breath through his nose, then suddenly his fingers clenched in John's shirt and pulled him close. He hesitated, then finally pressed his forehead to John's. His other hand was clenched against his own diaphragm.

'You've never lied to me.' His whisper was jagged.

'No,' John agreed gently, rubbing a soothing hand over Sherlock's fist in his shirt.

'You don't have some half-arsed swamp fairy living in your head. Do you?'

John puffed a faint laugh. 'No. I'm the only half-arsed fairy in my head.'

Sherlock managed a small laugh that was partly a gasp and pressed a sudden, quick kiss to John's temple. 'You are a fixed point in a mad world.'

John's hands were resting on Sherlock's shoulders now. One smoothed across those tense shoulders to cup the nape of his neck. 'Are you saying I'm dull?' The smile in his voice was obvious.

'Never. Although. I am learning to appreciate a little less unexpected drama in my life.'

'You love the drama,' John told him. He tilted his face so he could kiss Sherlock's brow, and then his mouth, which softened to accept the kiss. 'You live for it.'

'Mrs Hudson said– She said it can break me. Or it can change me.'

Sherlock didn't look at Audrey. She drew the blanket he'd given her closer around her limbs and wondered if it was something he really could choose. Perhaps he would break no matter what anyone said.

John had pulled Sherlock close. Sherlock's hands were folded between them, but now he moved, wrapping them around John's waist. He brushed his cheek alongside John's. He drew apart from him, far enough for grey eyes to meet blue.

'You changed. You didn't break.'

'No. And you're ten times smarter than me.'

'I don't think intelligence is the key, here.'

'Then trust the evidence of your eyes. Trust what you see and that we see it too. It's that thing you're always saying. Once you've eliminated the impossible, whatever remains, however improbable–'

'...must be the truth. But John. It's–'

'Not impossible. I've seen it. You've seen it. Percy experienced it.

Nick and Mrs Hudson live it. Your sister, too. You can do it. Change, don't break.'

Sherlock's breathing settled as he looked into John's eyes.

Audrey found herself wishing, hard: *Change, don't break.* Across the room, Nick, now dressed in her borrowed clothes, seemed to be wishing the same.

'Well,' Sherlock said, with a ghost of his old humour. 'If you can do it, I'm sure I can manage.'

John grinned. 'Cheeky bastard.'

The storm had passed, and immediately Myca's imperiousness returned.

'Excellent, Sherlock. You can now appreciate my urgency. I must ask you all to leave while my people attend to the results of this intrusion and remove the evidence.'

Sherlock released John far enough to glance back at that evidence– the body of a man with the head of a snake, its throat and wrist both torn and bloody.

John took easy, low-key command. 'Down to Mrs Hudson's would be best, I think. Sherlock, can you help her?'

He and Sherlock helped Audrey to her still-shaky feet. Sherlock carefully arranged the blanket around her shoulders, and she held it closed, less to hide her near nakedness than her useless, unwelcome frailty.

They assisted her down the stairs. Nick followed them, pausing to retrieve the key still protruding from the front door lock and open the door to Audrey's flat.

Audrey stumbled crossing the threshold and Sherlock had to steady her. His hand on her arm nearly undid her. He might have been killed. He and John and Nick all might have been killed, twice, today. She couldn't bear another loss, so soon. Or ever. She couldn't. She wanted so much to keep them all in sight, to be sure they were safe – but she also desperately needed to be alone for a moment; for the wolf and human both to lick their wounds, regroup, recover.

On the shelf beside her front door was a wooden box designed for playing cards. She struggled with it briefly before Sherlock took it from her hands and opened it, revealing a key.

'Take it,' Audrey said, before she changed her mind. 'I need to clean up. You take John and Nick to Conal's flat.'

Conal's flat, which had not been opened since she'd come to London after he and Travis and Tara and Siobhan had been murdered. Allowing the twins' flat to be let to Sherlock and John had been hard. Allowing Nick and John to take refuge in Siobhan's room belowstairs more painful still. Allowing anyone to enter Conal's space – the first of her adopted children, the one she'd loved the longest and held perhaps the dearest – still felt unthinkable.

But she must think it. She had almost lost these three today, to a killer sent by the same person, surely, who had ordered the executions of her family and of many more.

Time to open Conal's door to give them all space to plan their next move; to work out how to survive this unknown and relentless enemy. This M.

'I'll be along in a minute,' she said. 'Shoo. I mean it.' She limped towards the bathroom. 'I'm having a shower now. Go.'

Her front door closed. She let the blanket fall and held onto the nearest walls as she made her way to the shower. She steadied herself on the basin while the shower flow built up to a steaming spray and then, legs shaking, climbed into the tub and tilted her face up into the water.

She wanted to cry, but wanting to cry also made her angry and, besides, she lacked the energy.

Her thigh ached, but the wound had healed. Her whole body ached much deeper down from the un-mooned changes and the ensuing battles. Hot water sluiced the blood and venom from her face, hair and body. She could still taste Gus' blood at the back of her throat, mingled with the tang of raw, refrigerated beef mince. Audrey filled her mouth with water, swished it and spat it out, four times, five, then reached for her toothbrush and paste to do it twice more.

When she emerged, she knew at once that one of the three hadn't obeyed her instructions to leave.

'Cuppa's brewing!' Nick called out.

Audrey ignored the difficulty of stockings and buttons, putting on instead a simple jersey midi-dress with a tie at the waist, and soft moccasins. She made her way to the kitchen and sat. Nick watched her, wary of lending an unrequested hand but alert.

'Tea.' Nick placed the freshly poured cup in front of her. In it she heaped four spoons of sugar.

Audrey arched an eyebrow at her.

'Sugar's good for you after a shock,' Nick asserted. She added four spoonfuls to her own tea. 'Not as good as whisky, but I can't find your booze, so sugar it is. Don't give me that look.'

'I'm not giving you a look.'

'Maybe not. I still feel like you are. I keep feeling like you're my captain or my squad leader or something. Myca keeps saying things like it's coz you're my Alpha, but that's bullshit.'

Audrey sipped at the tea, expecting to hate it, but it flooded her mouth with warmth and comfort. She took a deeper swallow.

'Is it bullshit?'

'I don't know,' said Audrey.

'Now that *is* bullshit.'

'Even werewolves have a lot of myths about Alphas. Being the leader of a group of werewolves is said to be about being the one who bit all the others, as though spreading infection is like being a parent. But all that happens is that werewolves who like to bite, and not kill, are the ones who create groups of followers. But werewolf Alphas are more like humans. It's just leadership, and the most experienced ones will lead the inexperienced ones; and because the inexperienced are so afraid of themselves, they are happy to follow.'

'So I'm not under compulsion to follow you anywhere.'

'None at all.'

'Except that I'm scared shitless of myself, and you look like you know what you're doing.'

'That's right.'

Nick sipped thoughtfully, then shovelled some more sugar into her tea. 'It's a bit wanky, isn't it, calling you my Alpha.'

'A bit. I'm cursed anyway.'

'Calling bullshit again.'

'That's what they call me. The Cursed Alpha. Because so many of my packs–' Audrey pulled up short. Took a breath. 'They die, Nick. They all die.'

'Not today, they didn't.' Nick put down her cup and met Audrey's eye. 'I know how it feels, you know. Those bastards in Afghanistan shot John before I could stop them. They killed Percy right in front of me. All my life, people I loved left me; they dumped me and ran; they got shot and left; or they died. And I'm here all alone. Except I'm not and John's not, either. That's two to us, then. And we saved Johnny today. We stopped that snaky little shit from hurting him and Sherlock. Gus *and* his snake-bastard father. So that's twice more we won. Maybe we're unlucky sometimes, but we're not cursed. You got that?'

Audrey wasn't sure who Nick was most trying to convince, but she was heartened by the protest nonetheless.

'Anyway, you're less an Alpha than a den mother, aren't you?'

Nick grinned and Audrey was tempted to cuff her. Conal's name for her in another's mouth stung – but it softened her, too, with warm memories. So, instead, Audrey smiled back. 'You, Nick Murray, are a test of anyone's patience.'

'Yeah, but I got mad skillz in fixing car engines and turns out I move surprisingly fast for a gimp.'

'Don't call yourself that.'

Nick blinked at Audrey's stern tone. She swallowed. She sipped her tea. 'Okay,' she conceded. 'If you're going to go all Wolf Mother on me. Your eyes go all yellow. It's...' she tilted her head, 'impressive, actually. Kinda beautiful.' Nick took another breath and settled back. 'So do you think Myca will go out with me if I ask her, even if I threatened her and said she had flippers?'

Audrey had long given up trying to keep pace with Nick's twisting conversations. 'You also called her a beautiful mermaid. If you keep her guessing like that, you never know.'

'I should ask Mr Pretty if he has any tips. If Johnny will let him out of his sight long enough for a conversation. Last I saw they were practically velcroed together. I bet we find them in the spare flat humping against a wall and cooing at each other.'

Audrey found the mental image all too easy to conjure, and much more endearing than Nick's turn of phrase would suggest.

'That boy Sherlock went from 0 to 100 in about 20 seconds, when he came back up this afternoon,' said Nick. 'What did you say to him to make him make his move?'

'I merely pointed out the obvious.'

'What, that Johnny was five sixths already mad on him? That poor bastard really went down for the count on about day three. Some folks are like that I guess. Years and years of being unimpressed and then, *bam*, punched in the face by love. Oh well. Guess it's time to turn the hose on 'em if they've started undressing again, and think about who the fuck is doing this to us; what the fuck he wants with that looker Irene; and how to smack the bastard six ways to Sunday when we get her back.'

Nick shoved the chair back with a scrape and offered her arm to Audrey. 'I know you probably don't need it, being an Alpha and everything.'

Audrey rose as well, and took the offered arm. She felt stronger now, but there was relief in not having to keep pushing and pushing. She was only Nick's Alpha – her den mother – if Nick wanted that, but her heart warmed that Nick seemed to have chosen her already.

Once Audrey's apartment door was open, she and Nick could hear the Fisheries team upstairs, bumping furniture around and pulling up the tacks to remove the ruined second floor carpet. Nick darted ahead, letting herself into Conal's flat with a call of, 'Make yourselves decent!'

Audrey paused on the bare floorboards of the foyer; Myca's crew had already taken away the venom-soaked carpet. Ruby would probably have been glad to be rid of it, but it reminded Audrey of Irene, and of how this was properly Irene's home, not hers; then of how Irene was missing...

A loud knock rattled the front door in its frame. Suddenly hopeful, Audrey pulled it open, not to Irene Adler but to Gottfried Norton.

His clothes were dishevelled; his silver hair and beard in manic disarray; his eyes wild, red pinpricks. His sharp teeth were bared, with bloodied saliva strung between them.

'Let me in!' he demanded, pushing towards the threshold. 'Let me in at once!'

Before Audrey could open her mouth, Gottfried crashed into the invisible line which marked Audrey's domain and was instantly repelled into the street. He sprawled, ferocious and yet terribly pitiable at the same time.

'Please, Ms Hudson,' he beseeched her, his German accent thick with emotion. '*Bitte*. They've taken Irene. They mean to kill her. I need your help. *Please*.'

CHAPTER EIGHTEEN

GOTTFRIED NORTON WAS TALL, BROAD-SHOULDERED AND IMPRESSIVELY muscled. Augmented by the paranormal strength of a vampire, he should have been unstoppable. Instead, he was begging for help.

But Audrey had been around too long to automatically invite a vampire into her home, even a pleading one, no matter how novel the experience. 'Who took her?' she demanded. 'Where?'

'I don't know.' Gottfried scrambled to his feet and held out a beseeching hand. 'Four people in a van attacked our car. Shot out the windows with gas cylinders – wolfsbane and garlic. They dragged Irene away. Please let me in! You have to help me.'

Audrey began to move, ready at last to issue the invitation, but a heavy tread on the stairs heralded Myca Holmes' appearance. She was leading two of her team, who were burdened with a long roll of plastic-wrapped carpet with a Gus-shaped lump in its middle.

'Herr Norton,' said Myca, briskly approaching him and effectively blocking the doorway at the same time. Her sunglasses were firmly back in place. 'We've been searching for you and your wife after your ambush. We know your car was gassed. What happened?'

'You should know,' he spat at her. 'Our attackers' van bore Fisheries' livery.'

'Ms Adler's abduction is not our doing,' Myca said, as another

Fisheries van pulled up to receive Gus' concealed corpse. Her people shouldered firmly past Gottfried to get at it. 'We are as deeply concerned with her safety as you are, Herr Norton. If I am to help, you must tell me what happened.'

Norton twitched impatiently towards the door, but he could get no closer, especially with Myca blocking his path. He recognised that Myca was an immovable object, and resentfully launched into detail.

'They wasted no time on me, but took Irene at once. The moment I crawled free of the gases, I recovered strength enough to hunt them. I tracked them to the M40 but I was too impaired to follow the trail.'

The red of his eyes was highlighted by the watery blood that trickled from the corners. Vampire tears. 'So I returned to our car to seek their traces. I tracked a scent leading to the house at 224 Baker Street, opposite you, but it's uninhabited, and whoever I followed *there* has gone.'

'My Department has an alert out for the suspect,' she said. 'Also, Herr Norton, I should like to know: who is that in your teeth?'

Gottfried sucked belligerently on his fangs. 'I bit one of the men abducting my wife.'

'We found no bodies at the scene,' said Myca.

'His colleagues took him away. In their *Fisheries* van.'

'The Department of Fisheries, Wildlife & Parks had nothing to do with Ms Adler's abduction,' Myca repeated firmly.

'I know it wasn't *yours*. Your Department has a reputation, even in Frankfurt. My wife and her late father studied all your methods. Kidnapping in broad daylight in the middle of London has never been among them.'

'No,' Myca agreed drily.

Gottfried immediately resumed his entreaty to Audrey. 'Let me in, Mrs Hudson. *Helfen Sie mir!*'

To Audrey's annoyance, Myca spoke over the top of her imminent sympathetic invitation.

'While Ms Adler is a Department priority, you can't be given free rein of this household,' Myca asserted. 'Vulnerable humans reside here, Herr Norton. Mrs Hudson, if you'll permit, I have some knowledge of invitation lore.'

Audrey gestured for Myca to go ahead. It would be educational, if nothing else.

'Gottfried Norton, as a Guest in this household, I offer you entree under my auspices, a Guest of a Guest, guided and curtailed by the rules of hospitality. You may walk where I walk, only. You may do no harm. Of your own free will you must abide. Will you be so bound?'

Gottfried tilted his head, a hunter regarding puzzling prey. 'I've never heard an invitation like that. I'm a lawyer and couldn't have drafted it more effectively. I can feel its power.'

'I carry a powerful Guest within my own blood,' said Myca. 'She is much older even than this city. This is very like the oath she took when she inhabited me. Will you be so bound?'

'I will.'

Myca stood aside. Gottfried carefully placed a foot upon the threshold and entered, unhindered. With an air of curiosity, he tried to walk towards the stairs, but froze like his feet had been glued to the parquetry.

'Fascinating,' he said, though it clearly meant *aggravating*. 'Now, for mercy's sake, will you help me find my wife?'

'Let's combine our intelligence,' said Myca. She glanced at Audrey. 'It's time to consolidate our individual knowledge.'

Audrey led the way into Conal's flat, shoving the door open rapidly to counter the trepidation she felt. The motion kicked up the dust within, and Nick, who had approached the door as it opened, sneezed violently.

Past Nick's shoulder, Audrey could see the state of the neglected room. Dust covered every visible surface and motes of it hung in the air. Spiders had made webs in cosy corners. Moths had settled in the curtains. Sherlock and John stood shoulder to companionable shoulder, gazing down at the dusty kitchen table.

Conal had made that table from a wooden door he'd found in an overgrown lot. He'd come to London with her the week before their planned move south to install it. He should have stayed at Baker Street with her while she finalised other things. He'd be alive, still. Instead, he'd returned to Scotland to help his siblings with their packing. A good brother, a good son.

She almost wept, standing there, surrounded by his treasures, the things he'd found and made: the table and the set of spice jars by the stove, because he liked to cook. The chalkboard he used for grocery lists and little notes to himself. He'd inexpertly drawn a cartoon wolf in a chef's hat at the corner. A magnet of a kilted bagpiper held a local pizza shop menu to the fridge.

The thought of finding the man responsible for killing Conal made her predator's mouth water.

The table was covered in lines and markings. Sherlock had swiped his finger through the layers of dust to create a map of England on the dark wood. Other marks were smudged into the layers, several clustered on the part that signified Wales, and he was in the process of making another mark, roughly where Dartmoor was located.

'...Roylott's house here, and Gruner's mansion where he first took Mrs Hudson there. We need to get a list of the other properties he obtained by deception in case they add to our understanding. Myca, good, you're here. I need to know more about the events at Stoke Moran if I've a hope of finding where it fits in the overall scheme. Does it have one of those sacred water sources you were mentioning?'

'Nothing of note,' Myca said immediately. 'I could obtain an actual map for you, Sherlock.'

'I haven't the time,' Sherlock said. 'Unless you've brought it with you? But no, you've brought–' Sherlock finally looked at the stranger in the room. 'A German, recently arrived in London and even more recently involved in a fight.' He indicated the visitor's torn clothes and the blood on his face.

'This is Gottfried Norton. Irene's husband,' explained Audrey.

'What's this one? Another werewolf? A snake man? A water spirit?'

'Vampire,' Gottfried informed him with an unpleasant grin designed to show off his fangs.

John automatically put himself between Sherlock and the vampire. He was pale but steadfast as he did.

Gottfried responded to the challenge by tilting his head up and baring his glistening fangs even further.

Sherlock refused to be cowed. 'Put those away. Nobody's impressed. We've already beaten two snakes today, and their teeth were much larger,' he said, before ignoring Gottfried in favour of addressing his sister.

'And while I think of it, John and I have already downloaded the *Napoleon app* we found on Ormstein's phone. Users clearly need an invitation to access it. It automatically deletes from any device without approved login credentials. No doubt it's encrypted for use by a small group to plan, collude upon and execute criminal activities.'

'Like that thing in the news,' John suggested. 'The encrypted app that all those gangs used for organising hits and laundering money that turned out to be created by the FBI.'

'Exactly,' Sherlock beamed at John. 'And now, Myca, tell us about

Stoke Moran. What happened there? Clearly, it was much more than met my eye.'

And so the story unfolded, with Audrey adding to it when necessary: the Roylotts' imprisonment of the dryad and kidnapping of a Greek interpreter who could understand her ancient tongue. Sherlock's eyes widened on a semi-regular basis as he realised the snake tracks had belonged to Grimsby Roylott, and the wolf prints to his landlady.

He resisted comment, until: 'You killed a tiger in Wistman's Wood?'

'Only a very ill one,' Audrey said modestly.

Audrey finally told Sherlock the whole story of her family's murder. He listened, eyes closed, fingers steepled, occasionally nodding. She told him about Ruby and Irene, and how she had met Irene this morning – *only this morning, good god* – to discover that a kidnapping attempt had already been made in Germany.

'And now they've succeeded in taking her,' Sherlock noted. 'Sebastian Moran and this Professor must want her very badly indeed and for some specific reason. Myca, Ormstein's phone?'

Myca placed the phone into his outstretched palm.

Audrey waited for Sherlock to announce that he couldn't access the phone without Irene's thumbprint, but he simply entered a 6-digit code. 'I added it this morning,' he explained briefly, 'after you handed it to me then.'

His nimble fingers expanded, closed, flicked and swiped through screen after screen. He barely winced at what he found. He was playing it super cool, but Audrey could detect his rapid heartbeat and the scent of anxiety underneath it all. The way John stood sentinel at his side suggested even he was aware of how hard Sherlock was working to keep accepting his new world view – to keep changing instead of breaking.

Finally, Sherlock raised his head to meet Gottfried's gaze. 'You're very lucky to be alive, if that's the term for you.' A moment's discomfort crossed his features before he schooled them back to professional detachment. 'From the evidence on William Ormstein's phone and from Mrs Hudson's reports, their usual *modus operandi* is to kill supernatural creatures that they have no use for.'

Audrey winced, but Sherlock, in the middle of his summary, missed it and continued.

'I'm still piecing it together. Ormstein has clearly been an instrument of assassination in previous years, perhaps on the basis that one supernatural being is best placed to eradicate others. However, as soon as Ormstein himself became a liability, Moran despatched him very quickly. Really, Herr Norton, it's astonishing you're still here. At best, you're a threat. At worst, you're surplus to their requirements and an easy target which,' he waggled the phone, 'was Ormstein's favourite type.'

'Are you accusing me of something?' Gottfried demanded.

Sherlock's eyebrows rose. 'No. Is there something in this attack for which you can be accused?'

Gottfried's eyes glinted murderously, but Sherlock recklessly turned from him to address Audrey.

'I'm sorry, Mrs Hudson,' he said. 'I'm aware that this is a painful subject for you. Unfortunately, the information I have so far doesn't really bring us closer to why he targeted your family now, rather than at any time previously, or any time after. I'm still gathering data.'

Audrey calmed herself with a deep breath.

Sherlock paced the floor, speaking rapidly as he tried to knit the disparate threads of the case into a whole cloth, using his new understanding of how they might fit together.

'Adelbert Gruner was a collector of supernatural beings – or portions of them. Oh dear god, was that an *actual* zombie finger I saw inch-worming around its case?' He shuddered before continuing. 'We know from the letter we found that the Roylotts were supplying Gruner with at least some of those appalling trophies. I expect he paid very well for them. We may need to consider whether the Roylotts were the only ones who gained, or whether some of those funds went up the chain to Professor M, if we accept that "His Nibs" is the brain behind the operation.'

He turned on his heel for another circuit but paused to regard Audrey. 'You're clearly known to Ormstein. It's my working hypothesis that Ormstein gave your details to Gruner ahead of your kidnapping. I wonder if this means Gruner's other female victims are also supernatural. On the face of it, and judging by Kitty Winter, I'd say no. Gruner collected many things – cars, porcelain, women, cryptids. Given he aimed to take possession of Baker Street, we need to investigate what other properties he accumulated, and whether any of them relate to those poisoning cases, which I must now assume are related to Grimsby and Gus Roylott's peculiar venomous attributes. What kind of creatures were they, Myca?'

'Naga, a cryptid that originates in India,' his sister supplied. 'We know Roylott is from an Anglo-Indian background, though his behaviour is at significant odds with most of his kind. Gus, with his human mother, manifested less fully, as you saw.'

Sherlock stuttered to a longer stop.

'I'm as blind as a beetle,' he said with sudden violence. 'My ignorance of this material is profound and nothing I know can be relied upon. How can I theorise without data?'

'You know how to look for patterns,' Myca assured him. 'I can supply any details you lack.'

'All that study of folklore,' he said bitterly.

'Comparing reality with mythology,' she said. 'The latter can be surprisingly erudite, as well as riddled with human storytelling.'

'It's untenable.'

'It's the world as it really exists.'

'Quite.'

Sherlock turned away and his gaze fell on John Watson, and on Nick Murray at John's side. The two of them were peering with purposeful intent at the map of England drawn in the grimy table.

'What is it?' Sherlock demanded.

'I'm thinking about the M40,' said Nick.

'Nick was a driver in Afghanistan,' John reminded the room helpfully. 'She drove lorries in England before she joined up, too. She's good at maps.'

Nick swirled a dot in the grime to indicate London. She drew a line west then north, leaving a trail. 'So, the A40 starts in London, heads west, turns into the M40 and heads north outside of Oxford. Where did you lose the van, Norton?'

'Past Ealing.'

'You got that far on foot? You move fast for an undead guy.'

'Very.'

'Well, they could've taken your wife anywhere after Ealing. North to join the M1. They could have joined the M25 after Uxbridge too and buggered off to Woking. But if they kept on the M40, they could,' Nick continued to drag lines through the dust, 'end up a little south of Birmingham, or they could switch back to the A40 across Oxford and into Wales, or more likely swung around Birmingham on the M5 and then take the A5 to north Wales.'

'Why more likely?' Audrey began, but Sherlock had rushed to see where Nick's trail led.

'The roads that Nick has drawn all converge, ultimately, near Snowdonia National Park – and the cluster of places where the unsolved poisonings, and subsequent property sales, occurred. The properties that Myca said were all centred on sacred wells.'

Sherlock pulled out his phone and feverishly typed and swiped through Google maps. He leaned over the crude map and made a mark with his thumb. 'Snowdonia National Park, *Llyn y Dywarchen*, where you dro–' He faltered on "drowned", as he looked at his sister. 'Myca, does your soggy passenger have anything to say about the lake where she hitched a ride? What exactly does she want help with, did she ever say?'

Myca gazed at her brother's thumb print on the table. 'She was trapped. She needed to leave the lake.'

'Which she did, very effectively, by inhabiting you and being taken to Alltwen Hospital on the southwest coast, and then to London, as fast as our parents could take us.'

Myca became thoughtful. 'And goodness, didn't our trainspotting father complain that his inspection of the commercial and tourist railways of the region was not completed to his satisfaction,' she said meaningfully.

Sherlock responded instantly with sharp curiosity. 'Why is that important?'

'Wales is girded in iron,' Myca said. 'This section, leading to Anglesey and Holyhead, is effectively separated from the rest of England by rail. The Welsh iron trade was focused in South Wales, too, but the north-west – Anglesey and what's now Snowdonia National Park – was once bristling with branch lines from the main line to the east.'

'Didn't Beeching's reforms create breaks in the iron barrier?' Audrey asked.

'Beeching took away many of the trains but even with his best efforts, he didn't remove all of the tracks. Remaining stretches of rail are used by tourist steam train routes all through this area. The Welsh Highland Railway, Snowdon Mountain, Ffestiniog, Llanberis Lake, Bala Lake. Some stations on the regular lines have been reinstated, too.'

'You haven't explained why that matters,' said Sherlock impatiently.

'Iron is a barrier to the fae. North Wales was like a Faraday cage of iron to them. *Llyn y Dywarchen* lies to the east of Snowden Peak. Also of Bleinau Ffestiniog, which is linked by tourist train to Porthmadog on the coast. A line still runs all the way from Porthmadog to Colwyn Bay in the north via Bleinau Ffestiniog and Llandudno Junction. The spirit who shares habitation with me was apparently caught outside the iron cage.'

Sherlock studied the dust map with a frown. 'And five of the six properties related to the poisoning cases are west of that rail line. One in Anglesey, one near Beddgelert. Llanfairfechlan. Tregarth. Llanberis.'

'Llanberis.' Myca seized upon the name. 'It sits beside twin lakes. The Snowdon Mountain Railway begins there on the way to the summit. The Lake Railway is on the other side of Lake Padarn.'

'Is that another of your sacred waterways?'

'Not that lake, no, but one is nearby.'

Sherlock resumed pacing again. Audrey was dizzy watching him, and with watching how John watched him closely, with half a distrustful eye on the vampire in their midst. Nick was alert, too. Audrey was reminded again that those two had been in combat; had been irrevocably altered by the traumas of battle, violent injuries, and the brutal transformation of their dear friend Percy. Sherlock and Myca might have disappeared into a higher plane of clues, history, connections, inference and deduction, but others were more wary of the mortal dangers.

Gottfried avidly watched the siblings. While they unpacked, in their erudite fashion, the rail and fae history of Wales, his wife was in the hands of killers, taken alive for some terrible purpose.

Audrey understood his impatience.

'Another thing,' Sherlock was saying. 'I'm puzzled about this dryad. You said that the Roylotts needed a Greek interpreter to speak with her. Why would this – wood spirit, yes? – why did she speak ancient Greek? Doesn't England have its own wood spirits?'

'A good number, yes,' Myca agreed. 'We use the term dryad, but our own are not Greek speakers.'

'And yet Roylotts Senior and Junior and Sebastian Moran tortured a Greek dryad for information she would not give them, about the location of a sacred well. What do you make of that, Myca?'

'We don't know where she came from,' Myca admitted, 'but if they took her from the same area where they're now heading, she was surely part of their search for a sacred waterway. She must have been protecting one they can't at present locate. But how she became a guardian to a sacred well is a mystery. The Romans didn't get very far in that part of Wales; the Greeks never attempted settlement. Though certainly the Roman army would have had Greek-born soldiers in their number, and Greek traders would have come through the earliest seaports.'

'Fine. We'll leave that in the unexplained column with almost all of the rest of it. The next question is what is so special about Irene Adler that she's been kidnapped, after several failed attempts, including once in her childhood?'

'She's a natural born werewolf,' said Gottfried, who then had to explain what that meant.

'Rare, I take it?'

'Most naturally-conceived werewolves miscarry,' Audrey said. 'Most of the rest die in infancy. Only a very few survive to adulthood. Irene's the only one I know, and Ruby claims it was because she gave birth in wolf form at the height of the full moon.'

Sherlock appeared to take that in his ever-increasing stride. 'Curious. Given this Professor M's antipathy towards the supernatural, why would he want such a person alive?'

'The few who survive are subject to absurd rumours of extra powers,' Myca said. 'I've never found proof, but some records speak of the powers of the sun and moon residing combined, spiritually speaking, in the trueborn werewolf.'

Myca and Sherlock both fell into deep thought. The rest of the company resumed their watchful anxiety.

'So what you're saying,' said Audrey at length, 'is that Sebastian Moran has taken Irene north to Wales, because they think she has special spiritual powers. And they've been looking for a sacred well that's inside this network of iron.'

Sherlock beamed at her. 'An excellent summary of the working hypothesis.'

'What does it all mean?'

'I expect we'll find out more when we get to Wales. Myca, I imagine time is of the essence. Do your departmental powers extend to chartering a private plane?'

Chapter Nineteen

AUDREY HOVERED NEAR THE CESSNA'S PASSENGER DOOR, NO MORE ABLE to help Myca than Sherlock could. Compassion vied with frustration, with a kick of being annoyed at having to be concerned about the Fisheries head in the first place. Audrey was almost tempted to stomp down the aisle and damn well drag Myca onto the tarmac, to hell with the consequences.

Nick, John, the impatient Gottfried and their increasingly irritated pilot had already disembarked and were waiting in the shade of the nearby hangar for Myca to join them.

But Myca huddled – as much as a very tall, heavy-set person could huddle – at the rear of the sleek little aircraft that had brought them to Caernarfon Airport. Her already pale face was nearly bloodless beneath the hat and scarf. Her knuckles were white where they gripped the headrest of the seat in front of her.

Sherlock, by the door, regarded her with a kind of concerned, compassionate irritation. 'You have to get off the plane, Myca.'

'It was difficult enough to board,' she replied through gritted teeth. 'This thing is made of metal, you'll recall.'

'Planes are mostly constructed of aluminium,' he countered. 'Plus, you drive a car.'

'I am driven in cars,' she corrected him, 'on as few occasions as I can manage.'

'What is the morgen afraid of?' Audrey asked Myca from the door.

Myca shuddered. 'I don't know.'

'Whatever she was fleeing in the first place?' Sherlock gently suggested.

'I think so. She doesn't want to be here.'

'Yet here we are,' he said bracingly. 'You're stronger than she is.'

But Myca's fingers remained tightly clenched, no matter how deeply she breathed.

Outside, the pilot was arguing with John and Nick. John replied calmly, a steady counterbalance to the pilot's furious declarations that she needed to refuel and get onto her next chartered passenger while it was still light, because night flying wasn't allowed at this airport.

Nick overrode the pair of them with a heartfelt, 'Oh, for fuck's sake!' The next moment, Nick was up the four boarding stairs, a long black umbrella in one hand. She stuck her head past Audrey and into the cabin.

'Myca! I get it. The sky is way too big to look at. I've got a brolly. Let's go find Irene before Captain Hurry-Up takes a swing at John and Broody McFangface goes to town on the survivor.'

An expression of alarm broke through Myca's attempts at calm. Nick thrust the umbrella at Audrey. 'You know she's agoraphobic, you plonker. Plan better.' Then she marched back to the hangar.

Audrey passed the umbrella to Sherlock, who handed it to Myca. 'I hadn't forgotten,' he said.

Myca's hand closed over the handle. She levered herself up and walked down the aisle. As she came alongside her brother, Myca said, 'Broody McFangface?'

'Suits him,' Sherlock said.

Myca's lips quirked in a brief smile, then said, 'Vampires are never so straightforward.' A glance passed between the siblings that Audrey couldn't read. Then Myca waved Audrey to go first, and the two of them stepped onto the tarmac while Sherlock held the open umbrella over his sister. Then Myca grabbed it again, like it was a lifeline.

'Does that actually work? For the agoraphobia?' Sherlock asked, stepping down beside her.

'It doesn't *not* work.'

'Now you sound like Murray,' Sherlock complained.

Myca's mouth quirked in another suppressed smile. 'Quite. But I'm out of the aeroplane, so I'll take it. Where's the car?' Her eyes were firmly on her own feet as they crossed towards the hangars in close formation, Myca sheltered between Audrey and Sherlock.

'Parked on the far side of the hangars,' said Sherlock. 'I told your driver to take a cab back to town. I'll ferry us about as needed.'

The fuming pilot strode back to her plane. Her shadow was long on the ground; the air was growing cooler.

'You have plenty of time,' Sherlock called after her encouragingly. 'It's an hour till sunset.'

She flipped him the middle finger and kept walking.

Sherlock began a retort, but Myca elbowed him in his ribs. He danced away from her, pulling an outraged face, and they were so obviously siblings that Audrey had to smile.

Then she had to stifle an exhausted yawn. She was envious of Nick and John, who had snatched an hour's sleep during the flight. Nick claimed that the army had taught them how to sleep anywhere, any time.

They all needed rest – it had been a hell of a long day. Myca Holmes, Director of the Department of Fisheries, certainly pulled more weight than her title or department name suggested, but chartering a plane to fly north with numerous non-civil-service personnel on short notice still took time. The two-hour delay at least gave time for everyone to pack overnight bags before rendezvousing at the London Elstree Aerodrome, eight miles away. One of Myca's Department lackeys had even escorted Nick to her bedsit for a duffel bag.

Nobody was catnapping in the hangar now. John was keeping a watchful eye on the prowling Gottfried and Nick was standing over their heaped luggage, prodding at Sherlock's floppy backpack with her toe.

'Did you even pack anything?' she asked of Sherlock.

'Only the necessaries.'

'Socks, jocks, comb and condom?'

'I expect that's John's bag,' he said, without a blush. 'Mine is: canteen, magnifier, a jar of Allium sativum, and an evidence bag containing what I now realise is the severed finger of a Greek dryad.'

'I bet you're a riot on a dirty weekend.'

'I'm sure we'll find out in due course.' Then his ears went pink, then pinker as John, collecting the bags, gave him a saucy wink.

The six of them made their way between the buildings to their government sedan, with Myca in the centre beneath her umbrella. Sherlock unlocked all doors with a beep. Myca sat immediately in the broad back seat while John piled the luggage into the boot before calling shotgun and scooting into the front beside Sherlock. Nick scooted just as quickly to sit next to Myca in the back, between her and the door.

'Remind me to get my driver's licence back,' Nick muttered, wriggling to get more comfortable. 'I can still drive an automatic. Probably.'

'Use taxis. I do,' Myca said, eyes down.

'I hate other people driving me around.' Then Nick beamed at Myca. 'I could be your driver, eh?'

'We'll see,' said Myca, and her response took them both aback.

Audrey had no option but to get in beside them. Gottfried Norton stood by the open rear door, clearly reluctant to get them to budge up to make room in a car with front-and-rear flirting. Audrey couldn't imagine him squished up front between John and Sherlock. Were those two even flirting anymore, or just indulging in vaguely distanced foreplay?

'I'll meet you at the hotel,' he said curtly. 'Now, I look for my wife.'

'I'm sure Ms Adler will be here somewhere, but Wales is still quite large,' Sherlock said drily. 'Where will you begin?'

But Gottfried had already disappeared.

'Please don't tell me vampires have powers like homing signals for their One True Love,' Sherlock said as John buckled up.

'He's very motivated,' Myca said. 'He'll be faster than us in a grid search.'

'How fast?' Sherlock asked. 'How can you calculate speed and efficiency, with a vampire?'

'Ten times faster than a human; more without needing to get in and out of a car; supernatural senses for tracing scent, broken foliage, footprints. You know, I'm not sure how to quantify it, mathematically.'

'I refuse to believe you haven't tried.'

'I have attempted formulas.'

'I never doubted it.'

Audrey was sure that Sherlock was doing his best to distract Myca from her agoraphobia. Myca made the effort to accept distractions. 'Why do you have a piece of the dryad in your backpack?' she asked her brother.

'Curiosity. I picked it up at Stoke Moran without knowing its significance. I have no idea if it's of any use, but since it's the remains of an apparently sentient being, I thought at least it might be suitably interred.'

Sherlock's kindness was showing again. John patted Sherlock's leg, and

Audrey thought of John's kindness too, when he stood with her as they'd buried Conal's final remains.

Myca had arranged accommodation at a fairly central Caernarfon guest house. Sherlock pulled up in front of its early Victorian façade.

'Check in and wait for us,' he told John as he and Nick unloaded the car. 'My sister and I have things to do.'

'Such as?'

'Family business. We'll be back soon. Oh, I need that.' Sherlock got out to retrieve the jar of *Allium sativum* – garlic – from his backpack, and handed it to Audrey. 'Smear this on windowsills and door handles in your rooms.'

Audrey pursed her lips. 'Garlic. Really?'

'Is garlic as a defence just another myth?'

'It's quite accurate, but only because the odour is so intense it makes their sense of smell useless for an hour afterwards. But why do you want to defend yourself against Gottfried Norton?'

'I'm not sure how I feel about vampires, yet.'

Sherlock was trying to be dry and flippant, but his eyes betrayed a restrained alarm. At least he knew his sister, and to an extent his landlady, and John vouched for Nick. But what did Sherlock know of Gottfried Norton? Or Irene, who was the only person who could vouch for him. Audrey was tempted to think Sherlock was over-reacting, but then, she'd been living with beings like Norton for most of her life.

'He's desperate to save Irene. I don't think he'll cause trouble,' she said.

'The lore indicates that vampires cause nothing but trouble, usually of a devious kind.'

'Well, he is a lawyer,' Audrey drawled. Sherlock was doing remarkably well at not breaking so far, but she could allow for some paranoia. Hollywood and Hammer Horror had done no favours for vampires.

'Double-damned, then. Will you do it?'

'There isn't really much point.'

'Humour me, please. Would you?'

Audrey looked to Myca in the back of the car looking like she was trying to blend in with the upholstery.

'Fine.' Audrey pocketed the jar. 'You'll explain to the owners why their hostelry stinks to heaven?'

'They won't ask. Not if the Department of Fisheries has used this as a base before, which they have, or Myca would have directed us to the cheaper hotel down the road.'

He turned away and Audrey said, 'Be careful, Sherlock. We have an enemy that makes even a powerful water spirit afraid.'

Sherlock spoke a quiet au revoir to John, a squeeze of the hand, before driving off to their family business.

The rattling of the closed window woke Audrey from a fitful sleep. She'd only meant to rest her eyes, but now traffic noise had eased and the sky was dotted with stars: well, except for where the shape of the vampire at her window blotted them out.

Audrey checked but the other twin bed was empty. Nick hadn't returned from her long chat with John. Perhaps she'd fallen asleep there, or chosen one of the other rooms instead of disturbing Audrey's sleep.

Who was she kidding? Nick would certainly have tried to tip-toe quietly and awkwardly in.

The window rattled again. Audrey limped over to unlatch it and pushed the sash up.

'You could just use the door,' she said, grumpy.

'Everyone is asleep and I have no invitation.'

She refrained from pointing out that if he'd squished into the front seat he'd have received a key to his own room when they checked in. Which raised a question. 'How did you know this was my room?'

'This window and the next reek of garlic. This is the first I tried.' He was obviously offended, and not just by the smell.

'Any luck finding Irene?'

'I have found Sebastian Moran. He is alone.'

'You couldn't spook her whereabouts out of him?'

'Must we discuss this at a garlic-stinking windowsill?'

She pushed the window sash all the way up. Behind Gottfried, daylight glimmered on the horizon. She'd slept longer than intended, though not nearly as long as she needed.

Gottfried's face was a dictionary definition of disgust as he climbed over the sill and into the room. Audrey sympathised. The stench was awful.

'Where is Holmes?'

'We're not 12-year-olds having a sleepover,' she said tartly. 'Sherlock is sharing with John. His sister has her own room.'

A knock at her door drew their attention sharply.

'Mrs H?' Nick's voice penetrated the room in a stage whisper. 'You okay?'

'I'm fine, Nick.'

'Is that Broody McFangface I hear in there with you?'

Audrey almost laughed at Gottfried's new levels of deeply outraged. 'Yes, Nick, Mr Norton has returned.'

'Ask him if he saw Myca and Sherlock while he was out. They're not back yet.'

Audrey opened the door. Nick, still dressed in now-crumpled daywear, eyed Gottfried from the threshold. 'Well, did you?' she asked him directly.

'No,' Gottfried replied. 'And I must find Ms Holmes.'

John popped up at Nick's side. His clothes were just as slept-in as Nick's and his hair stuck up on one side. They'd clearly fallen asleep while talking into the night. 'The car isn't here. The other rooms haven't been used.' He glanced at his watch. 'It's nearly 5am. Damnit.' He scrubbed a hand through his hair, making a worse mess.

'Text him,' Nick suggested.

'I did. I can't believe I fell asleep.'

'Yeah. So rude. My stories are riveting, I'll have you know.'

'I'm not in the mood, Nick.'

'Yeah. I know. Sorry. So what do we do now?'

'We plan,' asserted Gottfried. He gestured impatiently for Nick and John to enter. 'Moran is camping in the national park. He is alone.'

'Waiting for a rendezvous?' said John. 'He must have left your wife somewhere safe nearby. Any woods around?'

'Yes,' said Gottfried. 'He was speaking on his telephone with great deference to someone. I searched the vicinity, but I could not find Irene.'

'Sherlock will,' John said encouragingly. 'If anyone can, he's the man for it.'

'He is a hunter,' agreed Gottfried. 'I count on it.'

And then, faster than even a werewolf could see or prevent, Gottfried Norton grabbed John by the throat, drew a canister from his pocket and sprayed gas at Audrey.

'Bastard!' Nick launched at him, but he casually knocked her across the room, sprayed gas in her direction, then tossed the canister, still spewing fumes, after her.

John struggled savagely, scratching at the vampire's relentless hand and trying to breathe, with no more effect than a rabbit in a fox's jaws. Gottfried dragged him through the open door, slamming it shut after, trapping the werewolves in the gas-filled room.

Audrey hadn't been fast enough to stop him, but she'd angled her face away from the particles to gulp down air. As the spray hit her face, her eyes streamed with tears. Her lungs ached as she tried to avoid taking another breath.

Nick was curled on the floor, her watering eyes screwed shut and her hand cupped over her mouth and nose, an inadequate filter against the gas.

Wolfsbane gas.

No.

Audrey's mind flashed to her family's home in Edinburgh. Her children, choking on gas before William Ormstein committed his appalling violence.

No. I will not succumb. I will not lose a single other person to this.

Audrey stumbled to Nick; hauled her up. A great cloud of wolfsbane gas sat heavily between them and the closed door.

In the far distance, John shouted then fell terribly quiet.

'Window,' she rasped to Nick, choking on the taste of wolfsbane. 'Jump.'

Nick coughed, her incredulous surprise turning almost instantly to determination. 'When my Alpha says jump, I say how high, right?'

With that, Nick lurched to the open window, swung over the sill and dropped.

Audrey didn't wait to see how Nick landed. She went over the ledge, hung on briefly and dropped one storey to the ground.

CHAPTER TWENTY

The shock of landing jarred straight up Audrey's leg into to her gammy hip. She stumbled with a cry, only to find Nick catching her, holding her upright.

'I got you, Mrs H.'

'You landed well,' Audrey puffed, recovering quickly.

'Good old PLF! Parachute Landing Fall.' Nick bounced lightly on her feet. 'All that army training still has some use, even when you've only got one leg. Now, come on. That skank is getting away!'

'Haring off after them won't help. Even with a hostage, vampires move too fast for us to catch him up.' Audrey limped around the side of the guest house to the front driveway. 'I don't suppose you have your phone? We must try to warn Sherlock.'

'Course I have my phone.' Nick drew it from her pocket and swore at the crack across the screen. It flashed on at a touch, however, so she sent a terse text message to Sherlock then crooked a grin at Audrey. 'And of course I have his number. John's hottie flatmate? I nabbed it from Johnny's phone so I could send him embarrassing photos of John, didn't I?' The grin wobbled. 'If that nightcrawling arsehole hurts my mate I'm going to smash his fangs with a brick and stuff his guts with garlic.'

Audrey would certainly hold Nick's coat while she did, and then take her own turn, but they had to find the bastard first.

At the driveway, Audrey halted next to the scuff marks where John had fought; had dug his heels in kicked up gravel as he was dragged into the night; the spot of blood where Norton had rendered John unresisting with a blow.

'Can you smell it?' Audrey followed the spots of blood to the road and sniffed.

'The blood?' Nick's voice was gruff with anger.

'The garlic. All over Norton's shoes. His trousers and coat too I expect. He was at my window for a while. It's seeped in.'

Nick sniffed experimentally. 'Isn't that just on us?'

Audrey's senses had been blunted by the wolfsbane gas, but the pungent odour was definitely ahead of her too. She would have howled except she couldn't shift her shape to make the right throat for her despair.

Nick's phone beeped just as the hire car slewed around the bend and squealed to a stop in front of them. Sherlock threw wide the driver's door and jumped out with the car keys in his hand.

'How long ago did he take John?'

'Five minutes,' Nick reported. 'Where the fuck have you been?'

'Gathering data,' he replied grimly, then into the car interior he growled, 'Oh, no you don't.'

Myca, surprisingly wet from head to toe, halted her awkward attempt to sidle from the front passenger seat towards the steering wheel, to which she was handcuffed.

'Get this iron off my wrists.' Myca's voice was quiet, fierce, and not quite her own.

'You knew this might happen,' Sherlock accused her.

'As did you,' said not-quite-Myca.

'I didn't know why they left him alive when they could have staked him after they'd gassed him. Surely it wouldn't have slowed them down that much. Also, I have no idea how I'm supposed to trust any of you fae.'

'I'm your sister.' Even she didn't seem to really believe it.

'My sister is in there, but you're not her,' snapped Sherlock. 'I've had enough of this. Enough lies. Enough hocus pocus. I want answers.'

Audrey had also had enough, right to the tips of her wolf ears which wouldn't manifest no matter how she tried.

'While you've been *whatevering*,' Audrey gestured sharply at Myca, 'Gottfried Norton has attacked us and kidnapped John.'

'Attacked; kidnapped: but not killed. We have time. You used the garlic on the frames like I asked?' he replied. 'Surely he got it all over himself when he tried the window. You're supposed to be a part-time wolf. Sniff him out!'

'Sherlock, he used wolfsbane gas on us. I can't shift my form. I can't follow the trail. He hurt John and now he's disappeared into Snowdonia.' Audrey clenched her teeth on rising panic. She did not panic. She was a grown woman, a werewolf who defied the moon, the Cursed Alpha, and she was not a panicker.

Sherlock paced back and forth. 'I know. But the mysterious Professor M doesn't want John. John must be a bargaining tool. M is after Myca, or the thing that inhabits her. And she is the only being that might know how to find John, Moran or the Professor. Omniscience being my sister's speciality.' He threw a venomous glance at the woman in the car. 'Isn't that right?'

'Oh, for fuck's sake.' Nick stomped closer to the car and glared at Myca Holmes through the windscreen.

Another inhabitant glared back at her from Myca's body. The water spirit filled those grey Holmesian eyes, not with unearthly authority but with fear. Myca's dark, wet hair hung around her face, not ethereal but bedraggled.

'What have you been doing to her?' Audrey asked, shocked at so powerful a creature seeming so wrecked. 'Where have you been?'

'Asking difficult questions,' Sherlock said. 'I'd suggested to Myca we put our heads together, particularly with her far greater knowledge of the fae world. We drove around Snowdonia Park to discuss what the Fisheries knows.'

'This doesn't look like a collaborative consultation.'

'No. Not a lot of consulting eventuated, so I handcuffed her and started again.' Sherlock sounded defensive, underneath his severity. 'The results were troubling. Myca went away and this thing began trying to persuade me to head south or east.'

The water spirit rallied enough to attempt sullen defiance. 'I hear Birmingham is lovely, brother dear. There's a sea aquarium, sensibly far away from the sea.'

Sherlock's lip curled. 'If this thing is a water goddess, then it knows things. Things like where this dryad came from.' From his pocket, he took the stump of the dead dryad. He displayed it between thumb and forefinger. 'Before Roylott murdered her.'

'You thought she could tell from a twig?' Nick asked, incredulous.

'Who knows?' Sherlock said. 'I have no idea what it knows, or how. I have no experience with the occult and supernatural, but I've read story books. If there's a skerrick of truth to them, I know that fairy creatures don't like iron. I know the folk tales are full of bones and hair that get turned into musical instruments that speak. I've read about tricking creatures with their secret names and rules of three and fickle fates. All speculation and all of it useless. But I took Myca to the lake where this creature drowned my sister, and when I got evasion instead of answers, I put iron on its wrists and asked again. It's been panicking ever since.' Sherlock glared down at the unkempt being. 'Shall we try again?'

'No.'

'Where is the vampire taking John?'

'I don't know.'

'I don't believe you.'

Sherlock leaned over to unlock one metal cuff from the steering wheel, and deftly snapped it around his own wrist before Myca could make a break for it. He headed down the drive, pulling Myca mercilessly in his wake. She snatched at him for balance, seizing his free wrist with her free hand. Water swirled from her unshackled arm to his, began to wash upward to his throat. Over it. Over his mouth and he – belatedly alarmed, belatedly afraid – strained away.

The water flowed over his nose and cheeks and eyes–

Audrey lunged at them, unable to change shape, but her blood was still full of the sleeping moon and the wolf. She scooped two fingers in Sherlock's open mouth, affording him a sharp, urgent intake of breath and to close his lips tight before the water closed over them again.

'Stop that,' Audrey commanded, even as the water splashed up her own arm. Nick reached for her. 'No, Nick, don't, someone has to be able to look for John.' *If the rest of us drown.* But the mermaid's fearful current had swirled to her mouth. Audrey drank it down in gulps, her human eyes blazing in rage. 'Myca!' she urged, then choked on inhaled water. She coughed. Tried again. 'She's killing Sherlock!'

Water covered her mouth, her nose, her eyes, and for a second she was drowning. Water in her belly, in her lungs, filling her ears.

And the tide suddenly receded. Audrey doubled over, coughed and retched up brackish lake water. Her lungs fizzed with a strange sensation, and her blood roared in her sensitive ears. She could hear night birds and distant cars and the cracking of Nick's knuckles as she clenched her fists. Beside her, Sherlock vomited water and thin bile by the roadside and drew a tortured breath.

'Sherlock?' Myca's tall, solid form shuddered and for a moment she seemed herself again. 'Sherlock, are you hurt? Please tell me she hasn't–'

He looked up into his sister's grey eyes. 'Myca. Why is she so afraid?'

And then the water sheened Myca's skin, changed the colour of her eyes, turned to mist where moisture met the steel of the handcuffs that still bound them together. Audrey watched, fascinated and horrified, while the two beings in that one body fought for control. The skirmish ended in a capitulation, though not a victory. Myca remained submerged, but the fight had gone out of the being that possessed her.

The water spirit in Myca flattened herself against the side of the car, trying to make that large body a small target. 'You don't understand.'

'This is what she did at the lake,' Sherlock lathered a sneer over his shock. 'Cowering and hiding from the sky. She really is terrified of the outdoors, and particularly of the dark, and that strikes me as very, very strange. This isn't Myca. Do you hear that, you waterlogged thug. My sister was never frightened of anything.' His tone was full of undercurrents again. Pride. Anger. Unaccustomed helplessness.

'It is not the dark that frightens,' said the morgen in Myca's body. 'It is what he can do with the stars.'

'He. He, who? Norton? No. He's a recent player. Ormstein is dead. Moran is a hunter, cunning but not supernaturally powerful. You mean the Professor. Talk to me!' He clasped her by the shoulder, bringing their chained hands up. More mist rose from the sprite's wrist.

Audrey made to intervene; she coughed instead. But with the cough, she felt it again. The fizz of something clearing in her lungs. A film of something gathering in her nose and mouth. Audrey hawked and spat more brackish liquid to the kerb, and at once she could scent Nick's fury, Sherlock's desperation, and the waft of garlic on the path, leading away from the guesthouse. The wolfsbane had cleared from her blood; her wolf was rising again. Being near-drowned by mystical lake water had done her the world of good. Her eyes grew tawny; and her nails had become claws.

'What's your true name?' she demanded of the morgen, before Sherlock could shake the prevarication out of it.

'I'm the mermaid of the mere,' the water spirit insisted. 'The Lady of the Lake, the–'

'You're not *The* Lady,' Audrey countered with certainty. 'A lady of *some* lake, perhaps. You're not the Queen. She wouldn't be afraid of any human. She wouldn't deign to possess one.'

'I am–' the morgen drew herself tall, her watery voice deep and terrible.

'You're a terrified water spook, I see that now,' Audrey spat. 'A Jenny Greenteeth, one of a legion, and if John Watson dies because you won't help us, I will tear out your throat and stuff it full of arum lilies and belladonna.'

'He is a god,' the Jenny whispered in sudden acquiescence. 'He is beyond gods.'

'Professor M?' Sherlock was incredulous.

'He could burn the holy groves to ash; boil the sacred waterways to less than the mists. He knows the names of the stars and how to scatter them to the void.'

'How do you know him? When did you meet him?' Sherlock crowded her against the car and Audrey had to pull him away.

'You're scaring her.'

'*I'm* scaring *her*?'

'Tell us what you did to him,' Audrey said to the Jenny.

'He came too near the sacred lake.'

'Which lake?' Audrey prompted.

'The dryads and I, we protected the waters. Mine to protect; mine to take my toll of the unwary. We kept the secrets of Our Lady and the Garland King.'

Audrey dreaded that she knew what 'take my toll' meant, in light of all that possessiveness. 'So this Professor M was too near your sacred lake. And?'

'He saw me on the banks, where I sought news from the ravens. The iron rails that had separated my sisters and I from our King and the Lady were slowly being stripped away. I wanted to know how soon I, *we*, would be free to return to court, to pay obeisance again. I didn't heed the raven's warning. I allowed this man to see me in my true form.'

'And he investigated,' said Sherlock, like it was the most natural thing in the world to pursue a supernatural creature you'd spotted lolling about with her scales and weedy hair and sharp predator's teeth, instead of running as fast and as far as possible.

Of course, Audrey thought. Sherlock would have done exactly the same.

'I slipped away but he followed me to the water,' the Jenny continued, 'and he stayed and he stayed. The sun sank low and he wouldn't leave. I sensed in him the curiosity that destroys in order to learn. I sensed his arrogance and how he would wait for me until he could catch and destroy me, and through me, the dryads, and my Lady. So I sang to him. I beckoned to him. He swam to me and I took him in my arms and pulled him to the deeps. I swallowed him and filled him and drank his mind and *oh oh oh*!' The singsong tale ended in wails of fear.

'He was cold, cold, cold like the emptiness between the moon and the stars,' the Jenny said, quietly, desolate. 'I could see his knowledge of the worlds beyond this world, the suns beyond this sun, and how he could split the tiniest particle, smaller than the sand, to unleash all-devouring fire on the air we breathe, burning even the water to nothing, to–'

'What is his name?' Sherlock asked, grabbing the Jenny's hand. A thin layer of water washed over his hand from hers and he snatched his away again, before she could attempt to drown him again.

But she didn't even try. 'Moriarty,' the Jenny breathed. Her eyes turned grey again as Myca resurfaced. 'James Moriarty. Astrophysicist. She's speaking of nuclear fission. He terrified her beyond all reason. She didn't understand what it meant. How could she?'

The Jenny rose up again, using Myca's voice. 'He showed me his power and I fled.' The skim of water over her skin pooled in her eyes. 'I spat him out and I dived so deep but he knew where to find me, he knew my lake, which I was sworn to protect, a sentinel to guard my Lady and the King, but he knew. So I ran. A coward, foresworn in my duty, I dived down and down and down and swam the deepest caverns past the sleeping dragons, away away away, between the diminished iron barriers, until I found another lake, abandoned by the fae.'

'*Llyn y Dywarchen*,' said Sherlock.

'There I bided,' the Jenny continued. 'There I hid. Cold Moriarty walked the moors, seeking me and my queen, for years and years and years, but he never found me. Then your sister came. So bright. She saw me in shallows, seeking news from the ravens. Not from the banks; never there again. She came down to fathom the motion she saw. I studied her, to see if she was *his*, for he had begun to send agents. Hers was not the curiosity of destruction. She would not cut me to pieces to understand the whole. So young; so full of knowledge and potential. She was the perfect vessel. Together, we could prepare against he who would burn the stars from spite, to harm us. Together, we could protect my queen.'

'So you lured my sister after all, and drowned her, and possessed her,' Sherlock concluded, icily enraged.

'I did what I must for the safety of the Green Realm.'

'You tried to drown Moriarty,' said Sherlock. 'Of course he fought back.'

'He's still fighting. For decades, he's been fighting.' Myca shook her head and water sheened clear from her skin and eyes. 'She tried to kill him and now he works to destroy all the fae. His is the hand I keep seeing, through my work. She barred that information from my conscious mind, the wretch.'

'Myca?' Sherlock sounded suddenly lost.

'I'm here,' his sister whispered. 'With her. We. She. She's kept things from my knowledge.'

'She's used you,' Audrey said darkly. 'After creating an enemy who has hunted not only her but all of us, for decades. He's slaughtered so many. He ordered the murder of my family, because you, you–'

Myca stood tall in defiance of Audrey's elongated snout, bared teeth, low growl.

'She did,' said Myca steadily. 'She did all of that. But if you could put aside tearing out my throat and stuffing it with arum lilies until later, we need to find John Watson and Irene Adler and put a stop to all of this.'

'How?'

'I have no idea yet. John and the vampire first. The rest will follow. We need to–'

Myca blinked again, dangerously taking her eyes from Audrey's to look around as dawn turned to morning.

'Where's Nick?'

Audrey resisted the urge to pounce, her instincts warring. Her fury at the Jenny could not be exacted on Myca, who was effectively a captive and, as Sherlock's sister, practically pack. Instead, she raised her chin to sniff the air.

Scenting wasn't necessary, however, as the slam of the guesthouse door announced Nick's return.

She was wearing a backpack, sturdy boots and a forbidding expression as she marched up to the trio by the car.

'You all done? Because that son of a bitch has got John, and even if I can't follow the garlic trail, you can, now you've got your wolf back.' A sharp nod of the head at Audrey on this. 'And you, Mr Pretty, if you've finished flapping your trap, you better be smart enough to find your boyfriend if she can't. And you.' Her glare at Myca was unfriendly. 'Sherlock's spot on, you water witch. You've got resources and powers we don't, so if you know where he is, you'd better say, because I swear to god, if anything's happened to my best mate, after I'm done with the bastards who took him, I'm coming for you. You got me?'

'Indeed.' Myca arched an eyebrow, but it was a ghost of her former dispassion.

'Right. Which way, Mrs H?'

Before Audrey could get down to following the trail, Myca spoke.

'I may know where Norton took him.'

'Then spit it out. I haven't got time for another bloody speech.'

Myca delivered one anyway. 'Norton knew the effect of wolfsbane gas on Mrs Hudson, yet in taking John, he clearly expected Sherlock could successfully follow, or there is no point in taking him.'

'But why does he want me?' Sherlock asked, then: 'Oh, of course. To lure Myca. He wants the Jenny.'

'Yes.' A wash of lakewater filmed her eyes, but Myca grit her teeth and remained uppermost. The revelations, on top of the effect of the steel handcuffs, had changed the balance. Perhaps, Audrey thought, because Myca understood the implications of the Professor's scientific knowledge in a way that the Jenny never had. Professor Moriarty understanding nuclear fission didn't mean he had the means to actually blow up the world.

Which didn't mean he wasn't attempting to destroy it in other ways, one cryptid at a time.

'He expects me to find him,' Sherlock continued. 'So what do I know about this area? *Llyn y Dywarchen*. But Myca and I were there, with no sign of Norton, Moran or anyone else. What else do we know?'

'The Jenny came from a sacred lake protected by dryads,' suggested Audrey.

'And the Roylotts, including Sebastian Moran, killed a Greek dryad at Stoke Moran after trying to discover her secrets.'

Sherlock retrieved the remains of the dryad from the pocket where he'd stowed it and stared. 'Who was the dryad protecting? Your passenger says she fled her post decades ago.'

Myca reached for the wooden fragment, eyes awash with the Jenny again. 'We protected the Garland King and the Lady of the Lake. All around these lands, surviving fae guard our most sacred places.' She held up her cuffed wrist. 'Remove the iron, Sherlock.'

'Not on your nelly,' Audrey muttered, but Sherlock took the key and unfastened the handcuffs from his own wrist and then, carefully, from his sister's.

'Do you know where to go? Will that thing inside you let you into its memory?'

'That wall has come down, Sherlock. I know everything she hid from me. I know everything I've done, thinking it was my choice when it wasn't. We're done with that. Aren't we?' Whatever reply the Jenny made satisfied Myca Holmes. 'Into the car. We'll find them at the oak grove.'

Chapter Twenty-One

Paved roads only went so far in the Snowdonia National Park. Sherlock had to abandon the hire car near Pont Pen-y-Benglog, so they picked their way north alongside the Afon Lloer river and over rocky outcrops. Myca, more nimble than her build would suggest, led the way.

Nick trailed behind, scowling. The flirting had definitely ceased. She chose her steps carefully, but her prosthetic still sometimes slipped on loose stones. She simply righted herself and ploughed on.

Audrey considered morphing into wolf form, now that she could again, so she could run ahead to find John, but he might not be at the grove, and what would happen to Sherlock and Nick in her absence if Myca was deceiving them? Nick wasn't the only one unimpressed by the Jenny's secrecy. Audrey was doubly irritated, because she should never have trusted Myca Holmes in the first place.

Audrey dropped back to help Nick over the treacherous scree littering the slope. Nick jerked away from her guiding hand and nearly toppled. With a grudging huff and a not-quite-apologetic grimace, she suffered to be assisted toward easier terrain, covered in tufts of grass.

Clouds scudded across the sky, congregating to conceal the sun, parting to reveal the brilliant blue morning, then closing again. Mists came and went around the nearby peaks, and sometimes in the hollows through which they walked, obscuring the hiking paths. The weather around these peaks was never really warm, even when the sun broke through, and the shifting clouds smelled to Audrey of pent-up rain. She hated to think how hard the walking might become for Nick then, with the mud and scree, damp moss and low alpine flora offering no handholds at all.

The Afon Lloer led to a lake nestled between three peaks – a site too exposed to be the sacred grove they sought. Myca led them ever more cautiously up the western slopes, circling towards the peak of *Pen yr Ole Wen*.

'*Pen yr Ole Wen*. Head of the White Light,' Sherlock muttered. He was perspiring freely but his energy hadn't flagged. He'd have overtaken Myca if he'd known where she was heading.

'Head of the White Slope,' Myca corrected him absently. She held up her hand. 'Wait.'

'I'm not in the mood to wait.'

'Sherlock.' She spoke his name gently and he looked away: a little brother fairly chastised by his big sister. But then he shot her a sharp glare.

'The vampire has had John for hours. He doesn't need John. He doesn't need me. He only needed me to bring you, and here we are. What are we waiting for? Tactical advantage? I don't believe we have any.'

'We have them.' Myca nodded at Audrey and Nick.

Audrey was sceptical about the level of tactical advantage they offered. Only one of them could turn into a wolf at will, and unless Nick had a backpack full of secret firearms, it was unclear what she was bringing to the fight. Their current goal was to find John Watson, but finding John alive – even getting him back – wouldn't solve their problems. Surely finding him (*please, let it be alive*) was just a step towards falling deeper into trouble. But like Sherlock, and like Nick, Audrey was impatient and angry, and that was fuel enough for whatever came next. But like them, she was not stupid. The urge to get their friend back was tempered with the knowledge that by travelling to the oak grove, they were following someone else's agenda.

Grudgingly, the three of them continued to follow Myca as she led them past a formation of jagged slate rocks.

Not quite past. A crack between two towers of dark grey stone suggested only a hollow, but Myca pushed between them and suddenly disappeared behind a sharp twist of the path. Sherlock and Audrey followed, fitting more easily into the unpromising gap. Glimpses of the changing sky were visible beyond the narrow gaps of stone leaning inward above their heads.

Immediately, the pungent whiff of garlic filled Audrey's nostrils.

Sherlock's nose wrinkled too and he peered about as Nick handed her backpack through to Audrey and slipped into the gap to join them. They halted, unable to progress while Sherlock bent to retrieve a reeking bundle stuffed into the cracks of the rocks. He shook out a coat wrapped around a pair of leather shoes.

'He's either marking the way or he couldn't stand the smell anymore,' Sherlock observed. He continued to examine the cloth while Myca waited impatiently ahead of them. 'No bloodstains.' His jaw tensed.

Audrey didn't need to point out that the absence of bloodstains didn't mean John was unharmed. Not with a vampire involved.

Without room enough to sling her backpack on, Nick clutched it to her belly, her expression hard. 'He'll be all right,' she said, tight and clipped. She and Sherlock exchanged a look, united in dread and ferocity. *He had better be.*

'Make no sound,' Myca warned them softly. She continued along the claustrophobic passage, the others close behind.

Myca stepped back into daylight.

'You came.' Gottfried Norton's voice sounded peculiarly flat in the hidden hollow that allowed no echo.

Still within the passage, Sherlock stopped so abruptly Audrey almost collided with him. She felt Nick's breath warm on the back of her neck.

'Of course I came,' Myca responded drily. 'You will return Dr Watson to me.'

A low moan indicated John's less than hale presence. Audrey couldn't see him, but nor could she smell blood.

A subdued gasp escaped Sherlock, however, who was ahead and could see whatever state John was in. The vampire heard.

'Mr Sherlock Holmes. There's no need to be shy. Come out where I can see you.'

Sherlock joined his sister in the clearing, allowing Audrey to see the Jenny's previous home. The place where it had tried to murder a nuclear physicist and set off this bloody chain of events.

She suppressed a growl and cast her hunter's eyes over the scene.

The clearing had no doubt once been lush, with trees growing all the way up the incline to frame the small body of water at its centre. The waterhole had long dried up. Now it was a murky depression edged with lichen and dying meadow-grass, a blackened stand of burned oaks forming a semicircle at one end. Scrubby tufts of singed alpine plants wilted between the trunks. Here and there, the bases of the ruined trees bore signs of trampled mushrooms. The faintest scent of ammonia lingered under the reek of cold ashes. The grove had been destroyed mere days ago: probably when the Roylotts and Moran had abducted that poor dryad. How many trunks here represented her murdered sisters?

The oaks had been old but not mighty, their stunted remains twisted like the peculiar oaks of Wistman's Wood. Was that another grove of dryads, protecting some sacred place? Audrey tucked that thought away to examine later – assuming later ever happened.

At the one end of oaken semi-circle stood Gottfried Norton, barefoot and coatless, his clothing in grimy disarray. Beside him, John Watson knelt in the soot, a bruise blooming on his forehead. He struggled to focus on Sherlock.

'Trap,' he managed to say. He blinked rapidly, then sagged, splaying his hands to catch himself before he could face-plant in the dirt.

'Yes, we know,' said Sherlock patiently, though his voice thrummed with repressed stress.

'I only need Myca Holmes,' said Gottfried.

'Why should I let you have her?' asked Sherlock.

'Moran will kill Irene,' Gottfried replied simply. 'He promised an exchange.'

'He lied,' said Myca. 'Whatever he and his Professor have planned, they will have more in store for a natural born werewolf than bartering her for a water spirit.'

'I'm not an idiot,' snarled Gottfried. 'She's valuable to them. But what choice do I have?'

'You could have worked with me,' said Myca.

'With the Department of Fisheries? The people who hunted Irene when she was a child and drove her out of England? Negotiate with a possessed human so compromised that she has spent a lifetime betraying humans and fae alike? I hardly think so.'

Myca folded her arms. 'I have no intention of handing myself over to you.'

Gottfried's fist closed around the back of John's shirt and he hauled John to his feet. 'You may not care if I tear out his throat to bleed to death in the mud, but I think your brother might.'

'Please, no,' began John, twisting in the vampire's hold.

The motion shielded John's right side from Norton's cold gaze – and

Audrey could see what John held in that hand, collected from the dirt in which he'd so deliberately fallen.

John stumbled gracelessly, untucking Norton's shirt from the waistband of his trousers. 'For God's sake, please don't hurt me.' John's left hand closed over Norton's shirt collar in what seemed desperate supplication.

With an irritated snarl, Norton adjusted his grip, as though it were distasteful to hold such a mewling human too close. It opened up the space between them a fraction: enough to allow John to brace himself against the vampire's body and drive the jagged, fire-hardened stick of oak in his right hand into Norton's exposed stomach.

Gottfried howled in fury and pain, the makeshift stake protruding from below his ribs. He released John to clutch at the wound. John wisely skittered beyond his reach, snatched up another scorched branch as a weapon and adopted a fighting stance.

From the far reaches of the burned grove, a deep and unpleasant laugh fell like a stone into the hollow, followed by a derisive voice. 'You need to stake 'em in the heart, you wally. You missed. And that monster'll snap your neck in a minute.'

A man dressed in black and grey camouflage fatigues emerged from the sooty shadows. He was grey at his temples and lines of hard living gave his tanned face a weathered, grim topography. His rifle was pointed lazily in their direction. At his belt were a holstered firearm and a sheathed hunting knife.

John cocked an eyebrow at the intruder, and then at Gottfried. 'I'm a bloody doctor. I know where to find a heart. If I'd meant to kill him, he'd be dead.'

Audrey thought it a bravura performance – John had hardly had time to aim, and penetrating the vampire's skin was almost certainly due more to the properties of the oak than the strength of the blow. But the confession distracted the recovering Gottfried from any attempt at revenge. Instead, the vampire's malignant glare turned onto the new arrival.

'Moran. *Du Hurensohn.* Where's my wife?'

'Exactly where we need her,' said Sebastian Moran. 'Nice work, luring the Fisheries bitch here. Pity you had to bring an entourage. Hello in there, lady wolf.' Moran waved at Audrey, who was not as concealed as she'd hoped. She slipped a hand behind her and gestured for Nick to withdraw down the passage. Nick wasn't much of a secret weapon, but she was all they had.

'Hello yourself, you murderous monster,' said Audrey, stepping out at last to join the Holmes siblings in the clearing. 'I've wanted a word with you.'

'I'm sure you have.'

'You and your father conspired with William Ormstein to murder my children.' Honestly, she was surprised at how calm she sounded. For all that, her fingers were now tipped with claws and coarse hair was raised in hackles along her spine. She knew her eyes had changed, too, and that Sherlock was trying not to look at her.

'That abomination wasn't my father,' Sebastian replied, lip curled.

'So you'll be pleased to hear that Irene Adler and I killed Grimsby Roylott yesterday.'

'Fairly pleased, though I'd been looking forward to doing that myself. That monster murdered my mother. I owed him.'

'Are you as pleased to know we've killed your brother as well?'

Moran's face convulsed in disgust. 'Gus was no brother of mine, either. That absolute fuckmuppet burned down this grove before he could be sure the dryad would tell us what we needed to know. You know, they thought to deprive me of my inheritance. Stoke Moran is *my* house. Lord Moran is *my* title. Fucking filthy pair of freaks. I'd have done for them years ago, if the Professor hadn't had use for them. Good riddance to the pair of them, and everything like 'em. Your time's up, wolf. Jim Moriarty's going to do for the lot of you. No more water hags to drown innocent folks, no more bastards with snakes for heads to destroy good women–'

'You were happy enough to use his venom for your own purposes,' Sherlock interrupted sharply. 'All those human deaths, while this Professor Moriarty of yours looked to control supposed sacred wells. And you *still* haven't found the one you want, have you?'

'Means to an end, and all in a good cause, Holmes. Oh yes, the Prof and I know who you and your boyfriend are. We've been watching you, like we watch the thing that used to be your sister. And we're getting close now. That waterlogged bint's going to tell us what we need to know.'

'I hardly think so.' Sherlock affected unconcern even more assiduously than Myca.

Moran lifted his chin at Myca, standing so pale and silent. 'Aren't you revolted at what that hag did to your sister, Holmes? After it tried to murder the Professor, it found a gap that Beeching made in the railroads and hid in some other muddy hole, till it could find another victim. Drowned and possessed her, didn't it? Doesn't it make you mad, that your sister is dead and her body hosting a parasite?'

'I lack data on the nature and likely outcome of that event, which has so far presented as a form of symbiosis,' Sherlock prevaricated. His eyes were darting around the hollow, checking where John and Gottfried stood, where Myca and Audrey were situated, trying to calculate what move to make. 'And my sister isn't dead. She lives alongside the Jenny.'

'For now. Like I said, the hag will soon be gone. The vampires too.' Moran nodded towards Gottfried, too weak to extract the stake from his body. 'Along with all those bloody werewolves. All kinds of ungodly brutes, weeded out of existence like they deserve.'

Audrey shuddered with horror, grief, and rage combined. 'Like you and Ormstein weeded out Siobhan, a child who had no say in what she became? Like you destroyed Ruby with poisoned meat. You coward.'

Moran raised an eyebrow. 'Ruby Stockton? Huh. Wish I could claim the kill, but she's not one of mine; that was well before my time. The Professor knows who was behind that one though, eh Ms Holmes?'

Myca dismissed Moran's accusations with a wave of her hand. '1995? Before my time, Mr Moran. Not yet in puberty, never mind encountered the Jenny.'

'What, the Fisheries doesn't keep records?'

'Not always.'

Audrey's body had begun to change without her will, responding to the emotional storm of her heart. Her snout crinkled at Myca's unhelpful reply. The memory of Ruby's horrific death and Ormstein's slaughter of her families in Bristol, and later in Edinburgh, howled in her veins. Remembered grief and fear mingled now with the way Moran pointed his rifle easily at Sherlock, and then at John.

John noticed, of course he did, and he stepped warily back, sideways, seeking the cover of the dead trees.

A bang, and dirt kicked up at John's feet. John stood very, very still.

Audrey sensed Nick's quick breathing behind her, but no motion.

'Hang about, Doc,' Moran said. 'I haven't got what I want yet. We've got a prophecy to fulfil, don't we?' He directed this to Myca. 'He remembers you, you know. The Professor remembers what you gave him.'

'*Fotze!* Give me back my wife!' demanded Gottfried. His voice rasped and his skin had darkened to a bilious black where the stake pierced it.

'Not bloody likely,' Moran said, amused.

'I have sold my honour for her sake!'

In that moment, Audrey found she could forgive him this betrayal, which had been done for Irene. She'd have done anything for Ruby; might have done it for Ruby's daughter, who looked so much like Audrey's love: from the curve of her shoulder to the delicate, dark skin of her throat and her golden eyes. Anything, that is, except trade others she loved.

'That's a nasty wound, there,' Moran said, ignoring Gottfried's plea. 'That idiot might have missed your heart, but he had the wit to stab you with oak. The Prof reckons the spookies use it for purification. Probably full of dead tree-bitch as well. You could get a nasty infection. Do vampires get those? Does it hurt? I'm not convinced any of you brutes feel more than a dog would, anyway. Guess we'll find out.'

As the last words left his lips, Sebastian Moran shifted the rifle a fraction and fired.

The bullet pierced Gottfried Norton's chest. His heart.

Gottfried's surprise barely registered before his entire form turned grey; crumbled in a dusty puff of air, created by the bullet powering through the cloud of his remains. The projectile slammed into the stump of the tree behind him. Splinters spat away at the impact and might have pierced John's cheek, if he hadn't thrown himself to the ground at the sound of the shot.

Moran laughed with gruesome delight. 'God, that never gets old. A little silver bullet dipped in holy water and pfffffffffhtt! Like a dandelion clock. Good reflexes there, Doc Watson. Wouldn't want to get that dust in a scratch. No idea what effect it has. Not one of the Prof's Areas of Study.'

The rifle was suddenly pointed at Audrey, who had crouched to spring.

'Nuh-uh-uuh, Hudson. Holy water doesn't damage werewolves as thoroughly as that, but I can fill any bit of you with silver and you'll be sick as a – haha – dog. Now you just heel, like a good mutt, while I finish with my tiger trap, hmmm?'

With the rifle trained on her, Moran pulled the revolver from its holster. 'I got bullets enough here for everyone, and you, water hag, have business to conduct with me and the Prof.'

'I will do no such thing.'

Moran grinned. 'But you came, and you obligingly brought your host's brother, so I gotta wonder what you think happens next. 'Coz you can give me what I want, or I can shoot him.'

'And then what do you have to bargain with?' Myca spoke in that voice which wasn't entirely hers. Her hair floated, her skin was dewy, her eyes green and murky. 'I'm not here to bargain. I'm here to destroy you.'

'Fine,' said Moran.

He fired, but John was already moving – had regained his feet while Moran threatened Audrey, and been running across the dried banks of the old lake. He flung himself at Sherlock.

Too late, of course. Bullets travel faster than people. Faster than werewolves too.

But not faster than sisters possessed by water spirits.

The silver bullet zinged past Audrey's cheek (too slow) but before it could drill through Sherlock's throat, it pushed into the sudden barrier of Myca's back, just as John tackled Sherlock to the ground.

Myca gasped, wavered, coughed, turned. Water swirled all around her skin; her hair swept into wet tendrils around her face.

Audrey fell to all fours, tangled in her human clothes but her snout wrinkled to bare her teeth. She could see the titanic struggle on Myca's face, the Jenny and the human vying for supremacy in that tall, sturdy body.

'You will leave Sherlock alone,' Myca gritted out, water and blood bubbling between her teeth.

'Didn't think silver worked on water hags,' said Moran. 'A note for the Prof. Or maybe it's the holy water.'

'If you harm my brother–'

'Come on, Fisheries bitch, you know what I want.'

'I am sworn to protect the Garland King and my Lady,' bubbled the Jenny, but Myca's voice spoke beside it. 'Anything. Leave my brother be.'

Moran laughed again. 'More of your sister left in there than I'd thought, lucky for you, Holmes. All right. I'll leave him be. You tell me where to find the right well, and I'll leave him and his boyfriend here. I'll even throw the wolf bitch in for you. She's hung around for years, another few hours won't make much difference.'

Myca touched her fingers to her lips. The blood on them washed away under the flow of green-tinged water. She was less water goddess now, Audrey thought. More drowned cat.

'*Croth y byd*,' Myca murmured. 'Sherlock, are you all right?'

He was sitting on the ground, John beside him. 'Fine.' He did not sound fine. 'Myca, what are you doing?'

'Saving what I can,' she said. 'Looking after my little brother.'

'Myca, this wasn't the plan.'

'What was the plan?' she asked, trying for humour.

'Ah, well,' Sherlock choked out a laugh. 'We were still working on that.'
John squeezed Sherlock's shoulder, and Sherlock shook his head.

'Yes.' She sighed; more bubbling. 'Come then, Moran, if you're coming.
I will lead you to the well. The Garland King and the Lady of the Lake can
protect themselves, I fancy.'

Myca heaved herself a step towards the hidden stone passage.

Audrey almost threw herself in the way, but Nick couldn't have been so
stupid as to loiter there. That bright young woman must have taken herself
to safety. Surely?

Stiff-legged and growling, hackles up her back and neck, muzzle drawn
to show her teeth, Audrey kept her body between Moran and her boys
until Moran and his bleeding guide arrived at the stone passage.

Moran gave her an unholy grin. 'Run while you can, mutt. You and your
kind will all be gone, soon.'

Then, shoving Myca ahead of him, they disappeared into the tunnel.

Audrey waited to hear a cry, a sound, any suggestion that Nick was
there, and had brought something more useful in her pack than a sunhat.

But not a sound emerged.

CHAPTER TWENTY-TWO

Reverting to her human shape was not an option. Even if rage and fear hadn't been burning through Audrey's blood, her torn and muddy clothes were insufficient cover now for that fragile, naked form. Instead, Audrey prowled in circles around John and Sherlock.

'Why did that hurt her?' Sherlock demanded to know, anger a poor disguise for his distress. 'Myca absorbed a silver bullet with no ill effects at Baker Street. Why should this one injure her?'

John had no answers for him. He sat in the dirt to examine his own injuries. A bruised head was the worst so far, though he favoured his scarred shoulder as well.

Sherlock gingerly reached out, fingers hovering above John's bruised brow before curling tightly into a fist.

'This is,' he began jerkily, 'this is why I don't– We came here without a plan because the vampire had you. And now. This.' He huffed a strained breath. 'Sentiment is dangerous. Emotions are a hindrance. Grit in the machine. A crack in the lens that keeps me from seeing clearly.'

John, whose face was already bereft, as the promised touch was withdrawn, now flinched at the hard words. Audrey wanted to howl at Sherlock's knee-jerk anxiety. He was frightened, but that was no excuse for cruelty.

But as John shrank away from the rejection, Sherlock lurched towards him. 'No, don't!' His hand closed urgently over John's shoulder in a strong grip. John gasped at the sudden pain.

'Oh! No. You're not hurt, John? Please say you're not hurt.'

'I'm not hurt.' John's hand settled over Sherlock's wrist, squeezing reassurance. 'That shoulder's always a bit tricky. I'm a little banged up, but I'm okay.'

'Yes. Yes, it's quite superficial.' Sherlock, relieved, stroked John's shoulder soothingly, and examined his bruised face closely. This time, he allowed his fingers to brush against John's face. 'It's as well Norton's dead already. If he'd killed you–'

John held and kissed Sherlock's fingers, then rose onto his knees so he could hold Sherlock close, pressing their foreheads together. 'And you,' he said. 'Thank god for your sister.'

Audrey finally stopped pacing and sat on her haunches beside them. She raised her head, sniffing the air for Nick.

'Heya, Mrs H!'

And there she was, the wayward cub, emerging from the rock passage with her backpack held tightly between her arms, expression alight with uncalled-for humour.

'Johnny, you okay?' Nick asked as she swung the backpack into one hand. Now, at least, she showed due solemnity for their situation. 'You're supposed to duck, remember?'

'I remember,' John replied. 'My head aches to buggery, but I'll live.'

Audrey resumed her pacing around Sherlock, John and Nick, uselessly patrolling a boundary in an effort to keep them from further harm. The danger had passed, yet still she felt it near, awareness of the threat making her hackles prickle upright. She seemed never to be able to keep her pack safe.

They talked as she prowled around them, ears swivelling, nose lifted, tongue hanging out to taste the air. A growl rumbled in her throat, but to voice it would bring danger their way, and as much as she wanted to have something to attack, it wasn't safe or wise. Not yet.

'Here.' Nick dropped the backpack in front of him. 'I brought your first aid kit along.'

'You don't have any weapons, I suppose?' Sherlock asked moodily.

'I stopped by the kitchen for a few sharp knives, a few other bits and bobs,' she said. 'It's not like John and I swan about with an arsenal in our pockets. The army doesn't let us keep that shit once we muster out. Oh, I picked up some more garlic, just in case, though I'm not sure how much use the stuff is. Where's Fangface, anyway?'

'That double-crossing bastard Moran shot him through the heart. He's literal dust,' John reported, poking through his kit for paracetamol and discovering bottled water and a few chocolate bars as well.

'Sorry I missed the show. I had to make a tactical retreat and I wanted to find out how that little shit Moran got here. Did a recce and found his wheels. Your hair's full of dust, by the way.'

'You didn't inhale any, did you?' Sherlock asked, alarmed. He took John's hand and held it tightly as he spoke, which made John smile despite everything.

'Don't think so.' His face scrunched up as he scraped his teeth over his tongue. 'Pretty sure it's bites and not dust that make you undead.'

Nick poured bottled water onto a gauze pad and wiped some dusty residue from John's hair. ' Hey, Mrs H!' Nick said as Audrey completed another uneasy circuit around them. 'We gotta worry about this vamp dust?'

'No,' said Audrey impatiently, forcing her wolf mouth to make human sounds. 'Worry about where Moran took Myca Holmes.'

'I know where they went,' Sherlock told her. 'Myca told us. *Croth y byd*. It's a sinkhole on one of the slopes south of Clogwyn y Tarw. We found it as children. How we'll get there on time to be of any use, I don't know. As Nick says, Moran had a vehicle nearby.'

'He's on foot now, though,' Nick said, with a devious and triumphant expression. 'I found his wheels, then I scuppered 'em. Hurt my soul to fill the tank of such a gorgeous motorbike with dirt, but needs must when a war's on, eh Johnny?'

Sherlock raised an eyebrow at her.

'Vagabund BMW all terrain job. Beautiful machine. I'd have slashed the tyres, but that could have made it obvious you lot had back-up. He might have come gunning for me, or gone back to eliminate you lot, so I took a page from the *Sneaky Bastards Book of Sabotage* and made it look like mechanical failure. Some dirt in the tank, a bit of fiddling with the engine, and all that sod knew was his bike wouldn't start. The look on his face! Ah!' Nick performed an exultant chef's kiss.

'What then?' asked John keenly.

'Then he made a phone call. Whatever the geezer at the other end said, Moran looked ready to warpath it back to you, but then a crowd came up from the valley singing cheery hiking songs in harmony. I guess he figured he didn't have time to tidy up loose ends before they reached us; coz he'd have to take out the choir too.

'Anyway, he'd already wasted minutes slapping the darbies on the Jenny and getting up to ride pillion. When the bike wouldn't start, he started marching her across the hills. Well, after he'd threatened to go back and shoot Sherlock in the head to make her go with him, the prick. The Jenny was not happy. She said she'd lead the way, but she was wailing and dragging her feet like a professional toddler. She'll have slowed him down as much as she can. I've no idea if that's Myca or the Jenny stonewalling, but it's a smart move. So if we can get hobbling, folks, we might even overtake them, since we know where they're headed. Crothy-bit?'

'*Croth y byd.* And we might, if I knew how to get there from here.'

'How would a local ordnance survey map suit you?' Nick produced the map from the backpack, like a magician with a particularly sparkly rabbit. 'Not just a pretty brain,' she grinned.

'The base commander used to call Nick "Eveready",' John said with delighted pride. 'She's always prepared.'

'Yeah. You lot can go haring off without water, food, maps or first aid, but I'm a driver. My job's to get you places,' She rapped her prosthetic leg with her knuckles, 'as alive as possible. Let's take a gander.'

Nick unfolded the map showing place names, roads, geographical features, and topography. She jabbed a finger onto Pont Pen-y-Benglog, where they'd left their car, then traced their path on the map to a sheltered, unmarked hollow.

'This is us.' she said. 'Show me where we're going; I'll see if we can find a short cut.'

Sherlock scanned the map then stabbed a finger further south, past a series of tight topography lines indicating the steep rise of Clogwyn y Tarw. To the west lay the lake, Llyn Idwal. The name *Croth y byd* did not appear on the map.

'That's just what Myca and I called it,' said Sherlock. 'We were learning Welsh at the time. It means "womb of the world". We found the sinkhole on our rambles, the day before Myca... drowned.' He closed his eyes and took a deep breath.

'She's not dead,' said John softly. 'She saved your life.'

'Moran shot her. When he shot her at Baker Street, she didn't even flinch, but this time she bled. I have no idea what she is. I have no idea if my sister is alive or a puppet of that water parasite. I–' Sherlock fell silent.

Audrey had not stopped pacing, and could not think how best to protect her fragile family. She wanted to hunt Moran and his professor down and tear them to pieces. She wanted to nip these ones in the heels and harry them back to London. She wanted to howl and run wild, or slink into a cave with her pack and snarl at the whole world.

But she heard the pain in Sherlock's voice and halted by his side. She bumped her nose against his shoulder, then her forehead to his chest. She made her long, toothy mouth make human shapes again.

'Myca lives,' Audrey said with difficulty, 'The Jenny isn't a parasite. She's the other. Symbiosis.'

'Symbiote.'

'Yes. I think they share,' said Audrey. 'The Jenny hides things from Myca. At Baker Street, Myca wasn't harmed because the Jenny was dominant then. Its goals and Myca's are not the same now. The Jenny would have let you die today. Myca took control to protect you. She was mostly human when the bullet struck.'

'So she really is hurt.'

'Yes. But alive. The Jenny needs her. So does Moran.'

'She was shot in the back,' John said suddenly. 'High up. One of the rhomboid or serratus posterior muscles. But she was walking and – wailing, did you say, Nick?'

'Like an overtired three-year-old,' Nick confirmed.

'So her lungs aren't badly compromised.'

Sherlock searched John's expression for tell-tale lies. 'Is this some kind of at-a-glance triage, John?'

'I was an army doctor. At-a-glance triage is my superpower. She's injured, but it's not immediately fatal.'

'She was still bleeding when I saw them,' Nick said, concerned.

'That's less good,' John said, sticking with his truth-telling policy. 'But she's moving and making a noise, and we saw how the Jenny was able to protect her at Baker Street. Whatever that water spirit intends, Myca is her transport, so it'll be looking after her body.' He cut a glance, equal parts concern and reassurance, at Sherlock.

Sherlock got to his feet at last, John following suit while Nick retrieved Audrey's torn, abandoned clothing.

'Are you all right?' John asked Sherlock gently. 'Not broken yet?'

Sherlock had finished brushing dirt from his trousers. He smiled wanly. 'Not yet. Still changing.'

'Good,' said Nick. She had folded Audrey's clothes and shoes and put them in the backpack with the first aid kit and other supplies. She still held the map. 'We can't have you losing your head, now.'

Sherlock's glare was deeply offended and Nick laughed. 'That's the spirit, boyo. We are going to stop that arse Moran and His Nibs the Professor doing whatever they've planned; we're going to get your gorgeous sister back; and we're going to find Irene Adler while we're at it. We, my lanky friend, are going to very solidly kick arse. Aren't we, Mrs H?'

Audrey knew there was no safety for them until they did exactly as Nick said. Moran and this Professor had orchestrated so many murders – human, werewolf, fae – without consequences. Hiding in a cave was no solution.

Audrey rose to her four feet, her front claws shimmering with cracked nail polish, her tawny eyes bright with fierce determination, and only a little fear.

'We go. Now.'

'Which way?' John asked.

Nick grinned. 'I can see a short cut. Come on.'

They left the oak grove and, led by Nick Murray, went in search of The Womb of the World.

CHAPTER TWENTY-THREE

Nick tried to shake off John's assistance as they clambered back down the slope to their hire car, but she'd worn her prosthetic far longer than the recommended hours. At the car, Nick reluctantly took the back seat with John while Sherlock took the wheel and Audrey rode shotgun, paws on the dashboard.

Audrey was aware of many things as Sherlock voided the rental car insurance by driving right off the road and thence up and down hills, across shallow creeks, slipping on scree and bouncing across tufts of grass, to get closer to their destination.

She was aware of Nick wrestling her prosthetic off, swearing vividly, to inspect the damage; and of how John was surprised that it wasn't worse.

That's the *were* in her, Audrey thought. Faster healing.

Audrey was also aware of Sherlock concentrating ferociously as he drove. Brow furrowed, eyes fixed on the terrain ahead. Ignoring her as comprehensively as if she didn't exist.

She didn't need to see her reflection to know why he was so single-mindedly refusing to see her.

Despite the daylight, the absence of the full moon, and the accepted mythology that tried to make sense of what she was – here was the true soul of the curse that lived inside Audrey Hudson, on the outside for all to see.

Rage drew on the curse in her blood and it shaped her. Audrey was not remotely human. She wasn't even truly wolf. She was *were*: the beast; the monster; the Cursed Alpha; a supernatural predator hunting those responsible for her suffering.

Audrey's claws dug into the dashboard and the upholstery for purchase as the car jounced over rocks and dips, every rough hair of her pelt bristling, a red light behind her tawny eyes, the constant low-level growl filling the cabin. Saliva was strung between her bared teeth in anticipation of a kill.

Sherlock wasn't the only passenger ignoring the abomination in the passenger seat. John assiduously rifled through the first aid kit to tend to the rubbed-raw skin of Nick's overused stump.

Honestly, it was a wonder Sherlock and John didn't simply bail out and flee at the first opportunity.

'I know we're dashing to the rescue and everything,' Nick said, looking away from where John applied cream and gauze, 'but what are we going to do when we get there?'

Sherlock ignored Nick, too. The car lurched sideways one way as the left wheels went into a furrow, then the other as Sherlock savagely corrected the steering.

'We didn't have a plan at the grove and that went tits-up pretty fast,' persisted Nick. 'We need something better.'

The car dropped briefly into a hole, perhaps a burrow, resulting in an almighty bang. Audrey dug her claws in but the others were jolted in their seats.

'Mrs H,' Nick tried a new avenue when she recovered from the knock. 'I know you've got your major mofo wolf on. But you're our Alpha. You–'

Only a bowel-curdling snarl greeted Nick's tentative query. Nick paled, but scowled back. 'That's not fucking helpf–'

The words were lost as the car slid down a metre of shale towards a creek bed, throwing the occupants every which way. Audrey instinctively reacted as though it were an attack, snapping her jaws and missing Sherlock's face by a gnat's breath.

Sherlock didn't even flinch. 'Sit!' he snapped, as though she were an unruly hound. 'And shut up. I'm *thinking*.'

Audrey could swear she heard John snort a laugh; and she saw how Nick went from deer-in-the-headlights to a fuck-me laugh at what she saw on John's face.

'You are so stupid in love,' Nick said.

'Yup,' said John. 'Do you want to see if you can get this leg back on?'

'Yeah, jam it on there. It feels better already.'

'That's because the chafing's already half healed.'

'Had to be an upside to being a hairy peg-leg of the night, yeah?'

'That's the spirit.'

Another lurch banged John's sore shoulder against the car door. He hissed in a breath and blew it out slowly.

'Wish we knew what this bloody prophecy was that Moran mentioned,' he grumbled. 'It'd at least give us context for what the hell he and that damned professor want Myca and Irene for.'

And then Sherlock drove into the shadows of Clogwyn y Tarw and the vehicle rattled to a wheezy halt behind an outcrop of stone.

'What do you think I've been deliberating?' Sherlock said, almost off-hand.

John sat forward. 'You know the prophecy?'

'No. And don't call it that. It's no doubt nothing more than a nonsense rhyme.'

'A little more intel before we walk headfirst into another trap would be welcome, love. If you don't know this so-called prophecy, what are you talking about?'

Sherlock paused in the act of unclipping his seat belt to absorb that unexpected endearment with an expression of bashful delight, then he put on his game face and twisted toward the others.

'When I put the iron on Myca's wrists last night at *Llyn y Dywarchen*, the Jenny became almost incoherent with terror. It demanded to be freed, that the end was nigh, and then it began muttering. All the drive back into town, when it wasn't trying to convince me to break speed limits to get it as far out of Wales as I could manage in an hour, it muttered. I'm not sure it meant me to hear, but my hearing is exceptional and frankly after the fifteenth iteration, it was impossible not to have memorised it.'

Sherlock began to recite.

Long is the day and long is the night, and long is the waiting of Arawn.
Fast is the river and deep is the lake, and long is the memory of Efallyn.
Come destroyer of heavens, Tylwyth Teg's bane,
And the hunter of Tylwyth Teg's light
With the throat of the daughter of sun and moon
And the heart of the exiled wight
And king and the queen asleep in the green will restore Cymru to right

At the end, he cleared his throat, uncomfortable with the collective stares.

'That's as close as I remember it. The rhythm is very ear-worming.'

'It *sounds* like a prophecy,' said John. 'Who's Arawn?'

'You have to stop watching those ridiculous films,' Sherlock said with a wan but affectionate smile. 'Arawn is, in Welsh mythology, a king of the underworld. I'm not familiar with Efallyn, but her name means something like "Living Lake". When the Jenny recited it, I think her fear imbued it with more meaning than it has. Or perhaps, a different meaning to that it might have held. The whole thing is very ambiguous.'

'By the sound of it,' said Nick, 'the whole thing got transferred from her head to the Professor's when she tried to drown him.'

'But did the rhyme live in her brain before then, or did it arise during that encounter, created by her fear?' Sherlock shrugged. 'The thing is, it doesn't matter if it's truly prophetic or merely a self-fulfilling, poetic panic attack. If Professor Moriarty is as obsessed with it as the Jenny, it has dictated his actions since they shared consciousness.'

'And that's what you've been thinking about all this time?' Nick demanded.

'Among other things.'

'And?'

'And I have some ideas. But first–' He looked up, to a towering spire of rocks that rose just to the east of Clogwyn y Tarw. 'We need to get in position before Myca leads Moran here.'

Two steep and twisting inclines led up to the summit of the peak that led to what the Holmes siblings had called *Croth y byd*. The forbidding, skinny cone of slate was not as high as Clogwyn y Tarw but much narrower and more jagged. When Audrey's thoughts were less honed on the here-and-now hunt, she fleetingly wondered how the Holmes children had found their way up here during their childhood explorations. What had their parents been thinking, to let a fourteen-year-old lead a seven-year-old on such dangerous adventures? (Or what parent could have stopped them, she also wondered, before fresh scents on the wind drew her back to the hunt.)

Audrey heard Moran and his prisoner approach long before she could see them, down at the foot of the steep stone formation. Human ears may not have heard, but to Audrey, Moran's voice was unmistakable as he spoke urgently into his phone.

'It's a bugger of a climb, Prof. Sure you can make it?'

The response at the other end of the call wasn't audible.

'Well, I'm already hauling the Fisheries bitch up, I can't drag you and Adler along at the same time. Well, tell her I've got hubby up there and I'll stake him if she doesn't come. Of course I bloody don't. Only good undead thing's a bucket of deader dust, am I right?'

Myca was breathing heavily, down there at the bottom of the slope. The breeze brought the whiff of silver and blood with it. Some fear, too.

'Hang on,' Moran continued. 'I can see you. I'm waving, can you see?'

Audrey stayed flat on her belly under the overhang of grey stone, divining events by the sounds she heard. Myca's wet, laboured breath. Two sets of footsteps approaching. Stopping with a crunch.

'Silver handcuffs?' Moran sounded impressed. 'That's Fisheries issue, that kit. Where the hell did you find those?'

'I've acquired things along the way,' responded a man's voice. His Nibs, Professor Moriarty. 'Iron won't do for werewolves.'

'Works well enough for this wet cow.'

'Where is my husband?' *Irene.* Audrey suppressed a whine.

'Shackled him up top. He did his part, bringing this soggy bint along to swap for you. Really, it was heart-warming to see him so worried about his dog.' This was followed by an ugly laugh in response to whatever expression of loathing Irene had directed his way.

'Come on, then. Lift your feet.'

Audrey caught a glimpse of four pairs of feet in an ungainly clamber for the summit, following the upward line of least resistance. Myca stumbled often and was often shoved on her way by Moran. Irene walked with steady grace, picking her way carefully and sidestepping whenever it seemed the Professor came too close. Audrey could see only his lower half: wiry legs and a white hand on a hiking pole to aid his ascent. An odour wafted from him – frightening in a way that felt both distant and skin-crawlingly familiar – which made her shudder. *The monster of whom monsters are afraid.*

Audrey waited until they were well past before slinking out from cover. She hoped John and Nick were safe.

She doubted it.

Audrey carefully followed the intruders up the rise, and paused when she heard Moran's laugh of surprise.

'Well, you're a turn-up for the books. Still hoping to get your drowned sister back?'

'My sister isn't dead,' said Sherlock Holmes coolly.

'How'd you get here first?'

'Myca said where she was taking you, and I've been here before.'

'And where's your boyfriend and your pet wolf?'

'John declined to assist.'

'He took off like a bleeding melt, didn't he?' Moran snorted. 'Little weasel. Thought he had more grit.'

'One can hardly blame him, given recent events,' Sherlock said levelly. 'Kidnapped by a vampire, confronted by a werewolf–'

'Where's she buggered off to, by the way?'

'Who can say? It followed me back to the road and then ran off after I got into the car and locked all the doors. I may be new to all this, but I'm not an idiot. What kind of suicidal maniac would let an angry wolf occupy a passenger seat on a rescue mission?'

'You sound convincing enough,' said a second male voice.

'And you, sir, must be Professor Moriarty,' said Sherlock.

'Indeed,' said the Professor. 'And really, young man, you must stand clear.'

'I must?'

'You stand in the way not only of me, as an individual, but of the completion of my very necessary endeavours, decades in the making.'

'Rather difficult endeavours, for a lone man to achieve,' Sherlock challenged.

'Oh, I've not been alone the whole time. Sebastian here has been a good right hand man, and we've had our ways of recruiting to the cause.'

'The Napoleon app,' said Sherlock. 'WhatsApp for unofficial cryptid hunters. I assume after the official ones proved unsympathetic to your cause?'

'What do you know of that?'

'Nothing, but there is no way the likes of the Department of Fisheries, Wildlife & Parks didn't know about you. You've been avoiding them for a long time, or Myca would already have known who you were.'

Myca's wet, ragged breathing became more pronounced. Then she said, 'Oh. Oh yes. I see who you must be. Everyone in the department thinks you're dead, Mr Musgrave.'

CHAPTER TWENTY-FOUR

MORIARTY'S LAUGH WAS SHARP AND WHEEZY. 'THEY STILL REMEMBER me there, do they?'

'You're held up as a Horrible Warning,' Myca said, voice strained. 'The consummate bad apple. You're the reason the Department changed its whole approach.'

'Oh, believe me, I noticed the subversion of their policies from eradication to containment.'

'We've never had an eradication policy.'

'They never explicitly *didn't* have one. It was all very coy.'

'And your behaviour pushed them very solidly in the other direction, the irony of which I find pleasing.'

From her vantage point among the sheltering rocks, Audrey sniffed again at Moriarty's peculiarly familiar scent. She'd never met the man, whatever name he used. Why did she recognise it? And why did it fill her with a dread that was steeped far back in time?

Why did it make her think of Ruby?

Myca coughed and Audrey smelled fresh blood. A bad sign. She suppressed another whine. She didn't like having to wait for a signal.

Myca continued to speak, despite the cost to her strength. 'The Department was established to manage and care for Great Britain's natural resources. It–'

'The fae as well as the fish, yes, yes,' Moriarty interrupted her. 'As though a grindylow was as good as a haddock, or a werewolf no worse than a garden pest, a larger aphid, or a once-a-month mole infestation.'

'What on earth did he do at Fisheries?' Sherlock asked Myca, curiosity finally getting the better of him.

'Musgrave was the king of euphemism. Even before he became Assistant Director, he built detailed registers of individual cryptids and their current habitats for "population management and care", which were used to damage and destroy cryptids. His last two years were full of "population relocation"; "waterways restoration"; "special treatments" and "transfers". The language of genocide, where he hid his kill squads.'

'No wonder Mrs Hudson doesn't like you,' said Sherlock.

'*I. Don't. Do. That,*' bit out Myca. 'The Department doesn't.' The painful cough had ceased but Myca was weaker. 'They've been trying for years to undo the damage this monster wrought; ever since he apparently died in a fire in Norwood. I wonder who they really found in the ashes.'

'Nobody important,' said Moriarty airily.

Myca's lip curled. 'I'm surprised you have to travel so far to hunt monsters when presumably you have a mirror available most mornings.'

'Sticks and stones, swamp-bitch.' Moriarty's almost playful tone vanished. 'You tried to murder me, until the superiority of my mind sent you running.'

Audrey, belly to the rough ground, inched closer until she could clearly see the tableau.

Moran, ruddy in the face from exertion, held Myca by the hair, a hunting knife at her ribs. Myca's skin was alarmingly white from the same exertions. She sagged in his grip, the back of her shirt moist with blood and water, and her lips were flecked with blood too. The Jenny was working hard to keep her host going.

Kneeling at the lip of the sinkhole at the crown of the peak, was Irene Adler, dishevelled and bound in silver handcuffs. Her wrists were rubbed raw with feverish reaction and her dark cheeks were flushed with anger and pain, and but even kneeling, she was chin-up, refusing to be cowed by her captors.

Moriarty stood by, a hunting knife held loosely in bony hands. His physique was wiry but strong. This old white man, who used to be Musgrave of the Department of Fisheries, was also the nuclear physicist of the Jenny's nightmares. Audrey salivated at the thought of her teeth in his wrinkled throat, but she held still.

On the other side of the sinkhole, which was even deeper and stranger than the term allowed, Sherlock maintained an expression so relentlessly neutral it betrayed the depth of his concern.

And why not? He'd briefly described that sinkhole as they'd begun their drive here. 'We lost four pennies down it before we realised the reason we hadn't heard them hit bottom was because they were still falling. Myca and I got as close as we dared to listen. We could sense how terrible it would be to fall in; how tempting it was, too.'

'That urge to jump is called high-place phenomenon,' John had replied. Nick had rolled her eyes, telling him they didn't have time to show his cleverness off to his boyfriend.

'It was more than that,' Sherlock had said, properly impressed by John despite the lack of time. 'It smelled like gardens, and the night sky, and sea caves and forests. Then a great flock of black birds – ravens and crows, mostly – wings beating the air in a panic or a rage, poured out of it like the possessed. It was terrifying and thrilling. We thought it a great adventure. That was the day before the lake.' And then he'd driven off the road and conversation had ceased.

In the here and now, Sherlock watched his once adored sister talking on and on, despite her injuries and the knife pricking at her skin.

Where were Nick and John?

'I am curious,' Myca said to Moriarty. 'Ruby Stockton and Dieter Adler. Your thug says you know about their deaths.' She steadfastly didn't look at Irene, who had inhaled sharply at the names.

Another reptilian grin. 'Oh yes. That was fascinating.'

'That was blamed on us,' said Myca.

'And rightly so.'

'Because you did it.'

Appallingly, the old bastard pretended to look shyly pleased. 'I thought it a failed experiment at the time. I'd hoped it might be a solution, but even at the best of times, I discovered, the symptoms might take a decade to manifest, though the end comes rapidly once they do. I believe werewolf metabolism delayed the onset of the disease far beyond the human norm.'

'You...' Irene's defiance slipped. 'You poisoned my mother?'

'Oh, I infected her and your father, though it took years for it to come to fruition. I'd read about human Creutzfeld-Jakob infections via medical treatments and naturally arranged for the Department to get hold of a research specimen. By then I'd learned of your existence, my dear atrocity, but my efforts to seize you weren't successful. I couldn't simply direct one of my squads to fetch you. They had no idea of the prophecy, let alone your role in it. I hadn't trained them to be a retrieval unit. Instead, I wore a wolf pelt to disguise my scent, went into your home while you were all scampering about one full moon, and introduced infected beef into that awful meal marinating in the fridge. Something pungent and foreign–'

'My father's *Glühweinbraten*,' said Irene faintly, aghast.

'All that mulled wine and garlic and spices and rubbish ruining a perfectly good cut of beef. But it meant, of course, they'd hardly be likely to smell anything I put into it, and you were about nine, I think. I noted at the time that a smaller portion of beef had been put aside for a less adventurous palate.'

'You infected both my parents–'

'Nothing happened for the longest time, which was disappointing. Fortunately, I'd embedded a bug in a photograph of their dear little girl, given their habit of moving so frequently. Your mother moved three times before I realised that she'd been luring my attention while your father spirited you away to Germany. I lost you for years, until you so unwisely pursued a singing career. What a clever beast you are.'

Audrey trembled there among the rocks. This man. This – monster. She knew that photograph. The faintest of faint scents must have clung to the tracker he'd placed in it. A scent she'd found in other places from time to time, she now realised with a shudder of horror-after-the-fact.

He'd come to her home while she and Ruby were moon-running. He'd tracked Ruby, intruded on their home to spy? Gloat? Ruby had harboured the seeds of her murder for 20 years before the healing powers of her *were* body at last failed to keep it at bay.

As Ruby had died, so had Dieter Adler.

Audrey pressed her muzzle to the soil and leaked a homicidal growl into the earth. If she was the Cursed Alpha, then Moriarty was the blight itself.

She would enjoy killing him, when the signal came. If she decided to wait that long.

'This is all very jolly,' said Moran into the charged silence. 'Terrific story, Prof. Now I know how you got hold of such excellent kit.' He nodded to the silver handcuffs binding Irene. 'But haven't we got things to do? That wrinkly old she-wolf must be around somewhere, and probably this git's boyfriend. Not that they can do much. Give us a smile, Adler. You and the Fisheries cow get to be the stars of the show any second now.'

Irene tried to be brave. 'Gottfried will–'

'Your dead husband's dust on breeze, bitch,' Moran responded with gruff glee. 'It's hilarious how vampires keep forgetting a shot through the heart with the right ammo will do for 'em before I'm even in biting distance. This is the 21st century, not some Victorian melodrama with sharp sticks. What a dopey wazzock. The look on his face!'

Irene's jaw clenched.

When he wasn't here, you realised Gottfried must already be dead, thought Audrey. Poor Irene, trapped between the man who'd killed her parents and the man who'd killed her foolish husband. Audrey had to remind herself to *wait for the signal*. She inched closer to the sinkhole. Where were John and Nick?

'Enough chatter,' Moriarty agreed. 'We have worlds to destroy. No, don't shoot the boy, Seb. Let him see what his sister *really* is.'

Sherlock waved a hand like that didn't matter. 'She's my sister, she's a cryptid, she is who she is and has been for most of my life. As siblings go, I don't suppose she's any worse than most. To tell the truth, I'm much more interested in what you think you're about to do.'

'I'm going to rid England of these abominations once and for all.'

'Yes, yes, but how?'

'It's all in the prophecy.'

'The one you plucked out of the Jenny's head when she tried to drown you. Which, in retrospect, seems a perfectly reasonable response to being in your head.'

Moriarty wouldn't be goaded. 'A blood sacrifice seems in keeping with their appalling rituals.'

Sherlock arched an eyebrow. 'Is that what you think the rhyme means?'

'*The throat of the daughter of sun and moon*,' Moriarty quoted, '*and the heart of the exiled wight*. That'll be Irene Adler, a werewolf who can change without the call of the moon, and the thing animating your dead sister, exiled from its lake to work from London.' Moriarty twisted his hunting knife, suggesting its likely use in a ritual.

'The *wight* is clearly the Jenny inhabiting Myca,' said Sherlock. 'This reprobate Moran is the hunter of Tylwyth Teg's light and you, with your knowledge of astrophysics, are clearly the destroyer of heavens. It's curious what a panicking mermaid might conjure in its brain. Maybe it did see the future, but I suspect you've misinterpreted the English version of whatever it communicated to you while you were drowning. Language is a tricky thing. So is punctuation, come to that.'

'I've spent my life studying that prophecy–'

'You spent fifty years contemplating an English translation of the ancient Welsh language that a frightened water sprite shot into your brain under traumatic circumstances. Why do you think it's destruction of Arawn and Efallyn that restores Wales? The rhyme can as readily be read that they are the ones to restore it to some previous perfection. And why would Irene be the sacrifice you need?'

Audrey noticed that Myca was making the best of Sherlock's distracting analysis. The Jenny's flow of water holding Myca's injured body up was also flowing over her arms and hands. And Myca, despite how the iron scored her wrists just as the silver scored Irene's, had braced the chain in her fingers and was trying to squeeze her hand out of the loop. Blood dripped from her torn and blistered skin.

Moriarty had had about enough of Holmes Minor. 'Weren't you listening?'

'What about Mrs Hudson?'

'If she survives the sacrificial cleansing, I'll see to that mad old bitch myself.'

'Well, not if it's her throat referenced in the poem.'

'Don't be ridiculous.'

'You've clearly lost track, and if the Roylotts knew what Adelbert Gruner discovered, they didn't tell Sebastian anything about it.'

'Those slack idiots,' Moran grumbled.

Moriarty was more focused. 'What did Gruner know?'

'I keep telling people it's a capital mistake to theorise without data, but there you go. Missing details.'

Moran pressed his knife against Myca's throat – she abruptly ceased her attempt to escape the handcuffs – and with his other hand pulled a pistol from his belt. He aimed it squarely at Sherlock's chest. 'Shall I just shoot him for you, boss?'

'Not yet.' Moriarty gritted out. 'What detail, boy?'

'Mrs Hudson doesn't need the moon to change either.'

'What?'

I'm a bitch, you rancid stain, but I am not the moon's bitch. She moved another fraction closer, still shielded by foliage and the landscape.

'As far as I understand these things, I believe it's a function of menopause,' Sherlock said.

'*What?*'

'And while I'm here, she's not the Cursed Alpha, either. Not really an Alpha, actually, in the way you mean it. The research asserting that wolves rule their packs through aggression was debunked. By the researcher hoping to prove it, himself. Pack leaders are parents, essentially. No battles to the death for dominance. No wholesale slaughter. Well, no more than in any other family.'

'Please let me shoot the gobby bastard,' demanded Moran.

'I haven't known about werewolves for long, but when wolf tracks became an element of my investigation into the kidnapping of the Greek interpreter, I did some reading. When the werewolf angle became apparent, it threw an interesting light onto the received wisdom of what people kept insisting was werewolf nature, despite their stories demonstrating the contrary.'

'Prof?'

'Let him finish. I'm fascinated.'

'Of course you are. You loathe the supernatural but you've been studying it most of your adult life. You're obsessive about knowing how its arcane rules work so that you can turn them on the creatures who live by them.'

'As any man of science should.'

Sherlock's scoffing was epic. 'Oh, please. You discovered something new about the world and instead of adapting your theories to fit the facts and accepting a new paradigm – as a true scientist would – you insisted that the world should be bent to fit your worldview.' Sherlock produced a crooked smile. 'Instead of changing – you broke. Shattered, I think.'

'So what is it about werewolves I have so wrong?'

'Everyone behaves as though wolves are inherently aggressive. That the werewolf curse, forced onto the human mind, is what makes those transformed murderous. There's an infection that gets transmitted through bite, of course, but I know of a werewolf who earned her curse when her werewolf friend saved her life with his actions, at the cost of his own. That wasn't the action of an unreasoning beast. That was courage, with unfortunate side effects. But then, courage can often have those.'

'Yours is about to have some,' muttered Moran.

'But then I saw William Ormstein's trophy assassination photographs. Cruelty is a peculiarly human trait, you know. Predators hunt and fight, but they do it for survival and to feed and protect the pack – the cubs – not out of spite. Ormstein was as cruel in human form as in that of a wolf, and you used him as a weapon until the weapon became unreliable. Until then, his aggression was very human. The werewolf curse isn't that it forces wolf natures onto human temperaments. It's entirely the other way around. The human is forced upon and corrupts the wolf. Well, in some examples. Mrs Hudson has found a balance.'

'Where is she?' Moriarty demanded.

'Oh, around, I expect. She's the pack leader, after all. The responsible adult. I suppose there had to be one.'

'You should have brought her,' Moriarty spat at Moran.

'How was I supposed to know? You said get the natural born wolf, I got her. You said get the sister, I got the sister. You're meant to be the brains of the outfit.'

'Well, you're clearly not.'

'Yes,' said Sherlock drily. 'You're clearly nothing more than another tool in the hands of a madman, just as Ormstein was, and the Roylotts, and even Gruner. Chess pieces in his game. Not even clever pieces. Pawns, all of you.'

'I'm not anybody's chess piece.' Moran raised the gun and corrected his aim towards Sherlock's forehead.

Among the stones circling the peak, Audrey detected John and Nick at last. The scents of sweat, dry blood, and dirt. The rare sounds of small stones moving underfoot.

The whiff of car fuel. The click of a cigarette lighter. Fire.

The signal.

Audrey sprang at Sebastian Moran.

Sherlock dived as Moran's gun discharged, chipping stone behind where he'd stood.

John broke cover with a bellowing war cry and rushed Moriarty. He'd ignited a petrol-soaked rag wrapped around the hire car's crowbar and now he wielded it like a battle axe in the fray. On the second pass, he swept the knife from Moriarty's hand.

Nick, limping but determined, launched herself at Irene, wrapped her arms around her body and tackled them both away from the lip of the sinkhole.

Everything went like clockwork, except–

Except.

Myca, wobbling with blood loss and strain, teetered by the edge of the hole, from which cold air blew up and fathomless darkness called down.

'Myca!' Sherlock cried out, alarmed, panicked.

And Myca folded, fell, tumbled down into the endless depths.

Chapter Twenty-Five

Audrey twisted as she collided with Moran, her wolf body morphing to semi-human so she could wrap wiry arms around his body. He fired again, left-handed, missing her completely, but at the same time he brought the knife in his right hand down in a sweeping arc. The knife reeked of holy water and silver nitrate – a weapon prepared for damaging supernatural beings.

Audrey pulled away from the stench, which saved her throat, but the blade scored across her snout, leaving a burning red line.

Recoiling in pain, Audrey sensed the chaos all around her.

John, having disarmed Moriarty, was rushing to her aid. Nick was shouting for Sherlock's help. Sherlock was supposed to have used this diversion to pick the lock of Myca's shackles, but he had frozen with her sudden fall. Now he lurched towards Nick to help free Irene instead.

Moran brought his gun to bear on Audrey as he regained his feet. Audrey stared right down its wicked barrel as Moran pulled the trigger – only for the shot to go wide again as John dropped the crowbar and tackled Moran, rugby-style, pulling him down and away. The bullet zinged through Audrey's ear, spraying blood, and Moran lost his grip on the gun as the two men crashed to the ground.

Moran slashed at John with the hunting knife as John retrieved the makeshift flaming torch. It had guttered out but John parried the knife with it, then swung its smoking end at Moran's ribcage. Moran spun clear and lunged again with the blade.

John danced nimbly away; aimed the crowbar at Moran's head. Moran took the blow across the meat of his shoulder, but grabbed the metal bar, wrenched it from John's grip and flung it away. He made another slashing attack.

'John!' Nick's panicked warning came a moment late.

John did the courageous unthinkable. He stepped *into* the threatened contact, right into Moran's space; inside the reach of the knife. Moran tried to enfold him with one arm and twist his wrist to get a killing angle. John stamped down hard on one foot and shimmied, twisting out and away from Moran's loosened grip. John was out of reach once more.

'Get back here you slippery mongrel.'

John turned on a pin, stooped for a rock, pitched it at Moran's face.

But Moran was too close.

'*John!*' – '*Johnny!*' bellowed Sherlock and Nick in panic.

Audrey leapt between the knife and John, just as Nick did the same, but Nick got there first, shifting as she moved. The adrenalin and desperation had dragged forth the wolf in her, manifesting a tailless, three-legged half-wolf creature, draped in ill-fitting clothes. Nick was turning, rising unsteadily on her single back leg to confront the attacker, when Moran's blade sliced viciously down her withers and into her shoulder.

Nick screamed as Moran pulled the blade out again. Blood gushed over her patchwork skin-and-bristles.

Audrey's hip jarred as she landed, off-centre; she tried to twist again to shield both John and Nick. Moran was driving a knife blow at Audrey's throat now, but to move would be to leave John and Nick undefended. Her pack, her *cub*s, vulnerable.

She tensed her haunches, ready to leap, to tear out Moran's throat or die in the attempt. The silver-contaminated cut across Audrey's snout made her eyes water, but she could see her enemy. She pushed through the pain; leapt–

And encountered only air as Moran was jerked backwards into the dirt.

Irene Adler, in half-wolf form, claws out, her black pelt bristling and vibrating with the deepest growl rumbling from her throat, crouched over him. She pulled away, snarling, trying to spit.

But she'd made her mark.

Deep gouges oozed around the thick links of a silver chain at Moran's neck. He touched fingers to the wounds and inspected the glistening blood on his fingers in annoyed confusion. 'That's always worked before.'

Irene was wiping her mouth and tongue on her fur, still trying to cleanse her burning mouth.

'Don' thin' it will thtop me,' she said around her efforts. 'You're mine now.'

Horrified realisation bleached his face of colour, but he gripped his knife more firmly.

'You bit me. You've *cursed* me. You've turned me–'

'*Only* if you live till the full moon,' Irene said darkly.

Audrey gave him a few minutes at the outside. She ranged herself across from Irene, cutting off his avenues of escape. John was behind them, worrying over Nick's wound. She heard Nick's sharp, shallow breaths, her whimper of pain. Sherlock was at the periphery of her vision, crouched low, moving away from the confrontation with Moran, and towards–

Oh hell.

A gunshot rang out. A second.

Irene fell with a cry, clutching a double-wound in her shoulder blooming blood.

Sherlock had remembered what she – what everyone – had temporarily forgotten. Professor Moriarty was far from a spent force.

A third bullet whistled over Irene's head and slammed into Audrey's left flank. She went down, cursing her own stupidity. She knew better than to think that because he was old he wasn't dangerous.

The Professor had recovered from the blow that knocked him down. Now he was on his feet, using the pistol that nobody had realised was in his possession.

John pushed Nick down as a fourth bullet sang overhead.

Sherlock found the Professor's discarded knife, but any attempt to use it was lost as Moriarty shifted his aim, centring on Sherlock's chest. But before the Professor could fire again, he sensed the same movement that Audrey did.

John, rising up, running at a low crouch, darting erratically to make a poor target as he ran for Sebastian Moran's gun lying in the shale. Audrey wanted to knock him down, cover his body with hers, make him stay still, out of danger, but her damaged leg wouldn't hold her up.

A fifth shot.

John stumbled. Ran two more steps.

Fell.

Sherlock cried out, and then the world was very still.

Not silent. Audrey's own breathing was loud in her ears, but she could hear Irene panting in bewildered agony. Both of them, silver burning in their blood, were caught half way between forms, two women with hairy arms and faces, sharp teeth in not-quite-human mouths, gnarled hands tipped with claws.

Nick, normally so robustly loud, was whimpering softly, back in her vulnerable human form. Sherlock was breathing deeply, trying to master himself. Nearby, John grunted as he pushed his hands over the wound in his thigh.

My cubs. My family!

Moriarty's cold eye fell on the three wolf-women. 'I didn't know about you,' he said to Nick. 'Another potential daughter of the sun and moon?'

'Too right,' she replied with a bitter laugh. 'I'm a special fucking moonbeam, you arse, and don't forget it.'

'Yes, you are, Nick,' Sherlock agreed steadily. He had drawn himself up, imperious and brimming with the relentless logic of deduction. 'Though *any* female werewolf is surely both of the sun and the moon.'

'You render the prophecy meaningless,' snapped Moriarty.

'It *is* meaningless,' Sherlock said coldly. 'I know that in the stories, the supernatural is woven through with all kinds of rituals and portents, but this is life, not fiction. Even if it looks like fiction.' This said with a sardonic lift of the brow.

'You know nothing, Holmes.'

'But I observe.' Sherlock's tone became acid with disdain. 'You have murdered my sister, vital to the prophecy you thought, and the supernatural world didn't care; because there's Irene Adler and Mrs Hudson, as werewolf as you like under a moonless, clear blue sky. Even Nick transformed without the benefit of the moon.'

Moriarty readjusted his aim, halting Sherlock in his tracks as he'd edged closer.

'You've only recently discovered the shadow world. I've studied it minutely for decades. It's my *life*.'

'It's your *obsession*,' Irene countered. 'For this, you murdered my mother and my father, who never did harm, with such cruelty. You murdered my dear Gottfried, who wanted only to protect me. For this obsession, you have slaughtered hundreds, without care for any who posed no danger.'

'You murdered *my children*,' Audrey added her wrath to Irene's; for her own unborn child and the children who could never come after because of her injuries; for all the children she had tried to protect afterwards. For Ruby; for herself.

'They weren't children,' sneered Moriarty. 'They weren't even *human*.'

'But you're a murderer of those you pretend to protect, too,' Sherlock said. 'In your efforts to locate the so-called sacred wells, you killed anyone who obstructed your acquisition of property. And you used the Roylotts' naga poison to do it. I don't see what makes you better than werewolves. Or Roylott, come to that.'

'I needed to act, to save England. That unnatural source of power must be destroyed.'

'Why?' John challenged, helpless and furious. His skin was clammy; blood welled between the fingers clutched across his bleeding leg.

'They are *unnatural*.'

'*You're* bloody unnatural,' Nick shot back contemptuously. 'You and your sick vendetta. I know your kind. Been dealing with you bastards all my life, thinking you get to decide who deserves to live and die. Like *that* homophobic, misogynist prick,' she jerked her head towards Moran, who had inched away from them, the silver-tainted knife in his hand.

'Well you can fuck all the way off. We're here, we're mostly queer, and some of us have monthly cycles that kick *all* the arses, you almighty cock-dribble. And you don't even know which of us your precious bloody poem's all about.'

Moran hefted the knife. 'Hardly matters,' he said. 'I can kill you all.'

But Audrey saw the way the Professor eyed his erstwhile right-hand-thug. That was the thing about unreasoning hatred. It took so little for someone who was an *us* to become a *them*.

And then Moran saw it too. The change. The way Moriarty now viewed Moran as a thing and not a person.

'Hey, Prof,' he said. Warily. Questioning.

Moriarty spoke like his whole body had not betrayed his sudden new contempt. 'Yes. Do it. Slit each throat and throw them into the pit. If it could be any of them, we will sacrifice them all.'

'Want me to do for the gobby queer as well?'

'Why not? Heart of the wight. That could indeed be him.' His gun remained steadily trained on Sherlock. 'Sebastian, didn't you tell me you couldn't do anything with Myca Holmes until you threatened this one?'

'That's right,' Moran agreed, eager to be of use, to be an *us* once more. 'The bitch took a bullet for him. Came quiet as a lamb after that.'

'So, by your own reckoning, Holmes, I should cover my bases. If your sister's death has effected no change, then yours should make up the deficit. Being the metaphorical heart of the wight.'

'What's to say your pet assassin shouldn't also be on your hit list?' Sherlock quickly countered. 'What is the role of "the hunter of Tylwyth Teg's light" in this fairy tale reading of your ridiculous rhyme? Particularly now he has been bitten. Surely he's damned, too, in your eyes?'

Moriarty hesitated only a fraction, but that fraction was – to an experienced hunter – enough.

'Sebastian is not to blame for his condition,' said Moriarty evenly, that fraction too late, 'and your attempts to further muddy the waters are very obvious.'

Sherlock shrugged. 'It's not particularly difficult. It's a quagmire to begin with.'

'Shut up, y' gobby shite.' Moran, on suddenly shifting ground where it came to the Professor, asserted his aggression in more obvious directions.

'I will tear out your throat,' Irene hissed at Moran, her mouth full of wolfish teeth, her amber eyes glinting red.

'No need for him to get so close,' said Moriarty, turning the gun away from Sherlock at last, and towards Irene. 'Modern firearms are marvellous and I have plenty of bullets left for you all.'

Irene shifted to four paws, despite her ruined shoulder. She snarled and crouched to spring.

Moran shifted his grip on the knife, ready to attack not Irene Adler but Nick Murray, lying close to him on the ground, wounded, human and without her prosthetic.

Moriarty aimed at Irene and began to squeeze the trigger.

Audrey had to decide where to jump. Who to protect? John? Irene? Nick? Sherlock?

Sherlock moved as she was choosing. He stepped in close to Moriarty and with a smooth drop of the shoulder, a sidestep and a turn, and with a swoop of his leg, Sherlock was suddenly grappling with the old man.

The gun fired into the sky; Moriarty twisted the weapon and pulled the trigger again, missed again; but the projectile exploded into the dirt by John's side – and Sherlock's savagely graceful motion took on a sharp urgency.

Sherlock grasped Moriarty's hand, twisted (another shot, zinging wide of any mark). The Professor's age belied his ferocity, his wiry strength, and the two of them staggered, locked together, to the lip of the sinkhole. Sherlock's precise movements used the Professor's own weight and momentum against him. Moriarty turned the tactic back on his attacker, his fingers clenched in the collar of Sherlock's shirt.

Seeing Sherlock's danger, John crawled towards them across the bloody ground.

Seeing Sherlock's danger, John's, everyone's, Audrey pushed herself to her wolfish feet and yelped with pain, dizzy with the terrifying options of where to go, what to do, *who to save.*

Moran lunged at Nick with his blade. Nick rolled, a rock in her fist, and smashed it against the side of his head as the knife flashed down. And then Irene's powerful body thrashed into his side, knocking him away from Nick. She closed her teeth around his calf and bit, hard.

Moriarty had tilted, foot slipping in the shale; he lurched dangerously, teetering over the sinkhole.

And Sherlock tilted with him. His face blanched, a picture of alarm, of terror.

Audrey leapt towards him, snapping her teeth to catch at his trousers or his coat or anything to keep him from falling.

Moriarty slipped and down he went, spitting rage like the deranged, his only aim to take someone, anyone, with him, and so keeping his fist tight in Sherlock's collar.

Audrey snatched a mouthful of cloth for her efforts, so that when Sherlock toppled, dragged over the edge by the Professor's deathly grip, every tooth in her jaw was jarred.

Even then, she might have held, but her injured hip and the wound in her flank gave her no hold. Her hind legs buckled under her and she was pulled, so so swiftly, in Sherlock's wake, into the horrific depth of that great hole in the earth.

They fell – all three.

Above, away, so far away, Audrey heard John's desperate, despairing cry. They fell.

Around them, cold wind blew, whipping icily into her eyes. The howl of it filled her ears, filled her nose and mouth, drowning out the Professor's scream, Sherlock's shout of terror, John's fading voice.

They fell.

Audrey heard Irene's voice up there among the rocks, rising in an extraordinary sound, a wild cry, almost musical, which suddenly echoed down in the darkness, winding around her, around Sherlock, around Moriarty as they fell.

They fell.

They fell.

And then.

And then.

Audrey was surrounded by a great wash of water, swirling, foaming, rushing and tumbling her over and over and over and over.

We do not fall to our deaths.

We drown.

Oh, my little loves, I'm so sorry.

And the water filled her lungs.

Chapter Twenty-Six

The torrent whirlpooled around Audrey's body, her limbs flung every which way in the tumultuous flow, soaking her fur to the skin, chilling her skin to the bone, filling her ears, her mouth, every inhale a choking gasp, every exhale a rasping cry.

And still she fell.

Through the swirling waters, Audrey caught flailing glimpses of other limbs, other faces, sodden clothes and tangled hair spinning, eerily glowing in phosphorescent light.

And still.

They fell.

Audrey opened her mouth to howl. To drown. A bereft sound rose from her throat, a plea. *Save my boy. Save my family. Save these ones, please. Take me and save them.*

And somehow she could still hear Irene – *singing*? Rolling notes, a beautiful lupine opera, uncannily clear where no voice should carry. Audrey had time for a single prosaic thought – *perhaps Irene's is the throat of the daughter of the sun and moon* – before Irene's bays, her own, and the roar of the water, mingled into one uninhibited heart-cry.

Audrey tumbled in the tempest until she could not tell if she was still plunging toward the hellish bottom or being borne upwards by the turbulence.

Then her face broke free into blessed air and she drew a ragged breath. She opened her eyes, streaming with tears, and looked for him. 'Sherlock!' but her voice was a raw whisper.

Her body fully human again now, Audrey trod water, turning frantically in the churning swell, seeking him, not seeing at first that she was in the midst of a great waterfall.

Not seeing that the waterfall was flowing–

Up.

'Sherlock!'

Hush.

Audrey twisted in the spirals of water that held her, trying to find the source of the voice.

Hush, daughter. All is well.

Audrey wished she could believe that voice, but her life had never been that simple, or that kind.

Peace, daughter. Do you hear?

Irene's beautiful, monstrous voice curled around her, through the waves, through her bones and blood, another fearsome, broken plea for justice. Beside it, Nick, not half so melodious and yet her human voice song enough, calling out in surprise and wonder.

John's too. 'Take my hand! Sherlock, take my hand!'

Audrey saw a long limb shimmering through the funnel of water, obscured by sodden cloth splayed wide by the pushing the current. Long pale fingers reached; a strong hand grasped them.

Another, thinner, more wiry form rose past her too, then a second which was taller and more stout. A swirl of water, glowing soft and green swept ahead of a much brighter light. Flowing upwards, up up upwards.

At last Audrey was deposited, as though her body was held in two strong hands, upon the shore of grey stone and spackled lichen at the peak of Clogwyn y Tarw. She coughed a gush of water onto the shale, which pressed against her fragile human skin. Against her aching hip and the place where the silver knife had pierced the muscle, now curiously free of pain.

Uncertain, Audrey felt for the wound, but her skin was whole.

Finally, she lifted her gaze.

The stones around the lip of the sinkhole were awash with clear water, running like a cheerful, babbling stream, bouncing over stones and rocks. It spattered down into the hole in the earth only to swirl and funnel up again, to begin the dance anew.

Irene was on her human hands and knees, clad in rags, with no sign of the appalling damage the poisoned bullets had wrought on her shoulder. Her extraordinary wolf-opera voice had faded into shaken, panting breaths.

Not far away, John was still holding tight to Sherlock where they both knelt in a pool of rushing water. Sherlock pulled away, but only so that he could press his forehead to John's. His hand strayed down to press flat against the tear in John's bloodstained jeans, where the skin was inexplicably healed and whole underneath. Audrey could scent no fresh blood; couldn't even see where the bullet had hit.

'I'm okay,' John was saying as though he could hardly believe it. 'I'm okay. You too. You're okay. Aren't you? Sherlock?'

'Yes. Yes. I am. Against all expectation. Yes.'

They huffed a shocked laugh together. Audrey's heart lifted, that they could still laugh, after the day they'd had.

But then they heard Nick – heard the two rhythmic puffs of air, followed by a gruff, grunting count: 'One, two, three, four, five, six...' and on and on.

Audrey followed Sherlock's gaze as he hesitantly turned his head towards Myca – who lay as though lifeless in the shallow water covering the shale. Myca's lips were blue. Nick was balanced awkwardly over her, counting chest compressions between puffs of air.

Oh, Myca. No.

John and Sherlock untangled themselves: John to assist Nick with the chest compressions, Sherlock, trapped between fear and hope and helplessness, to watch his sister.

John continued with the CPR – 'twenty-seven, twenty-eight, twenty-nine, thirty' – and paused for Nick to supply two more puffs of air before he began the count again. Sherlock didn't ask for a prognosis. John didn't offer one. Nick squeezed Myca's hand tight in the intervals between giving breaths to her.

While the terrible chant continued, the upwards-flowing water coalesced in the mouth of the sinkhole, and took form. Water and luminosity, ripples and shifting reflections, in a shape that somehow clothed the fathomless depths of the salty sea within a sparkling, dappled brook, emanated its own bright light.

To look on the true Lady of the Lake was dazzling. Painful. Yet it was as hard to look away.

Audrey wondered that any of them had ever mistaken the Jenny-possessed Myca for the true Goddess, whose radiance was so hard to look upon.

Peace, said the Lady of the Lake, without speaking, without the shape of her mouth moving at all. *All is well.*

'It's not *well,*' Irene countered angrily.

John was still counting compressions, refusing to be diverted by a deity in their midst.

'I begged for justice, and you bring him back with the rest of them.' Irene jerked her chin towards Professor Moriarty. He stood, bedraggled, on the other side of the sinkhole – as alive, and as wet, as the rest of them, though nothing like as grateful for the miracle.

We heard your song, daughter. Justice will be served, on our own terms.

'What about justice for my sister?' The hostility of Sherlock's demand was tempered by the way his voice cracked as he continued. 'You can't let her die.'

Nick puffed two breaths. John resumed his count.

What will you give for her? asked the Goddess.

'Don't, Sherlock!' Audrey said sharply, cutting across his intaken breath. 'Never make deals with the fae. That's one thing the stories have right.'

But before the stricken brother could offer himself, or think of something more clever to offer in the belief he could outwit a goddess, Nick spoke.

'Hasn't she given you enough?' Nick challenged. 'Didn't the Jenny take enough? Myca was just a little kid when your incompetent Jenny possessed her, for fuck's sake.'

Ah, my little dear. Such a fierce young wolf. So steadfast. Do you claim her, then?

Nick's expression twisted with distaste. 'She's not mine. She belongs to herself. Give that back to her. You *owe* her.'

John stopped counting long enough to give Myca two breaths of his own. Started again.

A sound, like a tiny waterfall over pebbles in the spring, suggested the goddess was merry. Before Nick could furiously accuse the Lady of cruelty, Myca coughed, turned away from John Watson and vomited cold water and bile on the stones next to Nick's bent knees. Myca took a shuddering breath and coughed again, clearing her lungs, and lay there with her eyes closed, wheezing.

Sherlock was momentarily undone, his expression naked in its hope. 'Myca? Are you hurt? John, is she still hurt? Myca, speak to me, please.'

Nick held and rubbed Myca's hands reassuringly. 'Hey, hey, Myca. Babe. Look at me, honey.' Myca's eyes opened blearily. 'That's it, my girl. John's gonna look at you, yeah? Make sure you're not still bleeding. Okay?'

Myca, dazed, nodded and leaned against Nick's thigh. Behind her, John quickly and gently examined the skin underneath the tattered hole in Myca's clothes.

'The wound's healed,' pronounced John immediately. He took Myca's pulse, checked the dilation of her eyes and the colour of her skin. Where a moment ago she had been blue around the lips, pinkness was returning. 'How many fingers am I holding, up?'

Myca was working hard to focus, and eventually came in with the correct count of, 'One. Your left index finger. It's as well you're the one asking. Ms Murray may well have given me the middle finger.'

Nick choked on a laugh. 'I'd never flip you the bird,' she protested. 'I'm always respectful. You're like the fuckin' queen.'

A smile pulled at the corner of Myca's mouth.

'You're doing very well, Myca,' John said in a warm, bedside manner.

Myca scrunched her eyes closed. Memory spurred her into keener awareness. 'Sherlock! Where–'

'Right here, Myca.' He had stagger-sloshed through the inch of water still flowing over the shale, to drop to his knees at her side. He caught her hand in his and looked keenly, worriedly, into her eyes. 'Are you alone in there?'

'Quite alone. It feels...' her look to him was beseeching. 'Dreadfully tranquil. Appallingly free. It's... rather lonely. I am not sure I like it.'

Sherlock wrapped his arms around Myca's hunched shoulders. 'You are not alone,' he whispered into her hair – a younger brother, making desperate promises to his big sister.

'No,' murmured Myca. 'I'm not.'

It was left to Nick to thank the goddess, which she did, gracelessly. 'Thank you, I suppose, but you shouldn't have made us beg for it.'

The Lady's light shimmered mirthfully. *Nature is not always kind, but neither are we malicious.*

'Coulda fooled me.'

You ask nothing for yourself?

Nick sniffed. 'Like Mrs H says, making deals with the fae is a mug's game.'

'I'll make a bargain,' said Irene sternly, her eyes fixed on Moriarty: a predator held back from taking down her prey by a force as yet unacknowledged.

Your bargain has already been made. You shall have your justice. Another shimmer, but the Lady directed her next offer to Audrey.

And for you, daughter?

'Don't call me that.' Audrey shivered by Irene's side, with cold as well as shock, her elderly, pale skin goose-bumped and bruised. She lifted her chin, defiant, refusing to succumb to her vulnerability. She was naked, old, afraid, and angry. But she still had people to protect, and she'd fight whoever she had to.

Yet you are my daughter.

Audrey's hands clenched convulsively.

'She is an abomination.' Moriarty's drowned-rat fury might have been comical except for the venom in his voice. 'You are all *abominations.*'

'Oh, do fuck off, Professor Doom,' said Nick wearily.

'You are an offense to nature.'

'They embody nature, you absolute bell-end.'

'You are an offense to *logic*,' Moriarty spat.

'What has logic to do with it?' Irene snapped at him. 'You speak without imagination, with a mind so small and frightened. You hide your terror behind this word; this *idea* of your logic.'

Sherlock's disdain for him was palpable. 'She's right. Your failure of imagination is unforgivable. What is logic to a fish would be death to me. I don't understand all of this yet, but while the logic of the supernatural is alien to me, it is not beyond comprehension.'

'Why do you defend them? These monsters will kill you in the end.'

'They have done nothing but protect me. You, on the other hand–'

'I shall bring destruction upon all of you.'

The ground heaved suddenly under Moriarty's feet, knocking him off balance. He righted himself before the ground bucked again.

The Garland King comes said the Lady. *Justice comes.*

Moriarty blanched but Audrey was impressed by the level of blustering courage he still managed to summon. 'I don't recognise your justice. I refuse it!'

'You *dare*?' Irene rose, her nakedness granted dignity by the threat in her stance and in her voice. Her brown skin gleamed with vitality, without wounds. She was graceful and unwavering and deadly.

'You are nothing more than a beast,' Moriarty sneered, even as the rocks and earth rose up beside him, elongating unhurriedly into a vaguely humanoid shape.

'You have butchered your way across this land, and you call *me* a beast,' Irene accused. 'You creep and crawl and curse yourself with every murder you commit. You make yourself a monster. *You* are the abomination.'

Audrey curled in on herself, feeling the stones bite at her skin, feeling weary beyond endurance. Unable to look any more, she hid her face against her knees. She had been made barren, had twice been made packless, her children slaughtered for this man's vicious schemes. Ruby, slaughtered. Irene, orphaned and widowed. John, Sherlock, Nick, almost dead today. And the Lady of the Lake had seen fit to spit him up again, untouched and unchanged.

'I stand by every act,' Moriarty said, 'and I will do more. I will destroy you. And *you*.' He directed this towards the gleaming goddess, while also sparing a venomous look for the subdued Jenny that ebbed in the Lady's shadow.'

You cannot destroy me any more than you can destroy the Garland King.

The shape of stone and earth stood taller than any of them now. The shale hardened like stony armour around the human-like earthen body. No features appeared on the oval of its face.

'I have resources,' Moriarty promised. 'Poisons. Explosives.'

You cannot hurt us.

'Uranium. Toxins.'

These too are things of earth and fire, water and air. What are we if not the makings of the world?

Audrey was glad to see Moriarty nonplussed by the Lady's calm, measured failure to be impressed by his threats.

Surrender, little one. The Garland King and the Lady of the Lake embody the land you claim to defend. Poison this well, shatter that rock, and we shall yet live, for we are in all places, all times. Neither water nor the earth is divisible. We are everywhere. For where flows water and air, there flow I. Where rests earth and fire, there rests the Garland King.

The giant earthen Garland King turned its faceless head towards his queen, with a sound like rocks being crushed to gravel. Eyes appeared in the stones, their black gaze resting on her. The Lady gestured towards Moriarty. The King grindingly turned his head to cast those obsidian eyes upon the man who wished to destroy the world.

The Professor gritted his teeth. 'Why doesn't the foul thing say something?'

Earth lasts long and its speech, too slow and deep for your hearing, may be measured in eons. The King could speak in fire, which is quick, but it would burn. Thus I, water and air, do our speaking, for the most part.

'Is this where you kill me, then? Like the monsters you are?'

The Lady tilted her head – light sparkled in the water that flowed over her form – and regarded the Jenny in her shadow sternly. The creature covered her face with her thin hands.

My morgen did you harm, and so you, too, are owed a debt.

'No!' Irene lunged for the Professor, but was stayed with a glare from the Garland King. Small green shoots had begun to appear between the stones that made up his body.

You may ask what you will of us, said the Lady.

Moriarty swallowed hard and considered the King with watchful eyes. What he said was, 'So the prophecy meant nothing after all.'

My sprite saw a future she did not comprehend, but its truth is here. My daughters raised their voices to ask gifts of me. My new daughter cried out for her friends to be saved. My lonely daughter cried out to offer herself that I may save the rest. My grieving daughter called to me for justice. Their throats combined in supplication to me.

'And what of the wight's heart?' Moriarty asked bitterly.

The heart of she, who for so long carried my handmaiden, begged that I should save her brother, the heart outside herself. The heart of the brother, who is the heart of the wight, cried out for the life of his sister and his companions and his beloved.

'All very sentimental.' Never had the word sounded so like profanity. A thought occurred to Moriarty then, and he pursued it. 'They all struck bargains with you. Aren't they supposed to pay?'

They have already paid, in their service to me.

'What do I get then?'

You are owed a debt. We must repay it, to keep the balance.

'Whatever I want?'

Whatever is in our power. May I offer you a choice?

'Go on,' said the Professor cautiously.

Our existence offends you. We can take the knowledge of that existence from you.

'That would leave an inconvenient gap in several decades of my life.' His tone was dry, cynical, recognising that such a choice would strip him of fifty years of memories.

Or we may offer you extended life, with which to study us further.

'Extended life? Do you mean years?'

Centuries. More.

'Immortality.'

As close to it as can be offered a mortal. Even mountains erode with time. But this is a gift from the Garland King, a gift of earth and stone.

'You would make me nearly immortal? So that I may study and grow to understand you?'

Yes.

'Yes. All right, then. I accept your gift, in reparation for your water spirit's attempt to murder me.' A gleam of triumph was in his eyes.

He thinks he's tricked them, Audrey thought. *He thinks he gets to walk away to live for centuries. And maybe he does.* She resolved then and there to find a way to kill him. Her family would never be safe until she did.

The Garland King towered over Moriarty, black eyes gleaming, straight nose lending noble dignity to the high carved cheekbones, the granite jaw. The King's blank face shifted like he was smiling – motes of dust drifted from the stone – and Moriarty smirked, sure of his own cleverness.

A mouth opened in that stone face, revealing two long, sharp teeth among all the pebbly nubs inside.

Before Moriarty could recoil, the Garland King – monarch of things of the earth, the long-lived, the near eternal – bit into Moriarty's pale, wrinkled neck, and exchanged the Professor's blood for a strange and terrible gift.

Moriarty would have fallen if not for the King's arms around him. When the King had finished drinking, he lifted his head – stone mouth smeared in blood – and Moriarty, waxen pale, opened his mouth to accommodate the unfamiliar shape of two sharp teeth within. A hoarse cry escaped him.

'You should have asked more questions,' said Audrey, entirely without sympathy.

Moriarty grinned horribly. 'They promised me immortality. What did you think they would give me? This isn't what I had in mind, but there's a logic to it.'

'You should be dead,' said Irene. 'This isn't the justice I called for.'

'No, it isn't,' he agreed. 'Especially when I think how I might use the gift.' With a smirk, teeth bared, he stepped towards Sherlock – intending only to intimidate; perhaps.

The Garland King seized Moriarty by the shoulders, a biting grip that allowed no forward motion. The green tendrils now growing all over the King's body began to twine around the Professor's biceps.

The King's gift of extended life is so that you may study and understand, said the Lady of the Lake.

She was smiling again, and it was terrifying, but Audrey couldn't tear her eyes away.

'You said you owed me a debt,' Moriarty said angrily.

You are repaid. You agreed to the terms. An eternity in which to study and understand.

'Why won't he let me go then?'

So that you may go with him and as long as your long life lasts, you will study. You will understand.

A great cracking sound echoed all around them and the ground directly beneath the Professor split open.

When the Lady laughed this time, it wasn't water over pebbles in sunshine. It was great, dark waves crashing on rocks in stormy seas. It was, like her smile, utterly, bone-deep terrifying.

Moriarty and the stoic green-shrouded Garland King dropped into the sudden trench. Moriarty shrieked. He dug his hands into the rocky soil and tried to climb out, only for the trough to crack wider, deeper, and only his head was above the rim.

The towering Garland King's form changed. Shrank but grew wider, fuller, less humanoid. Within the furrow, stone flowed like water, gathered and coalesced into giant shapes. Arms, shoulders. A face, a foot, an eye, a mouth, there and gone.

A dozen giant stony hands enveloped the Professor's body...

'No!' shouted Moriarty.

...and they pulled him under the earth as though pulling him below the ocean's waves.

And then the dirt and shale closed over the place where he had stood, and silence fell.

CHAPTER TWENTY-SEVEN

NICK EVENTUALLY FILLED THE SILENCE WITH AN AWED, ALMOST reverent: 'Fuck me.'

'Always with the *mot juste*, my dear,' Myca observed gently. Nick very nearly blushed, and then really did when Myca patted her hand.

'Is that a good thing?' Nick asked.

'Almost always,' Myca assured her.

Audrey twitched as something landed on her shoulders, over her back, but it was John draping his coat over her. She huddled into it, shivering suddenly, as Sherlock gave his own coat to Irene.

'I suppose this is the logic of the fish you spoke of, Mr Holmes,' said Irene bleakly as she pulled the soaking wet fabric around herself.

'Something of the kind,' he said, making conversation as the only recourse in the face of such overwhelming events.

Irene turned her face towards the shimmering Lady. 'That's the justice I asked for?'

It is. And it is both your justice and the repayment of our debt to him.

Irene averted her gaze, then jerked her chin defiantly up. She seemed to be daring the Lady to find something else to take from her.

Audrey knew how Irene felt: the defiance and the recklessness. An earth god had just swallowed and imprisoned the mad scientist. The water goddess stood ready to drown them all in an instant, despite having just saved them, because who knew how she judged her choices? But Audrey was infuriated to yet again in her life be cornered, helpless and afraid, with so, so much to lose.

She rose, threading her arms into the sleeves of John's coat, drawing it shut. The hem fell to the middle of her thighs, offering her some dignity. 'Well then?' Audrey snapped, with no caution at all. 'What do you want from us now?'

I await my answer, daughter.

'What was the question?'

What do you want as payment for your services?

'What if I want to be free?' she said brusquely.

What freedom do you need?

'From this curse, for a start.'

It is not a curse. It is my gift that you bear.

'A gift.'

Just as the frightened one received his gift from the Garland King.

'Gift?' Irene demanded. 'My darling Gottfried was a vampire, and he never knew it for a gift of any kind.'

The near-immortal-but-not existence of fire and earth is, like all honours, only as true as they who wield it. Your husband wielded his gift in your service, and his dust is embraced by the King's realm once more.

A soft cry caught in Irene's throat. Audrey wanted to slap the Lady for the unkind reminder of Gottfried's betrayal. He had been a fool, as far as Audrey was concerned, but he'd only had care for Irene. He'd acted in the least intelligent manner possible, the ass. The poor, silly, fearful, desperately in love, so-very-dead man.

'So Gottfried and Moriarty were served the lie of immortality,' Audrey mocked her. 'What lie have I been sold?'

The Lady, damn her, was amused.

In the early days of the world's greenness, a human woman begged at the well for the power to protect her family from beasts and men and the freezing winter. She was clever. She knew how to make an exchange. She asked for the power to keep them safe beyond her lifetime, and I gave it to her. I am water and air, more mutable than earth. My gifts are those of transformation. I gifted her this power, through the strength of the wolf.

Audrey's fists were clenched. 'You say gift but there's a price.'

Gifts have no price, it's true, but powerful gifts come with great responsibility. At first she and her kin selected carefully to whom it was entrusted. But as the time grew long and forgetful, the gift was not always shared or used responsibly. Today, my wolf children do not even remember their first mother. You think you are cursed, instead of honoured.

Audrey couldn't begin to know what to say to that.

Do you still want your freedom, daughter?

Audrey closed her eyes. 'I want to go home.'

Then go. But first...

The Lady reached a hand towards Sherlock.

Leave her for me.

Sherlock recoiled. 'You can't have her. She's my sister. I'm taking her back.'

No, little one. I want the one in your pocket. You brought her to me, the last of my dear guardian maids, brought to me by Demeter, who came with the Romans and brought me a grove of dryads. She is the only offering I ask of you.

'In my...?'

Sherlock felt in his trouser pocket and drew out the short stub of the dead dryad's remains. Where it had been dead and dry, however, now the wood was fresh and pliable. Little green shoots curled out of it.

'Oh,' he said. 'Dryads are all women, aren't they? Well. As much as gender applies to this sort of thing. Is this how they reproduce? From cuttings?'

The Lady burbled another laugh. *If that logic seems fit to you, I will say that it is so.*

'Even if it's not?'

Even so.

'Where should I put it? Ah. Her?'

Plant her by the mouth of this great fall, where I shall tend her, and she will grow strong and tall to be my guardian. This one—

Beside her, the all but forgotten Jenny dissolved and churned, showing only tiny glimpses of a face suffused with shame.

—will teach her.

'She doesn't get punished for what she did?' said Irene, angry.

'Don't punish her on my account,' said Myca suddenly. 'I learned so much.'

The Lady made no reply.

Carefully, Sherlock dug a hole in the soil, far enough from the lip of the sinkhole for his own comfort and for roots to take hold. He planted the cutting with all its sudden new leaves. The reincarnating dryad took hold immediately. Her tiny leaves lifted up; her little stem wriggled into the ground.

Audrey was deeply unsettled by the infant sentience shown by a twig.

The Jenny sighed. Myca reached for her, then halted and held her fingers up in farewell. The Jenny which had been part of her life – her body, her mind – for so many years vanished into the ground without a word.

'Will she be all right?' asked Myca.

She will restore balance.

'And I?'

You will be your self, as you have always been.

The Lady swirled, all light and motion, sparkles on water and the deep green underneath and then...

She was gone.

Leaving a bedraggled group behind.

Sherlock retrieved Nick's prosthetic and Myca helped Nick to settle her stump back into it.

'Where's Moran?' asked John suddenly. 'Shit. I can't believe we forgot about Moran.'

In the distance, an engine burst into life, then faded as it raced out of the national park.

'Oh, that bastard. He's pinched the hire car,' Nick said, scandalised, then she shrugged. 'At least we can blame all the damage on him, if they ever find it again.' She stifled a cry of pain when she tried to rise, and sagged back to the ground. 'Don't suppose Fisheries runs to sending a chopper to get me off this bloody mountain?'

Myca's quietly confident Mona Lisa smile was every answer Nick could have hoped for.

Myca sent John to commandeer a mobile phone from the first hikers he could find, on the basis that, of those who had sufficient clothing and could still walk, he had the most reassuring manner. John returned with the news that his call to Myca's emergency contact had prompted a swift response.

The cavalry that eventuated didn't exactly consist of an airborne evac team, but four members of a local Fisheries crew arrived with blankets, sandwiches, fresh clothes, thermoses of well-brewed tea, and strength enough between two of them to carry Nick to the foot of the mountain. Another offered a steadying elbow to Mrs Hudson.

Muddy runnels – the tracks of their vanished hire car heading west – were evident. Sherlock stared at them for a while, perhaps trying to deduce something through his exhaustion. John put an arm around Sherlock's waist and gently drew him away.

'We can take a look tomorrow, love, if we need to.'

'No, I, I must–'

'That Fisheries bloke is taking photos, see? We can look at them later. Come on. It's getting cold and I won't have you dropping like a stone with pneumonia after everything we've been through today.'

Sherlock bent a look of wonder on him. 'How are you so calm?'

'We're alive. None of us got turned into vampires or swallowed whole by the earth. I got shot but it didn't stick. Everything else is a bonus, yeah?'

'Well, when you put it like that.'

The ride back to their hotel was short, and still too long. Audrey slumped in her seat and looked blankly at Myca giving orders to their driver. Nick leaned into the back seat corner opposite Audrey, her pale face beaded with perspiration; her prosthetic in her lap. The stocking covering her stump was spotted red in patches, indicating how blistered and raw the skin beneath was. Nick's capacity for accelerated healing wasn't accelerated enough for the day's exertions.

Audrey wondered whether the cars would take them to the airfield instead of their hotel. Myca was not behaving predictably. Or maybe she was? Without the Jenny as her passenger, who knew what was typical of the head of Fisheries?

Myca Holmes had them brought to their Caernarfon lodgings. Instead of a debriefing, the Director of the Department of Fisheries sent her agents away with a few murmured words. Myca herself assisted Nick up the stairs.

Nick leaned into Myca's sturdy presence. 'Why aren't you buggered? I'm buggered. This has been the longest fucking day. Dawn was about 80 hours ago, wasn't it?'

'Around 14, I believe.'

'Impossible. I'm sure I've missed at least ten meals.'

'I will make arrangements.'

'If you can include a short ton of chips, I'll bloody kiss you.'

Myca blushed.

'Kiss you now, if you want,' offered Nick and while Myca was totally flustered, Nick clutched Myca's arm, stretched up and planted a kiss on Myca's cheek. 'There. Bring me chips and you'll get another.'

'I truly fail to understand why you want to. You were enamoured of the water sprite, weren't you?'

Nick considered this. 'Was she the one who looked like Boudica, Gwendoline Christie and Ronda Rousey combined? I'll answer that. *No.* That was all you. If anything, you made the Jenny look good.'

Myca blushed harder.

'Ah, sorry I was a bit brusque with that Jenny while she was hitching a ride,' Nick added. 'I was calling *her* names, not you. I was a bit worried about John.'

'No offence taken,' said Myca, bemused again. 'I was beginning to feel brusque with her myself. Your robust language provided one channel of material motivation for the return of my dominance.'

'You bobbed up and down a bit in there, did you?' suggested Nick mildly.

'That's an apt analogy.'

'Right. Glad to have been of service. This is me,' said Nick at the door to the room she shared with Audrey. 'Kiss for the road, then?'

Myca bent her head to shyly kiss Nick's forehead. Sherlock, who had been following his sister up the stairs with John and Audrey at his heels, didn't know where to look. Audrey would have been amused if she hadn't been so exhausted.

Myca departed, leaving John and Audrey to help Nick into their shared room.

'Need a hand, Nick?' John offered.

'Christ, no. You go and look after your pretty boy. You both need a snog after all that shite, don't you? Bung my leg in the corner for now. I can't face putting it on again at least till tomorrow. You good, Mrs H?'

'Never better,' replied Audrey, and suspected it was true, even as life was clearly the opposite for Irene, who had been directed towards the room allocated to Gottfried Norton.

Audrey didn't need wolf senses to hear her weeping through the walls.

Chapter Twenty-Eight

Audrey showered and changed into comfortable clothes and her robe, then sat up in bed to listen.

Next door, Sherlock and John showered together. She heard the murmur of their voices, then more intimate sounds, and tuned out of those. Irene had fallen into exhausted, emotionally drained sleep. Down the hall, after ensuring food was delivered, Myca paced her room, making phone calls. Fisheries business.

In the twin bed next to Audrey slept Nick Murray. Nick had fallen asleep before her short ton of chips were delivered, woke at the scent of hot food, stayed awake long enough to stuff her face and lick her fingers, then promptly fell back asleep. Those army-earned skills of being able to sleep anywhere, anytime, at play again.

Audrey was desperately tired, but although everyone she cared for was safe and sheltered nearby, sleep refused to come. Every time her eyes drifted shut, horrible visions rolled through her. Blood, bullets, swirling water, the earth opening like a fanged and muddy mouth to bite.

A gift for you, the Lady would say, and Audrey dreamed of being forced into wolf shape, howling, and unable to help anyone.

It was a relief to meet the dawn and not pretend sleep was ever going to come.

Nick was well rested, but she couldn't face attempting her prosthetic yet. John inspected the damage to her skin, which was less inflamed but not ready for the rigours of use. He and Sherlock helped Nick down to the kitchen, where Myca had organised a cooked breakfast.

'You really are Queen of the Fisheries,' Nick said approvingly.

John filled Nick's plate with eggs and bacon, sat down to enjoy his own and found that his boyfriend had already pinched all the bacon to make a bacon buttie. Audrey and Nick watched indulgently as two grown men had a spirited squabble over the trespass, which was only an excuse for being handsy at breakfast. They shared the sandwich anyway.

Irene made a late appearance, wearing dark sunglasses and drinking only black coffee. Myca let her be.

'Aren't you having breakfast?' Audrey asked Myca.

'She ate before we rose,' Sherlock pointed out. 'Egg on your shirt, sister mine.'

'There is not,' Myca protested, checking.

'Made you look,' grinned Sherlock. She rolled her eyes at him, typical elder sister, and his grin widened before suddenly subsiding into sincere, sober feeling. 'You haven't fallen for that since you were twelve.'

Myca, fingers still hovering over her spotless blouse, returned the look. 'I don't remember you trying it since I was twelve.'

They gazed at each other a moment longer, communicating wordlessly.

'It's good to have you back,' said Sherlock suddenly.

'I've always been here,' she replied.

'Always?'

'Not always uppermost, but always. I remember it all.'

Sherlock nodded. He looked at his hands. He looked as John's hand covered his own and squeezed. He looked at John, and whatever he saw in John's face, it prompted him to rise, to go to his sister. To lean into her with a sideways hug, and then move as Myca stood and turned in his arms.

They hugged. They hugged, not hard, but firmly, mindfully, gratefully. When they released each other, they were both subtly calmer, more settled.

Then Sherlock returned to the table and tried to steal the toast from John's plate. John gave it up without protest, choosing instead to hold Sherlock's hand.

Audrey concentrated on her breakfast, aware that the hoteliers were absent. The Fisheries Department was keeping a tight lid on events.

'Have you located Sebastian Moran yet?' Audrey asked pointedly.

'The car was abandoned near the A5. Blood traces and tyre tracks indicate he has appropriated a new vehicle. We haven't found its owner yet, I'm afraid.'

'Moran'll show up, probably around the time of the full moon,' said Audrey drily.

'We'd rather find him before he can do more harm,' replied Myca in kind.

'I'll find him,' promised Irene grimly. 'Give me the scent and I'll find him anywhere.'

'We would like to engage you in the operation, Ms Adler, if you would care to work with The Department.'

'I have a choice?'

'Of course.'

'And if I choose to return to Germany?'

'Your wishes will be respected. But I thought you might prefer to finish this business.'

Irene removed her sunglasses. Her eyes glowed amber. 'I would.'

'We'd like to take him alive, if possible,' said Myca gently.

'And whole?' Irene sneered.

'Alive is sufficient,' said Myca.

There you are, Director, thought Audrey. *It wasn't all the Jenny who made the Fisheries a force to be reckoned with.*

And then Myca's confident gaze met hers: challenging and only a little terrifying.

Audrey shot back an unintimidated and fairly alarming glare of her own. Myca smiled, pleased by the response.

'I have arranged transport back to London for everyone,' said Myca, all business. 'I take it you'll all be returning to Baker Street?'

'It is my home,' Audrey replied stiffly, before remembering. She turned to Irene. 'Though in fact it's your home. Your mother should have left it to you.'

Irene waved the protest away with a small gesture. 'My mother did her best for me. My home is in Frankfurt.' She swallowed. 'Was. My life was in Frankfurt and now I have nothing.'

'Stay with me,' said Audrey impulsively. 'I have so many rooms. They've been so empty.' That was an admission she hadn't meant to make, but having made it, she turned to Nick. 'You're very welcome, too, Nick.'

A forkful of egg hovered halfway towards Nick's open mouth. 'Really?'

'Of course.'

'I'm not sure I'm exactly safe,' said Nick, putting down the fork.

Audrey simply arched an eyebrow, and Nick laughed. 'Right you are then, Mrs H. Am I bunking with you or–?'

'Downstairs.'

'Siobhan's room?'

'Your room.'

Nick crowed a laugh. 'Hey, Johnny, gonna be your neighbour. You two better keep the noise down or the Alpha and I'll have to turn the hose on you.'

Sherlock affected to be scandalised but John only looked smug. 'I'll keep that in mind when you start inviting girlfriends around.'

'Girlfriend, singular,' said Nick. 'And I haven't asked her on a date yet, so sod off with the labels, yeah?' She had flicked a glance towards Myca with that line, startling the woman yet again.

'A date. With me?'

'Don't see any other queens worthy of my best date night plans, do you? You doing anything tonight?'

Myca opened and closed her mouth; said: 'Work.'

'Skive off. Let me take you to dinner.'

'If you're sure?'

'Why wouldn't I be?'

'Well, yesterday was trying.'

'Honestly, yesterday was only the third worst day of my life. All my mates are still alive at the end of this one, and I haven't lost any more limbs. Do you like Greek food?'

'Yes.'

'Great. You, ah, don't mind that I'm, you know,' Nick made a little growly face, 'not entirely human.'

'Neither was I, until yesterday.'

'Still–'

'I would be honoured to accompany you.'

Nick beamed. 'Pleasure's all mine. Let me know where to pick you up in my fancy wheelchair taxi and I'll be there at 7pm for dinner. We can do dancing another night.' Nick raised her teacup in a toast and Myca, bemused yet pleased, clinked her own against it.

Audrey waved for the teapot, which Sherlock passed to her rather than look at Nick and his sister.

'Why don't you be mother?' Audrey suggested, just to see the look on his face, which was everything she could have hoped for, before he decided on amusement and poured her tea.

'How are you managing with all this,' she continued, her gaze taking in Irene and Nick, John and Myca, and the various Fisheries agents coming in and out of the breakfast parlour.

'Meaning, you think I'm yet to break?' Sherlock replied.

'Meaning you seem to be doing quite well today. Yesterday, as your sister so aptly described it, was trying.'

Sherlock sat beside her. He took her hand in his and examined the chipped polish clinging to her nails.

'Until very recently, I would have sided with Moriarty in either dismissing the supernatural or finding it abhorrent. And yet this secret world has existed all around me, for all of my life. I'm one man in the middle of a modern metropolis, yet I am acquainted with three werewolves, a deceased vampire, and a former water spirit, that I know of. That strikes me as statistically significant. I wonder if I'm above or below average in my circle. If my experience is the mean, then the supernatural seems very much embedded in life, whatever its rules. It is therefore as natural and even as quantifiable as cats, roses, and politicians.'

Sherlock patted her hand, then, in a burst of chivalry, kissed it before releasing her. 'In adherence to the scientific method, therefore, I am changing my theories to meet the facts instead of going mad.'

'Good.'

'I don't suppose with this viewpoint you'd like to work for the Fisheries?' Myca offered. 'We have an opening for an interpreter of visions and prophecies.'

Sherlock snorted derisively. 'You mistake my decision to sow confusion to the enemy with having the slightest belief in divination. In deduction, it's unwise to put the cart before the horse. Reasoning forward to potential outcomes is one thing; trying to reason backwards with insufficient data is quite another. No, thank you. I have my own career.' He glanced at John and grinned. 'We have an agency to run. But I remain available for consultation as required.'

'Noted.' Myca checked her watch. 'Time for our flight. Nick, would you like to drive with me? I've sent one of my people upstairs for your bag.'

'Woo-hoo, ridin' shotgun. That'll do me till I get my license back. Bags Johnny and his pretty boy ride in the other car. I love you like a

THE SHE-WOLF OF BAKER STREET

brother, Johnno, but I don't want to listen to you two whispering sweet nothings all the way to the tarmac.'

John ignored her in favour of seizing Sherlock's hand, pulling him close for a kiss, then murmuring in his ear before retreating upstairs for their bags. 'I'll get yours while I'm at it, Mrs H!' he called back down the stairs.

Audrey finished her tea and let her inner wolf listen. Her cubs – John, Sherlock, Nick – were weary, but not anxious. Irene's grieving heart was for now quiescent beneath a grim determination to find the man who had robbed her of so much. The Department of Fisheries personnel kept efficiently to the background.

She brought her attention back to the moment and met Myca Holmes' confident gaze again.

'Moriarty is responsible for most of our evil reputation,' said Myca. 'I've done my best to correct his transgressions.'

'You mean crimes.'

'Yes,' Myca admitted with a small sigh. 'His crimes.'

'That Jenny committed a few of her own. With you in tow.'

'She... we did. She meant well.'

'Did she?'

'By her own lights. Mostly. I'm free to make better decisions, now. Or at least, my own decisions. I hope they'll be better.'

'So you're staying on with the Department?'

'How else might I make amends? I can't simply abandon my post without knowing whether my replacement will break or change.'

'Do you have someone in mind?'

Myca's glance flicked briefly towards Irene, but she replied, 'No. Nobody yet.'

Audrey rose to her feet. 'Perhaps we can talk again in London. Especially since you'll be paying court to Nick at Baker Street.'

'Paying court,' Nick snorted then grinned cheekily and put on a faux posh accent. 'We'll be stepping out, Myca. Promenading, even. Mayhap I'll get the chance to lay my coat over a puddle for you.'

'Mayhap,' agreed Myca, gamely attempting playfulness. 'And if I'm required to go into battle again, I'll wear your favours near my heart.'

Nick preened at the suggestion.

'And for the record,' added Myca, 'I've googled Rhonda Rousey and that Christie woman and I look nothing like either of them.'

'Yeah you do,' Nick disagreed cheerfully. 'You're queenly. Definitely a Boadicea type.'

By the time those two had practised their flirting all the way to the airfield, Audrey wished she'd travelled with the whispering boys. Or taken a bus.

She'd forgotten how very much *too much* families could be.

It made her so happy she almost cried.

CHAPTER TWENTY-NINE

AUDREY WAS FAR TOO DIGNIFIED TO YELL UP THE STAIRS BUT SHE WAS also indulgently aware that Sherlock and John's honeymoon period had not yet abated. She thought it might take a while – near death experiences with elemental deities had clearly inspired her upstairs tenants to many energetic encounters in the last week.

Nick, however, was not half as squeamish or indulgent.

'Oi! Johnny! Quit snogging, get your kit on and bring your favourite snack downstairs!' she bellowed up the stairwell. 'Or did you forget Myca's coming for elevenses?'

The barely audible sounds of let's call it romance faded from even Audrey's excellent hearing.

Nick's too. 'And brush your hair, you scruffy beggar,' she added in a shout. 'You're meant to be a medical professional and I'm trying to impress my girlfriend. Scruffy mates are not impressive.'

'John is very impressive and my sister is not–!' Sherlock's answering bellow halted abruptly, no doubt distracted by his impressive boyfriend.

Audrey raised an eyebrow at Nick, who mirrored the expression.

'Girlfriend? Already?'

'We totally went to the flicks together on Wednesday. I shared my fizzy pop with her, same straw and everything.'

'I shall believe it when you've written her name on your arm in biro,' Audrey challenged her.

Nick threatened to pull up her sleeve, and Audrey couldn't tell if she was bluffing, but then the doorbell rang.

'That'll be my queen!' Nick darted to the door and opened it with a grand flourish. 'Myca! You look a million quid!'

Myca Holmes' shy, pleased smile confirmed everything. She stood tall, having dispensed with the hat, dark glasses and long coat in which the Jenny had tried to hide. She wore her dark hair in a flattering bob, the fringe sweeping across her forehead in a way that drew attention to her grey eyes. Colour had invaded her wardrobe – claret-red earrings that matched a pocket square in her tailored double-breasted blue herringbone pants suit. She even wore a pair of elegant black shoes with a low heel. Nick practically swooned at the added height, particularly when Myca bent for a chaste kiss.

Audrey could hear Nick's heart racing. Myca's too, come to that.

What a love-sodden house she lived in now, with Sherlock and John above, and Nick in the room below being so inexpertly and sweetly courted.

Audrey glanced across the hall to the new spare room. Having been breached as a war room, she'd finally let go of Conal's ghost. He had barely stepped foot in this house. Her memories of him were in other cities, other places, but mostly in her heart.

Ruby's daughter had resided in that room this last week, little more than a ghost herself. Irene was not sodden with love. She was grief-addled and rarely emerged except when Audrey brought her meals which Irene hardly touched; or cajoled her into an evening walk through Regents Park.

Nick had opened the door wide to allow Myca into the house, but the Director of the Department of Fisheries, Wildlife & Parks waited respectfully at the threshold, like a vampire awaiting an invitation. As she had done every time she'd paid a call on her young lady this week.

'Mrs Hudson.' Myca nodded a formal, cautious greeting.

'Ms Holmes. Do come in.'

The Fisheries' black history had not been Myca Holmes' doing. Myca had been attempting to mend its shaky reputation; with varying degrees of success, true. But now without the Jenny's agenda overlaying Myca's own, perhaps more fences could be mended. Or built. Perhaps she meant bridges.

Audrey was saved from brooding further on the subject when Sherlock dashed down the stairs, John following more sedately; having brushed his hair, Audrey noted wryly. Sherlock took in his sister's appearance at a glance and, as she stepped across the threshold, he swooped in to kiss her cheek.

'I like the new look,' he said, stepping back. 'You've already lost your characteristic pallor. Lunch breaks and walking in the sunshine with your–' the hesitation was very brief, 'girlfriend.'

'My agoraphobia appears to have run its course,' Myca replied. Her habitual aloofness faded beneath a fond glance at Nick. 'And Nick is very particular that a Director of Fisheries, Wildlife & Parks should spend a good deal of time in the parks.'

'You look lovely in a park,' Nick asserted.

'Where you like to commit PDAs,' teased John.

Sherlock's momentary confusion vanished as he concluded, 'Public Displays of Affection.'

Myca's ears pinked.

'You can't talk, Mr and Mr Handsy,' Nick riposted. 'And anyway, English gardens are pretty to walk in. Speaking of which, let me lead you to our little back garden, sweetheart. I've poshed it all up: a tablecloth and serviettes and Mrs H's good china and I've been practising my flashest manners.'

'I am already charmed, my dear.'

'Sherlock, you lead the way. John, with me. You get to carry the trays. I've made scones.'

'Oh dear god.'

'Very funny. They're good. Aren't they good, Mrs H?'

'You've made excellent scones,' Audrey agreed, not mentioning the two failed batches that had preceded them.

Sherlock seemed about to comment – he'd come rattling down the stairs with a fire extinguisher when Nick had set the oven on fire the first time – but one look at the way Myca and Nick gazed at each other thwarted his intentions for factual disclosure. Perhaps he recognised the expression. Audrey certainly did – it mirrored that besotted delight with which John and Sherlock looked at each other most of the time.

Instead, Sherlock offered his elbow to Myca and guided her through the building while John and Nick vanished into Audrey's apartment to fetch the morning tea accoutrements.

Audrey tapped on Irene's door. Irene answered, dressed in clothes that weren't pyjamas today, but her eyes were still bruised with sleeplessness.

'We're having elevenses in the garden,' Audrey said. 'You are very welcome to join us.'

'Is that Holmes woman here?'

'Yes.'

'Visiting her brother.'

'And Nick.'

'She's staying for tea?'

'She is.'

'Good. I need to speak with her.'

Irene vanished briefly and returned with a chiffon scarf wrapped around her disordered cornrow plaits.

'Through here,' Audrey began.

'I remember,' said Irene, a little sharply, and headed towards the back door.

Audrey made the offer again. 'This house should be yours. Your mother–'

'My mother left this house to you.'

'But you're her daughter. I've no right.'

'You've every right,' said Irene. She turned to Audrey and met her troubled gaze. 'It is not your fault she and I were separated. It is not your fault she died. Moriarty is responsible for both of those things. He hunted us, and he planted his murder in her, before you even met my mother.'

Audrey was ashamed of the tears that spilled so suddenly down her cheeks. 'That should *not* have been your life.'

'No. Nor should it have been yours, to lose her like that.'

'I'd have done anything to save her. I wanted to be with her forever. I would have been with her to the very end.'

'I think she would be glad you were not. It was a terrible death.'

'She made that decision for me.'

'Yes,' said Irene softly. 'My mother did that a good deal. Made decisions for others. For me, for you, for my father. To keep us safe, she thought. She meant it with love.'

'I miss her,' Audrey blurted and drew another breath on a sob.

'Me, also.' And Irene folded Audrey in her arms and held her while they both wept for Ruby Stockton.

'You know,' whispered Irene as she held Audrey close. 'If this was truly my house, Gottfried could have entered without an invitation. We made that vow after he was turned; what was mine was also his. He knew Baker Street had been my mother's home. But he could not enter. This house is not mine. Mother left it to you. It's your home.'

'Are you coming, Mrs Hudson?' Sherlock's voice rang out from out back.

'It's *their* home too,' said Irene.

Audrey took a handkerchief from her pocket and wiped her eyes and nose. 'It can be yours too. For as long as you want or need it. I'd like for you to stay.'

'I'd like that.'

The back door opened and Sherlock peered into the hall. Whatever he deduced from what he saw, he simply withdrew again.

Audrey waited until the door closed behind him.

'Let's have tea.'

The tea table was indeed elegant, even if the ragged garden was in need of pruning. Tea was poured and drunk. Scones consumed and praised. PDAs were committed to the extent of hand-holding and a modicum of unabashed food-sharing. John and Nick told stories on each other, for the amused benefit of their sweethearts.

Then Sherlock and Myca did the same, tentatively at first, feeling their way back to their siblingship, before rediscovering a competitive streak while deducing the neighbour, Mrs Turner.

'Nurse, divorcee,' concluded Sherlock. 'Two children. One cat.'

'Three children. Remember the tiny socks beside second pair of wellington boots.'

'Damn, yes. They have a new puppy as well.'

'A labradoodle.'

'We should get a dog,' said John suddenly.

'Bit redundant, really,' said Nick, and she stuck her tongue out and panted, before remembering she wasn't the only wolf at the table.

'There is a dog I would like to my hands on,' said Irene suddenly. She directed a hard gaze at Myca. 'Do you know where I can find him?'

Myca, who had begun to add jam to another scone, set the knife and scone down. 'We have tracked Sebastian Moran to Australia. I am in touch with the Fisheries equivalent there. He hired a car in Sydney, but it was found abandoned in the Blue Mountains.'

'The full moon is coming.'

'Yes. We hope to locate him before then.'

'I will join that hunt.'

'Moran is out of our jurisdiction at present.'

'He murdered my husband.'

Myca folded her hands in her lap. 'I can only authorise your inclusion in his capture if you will consent to be governed by the Department's operational guidelines. Our work may be covert, but we are still answerable to laws and – and ethics.'

'I will consider it.'

'I hope you will.'

'Don't suppose you have a job for me?' Nick asked wistfully. 'I'm a crack scone baker!'

'You said you were a driver,' said Myca mildly but meaningfully.

Nick perked up. 'Yep. Driver, mechanic, detailer–'

'We had the shiniest SUV in the war,' agreed John.

'An excellent recommendation. As Director, my car ought to be the shiniest in service.'

'When do I start?'

'I thought you might begin on Monday.'

Nick's surprise – she had obviously been joking – turned immediately into a delighted grin. 'Do I get a uniform? I look pretty smashing in a uniform.'

'You are smashing either way,' Myca dared to say, then blushed as she continued, 'but I don't think there's a uniform.'

'I'll get a suit. And a fancy hat. Your chauffeur should look the part.'

'Is nepotism going to be a habit with you?' Sherlock asked.

'Are you also looking for employment?'

'No. I have a job already.'

'Consulting detective, yes.' Her eyes sparkled at her brother.

'That's right. For the everyday world. Ghosts need not apply. If they exist.'

'Well–'

'Ah. Of course they do. We'll alert you if a case brings up anything in your line, then.'

'We?'

John grinned at Sherlock and then at Myca. 'Part time locum, full time back-up to the consulting detective.'

'Speaking of which,' said Sherlock, plucking out his phone as it beeped at him. 'Bradstreet's calling. We have a case, John.'

Sherlock and John took off. Myca resumed the consumption of her scone.

'You really mean it, Myca? I can be a driver for you?'

Myca sipped her tea to help her swallow the crumbs, dabbed at her lips with a serviette, and said, 'Yes. I need a driver I can rely on who is already initiated into the world of the fae. The department requires more staff with direct experience.'

'I'm a diversity hire, then.' Nick snorted a laugh. 'I tick at least three boxes, I guess.'

Myca placed her hand over Nick's. 'Many boxes, my dear, including your many very valuable skills and the pleasure of your company. But there will be no PDAs during work hours.'

'Course not,' Nick protested solemnly. 'I'm a fucking professional.'

'Quite.'

'Want to take a stroll around Regents?'

'Please.'

They, too, left. Audrey started to clear dishes, but Irene took over. 'Allow me, Audrey. This is my home for a while, after all.' She smiled sadly. 'Until Myca finds a use for me, at least.'

While Irene carried the trays inside, Audrey sat in her little garden. Closing her eyes and extending her senses, she could scent soil and flowers, the neighbour's cat and the new puppy. The fading aroma of cream and jam, tea and scones, the burnt batch in the compost bin.

She could hear traffic on Baker Street. Footsteps on the pavement. Bees in the flowering weeds and birds in the bushes.

Audrey could hear clinking dishes in the kitchen, and Irene humming a poignant melody. What a beautiful voice she had, the same rich timbre as Ruby's, though clearer due to years of professional training and performance. The sound filled her heart. Hurt it too, a little. A pang of loss for Ruby. For her long dead parents and her estranged sister Ingrid. For dear Hugh and their lost baby. For Conal and Siobhan and Travis and Tara. For herself and all that she'd lost.

Then Irene's song lifted in tempo and mood. Something in German, but full of warmth and with a fiery edge. It sounded like a challenge and a promise. It sounded like hope.

And Audrey's heart filled up again with all that she'd regained. She had a family again. All of her unspent love had somewhere to go other than into grief.

Audrey opened her eyes to regard her unkempt garden. She planned to be here for a very long time. Long enough to tend to long-lived plants. She would plant a bay tree in memory of Conal. Some rambling roses for the twins. Lavender for Siobhan, which Sherlock would like because of the bees, which fascinated him. Perhaps she could persuade Nick to help her pave a small terrace and install a fountain for the birds. Ruby had always loved little bird-baths. They could add planter boxes for the more dangerous plants. Foxglove. Some Daphne. Monkshood, of course, for the tea.

Tomorrow, Audrey decided, she would return to the Chelsea Physic Garden. Donate to make up for her theft of the monkshood. Perhaps discreetly harvest some seeds or separate a plant at the root to transplant it here. Sherlock would likely enjoy assisting with that. Perhaps they wouldn't tell John until after the fact. Though perhaps, given how smitten he was, he might volunteer to be their lookout.

A sparrow flew onto the back of one of the chairs and cocked its head at her.

'Go on then,' she told it. 'I won't eat you.'

Skittishly yet bravely, the sparrow hopped onto the table to claim a crumb before flying off.

Audrey couldn't help a little laugh at how she had failed to intimidate this plucky London sparrow. She might not be an Alpha, if Sherlock was right about wolf packs, but Nick's cheeky choice of *den mother* seemed appropriate still. Though she could still put the frighteners on when necessary.

And if she was not truly an Alpha, perhaps she was also no longer cursed.

Listening to Irene and the bees and the murmur of life beyond the garden walls, encompassing all of Baker Street, Audrey thought she might at last be exactly the opposite.

ABOUT THE AUTHOR

Narrelle M. Harris is an award-winning writer of crime, horror, fantasy, and romance. Her 40+ works of fiction include 13 novels.

With Clan Destine Press (or our imprint Improbable Press) she has the vampire trilogy *The Opposite of Life, Walking Shadows* and the forthcoming *Beyond Redemption*; traditional Holmesian mysteries and Holmes/Watson romances – *The Adventure of the Colonial Boy* and *A Dream to Build a Kiss On*; the queer paranormal thriller-romance, *Ravenfall*; and a rock-and-roll urban fantasy, *Kitty and Cadaver*.

Her ghost/crime short story, 'Jane', won the 2017 'Body in the Library' prize of Sisters in Crime Australia's annual Scarlet Stiletto Awards.

Narrelle is also one of Clan Destine Press' star anthology editors, responsible for the Sherlock Holmes anthology, *The Only One in the World*; the feast of corvids that is *Clamour and Mischief*; the horror filled *This Fresh Hell*, with co-editor Katya de Becerra; and *Sherlock is a Girl's Name*, with co-editor Atlin Merrick.

www.narrellemharris.iwriter.com.au

Acknowledgements

This story began because I just really wanted to write a story with a hella BAMF menopausal woman. I had also been thinking about werewolf stories and what it had to say about human violence – often male violence – and how a menopausal woman might differ in the werewolf trope from most stories I'd read. I also loved Una Stubbs as Mrs Hudson in BBC Sherlock, though I admit the Audrey Hudson in my head is a lot more like Helen Mirren.

Naturally, all those thoughts coalesced and here we are with *The She-Wolf of Baker Street*.

My heartfelt thanks to all the screen Mrs Hudsons who have done so much with the very little Arthur Conan Doyle gave us; and to all the Johns and Sherlocks and Irenes as well. I've had so much fun giving all of Conan Doyle's creations, however briefly they appear, a different kind of life.

My thanks to my Patreon supporters who read the earliest draft of this story, and to my publisher Lindy Cameron for being excited about a lot of queer werewolves and their extended families.

My everlasting thanks to my editor, Atlin Merrick, whose acumen, wisdom and thoughtful suggestions have helped to make this a much better book.

Love always to my husband Tim and to my little band of Pixies – between them and Lindy, they always keep me right.

Thank you to my 2021 Patreon supporters who helped
to make this book possible.

Sarah Remy
Adelle Goettel
Donna Sams
Tim Richards
Mike Thompson
Kim Fasching
Blue
Carey Handfield
Dimitra Stathopoulos
Jane Tisell
K Caine
KRin Pender Gunn
Sarah Tollok
Beck
Lisa Christenson
Lora Timonin
Beth Zyglowicz

Kate Steere
Kimber
Sally Beasley
Melinda McCormack
Fennec12
Grant Watson
Jack Fennell
Kizzia
Sarah Drosendahl
Tansy Rayner Roberts
Sally Koetsveld
Richard Koehler
Stephen Harris
Julia Hilton
Champagne and Socks
Milane Duncan-Frantz

www.patreon.com/NarrelleMHarris

THE SHERLOCKIAN WORLD OF CLAN DESTINE PRESS

Since his first appearance in 1887, Sherlock Holmes has been the quintessential English sleuth, alongside his loyal companion and biographer, Doctor Watson.

But what if they had come from some other place in the world, or another time? How would they differ from Conan Doyle's creations? How similar might they remain?

Holmes and Watson are herein re-imagined in new cultural contexts, different genders and sexualities, and in stories rich in foreign detail that still reflect their origins.

Thirteen writers from around the world, with cultural or historic expertise, explore the possibilities with stories set in Germany, C17th England, Ireland, Australia, Russia, South Africa, India, Poland, USA, Ancient Egypt, Viking Iceland, and even the entire world.

You'll discover Holmes and Watson are not only unique in original canon, but the Great Detective remains singular in every world!

ISBNs: 978-0-6488487-8-3 (pb)
978-0-6489586-3-5 (eb)

Stories by: Kerry Greenwood & David Greagg, Greg Herren, Atlin Merrick, Jack Fennell, Lucy Sussex, Jason Franks, Natalie Conyer, Lisa Fessler, Katya de Becerra, LJM Owen, Jayantika Ganguly, Raymond Gates, JM Redmann.

Who would the Great Detective be if Sherlock was a woman?

That's the question posed in Sherlock is a Girls' Name, an anthology imagining Sherlock Holmes as female, in fabulous mysteries that follow the great detective across time and even space.

The eleven stories in this book, selected by Holmes and Watson tragics – aka long-time Sherlockian writer-editors – Narrelle M. Harris and Atlin Merrick, imagine Holmes in deep space, 1990s Russia, Victorian London, contemporary USA, worlds of magic and more.

Of course Holmes is not Holmes without Watson, and the many Watsons herein include ghosts, robots, a boy who doesn't speak, a teenage tuba player, a stranger on a plane. In each story Holmes and *her* Watson do what they do best: solve crimes and have adventures!

Stories by: Tansy Rayner Roberts, Eugen Bacon, SarahTollok, Verity Burns, Dannye Chase, Kenzie Lappin, JD Cadmon, Stacy Lawhorne, Karen Carlisle, Katya de Becerra, Narrelle M. Harris, Atlin Merrick.

ISBNs: 9781922904713 (pb)
9781922904720 (eb)

CLAN DESTINE PRESS ANTHOLOGIES
EDITED BY NARRELLE M. HARRIS

A driver picks up a hitchhiker on a dark road; a restorer develops a strange bond with a cursed doll; a visit to a cabin in the woods goes terribly wrong...

We all know how those stories end – or do we?

In *This Fresh Hell*, every story begins with a well-known horror trope but ends with a twist, bringing new life and unexpected resolutions to old ideas. Fears are interrogated, ghosts re-examined, and monsters reconfigured.

From chilling to quirky, the stories will appeal to dedicated horror fans and those trying the genre for the first time.

Editors Katya de Becerra and Narrelle M. Harris invited writers from Australia and around the world to reignite and subvert horror tropes.

The result is 19 genre-bending stories by: Eugen Bacon, Elle Beaumont, Jason Franks, Claire Low, Raymond Gates, Sarah Glenn Marsh, Greg Herren, Annie McCann, A.J. Vrana, Chuck McKenzie, L.J.M. Owen, Gillian Polack, Tansy Rayner Roberts, Clare E. Rhoden, Claire L. Smith, Candace Robinson, Sarah Robinson-Hatch, C. Vonzale Lewis.

ISBN: 9781922904348 (pb)
9781922904355 (eb)

A clamour of rooks. A mischief of magpies.
A storytelling of crows.

All the corvids – rooks and ravens, jays and jackdaws, crows and magpies – have the best collective nouns: from tidings and titterings, bands and trains, to a parliament, a party, and an unkindness.

And *Clamour and Mischief* is a veritable storytelling of adventures featuring corvidae, the bird family known for its intelligence and cunning, and its connection with folklore and urban legends.

Our storytellers come from around the world and include award-winners and fledgling authors in their professional debut.

Herein are 16 striking stories imbued with the humour, darkness, wisdom and magic of the birds which inspired them.

Stories by: Raymond Gates, GV Pearce, Eugen Bacon, Geneve Flynn, Alex Marchant, Jack Fennell, RJK Lee, Lee Murray, Dannye Chase, Narrelle M. Harris, R.D. White, Jason Franks, Katya de Becerra, George Ivanoff, Tamara M Bailey, Gabiann Marin.

ISBNs: 978-1-9229041-7-4 (pb)
978-1-9229041-8-8 (eb)